Broken Rules

this place.
more. Laughing.
contradictory thoughts.
thrives off dickheads like me.
ckets to watch porn in real-time.
I want to take her away from it all.

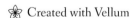

ROSALIE

Broken Rules

DON'T FALL IN LOVE SERIES

Author's Notes

Broken Rules is a standalone spicy romance, book two in the Don't Fall in Love Series which can be read in any order. Book two is based on the same timeline as Rule Breaker, so there will be spoilers throughout if you have not read book one.

Content Warning: Broken Rules contains explicit sex, voyeurism, a scene with BDSM, assault, emotional abuse, and mention of abortion.

CONTENTS

Playlist

Scan image below in Spotify to listen.

Time flies when you have a purpose, when you're committed, determined to reach a goal, and you're so close you can taste the finish line on your tongue—it's sweet, like peaches, and I'm ready to cross over.

e a purpose
you're committed
ermined to reach a goal
d you're so close you can tast
sh line on your tongue—it's sweet
e peaches, and I'm ready to cross over

PROLOGUE

Evie

"Take it off."

Goosebumps spread across my skin from his rough tone, his hungry gaze fixating on my last article of clothing, my lace panties merely decoration in his eyes, and I smirk while gliding my fingers along the waistband.

"Do you mean this?" I hook my thumbs inside, watching his every move from across the room as he slowly jerks off.

"I want to taste that pretty cunt of yours while I come."

"Hm, that's not part of the gig, Lex."

His dick stands tall as he stops his strokes to recline the chair he's sitting in until it can't go anymore. "What can I say? I'm not a watch and jerk-off kinda guy. Now, take it off, and sit on my face."

My gaze flicks to the timer.

He only applied fifteen minutes this session, which is almost up—quite tempted to give in to his request. I'd be lying if I said I didn't want to plop onto his lap to ride his thick shaft.

"I can't."

Lennox retakes his cock, slapping the tip along his abs, and my lips part as he rubs down the length to cup his balls. "This is the hardest I've ever been, Peaches, and it's all for you. It would be a shame to let it go to waste."

"Go to waste? You really are a cocky bastard."

"Nothing cocky about knowing what I like, and what I want is that lace on the floor and your ass bouncing off my chin."

I smirk, taking a few steps back until I'm against the wall. "You've come to the wrong place then." Using the tips of my fingers, I trail in between my breasts, tilt my head back and glide my palm up my neck. "Men who enter the box are to watch and only watch." I suck my middle finger, keeping eye contact as I glide back to my panties, and Lennox hums once I slip my hand inside the black fabric. "If you're staying in the box with me, you gotta follow the rules, just like everyone else."

His chest rises faster as I release a soft moan while

running my fingers over my clit, his eyelids falling heavy. "I'm not like everyone else."

Stopping, I stroll to the white line dividing us. "Then who are you, Lex? What makes you any different than the last man who sat in that chair and stroked his dick while watching me?"

Lennox stands, his cock jutting as he steps to the other side. "I'm the guy who'll come by every day, take every time slot, so no other man gets off in front of you." He takes hold of my wrist, and I hold my breath when he sucks my finger. "Mm. I'll gladly be a greedy bastard when it comes to you."

Tears threaten to emerge, and I blink them away. "You barely know me."

"No, I know you—I know the real Evie. *My wife.*"

The chime from the timer makes my heart leap, and I check the clock, taking a step back. "Time's up."

my finger

it comes to you.

You barely know me.

ow the real Evie. My wife.

the timer makes my heart leap

clock, taking a step back. "Time's up

ONE

PERFORMANCE
SATISFACTION

Evie

Beauty is in the eye of the beholder, created through one's perception—otherwise, beauty doesn't exist. As a Red Vixen, I'm nothing more than my looks, a man's most lavish fantasy come to life. Therefore, I only exist through my observer's eyes. A display for their viewing pleasure while they sit and form concepts full of stereotypes, giving hard-working women a bad reputation in an industry created to entertain adults. Many of whom choose not to see past their noses.

I'd rather live in a world where beauty's insignificant, outside perfection where people accept my ugly, but I learned at a tender age that flaws are a distraction in the way of success. So, every day, I hold my head high. Play out whatever my beholder desires as they watch, satisfying their needs before going home to their vanilla life while counting down the seconds to come back—they always come back, or else I don't exist.

"Once more," Kylo whispers, and I inhale a heavy breath, licking the fallen tears from my lips. "My job does not define me." I open my eyes, staring into his dark green gaze in the full-length mirror, and he lifts my chin, making me stand taller. Stronger. "Only I can define me."

"That's right." Stepping behind me, Kylo rubs my arms as our time together ends. "You did great."

I smile, nodding before drying my cheeks with my sleeve. "Thank you, Kylo, for taking me sooner and the extra time. This week has been draining, so our session was much needed."

"Of course. You're very welcome."

He gestures for me to leave the guest suite of his cabin, and I walk ahead of him toward the front door after spending two days here. The Kylo Kent Experience has a lot to offer— women request him for intimacy, companionship, and, if the moment arises, sex. However, with my profession, I come to him for the opposite effect. Being explicit all day takes a toll on my mind and body where every few weeks, I meet with my confidant, who knows what to say to ground me, decompress, and reset. Otherwise, I wouldn't function.

"Oh, I shared your business card with a friend of mine. I hope that's okay. She's been having a hard time lately, and I believe she'll benefit from the experience."

Kylo smiles and leans against the door frame. "If she submits an application online, I'll review it with my assistant."

Convincing my best friend Sadie to try the experience will be tricky, but she needs his magic touch. I nod, skimming my fingers across his bare chest. While I've made a rule not to date at this time in my life, I won't deny that Kylo's an attractive man and why women drool over his tall, muscular form, dark hair, and beard—just not me.

The afternoon breeze hits, and I zip my jacket as I walk toward my car, calm and relaxed, stopping when he calls out, "Wait, what's her name?"

"I won't say to keep the process objective. Use your better judgment."

Kylo raises a brow, and I grin, strolling along the circular driveway as a black car arrives, parking behind me. A man hops out wearing worn jeans, a black fitted thermal, and a matching beanie over his light brown hair that peeks out the front. Not the fit I'd expect from someone exiting a Porsche —a suit and tie, maybe. Like most of my customers.

He winks at me, and I roll my eyes once he passes, probably checking out my ass as I quicken my steps to my car. My shift starts in half an hour, so I leave Lake Oswego, drive to Portland in twenty minutes, and park in the back of the lot of Vivid Vixens. Mondays are typically slow. I'll have around five to six customers for a six-hour shift in the voyeur rooms, however, today the lot's full of expensive cars, and it's barely noon.

I walk toward the back exit, texting Julianne, our house

mom, to let me in so I don't have to run into Gin behind the
bar just yet. I'd like to keep my buzz going, at least until my
first customer. A moment later, the door opens, and a woman
with long dark braids appears, wearing black scrubs.

"Thanks," I say, holding the door as I enter, Julianne
likely assisting someone.

"No problem. I just got here too. You're Evie, right?"

"Yeah—sorry, I've seen you around after sessions but
never got your name."

"It's Petra, and no need to apologize. I usually keep to
myself at work. The less I get into it with people, the better."

"Smart thinking."

Petra smiles, and I stroll alongside her toward the
dressing room exit, waving bye as she walks straight through
the red curtains that lead to the main floor. Several Vixens
are freshening up at their stations, and I head for the locker
area further in the back to grab my duffle bag.

Sitting on the bench seat, I withdraw my phone from my
purse, missing a *'checking to see if you're still alive after
spending two days with a man in a cabin on the lake'* text
from Sadie, and I giggle, clearing my throat while dialing her
number with every intention to convince her otherwise.

"Hey, Evie."

"Girl, I feel like a million bucks. I'm telling you, book the
Kylo Kent Experience."

Sadie blows a deep sigh into the line. "Yeah? What did
he do to you?"

"I'm not saying. That's something you'll have to find out
on your own," I say while removing my clothes, the phone
pinned between my shoulder and ear.

"I doubt he can help me."

"Did you check out his website?"

"Yes."

"Okay, and you're not even remotely curious about what he has to offer?"

She stays quiet for a second. "He's an escort, Evie. Paid to have sex for a living. Seems pretty straightforward."

A lot of people tend to have this misconception of the experience. "It's not like that at all. We don't pay Kylo for sex. We pay for the ultimate lover experience."

"Which means?"

"Think—the perfect friend, husband, confidant, whoever you want him to be for two days. A man who'll pamper, make you feel like the most beautiful woman in the world, and I haven't fucked him, but I've heard he's a beast in the sheets. He'll melt your panties and stress away."

"Then, after two days, he cuts you loose and moves on to the next woman," she adds, huffing a laugh.

"Well, yes. That's the whole point. You get the experience, and there are no strings attached."

There's another moment of silence, sensing her hesitations before she says, "Sounds great."

Lies.

"Sadie...." Grabbing my soap and a towel, I head for the showers across the room, needing to quicken my pace since my first customer is coming in less than ten minutes.

"Really. I filled out the intake form last night."

"You did?"

"And he emailed me back."

Really?

I switch to video call, and Sadie appears slouched back on her couch. "Wow, so quickly? What did it say?"

"I haven't opened it yet."

"Kylo gets a bunch of applications every week and is

selective about who he takes at the moment. I'd jump on it fast before you lose your chance."

The screen goes to pause mode, and I wait by the first stall for her to return, rechecking the time. "Sadie, are you still there?" I ask, and she reappears.

"I was reading the email."

"And?"

"He wants me to come this weekend."

My brows raise. "Oh really? Kylo said he wasn't taking weekly clients for a while. He must be intrigued."

"Is that a good thing?"

"Anything with him is a good thing. Trust me. You're not going to regret this."

Sadie slowly nods a few times, which is not convincing, but I hope she'll give the experience more thought. "Okay."

"Good. I'm going to pick you up at six after my last customer. This news calls for some new sexy outfits."

She gives me a small smile. "Sure. I'll be ready."

I hate seeing her down, and I want to treat her tonight, get her out of her apartment. Even if she'd rather be home watching her comfort movies than going to the mall.

"Listen, I know this time of year is hard for you—all the bad experiences can be a lot to handle, but don't let the past stop you from healing. Take this opportunity and allow Kylo to work his magic. He's the next best thing to a therapist."

Her nose scrunches, and I kick myself, remembering the mess between her and Declan. "Best not compare the two."

"Right. Yeah. I'll call you later."

"Bye."

I frown—there's only so much I can do to help ease her anxiety and heal from the pain. She lost both parents and fell victim to a narcissist during her hardest times. However, I couldn't be more proud of her strength to leave him, and I'm happy she's back in Oregon.

Taking a quick shower, I get dressed in black skinny jeans that hug my curves, a white short-sleeved t-shirt swooping low in the front, heels, and a tan blazer. A casual outfit and every layer necessary for this customer's request.

Creating a simple makeup look with Vivid's signature scarlet red painted on my lips, I leave the dressing room to the main floor, which is a full house. Gin whistles when she sees me, and I sigh, tempted to ignore her call, though I walk to the end of the bar where she's standing behind fixing an order.

"I need you on the floor between sessions tonight."

My stomach churns. "What? Why?"

"Look around, Evie. Three Vixens didn't show up today. We need more girls here."

"How is that my problem? I'm not stretched and haven't worked the pole in forever."

Gin huffs a laugh. "Everly, please, don't fight me tonight. I'm already getting my ass kicked behind the bar. Now, do what you gotta do to make it work."

Gritting my teeth, I nod, then walk through the sea of hungry patrons with stacks of money to spend, ignoring the lavish decor I know like the back of my hand. Every velvet stitch, and the well-dressed men who occupy each seat, their expensive liquor and cologne permeating the air while I pass through. How they itch to touch, but a Red Vixen is untouchable—until I walk the floor as a Vixen.

I head upstairs and continue to the employee entrance of room three out of four. The vacancy light above the door is off, meaning my customer's ready for their thirty-minute session. My six-inch heels click along the floor as I reach the entryway to the open apartment layout, and I take a deep breath of the cinnamon spice incense. We are known for our vivid setups where we bring the customer's fantasies to life.

My first of the day is anonymous, and instead of using the bed or chair provided in the viewing area, they are behind the privacy box. They can hear, see, and talk to me, though I can't see them through the two-way mirror.

The request: *you had a hard day at work and need to release tension. Slowly strip your work attire and pleasure yourself to porn.*

Wandering to the middle of the room, I lean against the arm of the cream couch to take off my heels and toss them aside. The two-way mirror is diagonal to me, so I stroll toward the glass, using the reflection to check my lipstick, then draw the elastic from my dark hair, each wavy strand falling past my breasts. I fluff my hair before heading to the dining room table, peeling my blazer off in the process to hang on the back of a chair. There's a flatscreen TV displayed by the couch, the customer can see the screen, but they won't be watching the same show as me.

I sit on the plush cushion, moaning while rubbing my sore feet, then relax back with my eyes closed. The speed of my session depends on the timeframe and the customer's request—sometimes, I have to get right into masturbating. Where others, I can take my time and really build the tension before making them climax. The hornier they get, the chances of them requesting more time increase and the more I get paid.

A few minutes in, I start unbuttoning my jeans, my bracelets banging together as I shimmy the tight material down my thighs, dropping them onto the floor, feeling free, and I hum with approval. Looking at the remote, I hesitate a second before grabbing it, glancing around the room as if someone is watching me alone in my apartment, then switching on the television. I click through a few channels, innocent enough, then stop on a not-so-innocent show.

Leaning back further, I tilt my head, my gaze turning heavy as I watch a man glide his palm across a woman's ass before slowly dragging her panties down her thighs while she's on all fours.

"That feels nice," she says as he rubs his fingers through her slit, *blah, blah, blah.*

I run mine along the band of my black thong, snapping the elastic against my skin once, twice before easing one hand over the front to touch my pussy, and letting out a soft moan. I'm numb to pleasure—I have to be in order to work, so my orgasms are not real, though they'd never know.

The couple is fucking now, the female lead vocal as the man stays silent. What a wasted opportunity to get viewers hot since hearing a man express their pleasure through sound, whether by moaning or talking, is a turn-on for many.

Fifteen minutes left on the red clock against the left wall, so I grind my pussy on my palm, my chest rising with my increasing breath. Gripping the neck of my shirt, I drag it down to rest below my bare tits, rubbing and tugging at my nipples to get them erect while inching my other hand into my panties to massage my clit.

Some customers finish before their time is up, and the clock will sound to end the session when they press a red button, usually by the halfway mark. If they don't request more time through the club app, and their session ends without their climax, the performer's not responsible for giving a refund, even if their performance wasn't up to the customer's satisfaction.

I've yet to experience someone expressing their displeasure in the ten years of working here, but some girls have. That's where the camera facing our side comes into play, notifying security that someone has crossed the white line dividing the room, and they escort the customer off the premises. There are no warnings once they break the rules, they're banned from returning to Vivid, and that rule is in place for us too.

I'm getting bored, so I increase my speed, pumping inside my pussy as I moan louder, spread my legs wider, buck my hips harder, squirming beneath my touch as I sit on my heels to arch over the back of the couch, lifting my ass higher to give them a better view. Then as I'm about to finish, the timer ends at ten minutes left.

I never leave a performance hanging, so I breathe out heavy pants, moaning while rocking my pelvis forward, squeezing my thighs together until I come down from the *high*. Slumping back onto the cushion with a satisfied grin, I remove my hand from my panties, unsure if they're still watching, but I suck on my fingers anyway, humming while catching my breath, waiting a minute before standing to leave the room.

Performance satisfaction is what I aim for—wanting as many regulars as possible, to know what makes them tick means having more control over my sets and the faster I can leave. Customers can rate us afterward, and management checks our weekly scores to indicate who to keep on board. If an employee gets anywhere near three out of five stars, they're usually gone.

Grabbing a robe and slippers, I leave the room, taking the emergency stairs that lead to the back exit hallway. We're not supposed to, but I couldn't care less what Gin says. Pins and needles spread along my body as a chill hits me, and I use my keycard to get into the dressing room.

A Vixen turns to look at me with a raised brow, and I pay her no mind, heading straight for the showers. I have another customer in an hour, and there's only so much stalling I can do before Gin has Julianne drag me onto the main floor. Ten minutes tops, I clean myself, dressed in a black lace teddy bodysuit with a crisscross pattern between my breasts, and step inside the Red Gentleman's Club.

During the night, the lights dim to a warm red, setting an alluring tone, less so in the afternoon, which is why the dayshift is usually slower. Apparently, not today. I sigh, roaming the floor, working the pole during my rotation, ignoring side-eye glances, satisfying my voyeur customers, wash, rinse, repeat, orgasm for the sixth time before ending my shift. My thighs are aching, but I speed walk to my car with a purse full of cash, running late to pick up Sadie.

I beep the horn a few times once I'm outside her apartment complex, and she comes rushing out wearing a heavy grey sweater, locking up before waving at her neighbor who lives above her. Delores glances away, the old lady ignoring Sadie.

"Hurry your sexy butt up. The mall closes in two hours," I yell after rolling down the passenger window.

"You see me coming. You're the one who's late." She gets into the front seat, rolling her eyes as I narrow mine. "Delores will get me kicked out with a noise complaint."

Sighing, I drive into traffic. "Today was hectic between working voyeur and the main floor non-stop because *three* Vixens didn't show. I haven't worked the pole in forever."

"Really? The front's usually slow on Mondays, and why would Gin need you to perform?"

I let out a short laugh, threading my fingers through my hair. "On top of the regulars, a flock of customers came at noon, right before I arrived. You can imagine how pissed off the girls who showed up for their day shift were when a Red Vixen walked the floor, having an untouchable within reach, obtaining more money."

My grip on the steering wheel tightens a few times. "It's not my fault patrons were more interested in me, taking the opportunity to get a lap dance since it's against the rules for a voyeur to touch us, though I prefer not to mingle with them. No thanks. That's why I keep my ass in the box. Less drama, but Gin doesn't care how I feel."

"That's rough. I'm sorry."

"Yeah, it's whatever and over with—also, you know my father would never kick you out."

Dad owns the apartment complex Sadie's renting, and my name's also on the deed. While he's not living in Oregon anymore, Dad still feels he needs to provide for me somehow, even being twenty-eight and living in a house I bought myself. Maybe it's his way of making up for leaving me here as a child, though I haven't touched a dime of the revenue this place generates and never will.

The mall isn't far from her place, but the silence makes the drive feel longer than it is. I glance at Sadie every so often as she stares out into the distance, her eyes getting teary, constricting my chest.

"Hey, get out of your head, Sadie," I say, parking the car in the lot.

She blinks a few times, stopping her tears from falling, and I place my hand over hers, giving a gentle squeeze before flipping down the visor to reapply my makeup. "You alright?"

With a meek smile, she lies, "I'm just sleepy. Nothing to worry about."

I side-eye her, pursing my bright pink lips. "I'm going to pretend that's the truth, or we'll never get inside. Come on. I'm treating you today."

"No way."

Slipping into my purse, I smirk, withdrawing three thick stacks of tens, fives, and ones. "I got more than I need."

"That's great, but you're still not spending your hard-earned money on me."

"Listen, lady, when will you understand I like to spoil my main bitches? And when I say bitches I mean bitch, because you're the only one."

"Evie—"

"Ah! I don't want to hear it. Think of it as an investment for both of us since we wear the same size. Minus the lingerie, of course. That's not lasting through the night anyway." I wink at her, step out of the car, and Sadie follows me.

We browse through several stores, trying and buying a few items, sensing Sadie's ready to go home.

"There's no way," she says, waiting for me outside the dressing stall as I try on a royal blue mini dress.

"You're taking that one. End of discussion."

"This will barely cover my crack. Might as well wear nothing."

"That's the point."

I laugh, then walk toward the tall tri-fold mirror. Sometimes it's hard to look at me, seeing beauty yet having to speak daily affirmations that I'm more than my body, and lately, in doing so, I only come out feeling drained because those words are becoming harder to believe. Fixing one of the skinny straps that dip along my arm, I turn to look at Sadie, taking my mind away from this subject.

"What do you think?"

"Looks great on you."

"Looked even better on you," I say with a smirk, and she stays quiet.

Sadie's gorgeous with her long honey-blonde hair, freckles along her cheeks and nose, and deep brown eyes. She doesn't see how beautiful she is and tends to hide her slim figure, which has everything to do with her dick of an ex. Before she met Declan, she was more confident, outgoing, and less timid. I miss her spunk.

Heading back to the stall, I change into my skinny jeans and knit sweater, then pluck the pink lingerie from her fingers a minute later. "Wait, where's your pile?" Looking at the put-away rack beside us, I roll my eyes, grabbing everything. "You're getting them."

"Evie, you don't have to...."

"Come on, sexy lady. We still have one more store left before the mall closes."

She smiles, shaking her head, and I love to see her perk up, even if she's annoyed with me while heading to our next destination.

I take my time driving to her apartment, exhausted and

ready to knock out once I get home. Her phone rings, and she quickly silences the call.

"Was it him?" I ask while parking in front of the complex.

She glances at me and nods. "Nothing new."

"What a creep. How is he finding your new numbers, and don't you have a restraining order on him? Why not call your lawyer and see what you should do?"

"It doesn't matter. I can deal with a few calls a month."

My brows furrow. "Sadie, don't push this off like it's not a big deal. If he can find a number, what's stopping him from finding an address? It's better to nip the issue in the bud before the situation spirals into something worse."

Her silence is deafening, the stress pouring out of her. "I will. Soon."

I sigh and draw her in for a side hug. "Okay. I'll text you tomorrow. Don't forget your bag in the trunk."

She nods, grabs the clothes, and waves before striding to her apartment along the darkened pathway. I watch her until she enters her home, then pull into traffic, driving the five-minute distance to my two-story house. Living in Portland means my neighbors are close by, yet I have no desire to talk to anyone. By the end of each night, I'm just a body waiting to crash, forcing myself to leave work at the front door.

ore striding

darkened pathway

, then pull into traffic

tance to my two-story house

I have no desire to talk to anyone

myself to leave work at the front door

TWO

CHAOS IN A WORLD
OF PERFECTION

Lennox

I tend to drive on autopilot until reality kicks in every few moments like shit—how did I not die within the last five minutes of staring out my windshield thinking about anything other than operating heavy machinery? Because my mind knows where to go, taking the same route every day.

Wake up, work both jobs, sleep, and start again.

Earlier this week, while driving through Portland, I nearly ran over a woman crossing the street to an apartment complex on my way back to work from my lunch break—not my finest moment, and an eye-opener to be more careful. Proof my mind does run on autopilot, and I need to slow down.

I'm no jealous person, but what would life be like living a day in the shoes of a man who has his shit together? I have no shame walking in mine—there's just not much going on for me other than punching a time clock, no room for anything new, but that's because I've yet to find something worth occupying my time...someone.

Would I prefer the company of a woman next to me when I wake up? Sure, but there's a difference between hooking up and really finding your person. A woman who plucks those heartstrings in your chest with the slightest smile, how effortlessly the terms us, our, and we roll off the tongue because being around them is that easy, where autopilot no longer exists since you're invested in every moment together.

There are clients who stay at the cabin every week for the Kylo Kent Experience, and since I'm Kylo's assistant, I can introduce myself to women—find that smile. In twelve years, I've yet to immerse myself in any of them or have the urge to talk to anyone for more than a one-night stand—until she strolled by me with that gorgeous smile, and I felt a pluck.

Love at first sight is bullshit.

Parked in front of the cabin, I puff out my cheeks, exhaling a heavy breath while rubbing my hand over my face, still unable to get that woman from this morning out of my head—her cute face, that round ass, and the confidence in her step—*love at first sight is bullshit, right?*

Fuck...what was her name again? I really need to start putting more effort into knowing his clients.

I huff a laugh, then groan while getting out of the car, my knee aching, and I shake the sawdust from my jacket before heading inside the cabin instead of going home. Kylo overworks himself just as much as me, maybe more, but he doesn't see it. I hope he'll take my suggestion to cut back his client intake to once a month for a while—so much prep work and mental stimulation go into his sessions. He'll eventually get burnt out accepting clients without proper breaks in between, even if he doesn't fuck everyone.

How does Kylo keep his dick soft around a woman like her? Knowing he hasn't touched her that way makes me want to talk to her even more, yet the chances I'll ever formally meet her are slim to none. Strolling through the great room, I enter the kitchen and go straight for the peas in the freezer, snagging a beer from the fridge, then sit at the island.

"I need to quit before my knee gives out."

"Old at the age of thirty-one." Kylo chuckles from the couch and places the book he was reading on the coffee table.

"Yeah. Well, not everyone can work from home with their dream career. I was told to suck it up and get my ass to work straight out of high school."

"So quit. You make more than enough here."

I snort a laugh—*yeah, if only it were that easy.*

Laying the peas on my knee, I sigh, resting my elbow on the countertop while smoothing my thumb over the beer cap. "You know if I quit, I wouldn't hear the end of it from my pops. The old man wants his son to take over the family business bullshit."

"And logging isn't what you want."

"Got that right." I slouch further into the seat and plop my foot onto the next chair, staring out into the distance. "Trust me. If I could, I'd leave in a heartbeat."

Kylo stays quiet for a moment, and I look at him. "I'm going to need Lina to come in early on Saturday morning to clean and stock feminine products."

"Why?" I ask, straightening up in my seat.

"I have a client arriving afterward."

I furrow my brows and shake my head while breathing out a deep breath. Of course he is, even with the issue he's currently having with his recent client termination. His better judgment has been off, and safety isn't at the top of his mind right now, so I'll have to continue to be firm with him regarding certain aspects of the business. Having to force him to hire security to guard the premises being one of them —Adam used to guard the mill before dad switched to strictly security cameras, so I know he'll do his job right around here.

"Why do I bother?" My beanie falls off my head as I push my fingers through my hair. "There's a reason why I said once a month, Kylo. Hear me out. We raise the price to offset the loss of client intake; this way, you can have more of a break between sessions. Dealing with other people's stress can become emotionally draining without proper self-care."

He stands, strolling toward the cabinet drawer next to the range, and slides a bottle opener to me. "I understand your concerns, really, but I'd rather not lose clients, especially my regulars who need my service. Helping them with their mental health outranks my need for personal time."

I down half the beer after opening it. "Fine. It's your business, do what you want, but don't come to me when you're feeling burnt out."

Sitting next to me, he nudges his shoulder into mine. "Don't be like that."

"I worry about you," I say, picking at the bottle label as condensation forms along the bottom. "You're my best bud. Can't blame me for dwelling on *your* mental health."

I arch a brow at him when Kylo places his arm around my shoulders with a smirk on his face. "You love me."

Chuckling, I give him a wink. "You know it."

"I love you too, brother. I appreciate everything you do, don't forget that."

A sharp breath leaves me as I laugh and tip my beer at him before down the rest. "I'll call Lina in the morning. Just promise me you'll consider my proposition after this one."

"Done. I'll take the next month off."

"I'll believe it when I see it." I pat his shoulder as I stand, grabbing my beanie off the floor and placing the bag of peas on my shoulder to keep for later. "I'm heading home. Thanks for the peas and beer."

"Goodnight."

Leaving out the back door, I stroll along the front of the cabin until the deck forks, and I slip my hat on as a chilly breeze passes through, heading toward the guest house a few yards back. I could find a place of my own, but Kylo offered me to stay here—saying the addition would be a waste of space and having his assistant close is also better for the business. We started the Kylo Kent Experience a few months out of high school, and we never thought business would take off the way it has, a little too much.

My place is similar to Kylo's, an open concept, floor-to-ceiling windows throughout the first floor, facing the cabin, trees, and a view of the lake—rustic yet modern with red oak floors and black panels that separate each glass.

Kicking off my shoes, I hang my coat on a hook beside the door, head into the kitchen on my left, and store the peas in the freezer. There's a four-seater white marble island, dark cabinets, and stainless steel appliances.

The living area is where I spend most of my time across from the kitchen, my black leather couch facing the woods. Even though I despise my logging occupation, the view of the snow-lined trees swaying in the wind helps calm me after a hard day, and I'll lay back in my recliner with the fireplace going to unwind.

Since I grabbed food on the way home, I stroll upstairs toward the back, which leads to my lounge room, main bathroom, and bedroom suite. I plop onto the edge of my bed, rubbing my eyes, and my shoulders slump as I exhale a heavy breath.

Fuck, I'm tired. Exhausted, and it's only Monday.

I need to shower, but the second I lie back on the mattress, I groan, never getting up again.

Five days of my early morning routine, waking up at 4:00 a.m., drinking my coffee, and arriving at work at 5:00—I'm now thirty minutes in with my fourth tree of the day down and tons more to go. Our current location is on a slight incline, so many of our trees need to be cut with a saw, using the buncher, a more efficient machine, for the flatter surface areas. I've been doing the job of three men the past couple of weeks, and even telling dad we need more men, he continues to take his time hiring.

I'm close to losing my shit.

If this is his way of teaching me a lesson on running this type of business, working all aspects of the job, it's not very efficient on my body. Soon enough, there won't be a body left to take over. I get to work topping the few trees, clearing as many branches as possible in the timeframe I have to get the number of trees down.

Bones comes walking toward me, and I wouldn't be surprised or blame him if he ends up quitting like he says every day. I wouldn't get shit done on time if he wasn't here, so I hope he won't.

"Skidder's running."

"Alright, almost got these done, and you can chain them up."

What would usually take three days to fully load a truck with an appropriate crew takes Bones and me a week to get done alone. After five hours, I get a call from Gwyneth, Dad's secretary, that he needs me to finish paperwork after loading the truck and look over the newer applications. I officially lose my shit.

"Drop that log and take your lunch," I say to Bones and leave for my truck.

I don't use this vehicle outside work, but I drive back to the cabin, needing to put as many miles between me and the mill as possible before I do or say something I'll regret afterward. My heart's racing as I get to Kylo's front door, knocking, but I use my key instead, barging in before he can answer, striding for the bar in the kitchen.

"I'm done," I say, pouring vodka into a shot glass and taking it.

"What are you doing? It's eleven in the morning."

"Yeah? I'll have another five by noon."

I shouldn't be drinking, but I need something to ease the edge, to numb my mind. Kylo furrows his brows and walks beside me, taking the bottle from my hand when I pour another.

"What happened?" he asks, eyeing the liquid as I lean forward on the counter, letting out a low chuckle.

"Same shit, different fucking day." I take the shot, allowing the burning inferno to slide down my throat before I slam the glass on the bar. "Felling trees on top of loading them and paperwork at the end of the night, which isn't my job, while expecting me to get it done in an unreasonable time frame. I don't mind working as a feller. I prefer it, but we're understaffed, and my dad's taking his sweet time hiring more men."

I groan, rubbing my eyes, an ache forming deep within my gut, but I hold back the anger trying to take over me, a sick revelation that even though Dad's working me to the bone, I can't get mad at him, I don't want to disappoint him that I've resorted to liquor to stop my tongue.

"I wake up at four every morning, and the moment I get there, he's hounding me. I'm lucky to get a break at all, which I left for early today. I'm sure he'll have something to say about that once I get back."

"Lex, I feel for you—" The doorbell rings, and Kylo's eyes widen as he looks toward the front. "Shit. My client's here."

"Alright," I say, needing something else to occupy my

brain, so I scavenge around his cabinets to make myself lunch, not wanting to be alone right now.

"At least make yourself scarce."

"You want me to be more included, right? As your assistant, I should get to know the clients, so this is me involving myself—planting my ass right here."

There's knocking this time, and Kylo glances at me before jogging to answer the door. A few moments later, I'm by the range, ready to make a sandwich with whatever ingredients Kylo has on hand. A woman with long blonde hair slowly walks inside, glancing around the cabin. I try not to eavesdrop, but can't help myself when Kylo's voice differs from his usual tone when it comes to his clients, as if he's nervous or something. Since when does Kylo get nervous around women?

They stop by the short hallway between the living room and kitchen that leads to his office and the guest suite, then she looks at me, whispering to Kylo. They walk toward me, and I wipe my hand on my jeans before holding it out to her.

"Nice to meet you...."

"Sadie," she says, taking my handshake.

"Sadie." I smirk, tapping on my temple. "Gotta remember that."

Kylo turns to her. "Lex lives in the guest house out back, but your comfort is most important, so it'll be only you and me in the cabin during your stay."

Damn right, she won't see me after today. I don't need to witness whatever goes down during his sessions, though I raise a brow while watching them—the way Kylo's taking her in when she blushes like he wants to touch the rosy hues in her cheeks, and it's taking everything in him not to.

Interesting. Something about her is familiar, like I've met her recently, but I can't pinpoint where.

"Okay, that's ideal," Sadie says, and I take a sip of my water as they walk down the hallway.

Getting lunch situated, I'm sitting at the island eating my three-meat sandwich when Sadie rushes toward the front door, Kylo not far behind her.

"Wait," Kylo says, and she stops as she reaches the front door. "I'll help you."

Her brows move close together. "What about your rule?"

"It's in place for women who can't keep their end of the contract, but this, your request, is different." Sadie glances at her feet, and I take another bite of my sandwich as Kylo steps closer, gently lifting her chin to look at him. "You're requesting my service, it's new to me, but I'm here to help. I'll make you fall in love with me, but it won't happen in two days."

Make her fall in love...well, that's new and contradictory.

"Oh, okay...how long are we talking?"

He glances at me, and I pause my eating, investing in whatever is happening right now to grasp what scheme Kylo's trying to come up with on top of the hectic schedule he's already given himself.

"Let's start with a week."

A week?

How does my suggestion to take time off become more work added to his plate? Even she looks taken back as she blinks a few times, trying to figure out her words.

"A week...I work nights on the weekend, afternoons during the week when I'm needed, and having no car to travel back and forth makes being here difficult."

Kylo glances at me again, and I shake my head, continuing to eat, my input not necessary. "Where do you work?" he asks her.

"In Portland, at Vivid Vixens."

Isn't that the fancy strip joint on the way to my job?

"The strip club?" I ask with my mouth full.

I can't help being curious about that, though I don't miss Kylo's glare, narrowing my eyes at him before taking another bite of my sandwich. He already knows taking on more work is a bad idea.

Sadie turns away from me and glances at Kylo. "No, it's a Gentleman's Club and more...."

"Hey, it's okay. We'll make it work, and Lex can take you."

I choke on my food, coughing while pounding on my chest as the dry bread moves slowly down my throat, and I stare at him. "Lex will what? Did you forget I work crazy hours?"

"You come here during your breaks. Drop Sadie off on the way back, and pick her up when you're done."

"I'm not a chauffeur."

Kylo walks up to me and grips my shoulders with a firm massage. "C'mon, *you* need me time, and what better place than stopping for a beer after a long hard day at work while you wait?"

I shrug him off. "That place is too upscale for a drop-by. Make Adam do it, or you can take her yourself."

"You don't have to," Sadie says. "I'll see if my friend Evie can give me rides. We work together."

My brows perk up at that name, and I look at Sadie. "Evie...why does that sound familiar?"

"I'm sure you've met her. She's one of your regulars."

Then the name clicks, and a beautiful brunette I can't

get off my mind comes flooding from my memories—I stand, finishing my last bite while wiping my mouth with a napkin. "You know what, don't worry about it. I'll take and pick you up."

Sadie glances between Kylo and me then nods.

"Okay. Then it's settled," Kylo says, pleased with her answer. "We'll start with a week, work our way to more if needed, and I'll do my best to make you fall in love with me."

Good luck with the rule, Kylo.

That lasted no more than ten minutes as I'm currently driving Sadie home. One second I received a text message from Kylo with the idea of extending sessions to be more effective, resulting in him having lengthier downtown between each client, then the next, he's asking me to take Sadie home. I assume she changed her mind for a second time.

"It's times like this that make me realize I don't understand jack shit about women," I say, glancing at Sadie sitting beside me, then back to the road. "You want something, and then you don't, then you do again only to say you don't once more? Why torture yourself like that?"

"I'm not torturing myself."

"Sounds a hell of a lot like it. You desire one thing, then sabotage yourself from achieving it without giving it a chance."

She stays quiet for a second before muttering under her breath, "Maybe you should mind your business."

"Mind my business. Lady, this is my business. You're wasting our time and resources."

I feel like an asshole when she's quiet the entire ride to her apartment since I don't know her story, what she's been through, still probably going through, and once I park on the street to her complex, that feeling intensifies to a thousand. "This is where you live?"

"Yes. Why?" She shifts in her seat as I turn to stare at her. "What?"

"Are you the girl I almost ran over a few days ago? I knew there was something familiar about you."

She widens her eyes. "That was you?"

Scratching my head, I stare at the road while tapping the steering wheel with my thumb and Kylo saying I need '*me time*' sticks because he couldn't be more right.

"Yeah, my bad about that. I was rushing to get back to work and didn't see you crossing—I felt like a dick almost hitting you."

"Oh, it's fine. I was sort of zoned out myself."

I nod, giving her a tight smile, relieved I hadn't traumatized her. "Well, I'm glad I didn't kill you."

She snorts and holds her hand toward me. "Thanks, I guess, for not killing me."

Chuckling, I give her a firm shake, then lean back in my chair. *I like her spunk.*

"I thought you worked with Kylo? Being his assistant," she asks.

"It's a side job, but unfortunately, I also work in the logging industry with my dad."

"Unfortunately?"

"Yup. No need to get into details."

"Hm." We sit in silence, and the more we stew, the more

she looks like she wants to leave, though I don't want her to. "I should go—"

"Take the sessions," I say, facing her. "I've been a jerk since you arrived, and I apologize. Kylo and I don't always see eye to eye when it comes to the experience. However, the idea he pitched regarding your sessions, I believe, will benefit future clients and the business more than our current plan. Take the week. If you feel it's not working, you are in control of terminating the sessions at any point. Don't..." I sigh, then look at her to not make the same mistakes as me. "Don't let fear rule you. I sense you're hesitant, but I know Kylo. He's passionate, caring, and has everyone's best interests at heart, to the point of neglecting himself while helping others."

She raises her brows. "Doesn't seem like the best idea to take on a client like me then."

"That's true, but he's nervous around you, which never happens to him with clients, hell, women in general." I rest my head on the seat. "I know he won't take time off, so maybe if he focuses on one person in the meantime, it'll give him time to rest his mind, and possibly you can help me help him?"

"You want me to help him relax?"

"To realize self-care is important, and at the same time, you'll get the help you need. It's a win-win if you ask me."

The freckles along Sadie's nose wrinkle as she scrunches, which is adorable—I can see why Kylo's flustered.

"I don't know. My situation... it's complicated."

"So, make it less complicated. What's the worst that can happen?" She stays quiet, but I don't let her think for long. "It's the least you can do since you almost made me a murderer," I add with a smirk, and her jaw drops.

"You're not seriously playing the victim card."

I chuckle, then check my watch. "I only have a few minutes of my break left. So what do you think?"

Letting out a deep breath, she nods. "Alright. What time will you be back to pick me up?"

Proud of my persuasion superpower, I grin, starting my truck. "I'll be here around 5:30."

"Should I contact Kylo?"

"No. I'll take care of it. You worry about packing."

"Sure, and thanks for the ride. I'm going to talk with my friend to see if she can give me rides, too, so you're not the one always taking me to work."

No problem with that. Maybe I'll have a chance to talk to her if she does.

"Alright. We'll talk about that later. Give me your phone, and I'll call my number."

After the exchange, she leaves my truck, and I wave before pulling into traffic, driving quickly before coming to normal speed to head back to work because why rush?

The night ended up being another shitshow while I ignored Dad's lecture about my work ethic the best I could, got my day's load done, and now I text Sadie that I'm five minutes away from arriving back at her place. Once I pull up toward her complex, she's holding an orange cat, and I dial her number.

"Hello?"

"Are you trying to get me fired?"

"No?"

"Ditch the cat."

She scoffs. "No way. We're a package deal."

Groaning, I get out of the car, slip my phone into my pocket, and stroll along the pathway. "Kylo doesn't do pets."

"Jinx is an outdoor cat, so she won't get in the way. It'll be like she's not even there."

"Hey, I couldn't care less. Bring the cat if you want, but Kylo will tell you no."

"We'll see about that."

I smirk, arching a brow. *Yeah, we're gonna get along fine.* "Alright, where are your bags?"

"My suitcase and duffle are by the door."

Grabbing her stuff, I head for the Porsche, waiting for Sadie as she waves to her neighbor before getting in the car with her cat. "Keep her on your lap."

"Don't worry. I won't set Jinx loose to wreak havoc inside your fancy car."

Not my car, but if anything happened to the interior while I'm using it, Dad would probably disown me—not the worst idea.

"It's my dad's. Not my style, and I'm only borrowing it until my Mustang gets fixed."

"Ooh. Yeah, a muscle car suits you more."

I smirk, ready to create chaos in a world of perfection. "Alright, let's go surprise Kylo."

Sadie whips her head toward me, and her cat stirs in her arms when I pull into traffic.

"What?" she asks, her eyes wide, and I lean back on the seat without another word. Maybe it's a dick move, not informing Kylo Sadie's returning so soon, but being caught off guard will be good for him. He would've started planning immediately, worrying rather than relaxing and taking his time.

Plus, I'm an asshole.

r eyes wide

out another wor

die's returning so soon

He would've started plannin

y, worrying rather than relaxin

king his time. Plus, I'm an asshol

THREE

YOU COST ME
A PRETTY PENNY

Evie

The office on the second floor is being renovated. Last week the walls were re-painted white with a dark grey accent wall along the back. Today movers brought in a black desk, leather couch, other furniture, and a massive abstract painting as a focal point of the accent wall, with red, white, and black throughout. The interior is open, visible through the floor-to-ceiling windows that take up the office front wall, which means whoever occupies that space has eyes on everyone.

Red, the owner, rarely comes to Vivid. He'll drop by every few months to make sure everyone remembers who the boss is, but Gin has always been in charge. No one has used that office in years, so why the renovations?

It's another full house this weekend, and I end my seductive aerial act with a grin as I unwrap my body from the red silks. My blood's pumping, adrenaline coursing through my veins as the crowd cheers, both men and women coming to watch the show before they venture out to other aspects of the club, most of them heading to the basement, some voyeur, and I have a break before my first customer of the night at 7:00.

Once in the dressing room, I remove the sheer white one-piece that's riding up my ass and throw on my street clothes. I have an hour all to myself, and I'm starving, sneaking out the back door for my favorite taco shop down the street. Zipping my jacket, I stroll along the sidewalk and close my eyes as the wind blows, cooling my heated skin. The best way to come down from the high is good food and company as I enter the small building with several customers eating along the left wall.

"*Hola*, Evie," says Marina, the owner, who glances over her shoulder at the clock. "Is it 6:00 already?"

I walk toward the counter. "Hey, and yup. Busy day today?"

"Always. What can I make for you?"

Since I have a long night, I'll stick with something light. "Two carne asada tacos, please, and I'll grab a bottle of water."

She nods, rings me up, and I grab my drink, the food ready a few minutes later, devouring every delicious bite. I still have twenty minutes left of my break, so I take my time walking to Vivid, entering through the front.

A guy with dark hair barely hitting twenty-one sits in the security box and rolls open his window as I stroll toward the door. "Ma'am, you can't enter without a male companion," he says, and I raise a brow.

I haven't seen him here before, and our head of security usually gives newbies lobby duty.

"Are you going to stop me from entering if I don't?"

"Um…" I inch closer to the door, and he stands from his seat, rubbing his palm over his short curly fade, his gaze roaming down my body. "Yes. There's a door fee and dress code as well. No jeans permitted."

"Rules are made to be broken." Strolling toward the window, I unzip my jacket, my breasts bare underneath my low-cut t-shirt, and his deep brown eyes flick to them as I lean forward on the ledge, displaying a pout. "Please. I've got money to spend and lap dances to look forward to. Won't you let me in this once?"

"No—sorry. Rules say I can't. We don't close until 2 a.m., so there's plenty of time for you to change and come back with someone."

I giggle, pulling out my ID, killing enough time, and have to get ready for my regular, Vincent. "Good boy, Jr," I say, patting his cheek, which turns a shade of pink above his neat beard. "I feel safer working here knowing you're doing your job right. I'm going inside to get ready for my customer."

"Shit, my bad." He chuckles, holding out his hand, and I take his handshake. "I've only been here a week. My name's Nate."

"Evie."

Giving him a wink, I enter the main floor and get by Gin without her noticing me. Showered and standing at my station mirror, I apply Vivid's scarlet red to my lips and press them together, everything else on my body void of color as I air dry. Being nude is second nature. Roni, the new girl working with me for this session, comes bouncing to my side, giggling as she plays with the long brown hair she's wearing on top of her natural blonde.

I hate couple sessions—not that I have anything against her—she's a sweet girl. However, I prefer performing solo acts.

"Here," she says, handing me white lace lingerie with a blonde wig, and I raise an eyebrow at her. "New request came in from our customer."

Vincent is a long-time patron of Vivid who comes to me every Saturday and prefers I make the decisions—taking control is also second nature—he's never submitted last-minute changes to his girl-on-girl fantasy request and couldn't care less what we wear as long as our outfit ends up on the floor.

"Are you going to get dressed?" she adds, attaching the last strap of her black feathered garter belt to her stocking, mine having an identical style. "I'd like to head upstairs before the customer settles. I'm nervous but also excited to start my first couples performance."

I grab an elastic, securing my hair that I finished styling a few seconds ago into a low bun, and slip on the wig as best I can without a cap—it'll have to do for this fifteen-minute session. With only a few moments left to get ready, I slide on the lingerie and take one last look in the mirror before meeting Roni's excited grin.

"Let's get this over with."

Slipping on a robe, we leave the dressing room for the Red Gentlemen's Club, stopping by the bar, and my skin prickles as a flock of patrons turn our way with prying eyes. I scan the room, searching for Sadie before remembering she took off work for her weekend with Kylo, and I'm glad she decided to take my advice. That girl needs his magic touch as much as I need his words, but a few days of the Kylo Kent Experience is no longer enough to reset me. As if my mind's immune to anything positive trying to enter.

"Get to work," Gin says, tapping my shoulder, and I press my lips together to stop from responding—having control over my tongue is a concept I'm still grasping.

Roni nudges my shoulder with hers, nodding toward the stairs to our right, and I follow her. The four voyeur rooms change themes depending on how well a display does, and the more money a setup makes, the longer it stays. I walk ahead, climbing stairs and continuing to the employee entrance for room one. The vacancy sign fades off, so Vincent is inside, ready for us.

"I'm leading," Roni says as we enter the Vixen privacy box and hang our robes. "Customer wants a sixty-minute session and for you to be submissive while he directs me on how to pleasure you."

I furrow my brows. "Are you sure?"

"Yes. The new request had a few changes. Aren't you supposed to check the queue before each session?"

"Not when it comes to my regulars. What was the name?"

"Didn't say. They are anonymous."

Did I get my times wrong?

"Alright. Not what I was expecting, but I'll try to tone myself down."

Roni scrunches her nose, rubbing her palms on a robe hanging on the wall. "Believe me. Today being my first time, I'd rather follow you."

Grabbing hold of my hand, she leads us down the short hall, and the musty scent hits me first when we round the corner, never getting used to the old motel smell, though something new filters through. Tobacco, which customers aren't allowed to smoke in voyeur. The room is dim, but I know the setup—straight ahead is the same voyeur box in every room, where customers watch, touch themselves, fuck their partner, whatever they want to do except pass the white line separating them from the performers.

Customers have access to a dresser stocked with intimate items available for purchase, a bed couples mainly use, and a chair for the solos unless they opt to stay behind the privacy glass. The area brightens, and a man I haven't seen in years appears from behind the wall, leaning on the doorway, smoking a cigar.

You can't be serious.

Staying in the middle of the room, Roni turns to me, pressing her palm on my stomach, and waits for his instruction per his request. Jared, the son of the club owner, is wearing a black suit tailored to his body, puffing on the cigar and blowing smoke into the air as he drags the chair to the white line, relaxing in the seat with his legs wide open. Strands of his sleek dark hair fall onto his forehead as he cocks his head to the side, staring at me with his steel-blue eyes while snuffing out the cigar on the leather arm.

"Everly, it's been a while," he says, his voice deep and gritty, spreading goosebumps across my skin.

Only Gin calls me that, and I hate it even more off his tongue.

"Don't call me that."

I narrow my eyes when Jared shushes me, shaking his head while rubbing his fingers over his bottom lip. "Show me her tits."

Roni slowly circles my body, trailing her hand up my side before stopping behind me to release the clasp of my bra, and the delicate white fabric falls to the floor. He unfastens his belt and drags the zipper of his trousers down to expose his dark underwear, not once taking his eyes off me.

"I watched your performance earlier on the silks and wanted a closer look, catch up a bit," he says while unbuttoning his shirt. "You cost me a pretty penny to take this spot—"

"Don't expect anything other than a show."

He breathes out a low chuckle. "I know the rules, and as should you. Now, play your part and make me come tonight."

Drawing out his half-limp dick, he rests the length on his thigh, and I couldn't care less if he ever shoots his load. However, I let out a heavy breath, easing my expression before he gets me written up—I don't feel like dealing with Gin tonight. Licking my lips, I roll my head to the side as Roni kisses my neck.

"There you go. Not so difficult, right?"

I close my eyes for a moment, my chest heaving once she dips her hand to my breast, though it's not her touch riling me up.

"Tease her on the edge of the bed with your mouth. Take your time. Don't make her come until I say." He pulls out a vial of lube from his pocket, glancing at me as he drips the liquid on his palm. "Lighten up, sweetheart. Moan a little. At least pretend you're enjoying my presence."

Arching a brow, I put on a sweet ol' smile before following Roni to the bed across from the ugly brown curtains. She positions me on the edge, kneels on the shaggy rug, then spreads my legs wide, rubbing her thumbs along my inner thighs. Her pointed stare shows she knows I'm annoyed and not to cause trouble—*she doesn't know me too well.*

I lean back on my hands, letting out a fake gasp as Roni drags me closer, impressed by her strength and persistence. She unclips all my buttons, stripping me until I'm nude, and I look at Jared, who's now slowly stroking his shaft. He's a handsome man with a monster cock, and a cocky attitude to go with it, though it's not the attractive kind—a shame, really, that I ever liked a guy like him.

Roni's soft pecks along my hip bring me back, moving up my stomach, her tongue leaving a wet trail to my nipple before taking the peak into her mouth, which makes him quicken his pumps, his breathing increasing.

"Eat her pussy next," he rasps, and Roni spreads my legs more, continuing to kiss down my abdomen. "Harder."

Her kisses turn to bites, nipping her way to my core, and he moans, sweat forming on his brows as he works himself. I'm sure her mouth feels nice, but I feel nothing.

Jared chuckles again, slowing his strokes while dragging his teeth over his lower lip. "Are you always so stiff? Here I thought you were the best."

Oh, you want my best?

I grin, tilt my head back and hum, gripping the nape of Roni's neck as I rock my pelvis forward. "That's right, sweet girl. Go on and suck my pussy." She grabs my thighs hard when I draw her closer, lifting my leg over her shoulder and moaning loudly, "*Fuck,* just like that—make me come."

A slight wrinkle appears between Jared's brows as he watches every buck of my hips. "Slow down."

"What are you doing?" Roni whispers harshly, stopping her movements, but I continue to pant, holding her in place, squirming my body as if she's eating me out.

"Don't fucking come," he barks, but I don't let up, rocking harder, whining louder, staring him down.

Ripping my wig off, I toss the blonde hair across the room and unravel my long brown waves, each strand flowing past my chest. I draw out one last moan, run my tongue along the length of my fingers to rub on my tits, and finish my performance strong before slowly letting up. Jared cocks a brow, dipping further into the chair with his heavy gaze on me. Though his dick is still hard in his hand, I can't tell if he's upset I didn't follow his rule or further intrigued by my defiance.

I release Roni from my grip, paying no mind to the scowl on her face, and leave for the dressing room without another word. Grabbing my robe, I stride out to the hall and gasp as I knock into one of the cleaning carts nearly tipping it.

Petra rushes over from a supply closet with a box of gloves in hand. "Oh, I'm sorry! Wasn't expecting this room to finish so soon. Are you okay?" she asks, handing me the robe I dropped, genuine concern etched on her face.

"Yeah, thanks." I slip the robe on, heading for the main stairs since I don't have my keycard, ignoring Gin as I walk straight for the dressing room.

A moment later, Roni strides inside and shoves me into my station table, my makeup scattering. "What the fuck,

Evie?! Why couldn't you stick with the act and get it over with? Now we'll get a low rating and lose the customer."

I swallow hard, clench my jaw and straighten up, holding back the tears threatening to fall. "Fuck that guy."

"No, what you did in there was fucked up. How could you do that to me?"

I should feel bad, but I don't. Maybe that'll be my last couples session.

"Sorry."

She laughs and shakes her head. "No wonder nobody likes working with you. You really are a selfish bitch."

Strolling to my chair, I sit back, and my thin robe falls open, exposing my thigh as I cross my legs. "I work better alone anyway."

"Unbelievable. You're lucky Gin's your mother. She's the only reason you're still here." Roni spins on her heels and leaves for the shower room.

She's right about that. My mother is the reason I'm here, why I am the way I am. Looking over the mess on my station, I reorganize each item and fix the origami bird displayed in the corner. What was once bright white has dulled over the years, the little dove flawed but still beautiful. I unbend the wings and place my childhood treasure back in its place. Julianne strolls into the room—her long silver beach waves fall over her right shoulder, covering half of her tattoo sleeve. She crosses her arms and leans on the doorframe.

"You know Gin's gonna have your ass for that session. She and Red are about to tear each other's heads off out there."

My brows pinch together. "Red's here? He never comes to the club."

Red couldn't care less about what goes on at Vivid as

long as we're not performing illegal acts and he gets his money's worth. Everything falls on Gin.

"Go see for yourself. You know who that guy you fucked over in there is, right?"

"Unfortunately, yes." I stare at her and sigh.

"Yeah. You need to fix this now."

I stand, unfastening my robe. "Let me change—"

"Now, Russo," she says, raising a brow.

Julianne's the only person who can get away with talking to me that way, and using my last name means business. She's taken care of me since I was a kid, basically living back here while Gin worked.

"Fine."

Walking past her, I stop as she takes hold of my hand. "Between you and me, I'm glad you showed off to that jerk. Proud of you, kid."

I smirk, giving her a quick hug. "Thanks, Ma." Then continue strolling toward the bar in the front.

"You need to get her under control, or I will."

"Or you'll what?"

Stopping where the wall meets the counter, I peek around, finding Red and Gin face to face as they talk in low, harsh whispers. He chuckles, and Gin narrows her eyes at him. "This place needs more male authority. Since you can't handle your girls on your own, I'll have Jared keep them in order."

Oh, hell no!

"You'll do no such thing. I'm running my business just fine by mysel—"

Gin gasps, eyes wide as Red places his hand around her throat, tight enough to get her attention, and eases her onto the bar shelf. "You'll do great to remember this is my business, and you're only the whore who looks after it."

My fists tighten, pushing forward as if I just arrived, and they both look my way. Red's gaze falls down my body, his eyes almost dark gray in the lighting, and I fasten my robe as he backs away from Gin, crossing his arms—his diesel biceps almost bursting through his short sleeves.

"What do you have to say for yourself?" he asks.

Gin straightens her stance, her fingers touching her chest as she stares at me, *her spitting image*, and I look away to face Red. "I'm sorry. I wasn't in the right mindset and shouldn't have taken the session. It won't happen again."

He chuckles, then smirks. "Damn right, it won't. Because starting Monday, your new manager will ensure our revenue stays on the increasing end." He glances at Gin, then back to me. "You won't think twice about fucking with my business then."

I keep a straight face before giving him a slight smile, but deep inside, I'm fuming. He walks around the bar, then crosses the floor toward the stairs, heading to the office on the second floor. Gin releases a loud sigh, and I face her leaning on the bar, her chestnut hair covering her face as she breathes deeply, then looks at me with dark eyes like mine.

Cold.

"Everly—"

Not caring what she has to say, I stride into the dressing room and go straight to the showers.

I'm done with today.

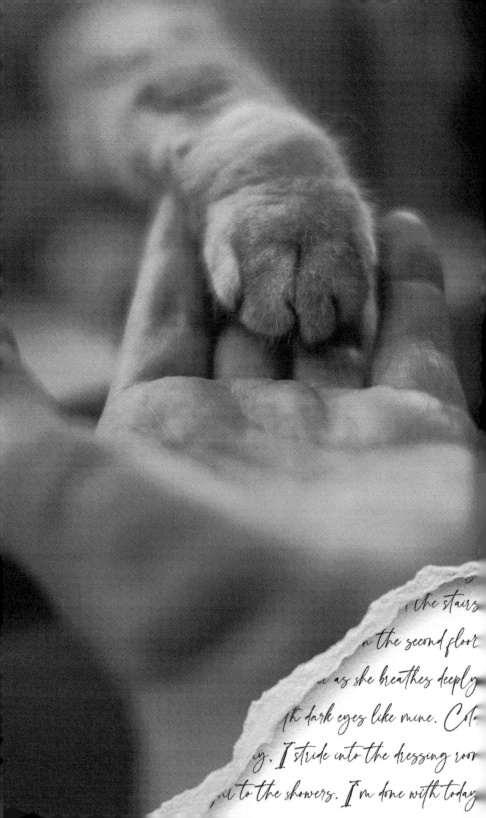

the stairs

the second floor

as she breathes deeply

th dark eyes like mine. Col-

y. I stride into the dressing roo

to the showers. I'm done with today

FOUR

SLOW YOUR ROLL, MISSY

Lennox

"**F**uck..." I groan, hanging my head as I immerse in the warmth of my happy place.

Slipping my arm behind my neck, I spread my legs over the sides of the tub, the heat of the water relaxing my strained muscles, unwinding from the shit show at work today—if I had bubbles, I'd give my balls some much-needed pampering, too. I rub circles around my aching knee, wishing the pain would subside quicker. My doctor was no help, telling me to ice and elevate my leg at night along with taking a few days off work, then slapped me with a hundred and fifty dollar bill, calling it a day. I'm simply overworking my joints like I didn't already know.

There's no luxury of *'taking a day off'* while working with my pops, not when we're understaffed, and I'm designated to take over the place when he retires.

Son, you're young. You can rest when you're dead. Put in the work now, so at my age, you're set.

I should tell him how much I don't want to run the mill— Jimmy's been there longer, better suited to take over fully since he already owns half the business. However, if those words were to leave my tongue, Dad would flip matters to make me feel like the bad guy for not having the same priorities.

Relaxing further into the water, I hum, dipping my hand inside to rest on my stomach. My priorities should be on crafting these ideas in my head. I'd rather spend my time working wood than harvesting them, but there's not enough time in the day to create. Maybe one day I'll have the guts to start my own business as Kylo did.

What went down in his office earlier when Sadie and I returned to the cabin makes me chuckle—she left the room beet red, and I'm glad I only walked into the aftermath, my plan in full effect. He's fighting his attraction toward her, and it's about time someone finally came along to stroke his heartstrings.

Evie comes back into my mind, and I dip my hand along my shaft. Damn. She's beautiful, from her long brown hair that reached just above her round ass swaying in those skin-tight jeans, but her dark, intense gaze caught my breath, which is why she's stuck in my head. When our eyes connected, I felt the weight of the world behind them, that her confidence was a mask to keep her moving, and now I want to know her pain, to relieve it for her.

She's branded in my mind, those pouty pink lips, unashamed to picture them pressing along my body until they wrap perfectly around my cock. I close my eyes, my dick quickly rising as she laps up the cum bead like the greedy girl she'll be with me. How deep can she take my length before gagging as I tangle my fist into her dark hair, feeling each strand while pushing my dick in a little further—

My head falls back over the tub as I stroke my shaft, moaning when she hums, her intense gaze making my pulse race and groin tighten, a pulsing sensation creeping to the surface, though I'm not ready for the finish line awaiting me. I don't want to win yet, not this way, because I want the real thing. *Her.*

Gritting my teeth, I stop pumping just as I'm about to blow and take deep, steady breaths, staying in the tub until the water turns frigate and my dick falls limp.

I'm done being alone.

4 a.m., and I'm waiting for the coffee to brew in Kylo's kitchen, hoping he or Sadie won't wake before I leave back to my place. Her orange cat prances toward me, the little bell on her collar jiggling when she jumps onto the island just as

the liquid gold pours into Kylo's fancy mug, and she watches me fix my coffee.

"The fuck you looking at?" I say, and she tilts her little head to the side, curling her paws into her body. "People eat here. You know that, right—and now I'm talking to a fucking cat." She winks an eye, and I arch a brow. "Slow your roll, missy. I'm not that desperate."

I pet her head, then walk outside to the guest house. Kylo's coffee is better than mine, and I have no shame waking up early on a Sunday to steal some. Reaching my door down the pathway, I glance at my feet, where the cat sits beside me.

"What the—go back." I shoo her away with my foot, but she doesn't budge, rubbing her head on my leg, then makes a weird noise while staring into my eyes with that cute face.

She bolts inside when I open the door—taking in a cat isn't what I had in mind with not being alone. I prefer the pussy that enters the premises to be less *furry*. Chuckling at my joke, I roam inside my home, leave the door cracked in case the feline decides to go, and take a sip of the steaming liquid in my mug.

"Damn, that's smooth."

The cat hops onto the back of the couch with a balled-up sock in her mouth, then lies on her side, kicking it with her feet.

"Go ahead. Make yourself at home."

Sitting in the chair beside her, I continue sipping, watching the snow-dusted branches sway in the breeze. My body naturally wakes at 4 a.m. every morning since I've been doing it for thirteen years, getting ready for my 5 a.m. shift at the mill. Sleeping in is nearly impossible, even if I try. My new guest jumps to the chair, purring as she steps onto my lap, and I scratch along her back.

"You're a good girl. Just don't eat my plants, and we'll get along fine."

She meows as I pet behind her ear, then bolts to the floor, running across the room. It'll be interesting having two nocturnal beings sharing space if she continues to come around. After a few hours of hyperactivity and lots of crying to leave, I walk into the cabin with the cat resting on my shoulder, walking toward Kylo alone in his kitchen.

"Mornin'. Where's the food for this beast? Maybe she'll shut up if I feed her."

He raises a brow at me. "First, why do you have Sadie's cat?" Kylo asks.

"She followed me home earlier when I came to steal coffee."

"You know, those grounds aren't cheap."

"Yes, and I thank thee for the full-bodied brew to touch my tongue—tastes almost as good as a woman. Almost—" I suck a sharp breath as the cat gears her claws into my shoulder and leaps to the floor, prancing up to Sadie.

"Hey, pretty girl. I heard you made a new friend," she says, glancing at me.

I don't usually come to the cabin when Kylo has his clients over, but something about Sadie is inviting. Or, it's because my best bud hasn't stopped looking at her since she entered the premises. Professional Kylo is definitely not in the building.

"She has good taste. I enjoyed her company until she took a shit in one of my plants."

Sadie gasps. "Jinx! I'm so sorry. She's an outside cat, so I don't use a litter box—"

Chuckling, I wave it off. "No big deal, she's cool."

"Are you sure? I'll replace it."

"It's nature. Animals shit on plants all the time."

I smirk as Sadie giggles and kisses Jinx on the head.

"Okay. While I have you, do you have a minute to discuss rides?"

Nodding, I gesture for her to sit on the couch and sit beside her. "What's your schedule like?"

"I work weekends 6 p.m., and I'm out by midnight, 2 a.m. the latest—"

Jinx turns her head toward the kitchen, scrambling from Sadie's hold to eat her meal when Kylo opens a can of food.

"Jinx!" Sadie groans. "Off the counter."

"Our girl is a handful."

She smiles and lets out a deep breath. "Yeah, this is all new for both of us. Sorry if she was bothering you over at your place."

"No bother. It was nice having the company."

"Okay. That's good, at least." Sadie's phone rings, and she silences the call, placing the device between her thighs. "Um, back to work. Don't worry if the pick-up time is too late. My friend Evie can bring me back, and I'm off on Sundays."

Evie...is it a coincidence that the woman who's caught my eye happens to be friends with Sadie? Even her name is beautiful.

"I'm not picking up the next two shifts, but on Friday evening, would you mind bringing me? You could come inside, grab a drink—on the house, of course."

Sounds like a good plan. "Sure, no problem."

"Great, thank you, Lex. I appreciate your help. I should

buy myself a car now that I'm on my own. I never drove when I was with—"

Her face drops before she glances at Kylo, and I bet her mood change has something to do with an ex. He must've been a dick if even the thought of him still affects her this way.

"Come with me," Kylo says, holding out his hand. "I want to show you something."

If anyone can make her forget, it's Kylo. Sadie's smile returns before she places her hand in his, and they head for the basement. I'll need to announce my presence before entering the cabin after today because they both got that twinkle in their eyes. Who knows what'll go down here at any given moment. Heading toward the back door, I stop before leaving, whistle, and Jinx runs to my side, walking with me up the pathway.

As I said, I enjoy the beast's company.

my presenc

kle in their eyes

at any given moment

I stop before leaving, whistle

walking with me up the pathwa

I said, I enjoy the beast's company

FIVE

ROOM SIX

Evie

Afternoons are slow here at Vivid, so fewer Vixens pick up shifts, but lately, patrons have been flooding the main floor, which means I've been summoned yet again to work the front between voyeur customers. Did a new business open around the area, generating a crowd that decided to take their lunch simultaneously? Since switching titles to Red, being a Vixen is the last job I want. My ass belongs in the box, away from people.

One Vixen stares at me as I pass, another giving her a knowing look as if me being out here was my idea. I'm barely acknowledging patrons, so what's their problem?

If that's how they want to act, I'll give them a reason to hate me.

It's not my turn, but I drag one of the smaller chairs to the main stage as Gemma finishes her set, placing the velvet seat in the middle. Multiple patrons set eyes on me, and I smirk, glancing upstairs to the office as Jared walks to the window that overlooks the main floor. Today's his first day as manager, and he sure looks the part, crossing his arms, widening his stance, watching me start a set, though will he intervene? Make me stop to prevent drama that could jeopardize revenue.

Go fuck yourself plays on the speakers, and my lips widen to a grin. Oscar, the DJ, knows what I like. I tussle my hair, making the long dark strands fall over half my face as I wine my body to the slow melody, the lyrics guiding my sensual moves along the stage until the beat drops, and I take hold of the pole to spin around. The faster I work, lifting into the air, stretching my body, the more every man inches off their seat to get closer.

Landing on my knees, I arch backward, peeling off my sheer black bra as I buck my body, then roll onto my stomach with my ass in the air. Each hungry gaze makes my skin crawl, their thoughts screaming, *I want to fuck you right here, right now.* I grit my teeth, stalking toward a blond man with thick-framed glasses, and grab his patterned tie.

Eyes wide, he presses his palms on the edge of the stage as I draw him close to my face and fog up his lenses with a deep breath. He goes to take them off, but I drag him on stage, which is against the rules. Oscar transitions to a slower sensual song and a few people whistle as I stand, making my patron crawl while keeping hold of his tie, then drop his leash.

Stepping behind the chair, I pat the back cushion for him to take a seat, and he obliges. I cup his stubbled cheek, taking off his glasses, and he blinks a few times before his heavy gaze finds mine as he tilts his head back. Trailing my thumb down his lower lip, I stroll around, dodging his touch when he reaches for my waist.

I put on his glasses, both of our vision blurred, and I place my hands on his thighs, leaning forward until our lips are inches apart.

"You want to watch?" I ask, and he nods, easing his glasses off my face before I slowly dip, dragging my nails down his expensive trousers until my ass rests on the floor.

Spreading my legs wide, I arch my back, cupping my pussy as I rock my body to the song. His chest quickly rises, dick begging to be freed while palming himself, and I extend my leg, resting my calf on his thigh. Crossing the other, I turn over and brace myself on the floor, face downward, my ass pressing onto his stomach when I hand-walk toward him.

He takes no time touching me, exploring the curve of my ass with his thumbs, gliding his palm up my lower back as I wind my hips. Gripping his knees to draw myself upward, I straddle his lap backward, continuing to grind, and he moans into my ear while palming my stomach and tits—an intimate show meant for a private room, and no one stops me. Everyone's watching at this point, including Gin. The rules have never applied to me, and they are all right. I'll never worry about leaving this place because I'm Gin's kid.

The song ends, and I slide off him, gather my clothes, giving zero fucks about the cash on the stage while striding to the dressing room. No Vixen approaches me as I walk to the costume rack, picking another of my scandalous outfits, then heading back to the main floor. Jared's outside the curtain and blocks my path.

"Room six," he says, his fingers trailing down my arm and landing on my hip. "Now."

I'm on the verge of tears, needing to keep them at bay. "Employees are off-limits."

He smirks. "We both know you don't play by the rules." Jared places his hand in his pocket, then heads for the back wall by the stairs.

One tear falls, and I quickly swipe it away, then look at Gin behind the bar. I stare deep into her eyes, my chest rising fast, longing for her to stop her flesh and blood from entering that room. The moment she turns away, tending to business, another tear falls, and this time I leave my sorrow, wandering across the floor to the private rooms as multiple hands touch my body in passing, and I give zero fucks. My body no longer belongs to me.

Standing in front of six, I stare at the closed door for a moment. I have the choice to leave right now. Leave this place—never look back, but instinct kicks in as I enter the room with my head high. There's a white semi-circle sectional along the back wall, red drapes drawn on either side, and Jared sitting in the middle, leaning back with his shirt half-buttoned and legs wide open. He doesn't say a word as I stroll closer, but his eyes roam over my body, drinking me in until I'm standing before him.

There are five crisp hundred dollar bills lined along the leather fabric. Jared takes one, folds it in half the long way, and slips it into the band of my tassel skirt. "One for listening. Continue, and you'll receive more." My brows raise a notch as he holds another in his hand. "Lose the top."

"Why are you infatuated with me?" I ask, taking a few steps back while removing my rhinestone bra.

The next hundred falls to the floor as he flicks it between us. "Because you're difficult."

I saunter forward and slide into a straddle to take the bill, snapping the band of my skirt against it. "And that turns you on?" Rolling onto my stomach, I prowl toward his legs, open them wider, and purr, "You want to tame me, don't you?"

He licks his lips, his erection bulging, and he lets out a low, gritty hum when I rub along his groin. "Unzip me," he breathes. "Slowly."

Staring into his steel-blue gaze, I try to find sweet Jared in those hues before he became a bully, but that guy left years ago.

Jared lifts as I stand, urging me forward by my hips. "There's one thing you should know about me," I say, shoving him down and pressing the ball of my stiletto on his dick. "I don't fuck, or suck to make a quick buck." Gripping his hair, I tilt his head back, and he groans as I lower my lips toward his. "When I'm out of the box." I press a kiss, leaving my red mark. "I make my own rules."

He grits his teeth, his chest rising faster the harder I step. "Is that so?"

Releasing my hold, I remove the bills from my strap, crumple them and toss each one at him while stepping back. "And if you ever touch me again. I'll leave this place without a single fuck given what happens to it."

"That easy, huh?" Jared rubs his dick, and I glare at him

as he chuckles, relaxing into the seat again. "We're done. Go back to work."

I snatch my bra off the floor, fastening it on while promptly leaving the room. My shift's over in an hour, but I'm already clocked out in my mind, heading straight to the dressing room.

The phone rings a few times, goes to voicemail, and I frown. Sadie didn't pick up a shift today, and Kylo usually ends his sessions before noon. Maybe she's spent after an exhausting weekend of wild sex—I'm going with that, the only acceptable excuse for not answering. I smirk, then sigh. Sadie deserves all the pampering to decompress from her ever-wandering state of mind because of her stalker ex-husband, who can't come to terms with the fact she no longer wishes to be in contact with him.

My phone lights up with her name, and I grin, answering Sadie's video call right away. "Hey, sexy lady. How did the experience go?"

"Um, it's still going."

"What?" Sadie goes off-screen as Jinx jumps onto her lap, getting a view of her surrounding area before she comes back. "Are you... you're still with Kylo?" I whisper, and she nods.

"A week."

"No way. How did you get him to agree to a week?"

"I didn't. It was his idea."

This time my jaw drops. "Wow. Out of the five years I've

been working with Kylo, he hasn't taken me or any of his clients beyond the two days he agreed, and he let you bring a cat. He must be very intrigued indeed." I wiggle my eyebrows, and she snorts a laugh, one thing we both have in common.

"Stop it." She grins, then it slowly falls into a smirk. "He said my request was new to him, and he needed more than two days to achieve my goal."

"Which is…"

Sadie presses her lips together and tilts her head to the side while rubbing Jinx's head. She's about to speak before Kylo's voice sounds in the distance. I should let her go.

"I'm heading home. Call me tomorrow…or don't," I say, giving her a wink, then hang up after blowing her a kiss.

If the glow on top of her flushed cheeks says anything, it's Sadie's having a good time, and I feel Kylo's got other plans up his sleeve. They would be good for each other, and I hope they explore one another further. Though I may lose my confidant, Sadie's peace of mind is more important.

Home isn't far from Vivid, so I'm parking in my driveway several minutes later. I close my eyes, trying to reset my mind after tonight, until a call breaks through the silence, and I answer, "Hey, Dad."

"Hey, glad I caught you tonight."

"Yeah, I'm just getting home."

"Long day?" he asks, already knowing my answer.

"When isn't it?"

Dad chuckles, then sighs, and I do the same. "How are you, baby girl? Job's still working you to the bone?"

I chew on my bottom lip, hating he has no idea I'm a Red Vixen, but he'd be disappointed if he knew—if he found out about everything Gin brought me into behind his back. "Yep. Drinks won't serve themselves."

He hums, the line staying quiet for a moment, and I glance at the time before he says, "Let me not keep you from the rest of your night. I just wanted to hear your voice before settling into bed."

"Dad, you can call me at any time. You're never a bother."

"Good to know. I love you. I miss you, and we'll talk soon."

An ache forms in my chest. "Yeah, love you too. Night."

The call ends, and I close my eyes, even further away from gathering myself, so I head inside instead. Running on autopilot, I close the front door of my home and lean on the wooden surface, glancing around the expansive living area.

My brain processes that every curtain is open, my neighbors visible on both ends of the room, but I slowly strip each article of clothing from my body, unfazed by the fact people could be watching. A chill creates goosebumps along my skin, but I feel nothing. Numb, deep to the bone. Some may say it's great to have self-confidence, but I'm so far gone, completely desensitized, that I couldn't care less if people see me nude.

My body no longer belongs to me.

I shouldn't complain since I'm choosing to be a Red Vixen. Right? No one's forcing me to work at Vivid, but it's all I know, following in mommy dearest's footsteps. Why not quit, and find something I'll thrive in? Well, Vivid is my home. Those walls have been mine since I was seven years old. When Gin separated from Dad, she took me and nothing but the clothes on our backs, running to her hometown in Oregon. I was devastated, constantly begging her to let me go back to my cousins in San Francisco since I barely knew anyone on her side.

Dad followed, bought property to stay nearby and help support me, to try and make a relationship work with Gin, though she didn't make it easy for him. She pushed for years to get him to leave, even serving divorce papers as the final blow. There's only so much a person can take, so he left soon after, *left me here.* I went from an amazing support system to sitting alone in the corner of a dressing room meant for grown women. Julianne kept me occupied, taking me outside and away from some of the chaos, giving me moments of a 'normal' childhood. Whatever that means.

Closing my eyes, I tilt my head back, my face scrunching while still trying to hold in tears threatening to spill, and I inhale a long breath through my nose, thinking of Kylo's words from our last session to ground myself. I blow it out, my skin prickling more while freeing my mind, leaving work at the door with the men who only see me as an object.

They don't belong in my head.

"My job does not define me," I whisper, taking another deep breath. "Only I can define me."

I stroll to the white silks in the middle of the room, swaying my body through the soft fabric hanging from two stories before climbing to the top. The beauty of dance, there's no right or wrong way to do it. Everyone has their style, skills, and flow. I enjoy silks nights at Vivid, the only time I look forward to performing on the main floor. It's still erotic, but for three minutes, it's where I feel most comfortable—empowered.

Moving through the air, I wrap around the fabric and lock into each pose, pushing my limits while the movements set me free. I close my eyes for a moment, suspending myself at the top, allowing gravity to stretch my body before I free fall and stop a few feet from the floor. Taking a few deep breaths, I unravel myself and lay on the hardwood.

Only I can define myself.

Kylo hasn't once judged me, made me feel uncomfortable, or tried to convince me to up my wholesome heat level —sex is the last thing I want after being around explicit content all day. Our sessions are a nice refresher, resting my mind after daily reminders from customers of how much of a good little slut I am when they get me alone.

I rise from the floor and stroll to my bedroom upstairs, standing in front of the full-length mirror. There's no doubt I have a nice physique, but there are days I hate my body, today being one of them. Hovering my palm over my stomach, I trace the lines of my abs with the tips of my fingers, the gentle touch doing nothing for me. I close my eyes, draw in a deep, shaky breath, and slowly let it all go, allowing the negative energy to pour out of me.

"I am brave, strong, capable, *kind*...of a bitch, but that's okay." I smile, tilting my head to the side, then sigh. "I am worthy." My eyelids slowly open as I look at my reflection. "I'm doing my best...my best at pretending everything's alright, to hide my flaws, to get through each day without adding more—"

Grabbing my throw blanket from the edge of the bed, I cover the mirror, then slip under the comforter. I suppress anything close to pleasure, fully aware of my body and self-worth, depriving myself because I don't deserve to feel loved, which leads to *anger*—being a good little *fucking* slut.

I'll always be flawed. There's no way around that.

SIX
DON'T TAKE
YOUR EYES OFF ME

Lennox

I can't stop the rapid beating of my heart as I park in the lot of Vivid Vixens, as if I've never been to a strip club before. Typically my days pass by quickly, but the last four felt like Friday would never come—the anticipation of bringing Sadie to work has been on my mind since she arrived. Turning off the engine, I lean back in my seat and curse under my breath because I didn't think to change my clothes.

"Would you like to come in?" Sadie asks, and I look at her. "My shift doesn't start until six, and I want to introduce you to security. They can put you on my pick-up list, and on nights I'm running late, you won't have to pay the fee to get through the doors. You can wait by the bar for me."

I nod, then look at my plain black shirt. "Will my get-up be suitable enough to enter the premises?"

She smiles and shakes her head. "If you were a customer, no, but since you're my guest, it's okay. Let's go."

Following her to the entrance, I sign a few forms with security, get a pass, then walk through a door leading into the upscale red club. I've been curious to see what the fuss is about, what makes this place better than the rest of the clubs around Portland. Besides the elegant decor, beautiful women are strolling around the floor with various outfits that leave nothing to the imagination, dancing on stage completely nude, entertainment I can receive down the street with a less hefty price tag attached.

As I continue to observe the room, we walk toward the bar, and Sadie stops by the end. My heart rackets my chest the moment *she* comes into view. *Evie.* She's leaning on the bar in a short robe, watching her phone while eating candy. I can't help staring at her smile when she snatches the bag away from Sadie in her attempt to take one.

"Don't be greedy."

Evie reaches for another, and I focus on her mouth as she slowly sucks on the sugar-coated substance before using her tongue to take it entirely into her mouth. My dick takes notice of her tease, and I adjust through my jeans before moving closer, nudging Sadie's side with my elbow.

"Are you going to introduce me to your friend?" I ask.

She raises an eyebrow at me. "Okay..." Then gestures between the both of us. "Evie, Lennox. Lennox, Evie."

I step closer to the beauty as she grabs another sweet. "Hey."

Biting the peach ring, Evie stretches the candy until it breaks in half, her eyes roaming down my body as she tilts her head to the side, her long braid falling over her shoulder.

"I like your eye," she says, pointing to my left one.

My brow moves up a notch. "You like my eye?"

"Yup. Just the one."

I chuckle, and she looks at my hand as I hold it out to shake. "You can call me Lex. It's nice meeting you, Evie."

"Nice to meet you, *Lex.*"

I swallow the knot in my throat as she purrs my name, places the bitten peach ring on my palm, and sashays to another room with the candy bag.

"*Fuck...*" The sweet substance lands in my mouth as I toss it inside, wanting more of what she has to offer. *Does her tongue taste just as sweet?* "Where's she going?" I ask, turning to Sadie.

"Changing for work. You don't have to stay. I'll ask Evie to take me back to the cabin."

I plop my ass onto the first stool and wave over the bartender, who looks just like the beauty who left. *Maybe an older sister?* She finishes with another customer and heads my way, arching a brow at Sadie before leaning on the bar. "What can I get ya?"

"Anything you have on tap."

"Tall or short?"

My gaze draws back to the red curtains blocking off the

room Evie went into. I'm nowhere ready to leave this place. "Tall," I say, looking at the woman.

She nods, then is back in a few seconds with my beer. "Sixteen."

"Oh, Gin, he's my guest—"

Sadie looks at me as I pull out my wallet and slap a twenty on the bar, sliding it forward. "Thanks," I say, relaxing back in my seat, and I look at Sadie. "I'm here by my own choice. That makes me a customer, no?"

"I suppose." She glances past me, and I follow as Evie strolls through the curtain.

Her tits are fully exposed, and she's wearing a black thong that matches the mesh bodysuit. My lips part the closer she gets. Pins and needles prickle my skin as her sweet flowery scent hits my nose. *Pure fucking seduction.* Evie's the complete package, and I want to unravel her slowly.

She glides her fingers down her long dark braid. "So, you're staying for the show?"

"If you're performing. Yes."

The corner of her deep red lips tug upward, and I'm standing the second she takes hold of my hand. I don't look the part, security's watching me since I stick out in the sea of well-dressed men and women, but they don't attempt to remove me from the premises as I follow Evie. Her plump ass sways before me while we weave through the velvet chairs, the crimson color matching the fabric hanging in the middle of the room over a circular stage. She stops at an empty chair next to the platform, and I take my seat.

"Don't take your eyes off me," she says, stepping back.

"You have my undivided attention, Peaches."

She quirks a brow before walking to the stage stairs, and the music transitions to *Never Tear Us Apart.* I follow her rule, my gaze sticking to her, not wanting to miss a second of this smokeshow's performance. Evie's slow steps around the red fabric are enticing, drawing me to the edge of my seat, and I stop breathing when she grabs hold with one hand, pressing her barefoot on my chest to push me against the cushion. My heart's beating rapidly and nearly falling out of my chest once she climbs the fabric with ease.

Fuck.

Her body bends and stretches in all sorts of angles, her strength impeccable to keep herself from tumbling to the stage—I'm nearly off my chair, my heart banging against my ribcage as she spins and falls, catching herself before the fabric completely unravels. She wraps, stretches, and poses until she places herself back on the floor. I finally breathe, relaxing as she dances on the solid surface, her sultry moves capture my very being, and I don't want to share, wishing the show was for me and only me.

How can I get her alone?

Heading back to the fabric, she climbs again, enveloping herself in a knot. My leg bounces as she hangs at the top, at least twenty feet into the air, slowly rotating, then quickly unravels her body to hover a few feet above the stage, and I exhale hard, relieved she's now safely on the floor, ending with a stroll around the fabric.

Shit, that was intense.

She smiles, fixing the mesh up her ass as she exits the stage and walks back to the room she was in before. Numerous people are still clapping, rising from their seats, wearing suits and lavish attire. Some head toward the red double doors by the VIP rooms, while others take the stairs to the second floor. I have no idea where either direction leads, but I know for sure these people got money to spend.

One seat over, a husky guy with greying hair, likely in his mid-sixties, is staring at me while knocking back the rest of his drink. "Your first show?"

"What makes you ask that?"

He smirks, then chuckles. "You were ten seconds away from hopping on the stage to rescue her."

He ain't wrong about that. "Yeah."

"Evie's the best of the best here at Vivid. Everyone wants a taste, but she's usually off-limits."

My jaw tenses, and the urge to keep this guy away from Evie intensifies. "What do you mean off-limits?"

"She's a Red Vixen, one of the untouchables, though rarely do we get a moment when one of them walks the main floor."

"What's the difference between her and the others?"

His eyes flick to my clothes, and he raises a brow. "It's not my business how you got past security, but I'm guessing by your attire and demeanor, this is your first time walking into this establishment. Vixens work the poles and private rooms on the main floor, giving us access to touch them...but a Red Vixen." He whistles through his teeth. "You're a lucky son of a bitch if you get close enough to breathe their air. They work in the box on the second level. For fellow voyeurs, to be exact."

"Voyeur..."

The man leans in closer, reeking of scotch and cigar smoke. "You didn't hear it from me, but the manager of this place removed this sweet thing's after-show block, so I got my hands on a shower session in about...five or so minutes." He stands from his seat, and I do the same. "But, the wife's been calling nonstop, so I gotta head out before she tosses my shit to the curb." He hands me a card key, then pats my shoulder. "Enjoy yourself, kid. It's on me."

I stare at the red silhouette of a naked woman on the front, then flip it over to a message, *fifteen-minute, voyeur room two* stamped in script along the backside. Evie strides to the stairs by the back wall, a scowl on her face as she rushes to the second floor, and I make my way in the same direction to see if she's okay. However, she's nowhere to be seen. Door number two is to my right, so I stroll toward it, insert the card above the handle, then enter the darkened room.

the front

sixteen-minute

script along the backside

she rushes to the second floor

tion to see if she's okay. However

e handle, then enter the darkened room

SEVEN
AM I CLEAN ENOUGH?

Evie

"Why did you clear my hour block?" I ask, crossing my arms after barging into the manager's office.

Jared looks up from the paperwork in front of him with his brow arched, then goes back to reading. "You don't need an hour."

"Five fucking minutes is not a break!"

He pushes his chair back, then stands, strolling around his desk to lean against it. "You have breaks between customers already. Why should you have extra because of a performance? Do you see any other employee having that benefit?"

"Is any other employee holding themselves twenty-five feet in the air with fabric?"

Jared walks toward me, and I take a few steps back until I hit the window. "You perform one song. If it were more, that's another story, but I won't spoil you like Gin. Are we going to have an issue, or do I have to remind you who's in charge?"

I narrow my eyes. "Are you threatening me?"

"Just because you're Gin's kid doesn't mean you get special treatment. Your hour's no longer valid. Now go to your customer before you get a complaint."

Looking him up and down, I turn away and head back to the dressing room. It's not that I'm exhausted after a performance, I could easily go on longer than one song, but the hour was for my mental health. Having a moment longer to myself helps me push on with my nights. Sitting at my station, I check the queue in the club app, finding an edit in the session, so I change into casual clothes, then head upstairs to room two.

The vacancy light is off, so I enter through the employee door for the shower theme room and halt my steps. "You..."

The guy who came in with Sadie is leaning on the wall before sitting in the chair with a smile. "Me."

My lips curve up as I walk closer. "My show caught your interest?"

"You can say that."

"Got a shower fetish?" I ask, stopping at the white line, and he chuckles, shifting in his seat.

"No."

"I'm going off a hunch this is your first time in the voyeur box. Your request was very vague. *Take a shower.*"

He rubs along his short beard, his gaze roaming down the outfit choice he chose. "Do your thing, Peaches."

I lift a brow as he uses that name again. *Peaches...*walking to the bathroom mirror, I lean against the vanity, looking at myself in the reflection, then my gaze pulls to the handsome man as he relaxes into the chair.

Maybe he has been here before because his face seems familiar. How does he know Sadie? Getting back to my task, I close my eyes, touch the hem of my cropped shirt and draw it over my head. I exhale a heavy breath, drag my jeans off, and slowly walk backward while finger-combing my hair until I press against the cool tile wall.

He's fully dressed, watching with his head tilting to the side. *Maybe he's an observer or one of those in the right-moment masturbators?* Lennox winks, and I turn away as a light flutter hits my stomach. Unclipping my bra, I drop the black cotton fabric to the floor, then hook my thumbs in the strap of my matching thong to slip them off next. I fixate on the mirror ahead, taking in my nakedness, not having to stimulate my nipples since they are already hard, which is new to me.

There's a slight knot in my throat, and I swallow, turning toward the glass door of the walk-in shower on the left. They are anti-fogging, so the steam doesn't obscure the customer's view, though the way my body reacts to his intense stares, I wish the glass would as I step inside. If I can't see him, that feeling won't happen again.

It goes to show voyeurism comes in all different forms. My instructions are to shower, as usual, nothing stating to touch myself. I turn the water on, stepping into the stream as it heats to a perfect temperature. Goosebumps rise, and I hum as the hot water soothes my body, enjoying the fancy jet setting for once—the shower heads in the dressing room don't compare. After a moment of bliss, I grab body wash, squeeze the fruity pink soap onto a loofa, and glide the liquid silk across my skin.

My head falls back as I slowly move down my throat, across my shoulders, suds forming in its path. I drop the puff and close my eyes, continuing with my hands, smoothing the bubbles over my breasts, inching toward my stomach. Once I reach my mound, I peek at him. He's still completely dressed, resting his elbow on the arm of the chair as he trails the tips of his fingers across his lower lip, legs spread wide.

Maybe I should raise the heat a notch?

Since his session has minimal instructions, I get creative. Opening the shower door, I grab a small towel before stepping onto the tile floor, the chill surrounding me making my nipples pebble more as I saunter toward the middle of the room while scrunching my hair. Lennox shifts in his seat, his chest rising faster as I glance down at my body. Bubbles drip between my breasts, and I gently blow, peeking at him as he watches them move further down, reaching my pussy.

"Am I clean enough?"

"I think you missed a few spots," Lennox says, acting laid-back, but his low, raspy voice gives away the tension he must be feeling. He's anything but relaxed while adjusting the bulge in his pants, which makes me smirk.

"Where?" I twist my body to check, then hum. "Oops. I hadn't noticed."

He chuckles, his gaze roaming from my pussy to my tits. "You should finish rinsing."

"As you wish." Spinning on my heels, I stroll to the shower and unhook the hose from the holder, making sure to hum as I pass the soothing jets over my body, avoiding the area his hungry gaze craves. If he wants me to come, he'll need to say it.

"More thorough."

There we go.

"You mean..." I trail the stream down my stomach, stopping above my pussy. "Right here?"

"Lower. Nice and slow, Peaches. Make sure you rinse it all."

I lick my lips, pressing my palm against the glass to lean against it, focusing on him as he widens his stance to adjust himself. Pleasure is work, never personal, though once the water hits my clit, my head bucks backward, the pulsating sensation makes my heart race, and I drop the shower head to the floor.

Fuck, that most definitely felt real.

"Everything okay?" he asks, concerned as he shifts onto the edge of his seat.

The timer goes off, and I haven't been happier about it in my life. "Time's up."

Lennox glances at the clock to his right, then back at me as I stride out of the shower toward the employee entrance. Grabbing a robe, I rush into the hallway, booking it to the emergency exit and down the stairs to the dressing room door, pulling out the keycard from my pocket. I head for my station, trying not to think about Lennox, about him making me feel *something*. There's no room in my head for pleasure while working because I'd never get anything done.

his right

employee entranc

to the emergency ex

the keycard from my pocke

him making me feel something

because I'd never get anything don

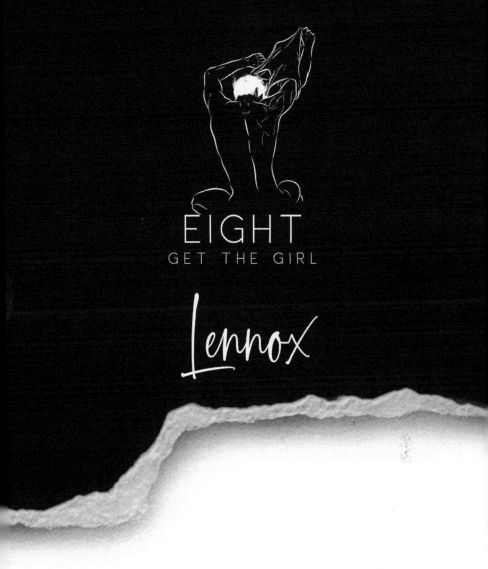

EIGHT
GET THE GIRL

Lennox

What happened? Why did she run out like that?
Stepping into the hall, I walk to the banis-
ter, searching around the main floor for Evie,
then head downstairs when I don't. People stare at me like I
don't belong, but I pay them no mind, walking to the bar to
look for Sadie. She's by the VIP section, talking to a woman

with short dark hair. Since she's busy, I walk to the exit instead. I'll try again with Evie another day when I look the part.

My dick's straining in my jeans, and I palm myself as I settle into the driver's seat of my car. It didn't feel right jerking off from afar, even if her beautiful body made my pulse skyrocket. Alone at home is one thing, but having Evie so close while not having her felt wrong. I'd much rather get to know her first and take care of her needs before getting my nut. I close my eyes, leaning back on the headrest as every curve seared in my mind replays with an itch to relieve myself now.

"Fuck."

I start the car and head out of the parking lot, needing to get away from this place, yet I can't wait to return to watch some more. Laughing, I shake my head. Such contradictory thoughts, though I understand the concept, how a business like this thrives off dickheads like me, willing to empty their pockets to watch porn in real-time. It's genius, and I want to take her away from it all.

The drive to the cabin is roughly twenty minutes, and I rush to the guest house, finding the beast waiting for me by the entrance like she always does. She meows, rubbing her body against my leg while I unlock the door, and she darts inside, heading straight for my room. I've been leaving clean sock balls just for her because if she catches a whiff of my workload, I'll probably lose her company.

Getting dinner situated, I eat, spend time with Jinx, then head off to bed with her. There's nothing much to do other than sleep while Sadie's here with Kylo. The guy's infatuated and, for the first time, doesn't know what to do with himself. Quite amusing catching him out of character, and

I'm curious to see how everything pans out by the end. My bet's on this sock-stealing roommate snuggling on my pillow, becoming a permanent resident. The thought makes me smile, and I run my fingers across her orange fur, setting off her purring, and it helps me drift, hopefully off to see my dream girl.

It's bright outside as I open my eyes, and my stomach drops. "What the fuck." I glance around my room, then at the alarm clock that says 7:00 a.m. "Shit."

Grabbing my phone, I click the sides, the black screen not lighting up, and I groan as the charger I plugged into the wall last night now hangs off the side of my bedside table with chew marks along the cord.

I never sleep in. Why the fuck didn't I wake up?

There are most likely numerous missed calls and texts from Dad, so I plug it back in, leaving my phone on the end table. No point in checking and adding more stress. Since I'm already late for work, I take a decent shower, might as well make it worth my while, then throw on a black thermal and worn jeans.

I won't push time by making breakfast, though I grab my travel mug and head out to the cabin, hoping no one's awake because there's no way I can function right without coffee. Jinx is a step behind me as I enter as quietly as possible, make my cup of joe, then sneak for the front door. Sadie's waiting on the porch swing as I step outside and walk toward her.

"Hey. Ready to make a break for it?"

She giggles and shakes her head. "Waiting for my ride. I need to check my mail and grab more clothes."

I'm guessing they are extending their time together. "I'm heading out, so I can take you."

Grabbing her phone, she checks the rideshare app. "Thanks, but she will be here in a few minutes. I'm surprised you're here so late."

"Yeah. Hopefully, my pops won't chew my head off, but what can I do about it?"

Sadie smiles, then looks toward the end of the driveway as a silver car pulls in. "That's her. I'll see you later."

"Wait—I'll pick you up tonight."

Her brows furrow. "Are you sure? Evie can drop me off."

"Yeah. The mill is closed on Sunday. I'm gonna come by, have a beer, and hang out for a bit."

"Oh, okay. Thanks. I get off at 2:00 a.m."

"2:00 a.m. Got it."

She nods, heads for the car, and I watch her leave. Getting into the Porsche, I drive to the mill in Northwest Portland, dirt clouds filling the air as I pull into my space next to Dad's spot and shut off my car. I rub my face, taking a deep breath before stepping outside and heading into the office. Gwyneth, Dad's secretary, glances from her computer screen, and her brows lift.

"It's not like you to be late, Lennox."

"Yeah. I overslept." I head for the time clock and punch in. "Where's my Pops?"

"Out in the field doing your job."

My head snaps toward her. "What?"

Her shoulder lifts before she leans back into her chair. "I told Tom, with his heart condition, that using a chainsaw was a bad idea, but he was persistent that trees weren't going to fell themselves."

"Fucking old man," I groan, rushing to my locker in the back room.

I grab my beanie and work gear, strapping everything on before striding to the door. If anything happens to Dad because I wasn't here to do my job, I'll one, never hear the end of it from him that he needed to fill in for his irresponsible son, and two, am putting him and the other men at risk of injury because he feels the need to prove a point. My work truck isn't where I left it yesterday, so I get back into the Porsche, then drive out to the field. Parking next to my truck, I grab a helmet, and chainsaw out of the back, then head up the trail to the marked trees.

"Yeah, start trimming as I get this tree down."

Dad's got his sleeves rolled up to his elbows, his gloves hanging from his back pocket, no utility belt, and his tools off to the side, which is a hazard, especially working with falling trees. Bones nods at me before walking away, and Dad shakes his head, putting on his hard hat as he walks toward the tree with the saw in hand.

"Tryna get yourself killed?" I ask, stepping in front of him. "The doc said to stay off the field."

"Well, if I'm gonna die, then it'll be by doing what I'm good at."

I stop Dad from starting the saw, and he stares at me with his dark eyes. "I'm here. Go back to the office—"

"After I've already started your job?" He shrugs me off. "Get out of here, kid."

"Dad, don't be stubborn."

He chuckles, getting ready again. "You sound like your mother."

"And what do you suppose she'll say to you felling in your condition?"

Sucking his teeth, Dad scolds me as I take hold of the handle, then he releases it. "Come late again, and you'll be drowning in paperwork. Give me my keys."

I sigh as he walks away, then I get to work. This time of year is perfect weather where the hard ground is the ideal texture to harvest the trees, but being out in the cold while sweating can take its toll on my body. The old man will feel the labor effect in the morning, that's for sure.

Nine hours later, my knee is throbbing as I step into the mill to punch out, Bones patting my shoulder as he leaves before me. There's shouting in Dad's office, Gwyneth standing with her arms crossed."

"What are you expecting to happen when you pile on so much responsibility? When has he ever been late?"

"All I hear are excuses. None I used when I was Lennox's age working the field."

"Have you ever once stopped to listen to him? Give him some slack before he leaves this place behind."

I turn back to my locker when she strides out of the office, and I sigh while storing away my gear. At least someone's sticking up for me.

"Lennox, get in here."

Closing my locker, I stroll to the doorway and lean on the jamb. "Yeah?"

He glances at me from the papers on the desk, applications he wants me to look over. "These two," he says, sliding two packets in front of the desk. "They start Monday. One is ready for the field, and the other is Jimmy's son. He needs to brush up on training and will work with you for a while."

"Why not pick two experienced men?" I already know his answer. He rather his men work the Thomas Hunter way.

"Are we gonna have this conversation?"

"Yes, because that's what adults do. When people disagree, they discuss the issue to figure out a solution."

"The solution is you train the man. End of story. Go home and rest so you make it to work on time."

"Great. Nice talk, Dad," I say, leaving the office building.

Another autopilot drive home, and I head straight for the guest house, letting Jinx inside first before stripping my clothes. I hang them on the railing, then walk inside in my underwear, ready for a hot bath to soak my body. Grabbing the bag of peas from the freezer, I head upstairs, running the water until it's hot enough, and get inside, resting my leg on the side of the tub with the peas on top of my knee. There's not much more I can do except deal with the pain until it subsides, which after icing and elevation, is relatively quick. Hopefully, that's the case tonight.

Either way, I'm heading to Vivid Vixens, already securing a time slot to see Evie at midnight. Even if seeing her this way doesn't feel right, I can't help myself—I'm ready to explore more of what she has to offer, but more so, I want to know who she is, what she enjoys in life, to see if her beautiful smile can calm my world of chaos. The anticipation is too much, so I cut my soak short, shower, then leave for my closet while securing a towel around my hips.

Sophisticated is not something I'd call myself, but when an occasion arises, I clean up nicely. I gather black jeans, a form-fitted button-down, and boots, grabbing my red underwear. Why not? Laying each article on my bed, I drop my towel to dress as Jinx watches me from her pillow. If she weren't a feline, I'd believe she was checking me out, or maybe my dick's a new toy she's been plotting to destroy. Either way, I'm not willing to find out.

I leave the top two buttons of my shirt unfastened, then stroll into the bathroom to style the mess on top of my head. Leaning on the counter, I stare at myself for a moment, my mind running a hundred miles a second. Evie's a knockout, easily the best-looking woman I've ever come across...am I even in her league?

"Don't start that bullshit, Lex. Get the girl."

With one quick nod to myself, I blow out a sharp breath, fix my collar, then grab my leather jacket before heading to the front door. Jinx is a step behind me as we make our way toward the cabin, going our separate ways. It amazes me the routine we've fallen into, and I'm glad she continues to hang with me.

Same route, but one I look forward to driving. I pay my fee to enter the building and take a seat at the spot I sat yesterday, the entrance to the dressing room only a few feet away. My time with Evie isn't for another two hours, but nothing a few beers won't help pass.

A woman with shoulder-length brown hair comes to the bar with a tray in hand, placing it on the counter. "Hey, Gin, can I get two rum and cokes, a vodka cranberry, and a tall domestic. The customer said it doesn't matter which brand."

She sits next to me while waiting, her bright blue eyes widen when they meet mine, and she quickly leaves toward the other end of the bar. I furrow my brows, watching as she gnaws on her bottom lip, bouncing on her feet as she waits.

It doesn't take Gin long to fill the order, placing each

drink on the tray, and the brunette carefully carries them away as Sadie watches her from across the room. The woman glances back just as Sadie waves at me. I do the same before facing forward, and Gin's leaning on the bar in front of me.

"Whatever's on tap?"

"And keep them coming," I say, resting back on the stool.

I'm not interested in watching the main floor, but I glance around the room at the dancers spread around talking to patrons. One woman is performing on the main stage with men seated in each chair surrounding her. Does Evie work in each area, or is her job upstairs, and the aerial performance? I can quickly gather the answers to questions from anyone in the room, but I would rather she gives me the details about her life. She chooses how much and how little information she wants people to know.

"16.00," Gin says, placing my beer in front of me. "You clean up well."

"Thank you." I slide my card to open a tab because I don't plan on leaving here anytime soon.

...formance

...yone in the room

...re details about her lif

...tion she wants people to know

...front of me. "You clean up well

...n't plan on leaving here anytime soon

NINE

NOTHING WRONG WITH
A BIT OF MYSTERY

Evie

You're the finest wine. The more of you I drink in, the better I feel.

My smile's instant as I read the cheesy message attached to my next request, a rare occurrence at work. Though, with Lennox back, I don't know how to feel about him. Maintaining control is essential to my job, and our session last night brought out a side of me that needs to stay away. With the number of times I 'come' in a day, I could easily slide into an addiction to pleasure if I didn't hold back, and I don't need that type of distraction. Once I leave this place at the end of my shift, I want nothing to do with touch or people.

As I enter room four through the employee entrance, I take my time strolling to the entryway of the elegant royal suite setup since he won't have access for another few minutes. Hues of purple and pearl line the room, with gold crown molding along the edge of the cream walls. There's a floor-to-ceiling faux window with satin curtains on the back wall, a king-size four post bed on my right, a crystal chandelier hanging in front, and a white vanity beside it. The deep plum chaise lounge and fur rug add to the elegant theme, a room that screams luxury.

I roam to the bed, loosening my black floor-length robe to expose the matching lace lingerie. It's a pain in the ass to attach every piece, but whatever the customer wants, I throw on. Closing my eyes, I blow out a deep breath to calm my racing heart and sit on the edge of the bed, watching the timer. Our session is fifteen minutes, the most requested time frame, though I was hoping to get a little more time with him.

The clock starts, and my stomach flutters from the click of a door closing, Lennox entering the room. *Damn, he cleans up fine.* However, I quite enjoyed the rugged look he wore last night. I swallow the knot forming in my throat from his intense stare, then get into work mode. He doesn't speak as he strolls to the chair, taking a seat, but his eyes never leave mine. His request is to enjoy a night's rest in luxury, nothing stating to masturbate or touch myself. Maybe he's shy or the type to initiate what he desires once he's horny enough—*is he vocal in bed or a silent lover?*

Smiling, I stand, strolling to the built-in electric fireplace to switch on the flames. The heat makes my skin prickle, and I hum, closing my eyes while running my fingers across my chest. Being alone with Lennox, I feel less anxious for the timer to sound, having a moment to enjoy the atmosphere without the pressure of satisfying the customer. I peek over my shoulder, and a minute has passed, one less spent with him.

Easing the robe down my arms, I let the light fabric flow to the floor, then head for the vanity to remove my pearls. I sleep nude but leave the lingerie on before crawling into bed to hug one of the many pillows, sliding my right knee higher. Rocking my ass to get comfortable, I'm ready to fall asleep, though I wish Lennox would ask for more before I actually do.

Only ten minutes left. By now, I'd usually have my customer halfway to climaxing during a fifteen-minute session. Does he plan on getting off at all? Straightening up, I lean on my hand while tilting my head to the side and thoroughly checking him out. His clothes are not overly tight, fitting just right to his muscular form, and I'm curious to see what he has going on under them.

"Why don't you undress or touch yourself while you're with me?" I ask, crawling to the front of the bed. "You can stay behind the wall if you're shy. I can't see you there."

Lennox raises his brow. "Shy isn't a word I'd use."

"Okay. Am I not doing enough to satisfy your needs?"

He stands, removing his shirt and dark jeans, showing off his lean body and the tent in his red boxer briefs which makes my cheeks heat. Taking his seat, he falls back, palming his erection.

"Proceed."

Does he want me to take the lead?

I keep my gaze on his lap while unclipping my garter belt from my stockings, easing each one down my legs, then unstrap the belt, dropping it into the pile. His dick's demanding attention, but he's still not touching himself. I widen my legs and lean back on my hand, focusing on him while trailing my finger along my inner thigh.

"What do you want, Lex?"

He cocks his head to the side. "What?"

"Tell me." I lick my lips, glancing down at my body. "What gets you off?"

"You."

"What about me?"

Lennox rests his head on the cushion, placing his hands on his thighs. "Everything."

Heat rises in my body, and my pulse picks up.

"So if I remove this...." I untie the strings of my bralette, freeing my breasts, then hold out the lace before it falls to the floor. "You'll touch yourself?"

His heavy gaze stays on my chest as he eases his hand along his bulge.

Now we're getting somewhere.

Each passing moment being here with him has me on edge, feeling every trace of my fingertips, up my slit, along my navel, between my breasts to caress them, moaning as my nipples harden. Touching myself feels better when he's around, so I need to get him going already and out of my box.

"Ditch the drawers, Lex, and stroke your dick."

Lennox closes his eyes and swallows deeply before

peeling his underwear down his thighs, looking at his thick shaft as it juts free. Taking hold, he meets my gaze, and his cocky grin stirs my insides as I thoroughly take in his handsome size while he glides his hand along his length.

"You see something you like?"

My brows raise as I huff a laugh, still checking him out. "It's a dick. Nothing special."

He breathes out a raspy chuckle. "I like you, Evie."

"Hm, no, you don't." I push off the mattress, caressing my tits while strolling closer, and stop at the white line. "Now, tell me. What do you want, so I can get that cum out of you."

"*Fucking hell...*" He rubs down his balls before retaking his cock. "To take you on a date."

I blink a few times, opening and closing my mouth before furrowing my brows. "A date?"

Using his thumb, Lennox rubs along the tip before resting his forearms on the armrests, his cock standing tall, ready, and rideable, my pulse rising at the thought.

"Yes."

"Why?"

"Why does any man ask out a woman?"

I glance at the timer with several minutes of this session left, needing to change the subject, so I do what I do best. Backing away, I head for the vintage vanity, pull a drawer open, and take out my glass wand, meant for pussy or ass play. His gaze falls to the bulbous object, his chest rising faster as I coat a healthy amount of warming lube on the toy, already deciding which hole I'll enter.

He seems like an ass man.

"Lex, do you know the rules?" Taking a seat on the leather chaise, I lie back, trailing the wand between my breasts, down my stomach, and stopping at the small patch of hair above my clit. "A Red Vixen is off-limits—untouchable."

His brow lifts, but his eyes never leave the toy as I inch the sleek shaft lower, rubbing the tip along my slit, and my eyes flutter close and open, swallowing while trying to keep control of the sensation. I may have taken over the session, but that doesn't mean I can't coax an answer out of him.

"Where do I go next, Lex?"

"Just keep doing your thing, Peaches." His response both excites yet irks me.

I stretch an arm behind my head, my breasts pushing forward. "I'm having a hard time figuring you out."

The tip of his tongue glides across his top lip as I place my foot along the small table in front while circling the wand on my clit, and I whisper a curse, my heart now beating rapidly at how good it feels. Forcing myself to stop, I glide toward my ass, continuing to rub.

"There's nothing wrong with a bit of mystery," he says, touching himself again, and I smirk.

"Well, in the box, you can be whoever you want to be. I'm your vivid fantasy come to life."

"And what if I don't want a fantasy?" I still my hand, staring straight into his eyes as he maneuvers to the edge of his seat. "What if I want the real thing?"

I drop the toy on the chaise and stand from the seat. "What are your intentions here? Because—"

The timer goes off, and I snap my head toward the clock. Lennox fixes his boxer briefs, his erection still prominent as he gathers his clothes, then winks at me before entering the private box.

What the hell was that?

A few minutes pass as I stay seated, replaying the last

fifteen minutes. Petra walks inside the room a moment later with her cart, putting on gloves, and gasping once she realizes I'm still here.

"Evie, shit, you scared me." Her cheeks brighten, a blush spreading across her warm brown skin as she takes in my nakedness. "Are you okay?"

"I don't know."

Walking toward me, she moves the wand to the table and sits next to me. "Did something happen? Need me to call Gin?" she asks, rubbing my back, and I look into her deep brown eyes.

"No, please don't." I smile at her. "I'm okay. I just had a weird session."

"Weird bad or...."

The issue isn't that Lennox makes me uncomfortable— he makes me feel good, and I don't know how I like that. "Just weird."

She slowly nods a few times, seeming genuinely concerned for me, and no one here besides Sadie and Julianne has ever comforted me like this. "Want me to give you a few minutes alone before I clean? The next customer isn't for another thirty minutes."

I stand, shaking my head. "Thank you, but I'm good. I just needed a second to compose myself before heading downstairs."

"Okay. I'm always around if you ever need someone to talk to."

"Thanks. I'll keep that in mind."

Leaving the room, I tie my robe and use the main stairs while glancing around the club. Sadie's talking to the new girl she's training in the VIP area, but I don't stop there, searching through every man, perhaps hoping he's still here, and my stomach sinks when I don't see him.

I huff a laugh while shaking my head and quicken my steps to the dressing room, straight for the shower to prepare for my next customer, using work as a distraction from whatever is happening to me.

VIP area

rough every man

when I don't see him

my head and quicken my step

er to prepare for my next custome

tion from whatever is happening to m

TEN
I NEVER LOSE

Lennox

I stepped out of the club when our session ended, waiting in the car for Sadie with my raging erection, trying hard not to relieve myself in the parking lot. The hours pass quickly, and my time with Evie replays on a loop during the drive home, fantasizing about her scent, how sweet she'd taste, and how loud I'd make her come by sucking her pussy alone.

Fuck...

Parking in the driveway, I close my eyes and let out a deep breath, needing to get ahold of myself. I don't even know her last name.

"Everything okay?" Sadie asks, and I stare at the cabin. "If picking and dropping me off is too much, I can find another way to and from work."

Glancing toward her, I shake my head. "No, it's fine."

"Okay. Then what's wrong?"

I drum my thumbs on the steering wheel, staring into the distance, trying to ease Evie from my mind. "How do you know if someone's interested in you?"

"Well, it all depends, I guess. Some people are upfront, whereas others may leave subtle hints."

"Hints, as in?"

"Little touches here and there, glances, smiles while giving you their full attention." I nod a few times. Evie has hinted at several of those, but what if she's like that with all her customers? What makes me special—I glance at Sadie when she adds, "Are you hinting at me because—"

"I like your friend, but I don't know if she does in return."

Her shoulders dip as she sighs. "Evie's a literal person. If she's interested, you'd have no problem knowing."

"So, do you think I'd have a chance if I asked her out?"

A few wrinkles appear on her nose as she scrunches it. "There's no harm in asking, but honestly, I don't think Evie's looking for a man at this time of her life. She has a lot going on."

Of course, she isn't, and I'm the dickhead being too forward without a second thought.

Sadie takes hold of my hand and asks, "Want me to talk to her?"

"No, but thank you. You should head to bed."

"You're a nice guy, Lex, and Evie would be lucky to have someone like you. She needs laughter in her life." Her genuine words ease my doubts, and I smirk, peeking at her. "Just how Kylo needs a woman like you to laugh with."

"He doesn't want to be with anyone either."

Huffing a laugh, I shake my head. "Looks like we're in the same club then. Interested in people who don't fall in love."

I smirk as the corner of her lips curve up, and then I nod toward the cabin. It's late—I'm sure Kylo's waiting for her to return home safely. We both get out, and I walk along the path to the guest house alone.

"Goodnight, Lex."

"Goodnight," I say, waving goodbye.

The sensor lights switch on as I walk along the deck, and my stomach sinks as something dark scatters into the woods the closer I get to the guest house—too big to be a critter, so it's probably the neighbor's black cat that fucks with the garbage bins. I narrow my eyes once the beast comes prancing toward me from the same direction and sits by the door. She perks my mood as I scoop her into my arms, and her head brushes against my chin while purring.

"Do we need to have the talk?" I chuckle, kissing her fuzzy face, then enter my home, which feels warmer tonight.

I had planned on asking Kylo to drop me off at the repair shop today to pick up my Mustang, but when Sadie hit me with her cat-sitting offer, I couldn't see a better way to spend my Sunday afternoon than with my favorite girl, though once I walked into the cabin to find the woman who's taken over my dreams sitting on the couch, I knew what Sadie was up to. Never thought this cat's obsession with me would come in handy one day, and I'm glad Evie didn't run for the hills when she noticed me.

We've been sitting for an hour, wanting this closeness with Evie since she placed that peach ring in my hand. The taste of peaches has been on my mind ever since, wondering if her tongue is just as sweet. Evie giggles as Jinx tries to catch the feather in her hand, and the sound is music to my ears.

She glances at me with those beautiful dark eyes, and the sunlight shining through the window brightens them to a warm chocolate brown. I could stare into them all day.

Jinx swats her hand, and Evie takes a sharp breath as her claws catch her skin. "Ow!" Observing her pinkie, she sucks on the cut, then looks down, smushing Jinx's face. "That hurt, you little beast," she growls playfully, rubbing her stomach next, making me chuckle. Evie glances at me and smirks. "Me being mauled is funny, huh?"

"No. I find you adorable."

Her nose wrinkles. "I've never heard that before, but this girly sure is." Kissing the top of Jinx's head, Evie pouts when she jumps to the floor, tired of the attention, and goes about her business.

Now that we're alone, I scoot closer, resting my arm on the back of the couch, and she glances at me before staring out the window ahead. "Want to play pool?" I ask.

"Kylo doesn't have a table."

"No, but I do at my place."

Her brows furrow. "Your place?"

"I live in the guest house, only a short walk from here." I point to the right, where the building resides.

"Oh. Well, I'm down if you don't care about losing."

Chuckling, I raise a brow. "One thing you should know, Peaches. I never lose."

Her eyes narrow, then she stands, crossing her arms. "Alright, prove it then. Just a fair warning, I learned from the best."

Standing from my seat, I move in close, and she takes a step back. "Once I win, what do I get as a reward?"

She huffs a laugh and places her hands on her hips. "Wow, you're a cocky bastard, aren't you?"

"Well, you ain't no princess."

Evie sucks her teeth, then she smirks. "Fine. If you beat me, I'll let you take me on that date."

Hello. "Deal—"

"Ah! But, *when* I win, you stop calling me Peaches."

Blowing a deep breath, I hold my hand out, and she shakes it. "I look forward to taking you out."

"We'll see."

I gesture towards the back door, and we both walk along the deck, Jinx a few steps behind us. As we reach my front door, I wait for both of them to enter, her sweet flowery scent urging me to walk in behind her and draw my nose closer.

"Love your place," she says, glancing around the open area, checking out a few art pieces I've crafted, and stopping at the coffee table. "Is this custom?" Crouching to get a closer look, she touches the multi-blue epoxy resin replication of water running through the wood. "I've never seen furniture so expressive. Such attention to detail, as if I'm looking at a canyon river through a photograph. Simply gorgeous."

Like you.

"Thank you. That one's my favorite piece. I stored away all the fancy shit Kylo had in here. Not my style."

She glances back at me with a smirk, then stands. "Did you make this?"

I nod. "Just a hobby. Something I enjoy doing on Sundays when I have time off work."

"Just a hobby?" Evie walks toward me. "You should expand that idea. I'd buy your art in a heartbeat."

"I'll keep that in mind."

Continuing to look around, she adds, "So, where's this pool table at?"

"Upstairs, in the lounging room."

Evie follows me to the stairs, arching a brow as I wait for her to go ahead. "I'm going off a hunch that you're an ass man. I hope the view's nice back there."

Chuckling, I, in fact, check out her ass as she sways her hips more than usual. "Ass, tits, smart mouths. I'm not picky."

She hums, reaching the top, and it's taking everything in me not to pull her aside and kiss those luscious pink lips.

Would she let me?

Entering the room, we both head toward the pool table, and she racks up like she's been shooting pool all her life. "I'll break."

Grabbing two cue sticks, I lean on the wall waiting for her to finish, then she walks toward me to take one, but I hold on to it. "Food, somewhere quiet, and we get to know one another."

"Don't get too cocky now." She smirks as I let her have the stick.

Strolling to the head of the table, she leans forward, closing one eye as she takes the shaft between her fingers, gliding it back and forth, then wacks the cue ball into the others. Two of them land into a pocket, and I give her a round of applause.

"That was beautiful."

"I'm only getting started. I got stripes."

I watch as she continues to sink each one, but my gaze mainly falls on her ass while she pokes it out each time. "You learned from the best, you say?

"Yup." Sinking another, she strolls to the other side and smirks. "My dad lives in San Francisco, and I used to stay with him, sometimes my grandma, during the summer. My cousins Enzo and Luca lived with her, and I would play in their basement whenever I visited. Enzo taught me how to win."

"Clearly. Are you close with your family?" I ask, enjoying her willingness to talk. She misses this time, and it's my turn to go.

"Only on my dad's side. Both of my cousins helped me get through my rough years. Enzo got me out of the house for fresh air, and to have fun, which I'm grateful for—Luca was a lot like me. Quiet, reserved...angry, and why I gravitate toward him when I need someone to talk to. He knows things about me I never told Enzo because he wouldn't understand, things no child should have to witness." She stops talking, her eyes glossing over. "Anyway, I love both of them more than anything," she says, changing the subject.

"Sounds like a great family." I smile and scratch the cue ball on purpose, wanting to know more about her.

She lets out a shaky breath, then smiles. "You never lose, eh?" Grabbing the ball from the pocket, she places it down, sinks number nine, and focuses on eight. "Say goodbye to Peaches."

Evie steps in close, trailing her index finger down my cue, then leans forward on the table, swaying her ass in front of me. I can't help moving in behind her, and she glances over her shoulder, then quickly gets ready to shoot. Gripping the end of the stick, I place it between her thighs, and she gasps, hitting the eight ball off the table as I gently press the butt against her pussy.

"Lex—" she moans as I gradually move along her leggings, and my dick swells.

Placing my hand on her stomach, I draw her back to my chest, and she wraps her arm behind my neck, rubbing her ass on my cock the more I stroke. I want to bend her over, fuck her right here on the table, but the view of her body pressing against mine, and her lips parting as she moans, is too beautiful to stop my tease.

With my free hand, I trail her stomach, lowering to the waistband of her pants, waiting for any signs of resistance. She hums, bucking her hips forward while raking her nails down the nape of my neck, and I dip into her panties. As soon as my fingers brush something metal along her clit, I drop the cue stick and groan—*a fucking piercing.*

Her hold on my neck tightens, and the perfect moans passing through her lips get louder as I sink through her slit, rubbing along her entrance before sliding back to her clit. I'm on the edge of coming, kissing down her neck, groping her tit as she grinds faster on my dick. Her scent sends my senses into overdrive until she rakes my skin again, pushing me further—every sensation causing a shiver down my spine.

"*Fuck*, come for me, Peaches—"

I intake a sharp breath through my teeth as she grabs my cock, firmly squeezing through my sweatpants, and then her warmth is gone when she hastily steps away. Moving to the other side of the room, she plasters her back to the wall, both of us panting, staring at one another. My dick's straining in my pants, and I lean on the table, palming my shaft.

"Don't call me that," she says, fixing her waistband.

Chuckling, I suck her wetness off my fingers, and she crosses her legs, rubbing her hands along her thighs. "Well, technically, *Peaches,* you didn't win."

She groans, narrowing her eyes before leaving the room. I take a deep breath once she's out of sight, then reach into my pants, drawing my dick out. It's always hard while I'm around her, and every night it's Evie on my mind, making me come. Right now, I'm aching while thinking about her, wanting her arousal coating my dick, the walls of her pussy squeezing around the tip as I ease inside, and she moans my name once I'm balls deep.

I sit on the chair in the corner, lean back, my head resting on the cushion as I stroke my cock. How would her ass feel swallowing it—does she enjoy getting fucked that way? *Shit.* I moan deeply, spreading my legs as far as they'll go, my hips thrusting in time with my fist, chasing the nut that's nearing.

Closing my eyes, I picture her bent over, open and slick, ready for me to take, moaning while running her fingers along her pussy as I ease inside her tight hole—I groan, cum shooting into my hand, grunting with each spurt.

My heart's pounding hard, and I take deep breaths as my dick gradually falls onto my thigh. There's something between Evie and me. I know she feels the draw, too, so I won't stop showing her how badly I want her because she's everything I've ever wanted in a woman.

ELEVEN
FRIENDS WITH A
SIDE OF DICK

Evie

Dammit, Lex, *fuck*, I'm on fire. I run my fingers through my hair, ready to leave this place once Sadie returns. Blowing out deep, shaky breaths, I lean on the counter, willing my body to relax, for my clit to stop pulsing before I rush back to that room and have

Lennox finish what he started. And that fucking name. Why does he keep calling me Peaches? Is he seriously that much of an ass man?

Doors slam in the distance, and my heart skips as I cross the room. Grabbing my jacket, I rush outside, passing between Kylo and Sadie while striding to my car parked behind Lennox's Porsche. The vehicle should have been the first give away that I wasn't going to be here alone, but my mind was so far gone that Lennox didn't register until he strolled along the deck to the back door with Jinx perched on his shoulder. I knew there was something familiar about him, the man who walked past me only a few days ago as I was leaving Kylo's session.

"Evie, wait. What happened?" Sadie asks, jogging toward me.

I narrow my eyes on her. If I knew Lennox was the man who worked with Kylo, I never would have agreed to come here today. He's too mysterious and tempting. "You know exactly what happened, liar."

She wrings her hands together, her nose scrunching. "Lex couldn't have been that bad."

I sigh, leaning on my car door, and stare at the ground. "It's complicated, Sadie. You know I can't do relationships, and that man is screaming long-term."

Sadie tilts her head so I see her face. "There's nothing wrong with making friends."

"Yeah. Friends with a side of dick." If only she knew what that man did with those hands, surrendering to sensations I've fought to subdue in mere seconds, and his words seared in my mind—so damn bold, so sure of himself, and those eyes, fuck, I'm silly putty to those golden hues.

She purses her lips, and I raise a brow.

"Don't give me that look," I say, crossing my arms. "Lennox is far from the guy next door type, even if he's literally the guy next door!" I roll my eyes, pushing at her arm when she smirks. "You little sneak."

"Sorry."

"Apology accepted. Now, go back to *your* side of dick. I saw that kiss."

Her cheeks brighten, and they lift her with a smile. *Good.* I'm glad the experience is working for her, and with how Kylo is around Sadie, I feel his client intake will be dropping immensely. It's a bit disheartening, losing my confidant, but seeing the joy in Sadie's eyes means more than my occasional session.

She hugs me and whispers, "It's okay to let your guard down, Evie." Drawing back, she adds, "To give someone a chance to prove they are worthy of your time."

I give her a small smile as she rubs my arm before heading back to the cabin, and I drive away. Far, far away, tempted to run, though Sadie's words and Lennox's touch have unleashed curiosity, hoping to see the guy next door in my backyard again very soon.

The mall isn't the ideal place to cool down, but it's better than stewing at home or being at Vivid. I'll go anywhere but there. Strolling down the long corridor sipping on a drink, I head into my favorite store and quickly duck out when a familiar blonde comes into view, not wanting to deal with Roni.

"Hey, Evie, right?"

I gasp, my back hitting the storefront glass as I spin, and the new chick working with Sadie stands close. "Fuck, you scared me."

"Sorry—didn't mean to sneak up behind you."

Looking back, I sigh as Roni walks this way.

Shit.

"Hey, Anna, you made it!"

Roni eyes me before hugging her, and I make my way out of there.

"Evie, where are you going?" Anna asks, jogging to my side. "Come shop with us."

"Thanks, but no. I have obligations that require me not to be in jail tonight."

"Jail?" I keep stepping, and my jaw ticks as she stops me again. "C'mon, you're always by yourself, and I know things with Roni aren't all that great, so maybe you two can settle your differences."

"Hey, I'm perfectly fine. If Roni's holding a grudge over me, that seems like a her problem, not mine."

She purses her lips, and it only irks me more. "Evie, please. I know I've only started at Vivid, but people talk, saying you're...*difficult* to work with, but I don't blame you. If Gin were my mother, I'd be using up my privilege to act the same way, too, though maybe you should try being a little more pleasant, then you'd have no issues getting along with people."

Blinking a few times, I try to figure out if what she said actually came out of her mouth. "One second," I smile, then huff a laugh. "Seems *some people* need to get their nose out of my asshole and mind their fucking business. And don't come to me talking like you know my mother or anything about me—better yet, I'd advise you to get far away from me before I go to jail for another reason, one this *privileged bitch* will gladly skip an obligation for."

Anna smirks, nodding a few times. "Okay, see you around, then," she says, strolling back toward the store.

What the actual fuck?

If I was on fire earlier, my body's a fucking inferno now. My heart's banging against my chest, tears threatening to emerge, but I bite down on my bottom lip to keep them away. I close my eyes, intake a long shaky breath, allow my lungs to empty, then repeat, but breathing isn't helping this time. With trembling hands, I ditch my drink, withdraw my phone from my jacket pocket and speed dial Luca, hoping he's not busy as I stride out of the mall.

"Please, pick up—pick up."

"Evie?" Luca's deep voice comes through from a noisy place, and a sob sits on the tip of my tongue.

"Tell me I'm not a fuck up, Luca," I barely whisper, sitting on a nearby bench.

"Jesus. You're not a fuck up, Evie." He sighs, a door closing to a quieter area before he adds, "Talk to me. What happened?"

I let out a shaky breath while bouncing my leg. "Sometimes, I feel like I am, you know? People talk their shit, but deep down, a part of me knows I deserve their hate, that I'm a heartless bitch who doesn't care how my actions affect others...."

"First, coming to this conclusion already shows you have a heart because the people who couldn't give two shits about others carry on in life without a damn worry, so pull yourself out of that mindset."

"Fuck... it's hard, especially when I'm reminded daily."

"No use trying to outlive your reputation. Use it to your advantage if you have to. Worked for me."

"Yeah, well, at least you have a successful business to show for at the end of the day. One I wish I could've been a part of instead of what I've been brought up into."

Luca sighs. "Evie, do you need me to come get you—"

"No. No, don't." I sweep a hair behind my ear. "I'll be alright. Thank you for listening."

"Are you sure? There's always a place for you here at Knockouts."

My smile is instant. "Yeah, I know. Thanks—"

Enzo's voice booms in the background. "Luca, this is no time to have your dick in your hand. We're swamped out here...wait, who are you talking to? Is it a chick? Let me see— ow, fuck, you're gonna snap my neck—"

Something heavy scratches along the floor, another object tumbling over, and I move the phone away from my ear as Enzo cackles on the line.

"I'ma add that to moments I wish I captured on camera. Oh, Evie, hey. You alright?"

He knows whenever I call Luca instead of him that I'm not. "Hey. Give me a few hours, and I will be."

The bustling noise from earlier comes back, then dies out rather quickly. "A few hours? Nope, let what's bothering you last no more than a few minutes."

Smiling, I add, "Nah, a few seconds at most."

"Yeah, that's more like it. Gone."

I giggle, then release a long breath. "Thanks, Enzo. You two always know how to brighten my mood."

"Anytime, Bratface."

"Okay, Zoey," I retort, rolling my eyes.

"Alright, I'll let that slide this time, but while I have you, what are you doing on New Year's Eve?"

"I'm working."

"What are the chances Gin would let you take a mini vacation?"

Slim to none. "Why, what's up?"

"There's a fight, two top contenders. Want in?"

It's been a while since I worked the octagon. "I would, but you know New Year's Eve is one of Vivid's busiest days of the year."

"I get it, same here at the bar, but the offer stands if you change your mind, though if you do, give yourself time to find security to accompany you. It's a requirement now."

"Thanks, I'll keep that in mind."

"Wait, here, I'll give you back to Luca—" They bicker for a moment before Enzo continues talking in the background. His voice becomes muffled and turns my smile into a grin.

My boys are just what I needed.

"Hey, sorry," Luca says with a sigh.

"It's okay. Tell Zoey I said bye."

He chuckles, and it warms my heart. "Alright."

"I love you, Luca. Talk to you soon."

"Love you too, kid."

We end our call, and I breathe with ease, ready to head home and put today behind me, like I do every other day. The faster I forget, the easier it is to push forward, living with enough control to get through tomorrow, the next day, and so on. My smile falters—what a way to live.

Running out of the office, I go down the main stairs, looking for Mom with tears in my eyes, but too many people are blocking my way. I'm not supposed to leave the dressing room, just as Jared's not allowed in there, but we have always found ways around that rule, sneaking through the emergency exits to see each other. Tonight, I needed him, to lose myself within him, but he was mean for no reason—that my problems were not his to fix and to leave him alone.

Mom's on the stage, and she looks so beautiful dancing, her tanned skin glowing under the bright lights, her long hair bouncing as she flipped the dark strands from her face, showcasing her wide smile. I want her confidence to be able to stand up for myself. Be powerful and brave, not the scared girl with her heart ripped in two. I can't stop the pain.

One look in my direction and her smile's gone in an instant as she rushes off stage, yanking me into the dressing room.

"Everly, what were you thinking going out there!?"

"I'm sorry," I cry, following Mom to her station. "I wanted to find you because—"

"You know you're never to leave this room while I'm working." Mom places her fingers on the bridge of her nose, breathing in and releasing the deep, shaky breath before adding with a calm assertive tone, "Do not leave this room again. Under any circumstances. Do you understand me?"

I nod my head quickly, taking in her disappointment in full strides before she leaves me alone. Tears roll down my cheeks, and I turn toward the table, resting my face in my arms while I weep, wishing I was home already. I pick my head up, only moments later to wipe my cheeks, and a little white paper bird is sitting in front of me. There are only a few Vixens around, freshening up, none of them paying me mind when I ask who left it here.

Picking up the little dove, I study each crease, how perfectly folded the paper is, not one wrinkle in sight. It's so beautiful, and I smile, the kind gift making the ache inside hurt a little less—

I blink a few times, glancing around the dressing room before staring into my station mirror, palming the paper dove I received when I was sixteen years old—how something so simple made me smile on a dreadful day. Picking up my phone, I contemplate calling Dad to brighten my night, pressing his number but end the call soon after, not wanting to bother him, especially while I'm here.

"I'm not working with her," Roni says, walking past me and leaving the room, Julianne staying behind, looking at me.

"What?"

"You know what."

I sigh. "I don't care if she's still upset."

"Evie, listen. I love your spunk, kid, but your careless attitude will only hold you back if you continue expressing yourself that way. Not everyone is against you."

"Yeah, well, even less are with me." I place the dove in the corner and stand from my seat. "For the sake of Vivid and everyone else, I'm better off working alone."

Walking past Julianne, I close my robe and head to the main floor, needing a change of scenery until my next customer arrives. I halt my steps and take a deep breath when the man who wrecks my mind, who won't stay away, walks through Vivid's front doors.

One look in my direction has my stomach stirring, a mix of needing to run out of here and wanting to stay for whatever request he has for me tonight—his smile quickly determines which direction I take, which isn't toward the dressing room.

"Dammit."

front doors
stomach stirring
and wanting to stay for
e tonight—his smile quickl
which direction I take, which isn'
oward the dressing room. "Dammit.

TWELVE
ENJOYING THE VIEW?

Lennox

Evie's standing by the bar in a red robe, beautiful as hell, even if she looks ready to run the closer I get. Will she give me the time to talk and apologize for yesterday?

"Hey." She doesn't acknowledge me, leans her back

against the bar, staring across the room, maybe at nothing. "I deserve that."

My remark gets a smirk from her, which is accomplishment number one. "What do you want, Lex?"

"Let's take a ride."

Evie glances at me, this time with her brow raised. "Can't. I'm working."

"C'mon, Peaches. You know you want to." I hold up my keys, finally getting my car back from the shop.

Her eyes narrow at me, then they lift toward the second floor to the office across from the bar. I follow her gaze to a man standing, watching us from the large window is uncanny, and I want to take her away even more.

"I got customers coming soon...." Her voice brings my focus back.

"And they'll survive one night without nutting. I'd rather you *come* with me."

She giggles, which is accomplishment number two, and what I love to hear.

Tilting her head to the side, Evie strolls closer, trails her fingers down my arm, and stops at my hand as she purrs, "Hm, you really want me to come?"

Fuck. "More than once."

My dick takes notice of the way she drags her bottom lip between her teeth, and the result is a smile before she snatches my keys. "Fine, but I'm driving."

"Uh, no. I just got her back."

"You want me to come, don't you?" She twirls a strand of her hair as she turns toward the dressing room, her thin robe barely covering her ass while she walks inside.

"You're wasting your time."

Turning to the feminine voice at the bar, I stare at Gin, who's wiping down the counter. "What do you mean?"

"I've been watching you, watching her." She places a towel over her shoulder and leans on the ledge. "You got relationship vibes written all over you. Sorry to say, but Evie ain't the one, honey."

I'll be the judge of that.

"Do you often give unsolicited advice to your customers?"

Gin chuckles. "It's not advice, kid, but a warning," she says, then walks to the other end of the bar.

Evie pokes her head out of the room she entered and nods for me to follow her inside. I do as she says, catching sight of one of the security guards standing nearby, but he doesn't pay me mind as I pass. The dressing room is nothing like the elegance of the main floor, with bare walls—not much more than lockers, stations, and outfits, as if the owner doesn't care what environment the girls get ready in.

I go inside unnoticed until one woman exits a shower, so I quicken my steps out the door Evie left through, which leads to a long narrow hall with an exit sign at the end by the stairs. There stands Evie, tossing my keys in the air, wearing jeans and a black coat with the zipper open.

"Where are we going?" she asks, moving her hand to her back when I go for my keys.

I glance around, no camera in sight, and tower over her petite frame. Her tongue glides over her lips as she stares into my eyes, and I inch closer, itching to touch her again. A soft, shaky breath passes through her once I take hold of her hips, and it's taking everything in me not to draw her to my body, to finally taste her.

"On our date."

She hums, tilting her head back against the wall. "You didn't win that bet."

"Maybe not, but we should give it a go anyway."

"Yeah?"

I nod, trailing my hand up her side, her lips parting as I hold her neck, caressing her cheek with my thumb. "Yes. I apologize for yesterday. Will you forgive my unruly behavior and go on a date with me?"

She smirks and holds up the keys for me to take. "Fine. One date."

"After you," I say, opening the door, and my skin prickles when she glides her fingers across my abdomen.

I blow out a deep breath before following her, unlocking my Mustang, and Evie picks up her step to the passenger side, smiling as she slides her hand along the carbonized exterior.

"She's beautiful."

My grin matches hers as we both get inside, and I fire her up. "Ready to go?"

Evie nods, glancing at me as I back out and head for the road. We have a few hours of daylight left, so I take the hour and a half drive up 101, making small talk, giving her the scenic view of Cannon Beach as I pull over to the side and park.

I should've packed a picnic or some romantic shit like that.

Rolling down the window, Evie leans out, and while she takes in the beautiful sight, I do the same, only mine's much closer, curvier, plump.

She peeks over her shoulder, catching me staring at her ass, and smirks. "Enjoying the view?"

"Very much."

Facing forward again, she widens her stance while swaying her body. "Come watch the waves with me, Lex."

I have a blanket from that one time I needed to stay overnight at the mill, so I pop the trunk to grab it, spreading the fuzzy red plaid fabric over the hood of my car. Strolling to her door, I open it and gesture for her to take my hand as she steps out. She kisses my cheek, and a fire ignites within me when her lips touch my skin. I swallow, assist her in climbing on top, and rest back on her elbows.

I'm next to her in seconds, and we stay silent for a moment, several cars passing behind us though the ocean waves crashing along the cliff drown out most of them.

"Thank you for taking me here. This view's much better than being at work."

"You're welcome. I wish I were more prepared with snacks, but I wasn't sure you'd say yes."

She glances at me, then continues watching the water. "I'm glad I did. This setting is beautiful."

"I'm happy you're happy, Evie."

Her smile is instant, bringing her lip between her teeth to mask it, and I wish it were mine instead.

"My dad used to take me here as a kid. Though it's not the same as our spot in Cali, this location is the closest he could get and was the only time I was happy. I assume that's why he tried to take me often. Maybe to ensure I'd never lose my smile." She sighs, maneuvering flat on her back, staring at the sunset sky. "I haven't been here since he left when I was twelve."

I mimic her, shifting closer, and she turns her head to face me. The sadness in her eyes makes my chest tighten, wishing I could ease her pain.

"My pops used to take me here before he took over his

business. We'd rent a boat and fish for hours, talking, not talking, just enjoying the atmosphere and each other's company."

Evie rests her hand on my palm, trailing her fingers with mine until they intertwine, and her touch feels perfect. I lift her hand to kiss the back, then we face each other more, and my heart skips as she raises her other hand to touch my cheek. The second her eyes flick to my lips, her gaze darkens, and the fire within burns even more. I take hold of her side, easing down to her lower back, and her lips part as I draw her toward me, her leg lifting to rest on my hip.

"Lex..."

"Yes?" I ask, moving my face closer as her breathing increases, her fingers pressing onto my chest and sliding up my neck.

"What are you thinking about? This very moment."

I knead the bare skin above her jeans, dipping the tips of my fingers into the denim. "How badly I want to kiss you."

She hums, then whispers, "How badly?"

Lifting to hover above, I sweep a few strands of hair from her temple, waiting for her cue, hoping she'll give me one, and the second she smiles, I do the same, dipping forward, capturing her lips with mine. There's no hesitation, no resistance, and my stomach flips when she moans, opening up for my tongue to enter. I want to be greedy and keep her all to myself—to be the first, last, the only man to taste these lips.

To never stop.

Our kiss turns urgent as she runs her hands along my sides, wrapping her legs around my waist to draw my body closer, and fuck do I want to be inside her. I buck forward, making her pant against my lips, our tongues lapping as my hardened cock digs between her thighs, and I do it again to hear her whine. Her head falls back, and I tend to her neck, kissing her sweet-scented skin, groaning as she pushes me lower, lingering between her perfect tits.

I gaze into her eyes before lifting her shirt, kissing her stomach, admiring her nipples as they pebble from the cool air, and take one into my mouth, making her squirm beneath my touch while I tend to the other. I want to taste more of her, so I move lower, kissing and licking her abdomen, digging my fingers into her sides as I place myself on the ground and hook my fingers into the loops of her jeans.

We're both panting as I wait for the next cue, hovering above her pussy, rubbing her thighs, ready to remove the barrier in my way.

She shakes her head, lowering her shirt and sitting straight. "I'm sorry, Lex."

My brows furrow and I stand, taking hold of the side of her neck. "No, don't be sorry. Everyone has their own pace, and I don't want you to feel obligated to do anything you don't feel comfortable doing."

Her teary gaze moves between mine. "Thank you."

"Anytime, Peaches."

She rolls her eyes, a slight smile emerging, and I'll take an annoyed smirk over her frowning any day. "It's getting dark," she says, sliding to the ground. "We should head back to Portland."

If only there were more time in a day. "Okay."

There's so much I want to learn about her, but the ride back feels like mere seconds, not much time to converse as I pull into the parking lot. I can't stop thinking about her lips, how she tastes, and when I can again. Would she let me kiss her goodnight? Will she get written up for leaving work early? Lose her job? Shit. I park my Mustang along the back where we left, and my stomach stirs when Evie doesn't attempt to leave just yet.

"I had a good time tonight."

"Same here. I'm glad I was able to convince you to come with me."

She presses her lips together to stifle a smile, and I want nothing more than for her to let it shine. "Is that one of your puns?"

I chuckle and smirk. "No pun intended. Though..." leaning closer, I whisper into her ear, "you would've definitely come with me."

"Oh yeah?" she asks, tilting her head to the side so our lips are inches apart. "And how sure are you about that?"

"As sure as I want to kiss you again."

Her smile brightens, and she lifts to swipe my hair away from my forehead before gripping a handful at the top. "That badly?"

"Mm, damn, you have no idea the things I'd do to taste those lips again."

"Anything?"

She prevents me from dipping closer, and I grin, smoothing my thumb along her bottom lip. "Just say the word."

Her mouth opens then closes before she inches away from me and whispers, "You make me nervous, Lex."

"Nervous?"

She nods. "I don't date. I've been fooled before, so I made a rule long ago not to."

The thought of anyone lying and using this beautiful woman for their selfish needs makes my blood boil. "Are you afraid I'll be one of those guys?"

Her eyes gloss over, and I want to take away her pain. "I'm sorry, Lex if I've led you on. For wasting your time—"

"Hey, no." I take her cheek in my palm and brush my thumb along a falling tear. "You could never waste my time. I've enjoyed every second spent with you."

She closes her eyes and turns away from me. "That's what they all say before dropping their pants."

"I believe you and understand your hesitation. That you need time. I've got plenty of that, and best believe I won't stop showing you I'm not one of those guys."

All it takes to ease any thought of never seeing her again from my mind is the radiant smile Evie displays. "Good to know." She leans forward, and I hold still as she presses her lips to my cheek. "Goodnight, Lex."

"See you soon."

Evie smirks before leaving my car and walks toward the back exit, quickening her step when someone comes outside. The woman doesn't hold the door, and Evie barely catches it. That Anna girl waves as she glances back, then rolls her eyes while counting a few bills. She enters a white Audi, and my stomach drops, recognizing that car parked in Kylo's driveway many times—belonging to a regular—one who broke the rules.

mes outside

e barely catches i

hen rolls her eyes whi

Audi, and my stomach drops

that car parked in Kylo's drivewa

g to a regular—one who broke the rules

THIRTEEN
MERRY FUCKING CHRISTMAS

Evie

"Breathe in, four, three, two, one...and release." I exhale, coming out of my bridge, and finish my yoga session with lotus pose. "Beautiful. Great class, everyone. Quick reminder for those who come once a week, we are closed next week from Christmas Eve until after the new year," the instructor Amy says as everyone prepares to leave except three other girls and me. "Evie, it's been a while since you came to one of my Wednesday classes."

I smile, resting on my hands as Amy unbraids the white silks for me. "I know. I need to come more often. Work takes up most of my time."

"Well, I'm glad you're here."

She takes down a few more, and I walk over to mine, running my fingers through the smooth fabric. I've been silk training since sixteen, falling in love with the art in this very studio, so this place holds a special place in my heart. As Amy teaches a class, I stay in the back, working on next Wednesday's Christmas special routine I've been practicing at home. I don't have the twenty-five feet height here, but the calming atmosphere is what I need most—to get out of my head and flow.

When I'm back on the floor, I grab a sip of water and find a few eyes on me, young girls who are rush-talking to each other before one is ushered out of their circle, hesitantly walking toward me. I give her a small smile as she wrings her hands together and stops in my area.

"Hello," I say, and her stance lightens as she smiles back.

"Hi," she replies, stretching her arms and her friends give her the 'talk to her' look, which I chew on my bottom lip to keep from giggling. "I'm sorry to bother you. My friends and I were wondering if you could maybe show us how you did that trick when you were in a hip lock and then rolled upward more."

"Sure. Come see me after your class, and I'll explain—if it's okay with your parents, of course."

Her smile widens. "Okay! I'll go ask."

I continue to practice until the class ends, and the girls

come rushing toward me, parents watching in the distance, which makes my heart race a bit. My skills are on the advanced side, but I show them a tutorial, giving tips on how to propel upward, some hands-on, and what core strengthening exercises to do to achieve the trick over time. When we're done, the girls are on their silks with mats underneath them, using the tips, and one of them gets into a hip key on the third attempt, and her excitement makes me grin, clapping along with everyone.

Amy watches me pack my gym bag and strolls over. "I'm impressed with your teaching technique. You must've had a good instructor," she says with a smirk, and I bump her shoulder with mine.

"Sure did." We both laugh, and I place the strap of my bag over my shoulder, feeling good. "I forgot how much I enjoyed being here."

"I hope to see you more often, and if you ever want to unwind, maybe teach a class or two, I could use a helping hand. The classes have gotten much larger over the years."

"Thanks. I'll keep that in mind."

She rubs my arm, then cleans the studio as I leave, walking the short distance to my car. The drive isn't far from my childhood home. Since moving here, I've lived in Portland and walked almost everywhere. I was supposed to go to work today, but I'm taking a personal day. I bet Jared's thinking of ways to make my life more miserable since I left Monday, too. My dislike for him grows more each second I have to endure him.

When I pull into my driveway, Gin's car is there, and I slowly put the car into park and get out. She doesn't waste time waiting for me to reach my door before she's standing next to me, smoking a cigarette.

"Evie, we need to talk."

"Talk about what?" I ask, crossing my arms as I face my mother, swiping away the smoke that filters around us. "Since when did you start smoking again?"

She huffs a laugh. "Can we go inside?"

"I'm surprised you remember where I live. I've been here for eight years, and you only came once."

"I'm not here to argue with you."

"Neither am I. We're having a conversation, and I've not once raised my tone."

Dropping the cigarette on my pathway, she presses her foot on it, choosing my battles, so I hold my tongue since she's littering on my property. "Are you going to let me in?"

"No. Whatever you need to talk about can wait until tomorrow at Vivid because I'm more than positive it has something to do with work, and I leave work at the door."

"I wouldn't be here if it was regarding work."

"What do you want?" I ask, losing my patience.

Gin breathes out a heavy breath. "Alright. It's obvious there's an issue between us that needs settling. So I'm here to settle it."

An ache creeps into my throat. "An issue...you think there's only an issue between us? Not you keeping me in the dark about why we left Cali, neglecting me my whole childhood, how you were always around but never present. Do you know how it feels to be alone in a building full of people?"

"That's not fair," she says, shaking her head. "I did everything to ensure you had a roof over your head and food on the table."

Tears spring to my eyes as I hold back a bitter laugh. "Fair? Nothing has ever been fair. My feelings never mattered, and every decision you made was to benefit you. Not me. Dad came here, and you drove him away. Why?"

Her jaw clenches as she looks down, not surprised that she would ignore my question, and I blink away the tears. "If you want to talk about our issues, '*mend the bridge*' between us to make *our* life easier, then come back when you're ready to talk like adults."

I unlock my door, leave her standing on the steps, and lean against the other side. Drawing out my phone, I dial Dad, waiting through the ringing, and his voice comes through—"Hey, it 's Marco. Leave a message, and I'll get back to you soon. *Ciao.*"

Ending the call, I slump to the floor and hug my knees.

I don't want to go!

Mommy's crying, making me leave my toys as she rushes me outside, Daddy coming in front of her when we reach our car.

"Marco, move out of my way...." Her voice sounds broken.

"Please, don't take our daughter from me."

I get out of her hold, running to hug Daddy's leg, and he crouches down, holding me close. "Daddy, I want to stay with you."

"Shh, don't worry, baby girl." He kisses my cheeks over and over. "I love you, and I won't be far—"

Banging the back of my head against the door, I chew on my bottom lip to bite back a sob, tears stinging the back of my eyelids as the memories run rampant, and I stand, heading upstairs to attempt falling asleep. Same shit, different fucking day.

Lennox is here when I stroll into the main floor for my Friday performance, sitting at the bar with a beer in hand, talking with a regular, which means he's becoming one, and I can't hide the butterflies that enter my stomach. However, I'm slightly disappointed his name wasn't in my voyeur queue tonight. A few spots are still available, which fills up quickly. There's still time. Oscar transitions to my song, and I glance at Lennox before heading to the stage, performing my act, adding an extra piece since I have time until my first customer.

He's watching but is still by the bar, which is unlike him.

I'm breathing hard when I finish, staying on stage a moment too long. *What am I doing?* I plaster on a smile as patrons cheer, trying not to look at him as I head for the dressing room. Leaning on my station, I close my eyes, unable to stop the doubt from settling into my stomach.

He's not toying with me. Stop creating issues that aren't there.

I look at myself in the mirror before walking to the shower, taking my time, breathing, then getting back to work —I return to work the next day, and he's here, Monday, Wednesday, Lennox is here, sitting at the bar drinking a beer, watching the floor, but he hasn't been present. Not once has he come to see me in several days. I've allowed myself to open up in ways I haven't with anyone but my small circle, and he's ghosting me in plain sight.

Why? Because I couldn't go further? I'm not as easy as

he thought, so why bother? Is he watching someone else? Tears form in my eyes, believing he could be different, that he's unlike the men I've attempted to keep in my life.

"Evie, you're up," Julianne yells from the doorway, and I quickly wipe under my eyes, retouch my makeup, and adjust my red satin bow lingerie that's supposed to replicate me as a present. No way in hell will it stay in place while in the air, though I'm to unravel myself like the gift I am. It's my job to get naked, but the air is my haven, where exposing my entire body is optional, unlike the voyeur box I'm heading for right afterward with the shit load of requests I have and none with him.

Merry fucking Christmas.

Closing my eyes, I inhale a long breath, exhaling until I can't anymore, allowing the performer within to come forth and push back the broken woman I try so hard to hide. I tie on my black lace eye mask with my head high, then walk toward the red curtain doorway, throwing on a smirk. *Shut up and Listen* plays the second I step onto the main floor, and all eyes are on me. I don't see anyone as I slowly move my body, staying focused while gravitating along the sultry rhythm not to meet his gaze in the head of patrons.

At the stage, I flow through the silks, gripping each one, then twist into the air on the beat of *Angelicca's* voice in an upside-down split, slowly swaying my legs, then front walkover onto the floor to climb halfway up the fabric. Working in the air, I allow the music to take control, freeing myself from all the thoughts, showcasing a genuine smile while wrapped in the silks that's keeping me stable, from falling, and relieving the emotions wreaking havoc in my mind, even for this moment.

I bend backward to untie my bow, my breasts on full

display as I gradually get lower to the stage, onto my knees, and open my eyes to Lennox in my direct line of sight. My heart flutters as fast as my tears emerge, every emotion rushing back, and I clench my jaw, the performer slipping as the broken arises. But I hold her back, blinking away the sorrow as I end my show on the floor—dancing while stripping the rest of the lingerie, focusing on every other patron but him.

Still, I feel his eyes on my body like a flame touching my skin, goosebumps rising, making me moan while trailing my fingertips across my breasts, between my legs, closing my eyes as if it were only us here. The lyrics affect me something fierce, wishing he'd come to see me again, hating how much he's taken over me, and I barely know who he is.

The song slowly comes to a close as I lie on my side, staring at the red lights on the ceiling, licking the tears that managed to escape through my lace mask, and I come into focus as everyone cheers. This time I don't look at anyone as I exit the stage, heading straight for the showers, ripping my mask off, and leaning against the stall while holding my face in my palms.

"Everly..." Gin says on the other side, and I groan, my mother being the last person I want to see.

"Please. I need five. You can at least give me that much."

She opens the curtain, and I roll my eyes, wiping away my tears as she looks me over. "Take thirty."

I huff a laugh, turning on the shower. "You pity me enough to listen for once."

"Stop making me out to be the bad guy. I'm your mother."

Facing the stream, I run my face under the lukewarm water. "Congratulations."

Gin takes hold of my chin and makes me look at her, her eyes glossing before whispering, "I'm trying my best here."

My brows furrow. "Trying your best...." I slap the water off. "You're not trying for shit! Where were you whenever I needed you? Huh? When I used to cry myself to sleep because you took me from the only people who actually love me? When I was tormented in school for being a slut because of where I spent most of my time? *She's bound to be a slut, just like her mother.* Well, I guess the apple didn't fall far from the tree while you spread your legs for—"

I gasp when Gin slaps me, and I press my palm along my stinging cheek. "Don't you dare disrespect me! You haven't got a clue what I've been through, what I've given up to protect you, shit I've done for you. I've tried to take you away but couldn't because working here kept a roof over our heads and off the streets."

Blinking back my tears, I turn to look at her, but she's already gone. I sink to the floor, already done with today. The trip to Vegas Enzo brought up is sounding better and better by the second, so I'll need to stay to have a chance of leaving then.

Taking a few minutes, I finish cleaning myself, then wrap a towel around my body, strolling into the dressing room, one of the newer Red Vixens eyeing me with sympathy, and my jaw drops once I reach my station. "Who the fuck did this?!"

Everything's crushed, all my makeup, a tube of scarlet red lipstick broken from someone writing the word slut across my mirror, and heat boils within, rising along my neck. "I know you bitches hate me, but c'mon, this is fucking low."

"Evie..."

I spin toward Sadie, hot tears brimming my eyes. "I need to get away, fuck this shit. Tell Gin I'm leaving early."

Roni comes striding out of the locker area, her brows furrowing while she clips her lace bra from the back. "You're not doing this again tonight. I'm *not* picking up your slack. Can't you stop thinking of only yourself for once in your life?"

Is she still holding a grudge against me about that day?

I get what I did was a dick move, but the hatred she feels toward me is a reason well beyond the move I made.

Sadie steps between us, turning to face me. "It's okay. I have a few minutes before the next room empties. I'll help you clean up."

Roni groans and walks back to the costume rack. A tear falls down my cheek, and I hastily wipe it away.

"Fine, I'll stay," I say, sighing as I get started on the mess, picking up my broken blush palette and tossing it into my trash can. "I do need a getaway. I'm thinking of taking a few days off, heading to Vegas for a fight."

"A ring girl gig? It's been a while."

"Yes, my cousin Enzo told me about it, and I think leaving town will help me clear my mind. Getting away from my crazy life for a bit."

"You should," she says, nodding. "When's the fight?"

"New Year's Eve."

Her eyes widened. "Will Gin approve the leave?"

She's not in charge but won't make it easy, especially after what happened.

"It's not up to her anymore. Everything goes through Jared now, and I know that dick will say no."

"Doesn't hurt to ask."

"Ask." I huff a laugh, dumping hundreds of dollars of

makeup into the trash can, then stare at the mirror, that word hitting me hard in the gut, my lip curling. "But I don't care what either of them say." The word smudges as I drag my fingers over the letters to make it unreadable, then clean my hand with a makeup wipe. "Are you still on a contract with Kylo? Do you think he'll lend me his security? It's mandatory to bring our own since the crowds have been getting rowdy."

"Adam?" she asks, blinking a few times, holding back tears, and I feel like shit not wanting to ask her why she's upset—she's my damn best friend, but I can't handle anyone else's sorrow right now.

"Is that his name?" I ask, pushing down the emotions biting the back of my throat. "The blond guy who stands outside?"

"Yeah. Want me to ask Kylo?"

"Don't worry about it. I'll come by and ask myself. You should get back to work. I don't need you getting written up for me."

"Hey, no way. You're more important."

I plaster on a meek smile, feeling even more selfish because she is the opposite, and I draw her into my side, her hug easing an ounce of my pain. Sadie helps me finish cleaning until Julianne strolls into the room, shaking her head.

"Sadie, Jared wants you in his office."

Shit.

"Ma, it's not her fault. I—"

She holds up her hand. "Don't get into it, kid." Turning toward Sadie, she adds, "Better get a move on it."

Nodding, she glances at me before exiting to the main floor. Julianne sighs, touching my cheek while looking me over. I'm sure my face is starting to form Gin's handprint.

"You okay?" she asks.

I lick my lips, adjusting the towel around my chest before smiling at her. "Of course I am. I'm a Russo." Huffing a laugh, I add, "We're built to endure misfortune...though best believe at the end of the day, we never forget."

"Okay, walk in, ask Kylo, then leave. Simple. Easy."

Except I stay planted in my car, staring at Lennox's Mustang in the driveway. I was hoping he'd be at work. He should be at his place. Everything is fine—I pep talk as I get out, walking to the front door. Sadie answers a moment later as I knock, the ache settling in my stomach eases when it's only her in the great room.

"Evie, hey, Kylo's in his office," she says, stepping aside so I can enter.

"Thanks." I take in her outfit and smirk. "Nice shirt."

She glances down at the oversized grey t-shirt that rests mid-thigh, her hair damp, and she can't stop the smile that draws from her lips. "His closet was closer."

I raise my brows. "Well, let me make this quick before Kylo decides he wants his shirt back."

"Oh, stop," she giggles, her cheeks turning pink.

We walk toward the kitchen, me turning down the short hall, and I slow my steps hearing Lennox talking. "Yeah, I figured we would. Love looks good on you."

Kylo chuckles, leaning back in his seat as I slowly round the doorway, and I stop when Lennox meets my gaze. He's slumped back in a chair, his legs wide open, just as he looks in our sessions, and I turn away as my heart beats faster.

"Hey...can I talk to you for a minute, Kylo?"

"Sure, what's up?"

I step forward and stop at the side of his desk, trying my hardest not to look Lennox's way, though I feel those golden eyes on me. "I may be overstepping, but I don't know who else to ask."

"Okay, how can I help?"

"I have a gig in Vegas, and I need to bring private security. Is there any way I can hire Adam for New Year's Eve?"

Kylo straightens up, his brows pushing together. "I'm sorry, but I can't at this moment."

Damn, I was hoping he'd say yes. "Okay, thank you. I understand it being last minute and all—"

"I'll go with you," Lennox says, and I finally look at him as he stands from his seat.

Why would he offer to come with me? "No thanks." I turn to leave, stopping by the burn his touch causes when Lennox takes hold of my hand.

"Hey, I promise you can trust me."

I've never been more confused about a man in my life. Does he still like me? Want to be friends? Fuck buddies? I sigh, crossing my arms, hating that I have nobody else to ask. "Fine. Let's go talk."

Turning to leave, I can feel him on my heels without looking back, and his arm brushes mine when he passes by, walking toward the back door. We pass Sadie setting plates on the island with sandwiches and step onto the deck. Kylo draws her close, and I can't help feeling envious of how easily they share and express their intimacy.

When Lennox and I meet the fork, and he continues

toward his place, I stop walking. "We can talk here," I say, and he turns around halfway, strolling back.

"Sure."

I want to talk about why he's ghosting me, but the words are stuck in my throat. Instead, I pull out my phone. "What's your number? Send me your info so I can text you the flight details."

"What time do you need to be in Vegas? I'll take care of the tickets, Peaches."

That name hits me harder than it ever has before. "No, you're not buying them."

He sighs, gesturing for my phone, and his fingers brush my hand as he takes it from me, typing in his number. "At least let me buy my own."

"Fine. I'll send you the flight information."

Lennox takes hold of my hand as I turn to leave. "Hey, are you okay?" he asks, rubbing his thumb across the back as he draws me closer, staring into my eyes. "Would you like to come inside for a bit?"

I search through those beautiful hues, wanting to get lost in them while running far away.

Am I okay?

"Yeah. I'm okay. I should get going. See you on Tuesday."

With that, I drop his hold, leaving back to my car, home, and Vivid. Wash, rinse, repeat as the next few days pass, only I make sure not to look around for him whenever I'm here—getting back into a routine, numbing myself deep to the bone because pleasure has to be work, never personal.

No more distractions.

Tomorrow's New Year's Eve, and I've been putting off telling Gin I won't be coming in—there's no way I'm going to

Jared. Throwing on a robe, I head out to the bar. Gin is finishing up an order as Anna takes the platter to VIP. I've been good to avoid this area, but Lennox isn't seated there anyway. Maybe he decided he's had enough of Vivid. I wouldn't blame him if he did.

"Hey, you got a minute?" I ask, and Gin looks at me, filling a tall glass under the tap.

"Yeah, make it quick. I got tickets almost out the door."

Just come out with it. "I'm taking off tomorrow."

Her head snaps to me. "What?—Not a fucking chance!" Roni and Gin say simultaneously, unsure how long Roni was nearby.

She takes off into the dressing room, and I sigh. Gin abandoning the liquor as she stands across from me behind the bar. "What are you talking about? It's New Year's Eve. You can't not be here."

"Well, Enzo got me a ring girl gig in Vegas—"

"Vegas? You're needed here, not there."

I place my hands on my hips. "I already took the job. My hotel and flights are paid in full, so I can't back out now. There are more than enough girls to cover my shift."

Gin pinches the bridge of her nose. "It's New Year's Eve. You, of all people, know how busy we are tomorrow—how many customers are coming to see *you*, and not only for voyeur."

"I don't care. I really don't," I say, shrugging my shoulders, then walk toward the dressing room. "Fire me for all I care, but we all know you won't."

"Everly—"

Heading for my locker, I take out my street clothes, tears stinging my eyes as I drag my jeans on and slip my arms through my button-up shirt. They flow so freely now as I roughly wipe them away. The hard shell I once built to hold my emotions is broken, along with the rules surrounding my life. Grabbing my phone, I sit at my station, propping my feet up along the ledge. No fucks given about responsibilities, about Vivid, anything—ready to leave for the night, but I need to wait for Sadie to let her know. So I scroll through MMA videos to brush up on the sport until Sadie appears in the mirror.

"Is Lex here?" I ask when she gets closer.

"No. Kylo dropped me off today."

I lock the screen and drop the phone on my lap. "Fuck. Okay. I'm sorry, Sadie, but I need to get away now."

"Of course. Don't worry about me. Kylo's picking me up tonight." She walks in front of me, crossing her arms while leaning on the table next to my feet. "I think you should do what's best for you, Evie. If you're not happy here, why don't you leave?"

The back of my throat burns, more fucking tears, and I quickly wipe my cheeks clean. "Vivid is all I know—I just need to focus on something else for a second. See my cousin Enzo. I'll be fine by Wednesday."

"Are you sure?"

I stare into the distance, then nod. "Yeah."

"Okay. I have to get back to work, but please call me if you need anything, even if it's just to talk."

Standing from my seat, I draw her in for a hug, and she holds me tight, rubbing my back which is just what I need right now. "Love you," I whisper before we part ways.

"Love you, too. Don't forget to let loose and have fun."

"New Year's Eve, in Vegas, you know I'm letting loose—the fights after parties are wild."

She wrinkles her nose. "Maybe keep yourself reeled, just a tad."

A genuine laugh leaves me, and I smirk. "Don't worry. Anyway, I'll be with Enzo and Lex. I doubt either of them will let me get shitfaced."

I'm unsure if she believes me, but she accepts my answer anyway. "I'll see you Wednesday."

"Let me get out of here before Gin tries locking a ball and chain on me."

We both look at the doorway as Jared strolls inside the room, and a chill hits me. Did Gin tell him already? His intense stares land on me as he leans on the doorway, and I turn to button my shirt while Sadie walks toward him.

"Hey, can I speak with you? It's about one of the employees—"

"No. Get your shit, and leave my club. You no longer work here."

"What?" Sadie and I say simultaneously.

"Why are you firing me? I've done nothing wrong."

He chuckles and pushes off the frame, standing before her. "I gotta say, you got heavy balls to continue stealing from me."

My brows furrow—what is he talking about?

"Stealing? You can't seriously be this dense and ignorant of what goes on in your club? Maybe if you stop eye fucking your employees from afar, you'll realize who's stealing from you because it's not me."

Damn, that's my girl.

Jared glances at me before he towers above Sadie. "I'm well aware of what goes on in *my club*, and my decision is final. Get. Out."

"Gladly."

Sadie strides out of the dressing room, and the rest of the Vixens follow when Jared nods his head toward the exit. I step back onto my station, not taking my eyes off him as he strolls toward me with his hand in his pocket. My chest rises faster as he stops inches from me, silent before reaching behind me and picking up my paper dove.

I want to snatch it back, but then I risk ripping it. "Don't touch that," I seethe, clenching my jaw when he chuckles, running his index finger along the delicate wings, up the neck, then smirks, placing it back on the table, leaving just as quickly as he came in.

It takes me a second to come to my senses, striding to my locker to grab my coat and purse, then to Sadie's next for her stuff. Bringing everything but her coat out to my car, I rush back to find security escorting Sadie out of the VIP area, where Anna is smirking.

"I have your bag in the trunk. Let's go," I say, and Sadie takes her coat from me.

"Thank you."

Gin's watching us with her arms crossed, but I don't stay a second longer as we leave straight for my car through the dressing room exit. "Why didn't you tell me you were having problems at work?"

"You're stressed enough, and I didn't want to add more to your plate. Kylo and Lex have been watching Anna while I'm here."

Watching Anna? Why would they?

"Kylo knows—wait, Anna...are you talking about Leanna, the regular Kylo cut-off? Drives a white car?"

"Yes. She's been stalking the cabin and most likely followed me here."

"I knew that bitch looked familiar—Leanna is Kylo's

longest client. I think since he started his business. They came to Vivid a few times, to the velvet room in the basement, but they stopped about two years ago because she wanted to start booking voyeur with me. Since we were both his clients, he didn't feel it was appropriate."

We jump inside the car as a gust of wind blows past us. "They came here together...did you forget how she looked?"

"I didn't pay her mind, but I remember she had long hair."

Sadie tears up, and it makes me frown. "She called me Love, Evie. Declan calls me that...do you think she'd go to the extreme of looking me up? Finding out about my ex-husband? Stirring shit up to get me away from Kylo."

That wouldn't be good. "I have no idea."

She leans back in her seat and closes her eyes, taking deep breaths while I drive out of there, getting her far away from this place. Somewhere I never should've brought her.

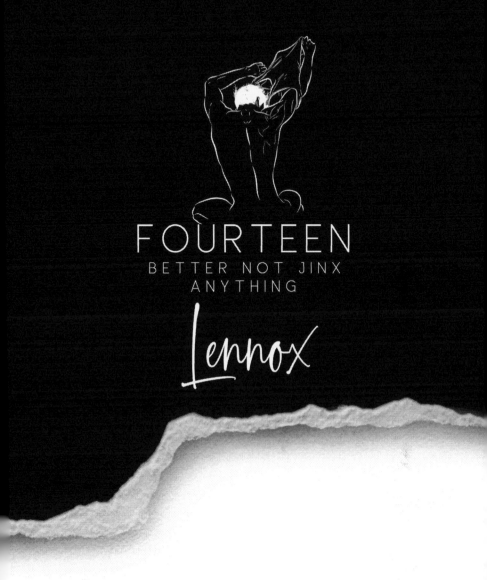

FOURTEEN
BETTER NOT JINX
ANYTHING

Lennox

I'm a patient man, but today that patience is running thin as I show Kevin how to work a saw. Brush up on skills, my ass. Jimmy's kid is starting from scratch. At least the other hire, Leonel, knows what he's doing.

"Alright, go on and start your conventional wedge," I say, and Kevin nods, doing a straight cut, then another at an angle below it, careful not to overcut, keeping it clean. "Good. Now, what's the next step?"

"The back, adding wedge blocks, and leaving a four-inch hinge."

My pocket vibrates, and I draw out my phone. "Good. Start on that."

Stepping aside, I keep an eye on Kevin while answering Kylo's call. "Hey, what's up?"

"Can you get off early today? I need to speak with you and Adam."

I look at my watch, it's a quarter to three now, and I'm usually out by five. "Uh, probably, yeah—whoa, whoa, stop! You're cutting too deep—" I rush toward Kevin, yelling to get his attention, and wave my hand to show him enough. "Ky, I'll call you back in five."

Ending the call, I place my phone in my pocket and run my hand across my jaw. Any deeper on the left, there would've been a big chance this tree kicked back as it fell.

"Did I do too much?" he asks, crouching to get a look at the side of the trunk. "Fuck, sorry, Lex."

"No, it's my fault. I should've been paying attention."

Kevin lowers his head, then picks up the saw, handing it to me, and I raise a brow. "Finish your cut."

"Are you sure?"

"You learn by making mistakes, now go on and fix yours."

He nods, a smirk on his face as he inserts the bar again, cutting the right side to match the left, then starts pounding the wedges with the ax, watching for movement until the tree tips on its own. We walk into our escape route, and I sling my arm around his shoulder as the tree fells beautifully.

"Good job. Start trimming. Then you can head home early tonight."

"Alright, thanks, Lex."

With our job done, I drive back to the mill, checking Dad's office, but he's not there. Letting Gwyneth know I'm heading out early, I get on the road. Since Sadie doesn't get out for another hour and a half, it's too early to pick her up, so I go to the cabin instead, though if it weren't for Kylo needing to talk, I would've stayed for a beer, see Evie. I've been trying to give her space, make her less nervous, and use Leanna as an excuse to stay away. To keep focus, but fuck was it hard.

During her Christmas performance, I felt something was off, just in her movement alone, pouring herself into the song, and I made my way to the stage as I saw the pain in her eyes, wanting to strip it away. She's so talented, so beautiful. I could watch her for hours and never tire. Now I have a chance to get to know her more, two days alone in Vegas, and I plan to get deep, to use up every second to make sure she knows how special she is to me.

Once I park in the driveway, I head inside, stop in my tracks to see Sadie here relaxing on the couch with Jinx, and I recheck my watch.

"Did you get out early?" I ask, and Sadie looks up from her phone as I stroll inside.

"Not exactly. I got fired today."

"No way. What happened?"

She sighs and shrugs. "People are assholes. Kylo's in the office."

I nod, walking straight there. Kylo's focused on the computer, and Adam's, by the window. Both look at me as I knock on the frame before entering.

"Hey."

"Hey. Can you close the door?"

Making sure it's closed, I walk toward the chair and sit. "Sadie said she was fired today...does Leanna have anything to do with that?"

"Good chance. Yeah."

"There wasn't much activity to report while I was there. With Sadie working upstairs, Leanna did her job, then went home. I wish I were able to be there tonight, but with Kev being new, I had to train—"

He holds up his hand. "Thank you, Lex, truly. You've done more than enough to help me, so please don't point the blame on you. What happened is all me, and I should've listened to your warnings a long time ago, and now this issue has spiraled into something much worse."

"There's no point in dwelling on what you could've done. What are we gonna do now to defuse the situation?"

Adam strolls over with his arms crossed, and we talk about his and Kylo's plan with Sadie's contract ending, both of which have negative results. Still, I agree that Adam's would be the quickest route, and ready to buy Sadie a ticket right now to get her out of Oregon. Kylo rests his head in his palms, threads his fingers through his hair, and lets out a deep sigh.

"Alright, let's do it," he says, and I can already hear the anguish in his voice.

"Are you sure this is the direction you want to go?"

He stands, sniffing while using his shirt to wipe his face. "Yeah, I want Leanna gone as fast as possible and out of our lives."

Adam nods, already getting his phone out to call his officer buddy, and I search for my flight to purchase another ticket while walking out of the office. Waving at Sadie, I continue to the back door, and Jinx is a step behind me as we head for the guest house, hoping this plan won't backfire.

4:00 a.m., and I'm awake as usual, sipping coffee on the deck, watching the lake with Jinx to pass the time, only I won't be going to work today. Sadie's belongings are by the front door, ready to load into my car, and in a few hours, Evie and I will be leaving for Vegas—hopefully, she can convince Sadie to come along. She thinks Kylo lying to her will backfire, and I don't agree or disagree.

Better not jinx anything.

My Jinx is the opposite of her name, bringing me more than good luck. I scratch behind her ear, and she purrs, rubbing her face against my chin, and I hope right now won't be our last moments together—that everything works out. Exhaling a deep breath, I clear my throat as a knot settles within and clean a tear from the corner of my eye with my thumb.

"Alright, ya beast. Let's get you fed."

Picking her up, I kiss the top of her head and stroll inside the cabin, filling her bowls and quietly making myself something to eat since I'm unsure when my next meal will be. I take my time, get Sadie's stuff in the car, and text Kylo about thirty minutes ago that I'll be waiting in the car at 6:30, ready to go with Jinx, which I am, to which he replied thank you.

Fifteen minutes go by, and I look at Jinx sitting in the passenger seat. "Let's go check on them."

I grab her, keeping the car running as we head inside the cabin—just as Sadie strides down the stairs, her face red with tears dripping down her cheeks.

Fuck. Quickest plan, yes. Easy? Not in the slightest.

Kylo's sitting on the top step with his head buried in his arms, his body shaking, and it's taking everything in me not to go upstairs, needing to do my part. So I leave him—leave my best bud to ride in his sorrows alone, and I hate it. I'll do my best to console Sadie. I text Adam to check on Kylo in a few minutes, then get in the car.

Sadie's breathing spasms every so often as I drive, taking the longer route while she stares out the window, Jinx resting on my lap. We arrive at her apartment complex, and I park, sitting in silence. I want to say something to make her feel better, give her even a hint that not everything is as it seems, and her name slips from my tongue before I can even re-think.

"Sadie—"

"Please, don't, Lex. I knew the rules, and I asked him to make me fall in love...and he did his job exceptionally well, that's for sure." She finally turns to look at me, wiping a tear that falls on her cheek. "I learned a lot this past month, more about myself than I ever have, and I'll cherish every great memory. I'm going to be okay."

"I know, but—"

"But nothing." She reaches to stroke Jinx's head before picking her up. "Have a good time in Vegas. Please look after Evie. She's not in the right state of mind right now."

I exhale a deep breath and nod. "I won't ever let anything happen to her."

"I know you won't, that you care for her a lot."

"Yes, but it doesn't seem like our feelings are mutual."

Her smile is reassuring as she takes hold of his hand. "You're a great guy, Lex, and Evie sees that too. She's just going through a lot right now with work, so give her time to unwind. Maybe she'll feel better after getting away."

"Thanks." I smile back, then pet the beast. "I'm going to miss her wake-up cries every morning."

Sadie giggles. "You can visit her anytime."

We both exit the car, and I grab her suitcase from the trunk before drawing her in for a hug while kissing her temple. "Happy New Year, Sadie."

She slumps a bit into my chest and sighs before pulling away. "You too."

I get in my car, and she waves Jinx's paw at me while I pull off into traffic, and an ache creeps into my chest. Though, heading to Evie's home makes the hurt less potent, really wanting to see my girl, even if she's not.

cing away

waves Jinx's pa

I pull off into traffi

an ache creeps into my ches

home makes the hurt less poten

nting to see my girl, even if she's no

FIFTEEN
YOU'VE WOUNDED ME

Evie

There's knocking, and I rub my sweaty palms on my jeans, blowing out a deep breath before pushing my shoulders back and walking to answer the door. Lennox is the last person I want to bring to Vegas, but there are very few people I trust—since Kylo relies on Lennox, getting him strictly as security shouldn't be a problem, even if he ghosted me after our date. I also don't like lying to Sadie, but whatever is happening right now seems serious, so I won't argue with them.

Lennox and I come face to face as I swing the door open, and I melt from his rugged look, leaning against the frame as he gives me a slight smile. A core memory of how he made me feel good without touching my body hits me hard. How does my mind react one way, but my body desires another? I want to drag him inside for him to do everything I've done to myself and enjoy it, to lose control, be vulnerable in the most delicious way possible, and break all the broken rules.

"Why did you stop coming to see me?"

He pinches his brows together. "What do you mean?"

"It's been a week. You're at Vivid, but not once have you booked with me." I stare at my feet. "Are you watching someone else?"

Gently lifting my chin to look at him, his expression softens. "Oh, Peaches. There's only you. I've just been occupied."

"Please give me a straight answer."

"Honest, I've been watching Leanna, ensuring Sadie's safety, though every second I was fighting the urge to spend time with you instead."

My mouth opens then closes as his phone goes off in his coat pocket. He glances at the screen and answers the call. "Sadie?" Lennox's eyes widen, sheer panic writing on his face, and goosebumps rise across my skin as he rushes toward his car. "Fuck, I'm coming, don't hang up!"

"What? What's going on?" I yell, grabbing my keys on the wall, and my body shakes as he reaches his car while I hop into mine, following close behind him.

We weave in and out of traffic toward Sadie's apartment,

my mind running a million miles a second, hoping nothing terrible has happened to her.

Once we're outside, Kylo and Adam are already by the door, as if Adam is trying to talk him down and leave. I exit, rush to the sidewalk, find Sadie's key in my loop, and jog to catch up to Lennox, who's almost at the door. They notice us rushing toward them, and Kylo already figures out something's wrong.

"What happened?" he says, pushing past Adam, but Lennox doesn't stop to talk, trying the knob, which is locked.

"Evie, do you—"

"Here." I hand him the key, and he's inside in seconds, heading for Sadie's bedroom—Kylo and Adam a step behind him as I stay in the kitchen.

Everything happens so quickly, from the yelling and loud banging, that I have no time to react until Lennox shouts at Kylo to go outside, shoving him from the bedroom. I shake from the blood pouring down his nose onto his shirt and the deep scratches on his arm.

"I'm gonna kill him," Kylo says, pacing back and forth near the island, and Lennox takes hold of the back of his head to look at him.

A second later, I spot her and rush inside the room. "Sadie!" I cry, pulling her in for a hug, Declan visible on the floor as Adam tends to him, then I draw back to look her over. "What the fuck—that asshole hit you!"

"I'm okay."

There are red marks already forming on her cheek. "When you called Lex, we left my house and rushed straight here—seeing all that blood on Kylo. My stomach nearly fell to the floor. I'm getting you out of here."

I hold her hand, but she pulls away from me once we

reach the front door, turning toward Kylo. He's leaning against the island, holding his nose, Lennox standing beside him with Jinx sitting on the counter. Lennox shakes his head when she moves toward them.

"Let's go, Sadie," I say, urging her to the door.

"I don't want to...Kylo, talk to me."

He doesn't answer and strides to the other room, and the anguish written on Sadie's face breaks my heart. "Sadie," I whisper, holding her hand, and she finally turns, following me out the door.

We make it to my house quickly, and I park in my driveway, giving her a moment before speaking. "Do you want to come inside?"

Sadie closes her eyes as she leans back on the headrest, then tips her head to look at me, pure defeat written in those deep brown eyes.

"Oh, babe, I'm so sorry," I whisper when her lip trembles, and she leans forward as I bend to hold her tight, letting her cry into my shoulder while rubbing her back. "Shh, you're okay. Declan won't find you here. I promise. The guys are taking care of the problem."

"How do you know?" she asks, and I wipe her damp hair off her cheeks to press a kiss, wishing I could tell her more, but that's not for me to explain.

"I—"

A car pulls into the driveway, and we both look back as Lennox steps out a second later, leaning on his door, not realizing Sadie has already left mine, striding up to him. "Why did Kylo come to my apartment after telling me to leave?"

"Shit," I say, getting out when she pushes him back.

"Why won't he talk to me—why is everyone so silent?" Lennox doesn't react, letting her pound on his chest with each question before she slumps forward with a vice grip on his shirt. "*Why* won't Declan leave me alone?"

He embraces her, whispering into her ear until she relaxes her hand. His heavy gaze meets mine, and I mouth a thank you to him before walking to my door. A moment later, Lennox has her inside, and she sits on my couch, grabbing a throw pillow to hold close.

I nod my head toward the kitchen along the back left wall, and he follows me—expecting him to take a seat at my table as I grab a few water bottles from the fridge, but he takes the drinks, placing them on the counter and wraps his arms around my waist, drawing me into his chest.

We stay hushed, though I feel this hug may be more for him than it is for me, that *he* needs a moment, so I give it to him. I lift onto my toes and rest my nose in the crook of his neck, inhaling his intoxicating woodsy scent while trailing my nails up the back into his hair, and he exhales a deep hum.

His hold strengthens before we look at each other, his face so close to mine, our lips only inches apart, before we jump back from a bang behind us. The door shakes from the wall, and Sadie is outside, crossing her arms as Kylo steps in front of her, caressing her hurt cheek.

"Did he hit you?"

There's no mistaking the anger in his tone, trying so hard to hold back.

"What do you want, Kylo?" she asks, backing away from him.

"Hey, let's give them a minute," Lennox whispers in my ear, and I nod, walking toward the stairs to my bedroom.

He's not far behind me as we reach the top, glancing at the white silks hanging from the vaulted ceiling. "You practice at home?" he asks, and I nod again, opening my bedroom door, making sure it stays open as I gesture for him to enter first.

I may have plenty of space in my home, but I live a minimal life—not much furniture or decor, no family photos lining my walls like at Sadie's apartment. Just me, my silks, and the essentials. Lennox strolls around, stopping at the practically empty bookshelf, and he picks up an old picture frame. The only photo I have is of me, my cousins, Gram, and Dad on my twelfth birthday, my first summer spent in Cali since moving.

He smiles, glancing at me. "Your family in San Francisco?"

I nod because it seems to be the only thing I can do right now. I'm surprised he remembers. Placing it back on the shelf, Lennox faces me, and I sit on the bed. We're supposed to be leaving for Vegas in a few hours, but now it doesn't feel right to go. Enzo's already there, and I'd hate to disappoint him, though I'm sure he'll understand. Of all places to be stranded in, let it be Sin City.

Lennox walks toward me, and I thoroughly take him in for the first time since he arrived. Neat short beard, to his black thermal and sweatpants hugging his body just right, down to his white kicks. He knows he looks good as I slowly make my way up his body, meeting his amused smirk and quirked brow.

"You like what you see?" he asks, lifting the hem of his shirt just enough to see part of his V-cut above the waistband.

I lean back on my hands, fixating while chewing my bottom lip, rubbing my thighs together as I shake my head, then squeak a laugh when Lennox lunges for me, straddling my hips, pinning my arms above my head.

"You've wounded me," he mumbles into my neck, bringing my hand to his firm chest.

His heart's beating fast, and I smile. "I think you'll survive."

He smirks, intertwining our fingers, his gaze flicking to my lips as I lick them. "I hope I do—"

"Evie?" Sadie calls, and we both look at the doorway as footsteps come upstairs.

Lennox straightens up, adjusting himself before gesturing for me to take his hand, and I do, standing beside him. Sadie walks into my room a second later and freezes.

"Oh, sorry, I didn't know you were both up here. Hope I'm not interrupting anything...."

"You didn't," I say, walking toward her, and I don't miss the hurt in Lennox's eyes as I look back before he quickly recovers.

Kylo enters the room a moment later, placing his arm around her waist, his bloody shirt draped over his shoulder, and he nods for Lennox to meet him outside. He follows, not before gliding his fingers across my thigh, below the curve of my cheek, sending a shiver down my spine.

Fuck me.

I need a minute, but Sadie comes closer. She's happier, which makes me smile. "Is everything okay now?" I ask, sitting along the edge of the mattress to cross my legs.

"We are."

"Sadie, I'm sorry—"

She shakes her head. "While I'd prefer Kylo didn't hurt me as part of his plan to set up Leanna, I understand now why he came to his conclusion, and nobody knew Declan was at my apartment. Hopefully, that's the last time I ever see him again, and I want to be a part of the new solution to get rid of Leanna for good too."

"Okay, what are we thinking?"

She shakes her head again. "I got this, Evie. You worry about your time in Vegas. Relax, and take time for yourself. Have fun..." Peeking at the doorway where Lennox stands with Kylo, she whispers, "Lots and lots of fun."

Two days with Lennox in Sin City—the unknown of what could happen while we're there scares me. How much I want to run the other way, far away, but he catches me with one glance from those beautiful eyes, and I nod.

...e in Vegas

...elf. Have fun...

...s. "Lots and lots of fun

...of what could happen while n

...uuch I want to run the other way

...ce from those beautiful eyes, and I no

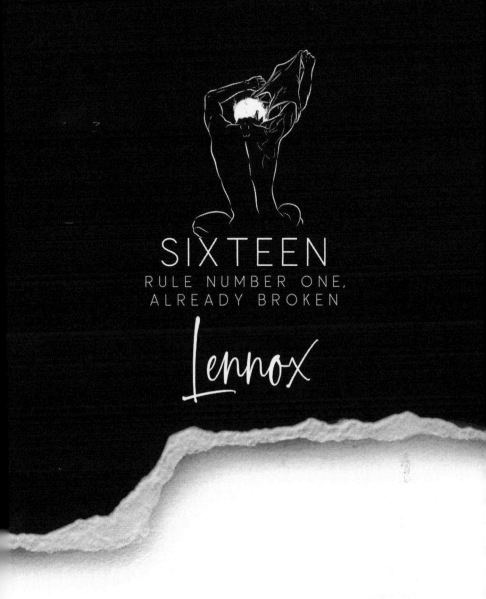

SIXTEEN
RULE NUMBER ONE,
ALREADY BROKEN

Lennox

My leg bounces in the back seat of our ride, waiting for Evie to come outside. We have plenty of time to get to the airport, but I can't stop the nerves from hitting me. Evie's throwing mixed signals, and I don't know in which direction to lead—keep pursuing, or fall back? I don't like option two. I don't want option two.

I want her.

Fuck, I want her so damn bad.

Checking my watch, I glance at the door again, and Evie rushes outside with her duffle bag on her shoulder, turning to lock the door. I get out, jogging up the pathway, and she gasps when I grip the strap of her bag to take to the trunk.

"Sorry. Didn't mean to scare you."

She smirks, removing her key. "Not scared. You surprised me."

I nod, gesturing for her to go ahead, and this time she laughs, shaking her head. "A kind gesture, or getting your peach fill?"

"My peach fill?"

"Yeah, that's why you call me peaches, isn't it?" She runs her fingers through her hair, swaying her hips while walking. "You can't get enough of my peach."

Damn right, I can't.

"Would you be disappointed if I said it wasn't?"

She peeks at me over her shoulder. "No. More like intrigued."

We reach the car, Evie gets inside, and the driver pops the trunk. I brought a few snacks for our flight, so I dip into my duffle, drawing out her favorite sweets, and slip it into my pocket.

"All set," I say to our driver once I settle in my seat, and he instantly backs out of the driveway.

Our bodies rock once he takes a sharp turn onto the road, and I glance at Evie with wide eyes as she places her hand over her smile.

She shifts closer, pins and needles prickling my skin,

when she leans into my side to whisper in my ear, "Angry much? I didn't take that long, did I?" His eyes flick to the rearview mirror, and Evie's cheeks burn red before hiding her face into my shoulder, trying to hold in her laugh. "Oh shit."

I chuckle, missing her scent as she slides back to her side. "You know the middle seat is the safest spot to sit. As your official bodyguard for the next forty-eight hours, I advise you to slip on over here."

Crossing her arms, she smirks, leaning her back on the door. "Is that right? But then I wouldn't have a window to stare out to help pass the time."

I wiggle my eyebrows. "I have something to help pass your time."

Evie rolls her eyes and faces the window again. "I'm sure you do."

Drawing out the peach rings, I make extra noise while opening the bag. "Suit yourself, then. I'll finish these all on my own."

She gasps, scooting to my side in seconds, staring at my hands, and I hold up the bag when she reaches for one. "Hands to yourself, missy."

"Please," she pleads, and I grin.

"Alright, I'll give you one, but you gotta close your eyes and hold out your palm."

"What? Really?" I don't budge until she sighs and does as I say. "Fine. Can I have at least a couple?"

Grabbing one, I take half of it between my teeth, stretching it until it breaks and placing the other half on her palm. "There you go, Peaches."

She looks down, her brows furrowing before she gazes into my eyes. "Peaches..."

"The best-tasting peach I've ever put in my mouth."

Her smile's instant, then she takes the peach ring between her teeth, my grin fading when she pushes forward, her hand pressing on my thigh, tits touching my shoulder as she pauses by my lips. I swallow hard, my dick growing harder as I close the distance to retrieve the sweet substance from her mouth, my tongue brushing sugar from her bottom lip, but she inches back before I can taste her sweetness.

"Mm, you're right," she purrs, chewing the candy. "The best-tasting peach I've ever put in my mouth."

Before I can respond, the driver arrives at the departures drop-off, and Evie leaves the car.

Fuck, what just happened?

Having the row to ourselves means naughty ideas appear— it'll make sliding a finger or two inside her more effortless, but I won't, even with my dick on standby since Evie's teasing in the car earlier. Evie watches the clouds outside, rubbing her leg, dipping between her thighs, wishing my hand was resting there instead.

She looks at me and raises a brow. "What?"

"You're beautiful."

Letting out a deep breath, she turns back to the window. "Thanks."

"You don't like compliments?"

The shade slides shut, and she turns toward me. "Okay, I know we've been more than teasing each other lately, and while I appreciate you coming with me, we need to set some rules while we're here."

"Rules..."

"Yes. First, no more touching—we should consider this a business trip."

"I gotta be paid for this to be business, Peaches."

She purses her lips. "That can be arranged. How does a thousand sound?"

"I'm not taking a penny from you."

Evie leans back on the window and crosses her arms. "Why did you agree to come with me then?"

"To keep you safe...get to know you more. If you haven't noticed, I like you, Evie. I *really* like you, and if anything ever happened to you, I don't know what I'd do."

Looking down at her lap, she swallows deeply, clenching her jaw, and maneuvers past me to the aisle. "I'm sorry. Me letting you come was a mistake. Excuse me."

"Evie—" *Shit.*

She heads for the bathroom toward the back of the plane, and I follow a moment later, passengers eyeing me as I pass by, then I knock on the door. It opens, and I place my foot inside before she closes it, entering the tight space while locking the door behind me.

"What are you doing?"

Her chest rises fast as we're practically flush with one another, and I place my palm on the small of her back to close the distance between us—rule number one, already broken—as it should be.

"Lex..." She gazes into my eyes through heavy lids, our lips inches apart as she breathes, "Wait. Please."

Holding the side of her neck, I tilt her head back, caressing her cheek with my thumb, and her eyes flutter shut as I draw her lips to mine. She hums, gripping my shirt when I shift for her to sit on the sink, spreading her legs wide to settle between them. The faucet turns on, and she gasps, clinging to me as she tries to move away from the running water hitting her ass.

"That's col—*oh*," Evie moans, the back of her head hitting the mirror as I rub her pussy through her black leggings. "Wait..." she pants against my mouth, "*fuck—wait.*"

"You want me to stop, Peaches?" Her breaths turn jagged the more I touch her, feeling how wet her pussy is through the fabric, continuing to rub her clit with my thumb, teasing her plump lips with mine. "Tell me, baby."

"Yes...no—" Tears pool in her eyes as she whimpers, "I don't know."

I don't know how to respond to that, so I stop. "Do you want me to fall back?"

Her eyes flood more, and she blinks, turning her head away from me. "I don't want to answer that."

My brows furrow, and I swallow the ache in my throat, dipping my head. "Alright, then don't."

The captain sounds on the intercom that we will be landing in Las Vegas, then to fasten our seat belts. Unlocking the door, I glance at Evie sitting on the sink, staring at the ceiling, then I leave the room, running my fingers through my hair as I head back to our seats. Evie takes a moment longer before she arrives, and I get out to let her inside rather than her climb over me.

"Thank you," she whispers as we fasten our seatbelts, ready to land in Sin City.

...g the door

I leave the room

I head back to our seats

...ment longer before she arrives

...side rather than her climb over m...

...seatbelts, ready to land in *Sin City*

SEVENTEEN
I'M DRUNK
OFF THIS MAN

Evie

If the captain didn't land the plane when he did, I don't know what would've happened in that bathroom. Lennox—damn him and those fingers of his. It only took him two seconds before breaking the rule. I huff a laugh and shake my head, already knowing the rule never stood a chance. Maybe it was wishful thinking, hoping to have a barrier between our magnetic pull to make it easier to stay away when all I want to do is draw him near.

But I can't—I shouldn't. Lennox deserves someone better than me, someone, less flawed.

Striding as far away from him as possible, I search for Enzo through the bustling crowd. As I reach the escalators, he's there, smiling, wearing a plain black t-shirt and jeans, his short dark hair styled in his *I just woke up from a nap, but finger combed my hair for the public* way, holding a small sign saying:

Looking for Bratface.

I snort, shaking my head, then cover my mouth with the back of my hand as my face scrunches, tears building, and I run, jumping into his arms. "Fuck, I missed you." Holding him tighter, I whisper, "So much."

"Back at ya, Brat." Smacking his shoulder, I laugh as he places me on the floor, using his shirt to wipe under my eyes. "Don't start with the tears, or you're gonna get me going."

"You better. It's been like, what, eight years since we met up from the last fight and even longer since I've been to Cali."

His brows push together. "Wow, has it been that long?"

I nod, hugging him again around the waist, finding Lennox in the distance with our bags, who's watching the exchange between Enzo and me. He runs his fingers through his hair, looking at the floor while strolling toward us, and I back away from Enzo's hold.

"I thought I lost you," he says, placing his hands in his pockets. "I'm guessing you don't need me here after all."

Is he jealous?

Well, I was embracing a man, one I never mentioned we were meeting here. As I look into his heavy gaze, I take my bottom lip between my teeth to mask my smile.

"Lex, this is Enzo."

Holding out his hand, Enzo gives Lennox a firm handshake and says in a fatherly voice, "Nice to meet you, Son. I hope you're treating my daughter well."

Lennox raises his brows, looking between us, and I roll my eyes, smacking Enzo in the back of his head, both of us bursting out in laughter. "Stop it. You're ridiculous. He knows you're my cousin."

"That's it, time out for you, young lady!" He chuckles, rubbing his scalp while running away from my second attempt to whack him.

I shake my head, then walk closer to Lennox. "Enzo's the one who got me in the fight."

He nods, his shoulders visibly relaxing, though him being jealous is oddly heartwarming.

"We should get going," Enzo yells, riding the escalator to the bottom floor. "The fight starts at 5:00, and traffic is a bitch around this time."

"Okay, we're coming."

"Didn't need to know that!"

The crowd tonight surrounding the octagon is outrageous. Here to see two of the top contenders in the medium weight division for the biggest fight of the year, and my stomach is full of knots. I've become accustomed to the crowd at Vivid, and anything exceeding the limit allowed in the building rattles my nerves even after getting in some practice time.

Several girls are getting ready in the dressing room, smiling and greeting me as I enter, and I wave back, heading for an empty station to doll myself up.

A guy with neon pink and black spiked hair comes striding into the room, talking on a cell phone between his ear and shoulder. He's carrying a few packaged outfits, passing them around, and giving me mine last.

"Excuse me," I say, and he looks at me as I hold up a tiny red halter bikini top with matching boy shorts that'll barely cover my cheeks. "Do you have a large? There's no way I'll fit a size small."

"That's the last one, sweetheart. Make it work, or the next girl will."

My eyes widen, and I blink a few times as he leaves the room as quickly as he came.

Great.

One of the girls with straight dark brown hair holds out her outfit. "Here, you can have this one. I'm not working tonight. Just came to watch my man fight."

The package says large, and I smile, taking it. "Thank you."

"No problem. I'm Janelle. Is this your first fight?" she asks, leaning against my station.

"Evie, and no. I did a few in my early twenties when my cousin was an active fighter."

Her hazel eyes light up. "Oh yeah? What's their name?"

Finishing applying a natural eye look, I glance at her before choosing a nude pink lipstick. "Luca Russo."

One girl gasps, and I close my eyes as she whispers to another, "She knows Loco Luca."

Letting out a long deep breath, I keep my cool, though it irks me how people still perceive Luca as a bad guy when he's anything but that.

"Hey, don't pay them mind," Janelle whispers, and I lean back in my chair while twisting the tube in my hand.

I nod and finish the rest of my look—Janelle adding curls to my hair as we talk, then I put on my uniform. She checks me out, twirling me around.

"Dang, you got a body, mama. You must work out like crazy."

"Thanks. With the nature of my job, staying flexible and fit is important, or I wouldn't last thirty seconds in the air."

"Let me guess...aerial hoop?"

"Silks."

"Nice. Maybe one day I'll get to see you perform."

I press my lips together and bow my head. Unless she's into gentlemen's clubs, it's unlikely she'd ever see one of my performances.

"Yeah, maybe."

"Five minutes, ladies!"

Janelle smiles, fluffing my hair. "I should get out there to cheer on my guy—if you're not busy later, you should swing by Hotel A. Wellington. He's throwing an after-party in the penthouse."

"I'm staying there, so I'll make my way up for a bit."

"Sounds good. Here..." She grabs a piece of paper and a pen and writes her number down. "Text me before you come, so I'll remember to put your name on the list. See you later."

"Will do."

She waves, and the other girls head out behind her while

I stay a moment longer. Taking a few deep breaths, I text Lennox I'm ready, then head out to start my night.

I've forgotten how exhilarating walking around the octagon can be and watching the fight front and center. Also, having Lennox, Enzo, and my new friend nearby made tonight ten times more fun. Janelle cheers loudly, jumping and hugging me when her man wins the fight, and I'm thrilled for her. She leaves my side to congratulate him before I turn toward Lennox, not finding him or Enzo, which makes my heart race.

As the crowd leaves the arena, I glance around in search of either of them with no luck, then head back to the dressing room to change, hoping they'll come looking for me here. After getting through the midst of the crowd, I round the corner and nearly run into someone.

"Sorry," I say, and the tall man continues to block my path. "Excuse me, sir. I'm trying to get by."

The guy towers over me, my pulse spiking as I hit the wall when he attempts to touch my jaw. "Back off!" I yell, barely able to push him away while searching for Enzo, Lennox, or anyone.

Drawing my eyes toward him, I take in his features. Clean shaven, salt and pepper hair that's neatly styled, dressed in a tailored shirt and slacks, and has to be at least six foot, mid to late fifties.

"You'll do beautifully," he says, and a chill shoots up my spine when he nods, then walks away from me.

"What that fuck?"

A few seconds later, Lennox appears around the corner

from running and strides over to draw me into him. "Evie. You scared the hell out of me."

Heat rushes across my neck and cheeks from his closeness. He pulls away, staring into my eyes. "Why did you leave?"

"I didn't see you."

"I was by your side the entire time, Peaches."

"You were?" I ask, and he nods, caressing my cheek with his palm.

"Oh...thank you. For coming with me, Lex," I whisper, leaning into his kind hold.

"Of course."

Enzo appears a moment later with a scowl. "Well, I didn't see that fight ending that way." He turns to me. "You did great, Evie. Ready to head to the hotel?"

"Yeah. Let me get changed. I'll be right back."

It doesn't take long to get ready as we drive to the hotel, and even if it's New Year's Eve in Vegas, I'm ready for bed. Lennox walks with me to my room door, Enzo already entering the room he's sharing with him across the hall, and I open mine, pausing as Lennox stays with me a moment longer.

"You're officially off duty, so go relax."

He smirks, leaning his arm on the frame as I press my back against the door, looking up at his handsome face. "I'm not off duty until we land in Oregon."

"Is that so?" I ask, dipping my head with a smile, and he gently lifts my chin with his index finger.

"I'll always have your back, Evie. Even there."

Licking my lips, I stare into his eyes, wanting to believe every word he says. "I should head to bed."

"Would you like company tonight?" he asks, smoothing

his thumb along my jaw, and I close my eyes, tilting my head away from his gentle touch.

"I shouldn't," I whisper, feeling him close—a part of me wants him to stay, but I push inside more before he can press his lips to my cheek. "Goodnight, Lex."

He smirks, walking backward. "I'm only a few steps away if you change your mind. Sweet dreams, Peaches."

Lennox enters his room, and I lean against the door once I get inside mine, banging my head a few times against the wooden surface. *Why can't I let him in?* He's a good, selfless, caring guy, yet I continue pushing him away. Sighing, I wander across the room and flop onto the king-size bed, staring at the ceiling, wishing I could be brave, just once allowing someone else to take the lead instead of needing constant control of my heart.

A ringing sounds in my purse, and I take out my phone, ignoring Gin's call. It's 8:30, the time Vivid starts to pick up, but I don't want to think about work tonight—another call comes through, and I sigh, answering it to get the lecture over and done with.

"Yes?"

"9:30, at Seclusion. You have a private customer waiting for you."

My brows furrow as I check my phone, gripping it tight in my hand. "You got to be fucking joking?" I say to Jared, lifting to a seated position. "I'm not going anywhere."

"You are, and you will. Thousands of dollars in revenue tonight, Evie. That's what you owe Vivid for not showing up to do your job."

I laugh from deep within my core at how comical he is. "You're sick in the head. You know that, right?"

He chuckles. "You and I both know who's sicker and

who will receive the end of his wrath if you don't make up this money."

I grit my teeth, hating that he's using Gin to get me to take this job. "Fuck you," I seethe, ending the call, and lie back while resting my forearm on my eyes as tears emerge.

Holding my breath, I bite back the sting, hating that even an ounce of me is willing to go, that deep down, I can't say no. *Maybe I'm the sick one?* My lip trembles as I open my maps, typing Seclusion into the search, gasping at the results.

No fucking way.

My hands shake as I drop the phone, holding them over my mouth as the dam breaks and tears fall freely. I need a drink. Several fucking drinks in me right now. Rushing for the mini bar, I take back the first nip I get my hands on, coughing when the brown liquor burns down my throat before I take another two. I'm in Sin City on New Year's Eve. I might as well end this shitty year the right way and start the new one just as shitty.

I crawl to the bed, grab my phone, sit on the floor, and sip on the next drink while texting Janelle that I'm heading upstairs in a few minutes. My duffle bag is on the chair next to the dresser, so I tear it open to grab my sluttiest outfit and drag the pearl tulip mini dress over my body. The hem rests slightly above mid-thigh, my tits perking up in the ruched shiny velvet fabric, the back swooping dangerously low as I check myself out in the mirror.

A perfect outfit for a slut, because that's all I am—a whore built strictly for man's pleasure. Tears continue to fall, and I roughly wipe them away. *Fuck men.* Applying dark, seductive makeup to cover my defeat, I slip on my stilettos and make my way across the hall. It only takes Lennox seconds to open the door, and his jaw drops when he gets a look at me.

"Evie..." he says, and Enzo appears beside him, his eyes widening.

"Get dressed. Both of you. We're going to a party."

One, two, three, who knows how many more shots I've taken within the hour, but the buzz is glorious. I lean back into Lennox's chest while sitting on his lap, feeding him another, and he takes the shot with no problem, his arm wrapped securely around my waist.

"Are you okay, Evie?" he whispers into my ear countless times, and I press my hand over his mouth before resting my arm behind his neck.

"*Please*, don't ask again. Just enjoy tonight with me."

I gaze into his eyes as he does the same, and I breathe out a breath when he nods, holding me closer.

Janelle comes around with a bottle of champagne, filling several glasses, and she smiles at me as I hold out mine. Her brow quirks while eyeing me sitting on Lennox, then she drags her teeth over her bottom lip, filling my glass to the brim.

"Drink it up, girl!" she yells, and I laugh, enjoying myself for once as I drink three-quarters of the glass before coming up for air. "Oh, c'mon, you can take it all. Tell her," she says to Lennox, and his eyes widen as I raise a brow at him, waiting for his response.

He presses his lips together and glances away, which

isn't a *'no, we're not together, and she hasn't sucked my dick'* answer.

Okay.

Turning to straddle his lap, I press my hand on his pec, and his gaze darkens as I slide my palm up his deep red shirt to grab hold of his throat, his hands gravitating to my hips that are barely concealed by the dress riding up my thighs. I hold the glass over his mouth, and his brows pinch together when I pull the champagne away just before he can drink the liquid. Instead, I knock back the rest, placing the glass down on a chair, his heavy breath hitting my lips with a low moan as I grip his neck tighter and spit the sweet substance onto his tongue once he opens for me.

Everyone erupts with cheer, but not a single person is present when that sweet tongue enters my mouth. It's only me, Lennox, and the liquor guiding us, our hands roaming, yanking at the clothes in the way of our bodies—and I can't get enough. I want more of him, so much more.

"Ohh, Luca's gonna kill me. Bar Babe! Give me another round. Gotta make sure I'm still drunk when I get home."

Enzo's voice splits through my drunken haze, and I break the kiss, staring into a pair of golden hues, mesmerized by the specks of green in the left, one of the many sexy things about Lennox that I really fucking like—*shit.*

"Wanna dance?" he asks as the music turns up.

I nod, inching off his lap, and Lennox fixes the hem of my dress before he stands. Placing one hand on my stomach, he draws me close to his body, the other threading through my fingers. It takes a moment to relax and lean into him, allowing him to take control and give my trust in my current state. The song is sensual, the rhythm moving us as he slowly matches my pace, entirely in sync. I rest my head on his shoulder, and Lennox takes the chance to run his lips along my neck while I grind harder on him.

His erection has already grown thick, and a shiver shoots up my spine as he takes hold of my throat, stroking his thumb across my jaw. The warmth within my belly from the many drinks turns into a heat of desire as Lennox turns my face toward him, dipping forward, and I close my eyes as our lips connect again.

Facing him, I moan into his mouth when he draws me flush to his body, walking me backward to press up against the wall. Lennox grabs a fist full of my hair and tilts my head back, our kiss breaking as he hovers above my mouth, gazing into my eyes. His teasing tongue brushes against my lips, and I whimper for more, making him grin.

"What do you want, Peaches?" Slowly he trails his hand down my spine, urging me into his hard dick by my ass. "Tell me," he moans, breathing me in with a firm kiss. "Tell me you want me as bad as I want you, baby."

"*Lex...*"

I rake my nails along the nape of his neck, and he crushes his mouth on mine. Climbing him while he lifts me, I wrap my legs around his hips as he keeps hold of my bare thigh, kneading my ass, pressing forward, grunting loudly against my lips, our kiss turning unruly. Nipping, sucking, unfazed if anyone's watching because I'm drunk off this man, needing to know what he can do to me, to let him in just this once.

Let him in.

What's the worst that can happen?

There's a weight on my finger that wasn't there last night—it's suffocating. My heart drops the second I touch a ring.

"What the fuck?" I mumble, my mouth tasting like death, and I raise my head too quickly. "Okay, that's not happening."

Taking a few breaths, I attempt at a slower pace, and there, on my left hand, resides a diamond ring.

This can't be real.

"Mornin', wife."

I gasp, whipping around, and instantly regret my decision as my head sways.

"Lex, what—" I hold my tongue as he leans back on the wall, focusing his gaze on my chest while sipping his coffee. Glancing down, I roll my eyes, grab the sheet, and cover my bare breasts. "What happened last night?"

"Looks like we got hitched," he says, then nods to the end table. "Got you some water and pain meds."

I squeeze my eyes shut, willing myself to wake up from this dream, then glance down at my finger again where the rock still sits. "No, we didn't."

Pushing off the wall, he strolls to sit next to me. "I'm in the dark just as much as you are, but photos don't lie."

"What photos?"

Lennox draws his phone from his pocket, brings up his photo app, then hands it to me. There are numerous pictures of a wedding chapel—some of us standing with an officiant. Enzo's next to me with a bowtie secured around his head instead of his neck, wearing a flower crown, and holding a bouquet with a blonde chick attached to his hip.

"Oh my—I'm gonna be sick." I press my hands to my mouth as I burp, whatever content is still left in my stomach rising, and I swallow it, scrunching my nose at the aftertaste. "*Fuck.*"

"That was sexy," he says, then chuckles as I glare at him.

"How do you know we actually got married?"

"If the photos and rings aren't proof enough, this is." Pulling a paper from his back pocket, he unfolds it and hands me the crinkled sheet. "We'll receive our marriage certificate in three to four weeks."

I look the forum over and groan. "No, we won't because this marriage isn't happening! We're getting it annulled. We weren't in the right state of mind."

He stays quiet for a moment, staring into his mug, then looks at me. "What if I don't feel the same way?"

"What? Lex, we can't stay married—we're not even together!"

"We can be. We'll make it work somehow."

A laugh bursts through my lips as I shake my head. "No way, not happening."

My head feels like it's going to explode as I climb off the bed, dragging the top sheet with me, and the coffee spills on Lennox as I yank the white fabric out from under him. He jumps, pulling his drenched shirt away from his skin, and I feel awful.

"Shit. Sorry."

Grabbing my phone, I continue to the bathroom and lock it behind me. This can't be happening right now. I can't believe he wants to stay married. That makes zero sense. Looking in the mirror, I scrunch my nose at my pale cheeks, dark circles, and smudged makeup, in need of a long hot shower. Letting out a shaky breath, I look at the ring closer and slip the silver band attached to the oval diamond off my finger.

It's simple yet beautiful—exactly something I'd pick out. I set it on top of my phone and head straight to the shower, putting the temperature on high. There's a knock on the door, and I wrap the sheet around me before I pull the door open a smidge.

"I ordered room service. Lunch is on the table," Lennox says.

Staring at his bare muscular chest, I gaze lower to the deep lines peeking out from the band of his underwear. "Um, lunch?" I ask, then look at his smirking face. "What time is it?"

"It's one in the afternoon, Peaches."

"What? We're gonna miss our flight!" My temples pulse, and I press my hand to the side of my head. "I should take those pills."

"Don't worry, I—" Lennox stares at my hand, his heavy gaze pulling back to mine before he walks away with his head low. "I called and booked us a later flight. Hope you like burgers."

My stomach sinks as I touch my bare ring finger, then watch Lennox plop onto the couch, rubbing his hands over his face while staring at the wall. *Why does he feel so strongly about all this?* There's nothing between us besides a few intimate encounters. Why would he possibly want to stay married to me? Closing the door, I sit on the toilet, carefully relocating the ring onto the vanity, then grab my phone, pulling up over fifty unread messages in the group text with Enzo and Luca. These don't look too good. I skim through numerous blurry photos and texts, reading some of them.

> LUCA:
> You let her get married!?

> ENZO:
> I was beautiful…I mean, look, Evie's beautiful, isn't she?

> LUCA:
> You're drunk! You're a fucking dead man!

Oh no. Skimming a few more, I stop at a voice recording from me.

"Lorenzo…where did you go, Zoey? I need you, my maid of honor."

I snort at the nickname he hates, and Maid of Honor? How much did we all drink?

"Luca, you're gonna be so mad when we tell you…ohh, wait, we don't tell him!"

There's a variety of emojis, including champagne with a long row of eggplants, and I groan, rubbing my eyes. "Fucking idiot I am."

Pressing on the message bar, I hesitate before sending a sober text.

> ME:
> Please, give me 24 hours before any new replies. I know. I'm in deep fucking shit.

I open a text for Enzo and type a message.

ME:

I'm safe. Please text or call me to let me know you're okay.

Scrolling through my contacts, I stop on Dad's number, wanting to call him so badly, but set my phone down instead, laying my face in my hands—*what a mess I am*. I should've kept my ass in Oregon. The room fills with steam, so I enter the shower, letting the water roll out my stiff neck. What happened after the fight? I know there was an after-party, and things get fuzzy after—I gasp.

Jared.

Tears instantly emerge. That asshole has the nerve to think I'd meet a stranger for a private strip show, not just at any place, but a room at a brothel! Does Gin know? Is that why she called me first?

I hold my arms over my chest, leaning back on the cool tile, and weep, "My life's complete shit—" Falling to my knees, I heave into the drain, but nothing wants to come out. "Lex!" I cry out, shaking while hyperventilating, and seconds later, Lennox rips the curtain open, stepping inside the tub to hold me close.

"Evie, it's okay." He strokes my damp hair off my face and kisses my temple, rocking me. "Shh, you're okay, baby."

His words are comforting, making me sob into his chest even more. I've dragged him into all this mess. "I'm sorry, Lex," I choke, taking a shuddering breath. "I should never have come here. This is all my fault—everyone's right about me. I'm a fucking loose cannon, a fuck up, and taking off my clothes is all I'm ever good for."

"Hey, no. Look at me." He places his hands on my face and swipes his thumbs along my cheeks. "First, do not apologize because you've done nothing wrong. Second, don't listen to any of those assholes, they can think what they want, but nobody can define you—your work does *not* define you."

I lick the water off my lips, staring into his eyes as his words hit me deeply, and I whimper, "Only I can define me."

Lennox smiles. "Yes, only you." He leans closer, his mouth inches from mine. "And tell me, Peaches, what do you see in yourself?"

Taking a deep, shaky breath, I blow it out and shrug my shoulders. "A woman who needs work," I whisper, lowering my face. "Needing to figure out her purpose in life. Alone."

"I can help you, baby. Let me in, and we can figure it out together."

I draw my bottom lip between my teeth and slowly back away, hugging my knees. "No. I won't drag you into my mess any further."

"Let it be our mess now."

"I'm sorry, but it can't be, Lex."

He sighs, bowing his head. "There's something here, something between you and me—I hope you'll allow yourself to see what I see one day."

Turning the water off, Lennox holds out both hands, and I take them, standing nude before him. He doesn't glance down this time, his gaze staying on my eyes, and he trails his knuckles across my cheek before walking out of the bathroom, leaving me alone, just as I wanted.

see one day.

...as out both hands

...anding nude before him

...is gaze staying on my eyes

...is knuckles across my cheek befor...

...m, leaving me alone, just as I wante...

EIGHTEEN
CALL ME COMMITTED

Lennox

M y heart's pounding as I pace the hotel floor,
water droplets still dripping from my hair.
Hearing Evie screaming for me with such
panic made my pulse skyrocket. It pained me to see her
panicking that way, and my first instinct was to jump inside
to console her. I never want to see her in that state ever again

—I'll do anything to ensure it never happens again, even if she's pushing me away. Evie holds my last name, that beautiful woman in there is my wife, and now I must protect her.

That's my duty as her husband—until death do us part.

Evie strolls out of the bathroom, holding her towel close to her chest, and I smile, facing away for her privacy. I've seen her body countless times, but right now, she's vulnerable. I want her to feel comfortable with me, so I sit on the couch to wait. A moment later, the cushion dips, and I turn to face her as she sits next to me, fidgeting with the diamond ring that was once on her finger.

"Thank you...for helping me in there—normally, it's easy for me to restrain my emotions, but that's an issue in itself. I'm thankful for what you said to help get them under control."

"Evie, I want you to be comfortable talking to me. I know I can be forward with you, but that's because I enjoy your company, having you near." Taking hold of her free hand, I add, "You are amazing, and I'll do anything to show you how special you are to me."

Glancing at the ceiling, she blinks back the tears threatening to spill, then lets out a shaky breath before looking into my eyes. "And I appreciate that, but this." She holds the ring in her palm toward me. "I can't keep this. We can't stay married."

"I have to disagree, and that ring belongs to you."

She drops her hand onto her lap. "Lex, please, don't make this situation harder than it needs to be."

I swallow the knot forming in my throat, not ready to give her up even if she believes getting married was a mistake. "Will you at least give me a chance to prove I can be a good husband? We don't have to be together right away, but—"

"I have no doubt you'd be an amazing husband, but mentally, I'm not ready to be in a relationship with anyone." Holding out the ring again, she pleads with her eyes for me to take it, and I can't stand the pain behind them, so I do. "Thank you," she whispers, leans forward, and draws me in for a hug.

My chest constricts, and I close my eyes, palming the precious metal in my hand before pulling back to wipe the tears that escape down her cheeks, leaving a kiss in its place, hoping that'll show I won't give up, that I'll be here for her no matter what title we hold.

"Please know I'll never be far, and if you're ever feeling lost, you can look for me to help guide you home."

Her head dips before she looks at me with tears brimming in her eyes. "And where's home?"

I place her hand on my heart. "Right here, baby, whenever you're ready. My door will always be open."

She quickly wipes under her eyes, then stands, walking toward her duffle bag. "I need to pack."

My stomach drops from her first attempt at distancing herself, hating the wall she's building when all I want to do is hold her close. Standing, I stroll toward her while pocketing the ring, and she doesn't look at me as I kiss her temple, then leave the room.

The truth is, there's no leaving Sin City the same person you were going in, and for me, I'm not the same man I was yesterday—hell, a month ago. I understand why Evie's pulling away. We've barely had the time to get to know one another, and it hurts that we can't. I want to shout from the rooftops what happened in Vegas because I can see a future with Evie, but her hesitance, the uncertainty in her beautiful brown eyes, says it all.

She won't.

We must forget we ever shared vows, that our marriage can't be, our actions are nothing more than a mistake, but the truth is... I've fallen in love with a woman who doesn't want to fall in love. Palming Evie's ring in my hand, I close my eyes, hoping one day I'll be able to glide it back onto her finger, to proclaim my love to her, to the world, to tell all how lucky I am, how wonderful my wife is. She's only a few feet away, yet the distance feels like miles between us. How can we give up on something that's yet to begin?

"My house is the white one there," Evie says to our driver, and he stops in front of her two-story home. "Thank you."

I leave him an extra tip, then exit behind her. We stand in silence at the end of her driveway, my Mustang a few steps away, but I don't want to leave, not like this.

"Evie—"

"Thank you for accompanying me, Lennox. I want to pay you for your time. Will you take cash?"

My brows furrow, her words punching me in the gut, and the ache forming within is agonizing. She's really going to throw money at me as a way to push me away. *Sorry, Peaches, but you won't get rid of me that easily.*

"No."

"Oh, a check then?"

"I'm not taking money from you, Evie."

She sighs, crossing her arms. "Please. It'll make me feel better knowing you are compensated for your time."

"I told you on that plane I wouldn't take a penny from you, especially when it came to ensuring you're safe."

"Just like I told you what this arrangement was. A business trip."

"How can you say that?" Walking closer, I take hold of her hand, running my thumb along her bare ring finger. "How can you truly believe what we've been through is strictly business? For fucks sake, Evie, I'm holding your damn wedding ring—stop lying to yourself. There's no pretending what we went through didn't happen." I caress her cheek and whisper, "It's okay to be afraid, baby. Please, don't push me away."

Her bottom lip trembles and she steps back from my hold, glancing into the distance. "I think you should go... thank you. I'll mail you the check."

"No," I breathe, shaking my head. "Keep your money." Drawing out my keys, I stride toward my car and leave without a glance in her direction.

The drive to the cabin is one long distraction, walking along the pathway to my home with no course of action. There's no dealing with a situation when it revolves around a person's lack of acknowledgment—giving me no other option but one, which won't do. Leaving wasn't me giving up, but giving space. Time—I'm a patient man with plenty of that to offer. To show her why I'm worth trusting, and if my only way is watching her from a distance, then so be it.

Does that make me selfish?

No.

Call me committed.

...on but on

but giving spac

plenty of that to offe

th trusting, and if my onl

her from a distance, then so be i

me selfish? No. Call me committe

NINETEEN
YOU WON'T BE TOUCHING YOURSELF TONIGHT

Evie

There's no escaping when it comes to a business like Vivid. As much as I want to run away from these doors and what awaits me, I step inside. The truth is, I am Vivid, these walls have been mine for as long as I can remember, and there's no turning away, no running from who I am when my entire life is etched into every crevice.

I cross the main floor, meeting Gin's heavy gaze before I walk straight for the stairs, taking each step toward the office with one goal. Jared will take accountability for his actions.

These broken rules have ruined me beyond repair.

Without knocking, I enter the office, Jared's head snapping up from his phone as I stroll to the front of his desk. He meets my upturned face, my jaw clenching when a slight smirk creeps into his lips, and I want to smack it away.

"Do you believe you still have a job here, Evie?" he asks calmly.

I tilt my head to the side and lean on the desk, plastering my own smile. "Thousands of dollars in revenue. That's how much Vivid lost after one night of *me* not working." Swiping his supplies off the desk, I climb on top to grip his collar. "You have no say in my place here, not one." My eyes gloss over as I tighten my hold and yank him closer, my throat constricting. "*You* have no say in my ethics or role here. Do you understand me, or do I have to walk away to make you understand?"

Jared chuckles, fixing his shirt when I let him go, then leans back in his chair. "Do you feel better now?"

"Fuck you." I shake my head, wiping under my eyes, unable to hold back my tears. "Why? Why did you do it?"

His brows furrow, then he looks at the door when someone knocks, his face softening. Petra walks inside the room, her hair no longer in braids and curls now resting at the tops of her shoulders.

She eyes me with a piqued brow and then to the mess on the floor. "Sorry for interrupting whatever this is, but I need to speak with you, Jared."

"He's all yours," I say, striding out of the room and down the stairs to get ready.

When I enter the dressing room, I slow my steps toward my station, touching another paper bird placed next to my dove, which is black and shaped like a raven.

"Can't say I'm not surprised you came back," Roni says, strolling out of the showers wrapping a towel around her chest, and stopping at her mirror.

Closing my eyes, I knock the bird down and walk to my locker while stripping my clothes. I have a few regulars coming tonight and one new customer settling in, enough to keep me distracted before my shift ends. My phone pings, and I draw it out of my coat inside the locker, quickly swiping away a text from Lennox. I can't think of him right now, not while I'm here. The queue says Hunter wants me alone, a sixty-minute session in room four that recently got updated to a kitchen set up, so I put on the requested night out outfit, then head onto the main floor.

"Evie," Gin calls out while fixing a drink.

I quicken my steps away from the bar, ignoring the stares as I make my way upstairs to the box. Taking a deep breath, I enter through the employee door since the customer has already settled in, but I take my time in my private box.

The request: *you arrive home after a long night of celebrating and make yourself something to eat. Look through your phone, and call me, the guy you met at the party. Let's see where the conversation leads.*

I've never had a full-blown conversation with a customer like this before, and I could use a laid-back session with everything that's happened the last couple of days. Standing before the doorway leading into the room, I rub my hands along my halter metallic gold mini dress, slip off my heels, then stroll inside with them draped over my shoulder by the straps.

The L-shaped kitchen layout to my right is a cute modern style design, with recessed lighting, white cabinets lining the walls with black granite counters, the stove against the back, a fridge to the left, and a farm-style sink to the right of the cabinets. In the middle is the island that seats four, a white countertop with the chairs stowed away underneath, and above are stainless steel light fixtures that match the appliances.

Dropping my heels by the doorway, I look to my left, where the voyeur box resides straight across from the setup, my customer hidden inside the private room. I rarely get an hour request and wonder if we will take up the entire session or not. I guess it depends on where our conversation leads. Strolling into the kitchen, I deposit my purse on the island, walk to the sink, and touch the velvety purple peonies in a vase by the faux window. My smile is instant when I look outside at my ocean view, admiring how the water shines in the moonlight with the subtle sound of waves crashing in the distance. Goosebumps rise on my skin, and I close my eyes while rubbing them away.

Get back to work, Evie.

I'm hungry after a long night of celebrating. It must have been a hell of a party if a man had charmed me enough to exchange numbers. The fridge is fully stocked with fresh produce and other ingredients to make meals. However, coming home late at night calls for something easy, so I grab a frozen pizza from the freezer and preheat the oven.

While waiting, I grab the prop phone from my purse and lean on the island, my body in the voyeur's line of sight as I poke my ass out, slowly swaying while scrolling, making him wait until I get my pizza in the oven, then return to my phone.

"Maybe I should call Hunter and see what he's up to right now," I say, scrolling down a list, and press on private room four, holding the phone to my ear.

The dial tone sounds through a speaker along the private box, and I wait for the customer to answer.

A deep voice comes through seconds later. "Hm, I was hoping you'd call me tonight, Beautiful."

I try hard to stay in character and not roll my eyes at the term of endearment. Since he's in the private box, I have no idea how Hunter really sounds, but it doesn't matter anyway. We'll eventually be coming, no matter how we sound to each other.

"Lucky you, then."

Hunter chuckles, and I glance at the window while chewing on my thumbnail, unsure what to talk about since I don't date.

"Did you enjoy the party?" I ask.

"I did since I met an amazing woman tonight."

Strolling to the end of the island, I lift to sit on top, facing the private room, and the slit that opens up to my hip bone exposes my entire right thigh as I cross my legs. "Oh yeah? Tell me about her."

He clears his throat as I adjust my plunging neckline, the delicate gold chains attached to the front of my dress tickle in between my breasts, and I hum from the pleasant sensation, though hating how sensitive to touch I've become. I need to shut that down real quick.

"Well, she left soon after we shared a kiss at the New Year's countdown, and I didn't get a chance to get to know her very much."

Tears threaten to emerge as fresh moments with Lennox

come to mind, and I take a deep breath, slowly exhaling to get my emotions in check.

"Are you okay?" he asks, sounding generally concerned.

I smile and lean back on my hand with the phone propped on my shoulder and ear. "Yeah, just tired is all. It was a long night."

He hums, and we stay silent for a bit—I glance at the clock to my left, and only ten minutes have passed. This session is becoming more difficult than I thought. "So, Hunter. What do you do for a living?"

There's a slight pause before he says, "I'm a logger."

My brows raise. "Ooh, a Lumberjack you say? Does that mean you're an expert at handling wood?"

Hunter chuckles this time. "Something like that. Nothing too interesting."

"I think it is, and sexy."

"Do you?"

"Mmhm." I close my eyes, trailing my fingertips between my breasts, focusing on the movement rather than the sensation my touch creates. "I can imagine how strong you must be to knock down trees that are stories high. How many people can say they have in their lifetime?"

"I suppose you're right."

Pleased he agrees, I ask some more. "Now, do you prefer using an ax or a chainsaw?"

"Both have their purpose. Having an ax on hand is a good idea, but a saw's more efficient to get the job done."

"Yeah?" I graze along my neck, then travel back between my breasts. "How hard does the job get?"

"It can get pretty rough on the field. Logging can be dangerous if you don't pay attention, and every detail matters. Weather, obstructions, if the tree's healthy, the height, and girth. Did the trunk grow straight, or does it lean to the side? All this determines how hard or easy a cut will be."

I smirk, uncrossing my legs to dangle them. "Sounds tough and dirty."

"Oh, definitely a dirty job." He chuckles, and my lips tug into a full smile. "You have a beautiful smile, Evie."

His statement instantly draws me back to reality—I'm not talking to someone over the phone but to a man behind a mirror. "Hunter, if we've only briefly met tonight, how would you remember something like that?"

"Honey, with a smile like yours, it would be hard to forget those lips."

Heat creeps up my neck, landing on my cheeks, and I swallow hard, needing to change the subject. Get Hunter feeling hot instead so we can end this session. I widen my legs, dipping my hand toward my stomach.

"Tell me then. Did you enjoy kissing them?" I place the phone on the counter and stare into the mirror instead. "Wish I was sucking something else rather than your tongue?"

"*Damn...*" he breathes, his exhales into the mic getting louder.

"Tell me, Hunter." Sliding down my thigh, I stop at the hem of my dress. "How badly did you want to lift my skirt," I inch the fabric upward until I reach the band of my lace panties, "and feel how wet my pussy was while we kissed?"

He stays quiet, so I continue, "Did you touch yourself thinking of me when you got home?"

"Yes," he answers, his voice husky even while masked.

"Are you hard now? Stroking your dick this very second?"

"Oh, I'm hard, but I won't come unless you come first."

I purse my lips, peeking at the timer, and only five more minutes passed, forty-five to go.

Trailing my fingers along the lines of my underwear, I inch closer to my mound. "Are you asking me to touch my pussy?"

"No. You won't be touching yourself tonight."

My brow piques. "Your request is very contradictory then, don't you think?"

He laughs, then lets out a breathy hum. "You're gonna explore your pussy, honey. Tease every inch of your wet slit until you're screaming, begging to come."

I don't like this idea—I need to regain control of the session.

The oven beeps, and I peek over my shoulder, my stomach growling for real. "As nice as that sounds, pizza's calling my name."

"Go on. We got time."

Forty-three minutes to be exact.

So, I take my time eating, making small talk with him, then cleaning my dishes, and ten more minutes are gone.

"Can I ask you a question?" I say with the phone back to my ear and facing the window.

"Sure."

"Do you like the ocean?"

There's another pause. "Yes."

"What aspects?"

"Honestly?"

His question makes me glance at the mirror. "Completely."

"I like how free the ocean is, how much power the currents hold. The waves can be unforgiving one moment, then calm the next, and never be judged. That even though the sea looks empty from the horizon, there's so much life deep inside, still so much to explore."

I glance down to mask my smile. "That was very vivid."

"Yeah. I like vivid."

We have gotten way off track. I'm supposed to make him come, not pour his heart out. Exhaling deeply, I hold my head high and return to my seat.

"I've had a great time talking to you, Hunter, but I think we got off course a bit."

"Remind me...where were we heading?"

"Well, since you've already tasted my lips, there's only one direction to go." I unclip my dress at the nape of my neck and let the material fall to my lap, exposing my breasts. "If you were here right now, what would you explore next?"

"Your mind."

I press my lips together, looking at the clock, and feel like time's going backward with twenty minutes left. "Hm, I could've sworn you were headed south."

"Honey, you are headed south. I'm right where I need to be."

Tilting my head to the side, I lean back on my hands and stare at the mirror. "You're a very strange man, Hunter."

"Does that make you uncomfortable?"

"No, more like—"

"Intrigued?"

"Yeah..." I whisper, then look at my chest, how my breasts rise with each subtle breath, my nipples pebbling the longer I stare, creating pins and needles across my skin.

"You control the currents coursing inside you. Free yourself."

"Tell me how."

"Grasp something that makes you feel safe, at ease."

Closing my eyes, I hum, dragging my bottom lip through my teeth while tipping my head to the side as my body heats, and I whisper, "Peaches."

I moan, brushing against my nipple as if Lennox were here using his tongue, and an ache surfaces from deep within my core as I cry, tears springing forward. Unable to suppress any longer, I leave the room with fifteen minutes left on the clock.

...y my eye,
...eeth while tippin...
...d I whisper, "Peaches
...x were here using his tongu...
...s I cry, tears springing forwar...
...with fifteen minutes left on the cloc...

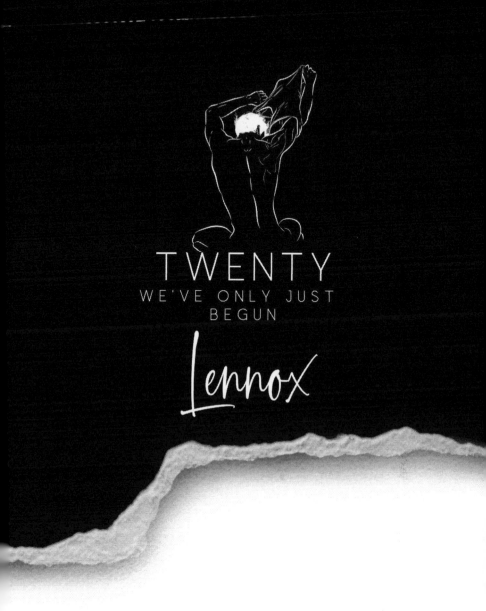

TWENTY
WE'VE ONLY JUST BEGUN

Lennox

Peaches. Drawing my brows close, I stare at the spot Evie once sat seconds ago, then look at the doorway she left from. Fuck, I wasn't expecting her to say that. It's taking everything for me not to leave this room and go after her, to kiss away her tears. Am I wrong for hiding my identity? That I want her to feel my love even if it's through a mirror, through another man? Everything I spoke was the truth.

I am Hunter—she is Hunter.

Waiting until my time is up, I exit the private room finding a woman with dark curly hair pushing a cart wiping under her eyes, and she gives me a meek smile. "Hello."

I nod, quickening my steps to leave, and find Jared by the stairs, resting his forearms along the railing while watching the main floor. He doesn't say anything as I near, only turns his head, peering at me for long seconds—his icy eyes are piercing, yet I'm not intimidated by him in the slightest. Straightening to his full height, we are at eye level as he smooths his palms along his white dress shirt, plastering a managerial smile.

"Mr. Hunter. I hope my girl was up to your satisfaction."

My jaw ticks, keeping the acid on my tongue at bay before I say something that'll get me banned from coming back. "I'd prefer to keep my business private."

He huffs a laugh while rubbing his stubbled jaw. "Of course—my apologies. Just making sure my girls are performing to Vivid standards. While Evie may be our most requested Red Vixen, her recent scores have been quite low."

"I can assure you those scores are wrong."

"Huh, well, I may have to check for myself then."

My fist clenches at my side, temples pulsing as blood rushes to my head, trying to keep my breathing even before I yank him close and ensure he never lays eyes on my wife, ever. I should leave, especially with the anger coursing through me, but I need to ensure Evie's okay. Instead, I take the stairs and sit by the bar.

Gin has a tall beer ready and placed in front of me without a single glance given to her. Officially becoming a regular, and I don't know how to feel about that. Sadie no longer works here, and right about now, I wish the same would happen for Evie. I won't force that kind of decision on her. If she leaves Vivid, it will be on her terms, not mine.

When a half hour passes and Evie has yet to come through those red curtains, the temptation to book a session under my first name grows, just so I can see her, so she can see me. I draw out my phone and pull up the club app, scrolling through the list of names. Some, perhaps, are aliases. Evie's idle, so she's not available at the moment. I press on her gorgeous photo, which takes me to various programmed sessions with different content levels ready to select.

I'm sure a lot of customers want something simple and to the point, but for those who have a specific kink, a role they would like their Red Vixen to play, they customize their session for their needs—I click the link, hoping she'll have an opening tonight though her schedule shows as max. No one else can get in. *Shit.*

I won't be able to book for tomorrow until midnight, which is several hours away.

"She's not here." I look to my left at a blonde woman standing at the end of the bar. "You're here for Evie, right? She took off about a half hour ago." She walks toward me wearing a short robe that's open in the front exposing her red lingerie. "Not surprising." Taking in my appearance, she smirks, touching the collar of my black dress shirt. "I have half an hour if you need to blow off a little steam."

"Thank you, but no. I'm about to head out—"

"C'mon, you look tense." I stiffen when she sits on my lap, gliding her fingers across the nape of my neck. "It's not every day I walk the floor as a Vixen. We can go to a private room."

Removing her from my lap, I stand and give her a polite smirk. "As I said, thank you, but no. Have a good night."

I place a twenty on the bar, Gin watching the exchange before I turn to leave the building, a place I'll return to tomorrow, and the next day, until Evie understands I'm not going anywhere.

I chose room four again, keeping the ocean view in the kitchen for tonight's session. I don't enjoy sitting behind a glass wall, but once I settle in and the click of the timer begins, everything around me disappears because there's only her.

My request: *You arrive home and pour a glass of wine, deserving every last drop and relaxation. Our previous call ended abruptly, and I call you tonight to continue our conversation.*

Evie storms inside the room, tossing her purse on the island, and heads straight for the fully stocked liquor cabinet by the fridge. Is she in character, or is there something truly wrong? My gaze is glued to her, how she grabs a shot glass and Tequila instead of the bottle of wine, pours the liquor to the rim then knocks the shot back in one gulp. No salt, no lime, just straight chasing the buzz.

Evie leans against the wooden edge, dipping her head to her chest as her face puckers, taking a sharp breath through her teeth before lifting to look at the ceiling. Her long hair is high in a messy bun, her eye makeup smudged as if she was crying only moments before, and a pang hits my gut, unsure if any of this is real. I lift from my seat, standing closer to the mirror, watching her every move as she slowly pours another shot and eyes the liquid in the glass.

"Fix my life," she whimpers and closes her eyes. "Make me forget."

Forget what?

"Evie," I say, but she won't hear me unless I turn on the mic.

Opening the app, I promptly enter the section for room four, press the call button, and a ringing sound comes from the island. She jumps, glancing over her shoulder, contemplating answering as she stares, not one motion to pick up the call, and the sound dies out. Turning to lean on the bar, she continues to stare, breathing harder—should I try again or wait to see if she'll return the missed call? I let three seconds pass before I dial room four once more, and she allows it to ring down to the last round before quickly grabbing the phone out of her purse.

She answers, still trying to regain control of her lungs, so I take the lead. "Breathe." One deep strenuous breath through her nose, and she empties, holding two counts before taking another, and another until she's back to a stable rhythm. "There you go. Nice and steady."

I take my seat as she does the same after grabbing a beer from the fridge, removing her long sleeve sweater, and tossing it to the side. Her white bra is simple, with no lace, everything covered, yet she's never looked sexier.

She picks at the label, then takes a quick sip. "Have you ever felt like you're not living, only existing?" Evie asks, her voice strenuous and low.

"All the time."

Her deep brown eyes flick to the mirror. "I like only existing."

My brows furrow. "What do you mean?"

"Existing is safe. I only have myself to worry about." She shakes her head, looking at her left hand, and her lip trembles. "Living is unpredictable. It's hard, so fucking hard, and scary, and wonderful...but I don't know how to live, how not to hurt people who want to share my existence."

"So you choose to be alone?"

"It's safer for everyone if I do."

I open my mouth then quickly close it, unsure how to respond without giving away who I am, how much I want to show her I'm here, that it's okay to be afraid and uncertain. Life's a rollercoaster, some parts are a smooth ride, and others, we'll hold on tight while we get through the bumps— no matter which parts we go through, I'll be by her side, making sure she's secure.

"What if living was safe? Would you try?"

Her lips press together while resting her chin on the bottle. "I did try, and...."

"And what?"

"I hate that I still want to, that no matter how hard I try, I can't go back to only existing."

Tears spring to my eyes, seeing the pain behind hers. *Then don't—live, Evie. Explore, be creative, do what you love without reservation, do it for yourself...*is what I want to say, and I lean back in my seat, rubbing my palms down my face, ready to run out there, rules be damned.

"I hear you." That's what I got—all Hunter can say.

A tiny smirk lifts from her lips. "You see me too."

I chuckle into my fist while leaning on the arm of the chair. "That I do."

"Thank you." She straightens up, pushing the beer away from her. "For listening, and I'm sorry for hijacking your session. This one's on the house."

"Nah, we got time."

Her smirk turns into a full smile as she unravels her hair and draws one knee to her chest. "Ten minutes down, fifty to go—my mind's a bit fuzzy, remind me, where were we heading?"

I hum, smiling against my knuckles. "In a new direction."

She tips her head to the side while trailing her fingers down her leg. "And where does this new direction lead?"

"Anywhere you want. Pick a place, and we'll go."

"Anywhere on my body, or...."

"In the world."

The tip of her tongue glides across her full top lip, and I follow the motion. "Italy?"

"I like Italy."

Her smile widens to a full grin. "My grandma always talked about her home there, how much she missed the air, and said she wanted to take all her grandkids to breathe the Amalfi Coast, ready to buy tickets. I was so excited...though she never had the chance. She passed away shortly after my sixteenth birthday, and it hurt I wasn't there during her final moments."

"I'm sorry for your loss."

"I am, too, for not fighting harder to go back home, to spend more time with her before she got sick. Summers weren't enough. I often think about how my life would be if I ran away when my dad moved back to Cali, but I couldn't. I couldn't leave my mom here to be alone by herself." She huffs a laugh, wiping under her eyes. "To this day, I still do. We're all—"

"Just existing."

Evie nods, hugging her knee tighter while staring at the counter. "And you?"

I'd live for you. "Well, right now, I'm observing and kinda hungry for something sweet."

She giggles, hiding her smile behind her hair as she presses her cheek on her thigh. "Shall I torture you for the next forty-five minutes while I eat?"

"You take pleasure in my pain. Don't you?"

Standing from her seat, she smirks, walks to the fridge, and a moment later strolls back to her chair holding a peach. She blinks a few times, and I hold my breath. What is she thinking about?

"Do you like peaches, Hunter?" she asks, rubbing the skin with her thumb, then looks at the mirror.

Do you see me? "Very much I do."

"What do you like about them?"

"Their sweet scent. How highly addictive they are, the best-tasting fruit I've ever put in my mouth, and I'm tempted to come take a bite."

"Careful." She takes one of her own, licking the juice off her lips, and I want to do the same. "Cross the line, and our sessions will end indefinitely."

"Hm, can't have that now." I straighten up in my seat as she does the same, staring right at each other. "We've only just begun."

five months later

Time flies when you have a purpose, when you're committed, determined to reach a goal, and you're so close you can taste the finish line on your tongue—it's sweet, like peaches, and I'm ready to cross over. Five months, and I'm in so deep, so utterly in love with the woman on the other side, with my wife. There's no more hiding behind a mask, and I need to tell her even though I'm sure she's already figured me out, even if revealing the truth could end everything. I can't continue having her near, yet she's so far away.

I sit behind this glass twice a week, staying in room four with each change, now a cabin as of last week, in the midst of Spring. We've fallen into a routine, and every time I see Evie, I fall deeper, almost to the point where it'll be hard to climb out if I continue further. Our sessions have been mostly mild, but in the last few, Evie's stepped up the heat, and I can't take the distance any longer.

Tonight, I settle into the chair behind the white divider, unbuttoning my shirt.

My request: *are you merely existing or ready to live?*

o a routin

hard to climb ou

have been mostly mil

take the distance any longe

ite divider, unbuttoning my shir

e you merely existing or ready to live

TWENTY-ONE

DON'T LET FEAR RULE YOU

Evie

The vacancy light is off, causing my heart to flutter, though I take my time entering room four, making him wait for me. My cheeks burn as I walk inside, and I lay eyes on him in the chair. Didn't take long to figure Lennox out—his way of staying close while giving me the distance he had no choice but to give. Five months, that's how long *Hunter's* come to see me.

He relaxes into the chair, his gaze heavy as I stroll to the middle of the room. "Good evening, wife."

"Don't do that."

He draws out a piece of paper from his pocket, slowly unfolding it. "Mrs. Everly Russo-Hunter."

I cross my arms over my chest and lean to one hip. "What happened in Vegas never should've happened."

"Still have to disagree."

Shaking my head, I consider leaving the session that's already halfway through but take him in instead, having not seen Lennox since the night we came home. His hair is longer, his beard fuller, legs wide open like his black button down, those eyes still hypnotizing. I never questioned why I stopped seeing him at Vivid or sitting at the bar because I already knew where he was.

Waiting for me, months of talking behind a mask, opening up to a stranger who wasn't a stranger that led me to this very moment—a time for choosing. Existing is safe, living unpredictable, yet Lennox is both. He makes me feel safe while wanting to explore outside these walls, and every time I feel myself spreading my wings, I find reasons why I can't, why I haven't, and why I won't...*why, why, why.*

"Why now?" I ask, untying my robe and letting the satin fabric fall to my feet.

His eyes darken as I stand before him in the outfit he chose for this evening, to wear something that makes me feel powerful, in charge, that'll get him on his knees.

"Because I've missed calling you peaches, Peaches." He removes his shirt and drops the fabric to the floor beside the chair, staring at my black leather Teddy bodysuit that hugs every bit of my curves. "How long did you know?"

We've been playing this game the last few weeks—ask a question, lose an article, and I've always stopped at my panties. "I always knew," I say, unfastening the strings between my cleavage enough to expose my tits, then slipping off my heels and stockings instead and dropping them beside me. "Why didn't you come as yourself?"

He leans back further in his seat, rubbing along his scruff. "I did. Every detail down to the name was all me. You asked for space, and I gave you time—five months' worth. I'm done waiting. I want you, Evie. All of you."

Moving to his buckle, he unfastens the strap, and his zipper, slowly eases his pants down his thighs, kicking off his shoes. I stare at his dark underwear, the prominent bulge that becomes larger the longer my gaze lingers.

"What are you thinking about? This very moment," he asks, palming his erection, then trailing up his lean muscular torso, one only manual labor could build.

"Honestly?"

"Completely."

I glance around the cabin theme room at the faux fireplace, the logs in the corner, the shaggy rug, the rustic atmosphere, and the comfort that comes with it. "So, you're a real Lumberjack?"

Lennox lets out a hearty chuckle, raising a brow with a smirk. "You answer my question with a question."

"You want me to strip for the answer? So you can stroke your dick to me, Lex?"

"Mm, keep going because we're down to nothing now, Peaches."

"Fair enough." I take my time loosening the rest of the

laces, one tantalizing notch after another, my entire front now open, and I keep my eyes on his. "Seems you have a question sitting on your tongue."

"I do." He grips his shaft through the fabric of his boxer briefs. "I'm waiting for you."

The thick material slips down my hips as I drag off the bodysuit and let it fall to my feet. All that's left is my black lace thong.

"Are you going to take it off?" he asks, peeling down his underwear, his dick springing free, and heat pools in my core when he takes hold of his length.

I run my teeth along my lip, slowly backing away from the line. "What exactly?"

"Take it off."

Goosebumps spread across my skin from his rough tone, his hungry gaze fixating on my last article of clothing, my lace panties merely decoration in his eyes, and I smirk while gliding my fingers along the waistband.

"Do you mean this?" I hook my thumbs inside, watching his every move from across the room as he slowly jerks off.

"I want to taste that pretty cunt of yours while I come."

"Hm, that's not part of the gig, Lex."

His dick stands tall as he stops his strokes to recline the chair he's sitting in until it can't go anymore. "What can I say? I'm not a watch and jerk-off kinda guy. Now, take it off, and sit on my face."

My gaze flicks to the timer.

He only applied fifteen minutes this session, which is almost up—quite tempted to give in to his request. I'd be lying if I said I didn't want to plop onto his lap to ride his thick shaft.

"I can't."

Lennox retakes his cock, slapping the tip along his abs, and my lips part as he rubs down the length to cup his balls. "This is the hardest I've ever been, Peaches, and it's all for you. It would be a shame to let it go to waste."

"Go to waste? You really are a cocky bastard."

"Nothing cocky about knowing what I like, and what I want is that lace on the floor and your ass bouncing off my chin."

I smirk, taking a few steps back until I'm against the wall. "You've come to the wrong place then." Using the tips of my fingers, I trail in between my breasts, tilt my head back and glide my palm up my neck. "Men who enter the box are to watch and only watch." I suck my middle finger, keeping eye contact as I glide back to my panties, and Lennox hums once I slip my hand inside the black fabric. "If you're staying in the box with me, you gotta follow the rules, just like everyone else."

His chest rises faster as I release a soft moan while running my fingers over my clit, his eyelids falling heavy. "I'm not like everyone else."

Stopping, I stroll to the white line dividing us. "Then who are you, Lex? What makes you any different than the last man who sat in that chair and stroked his dick while watching me?"

Lennox stands, his cock jutting as he steps to the other side. "I'm the guy who'll come by every day, take every time slot, so no other man gets off in front of you." He takes hold of my wrist, and I hold my breath when he sucks my finger. "Mm. I'll gladly be a greedy bastard when it comes to you."

Tears threaten to emerge, and I blink them away. "You barely know me."

"No, I know you—I know the real Evie. *My wife.*"

The chime from the timer makes my heart leap, and I check the clock, taking a step back. "Time's up."

"I don't think so." He steps past the line. "Our time has just begun."

"Lex...stop." Placing my hand on his pecs, I prevent him from walking further. "There's a camera on my side," I whisper, my heart pounding against my chest. "Please leave before you get banned from coming back."

The corner of his lips slightly lifts. "Are you afraid for me, Honey? Of not being able to talk to me here?"

I swallow, my eyes widening when he presses into my hand more, towering over me. If I say yes, admit how much I look forward to his sessions, my confidant, how I'd miss our conversations, the way he makes me feel, he'd have no regard for Vivid's rules.

"No." My eyes gloss over. "You need to go."

Lennox clenches his jaw, and I don't miss the hurt in his eyes as he nods and then moves away from my touch. "Your call." With that, he gathers his clothes and leaves the box.

"Evie?"

Leaning into the leather sofa, I tilt my head to the side, my heavy gaze staying on the mirror while trailing my fingertips over my tits, the fantasy behind our sessions no longer a factor as we speak freely with one another. "Yes, Hunter?"

"Come closer."

Pins and needles prickle my skin, and I take strands of my hair to twirl, letting the pieces fall to the peak of my breast. "Why?"

"Those panties are still securely around your hips, so no more questions unless you follow through."

Dragging my lower lip through my teeth, I smirk, opening my legs to show him my covered pussy. "What are you gonna do if I don't?"

"Keep going, honey, and you're gonna find out."

Our session has only ten minutes left, and I keep glancing over at the clock, so time doesn't go by fast. "How if we're worlds apart?"

"I have my ways. Now, come closer."

I squirm my body, stretching my arms above my head before relaxing further into my seat. "Hm, I'm quite comfortable. I think I'll stay put."

He chuckles, breathing out a husky growl, and fuck, this session is making me sweat. "You have no idea how badly I want to cross that line with you, Evie."

"How badly?" With my legs wide open, I bear my heels into the cushion, slowly grinding my hips. "So you can fuck this wet pussy? Bury your face deep between my legs to make me scream your name after months of watching? You don't deserve that satisfaction, 'Hunter'. Not when you've yet to come with me."

"Who says I haven't?"

"You. The speaker masks your voice but doesn't hide the ragged pitch of a moan. My panties stay on because we've yet reached that point of no return, that blissful sensation just before finding release."

There's a pause, a long pause, one, two, three minutes passing without him speaking, and my stomach sinks. So I stand, strolling toward the mirror to press my palm against the *glass, peering as if it were possible to see through. To see him after five months of watching my reflection.*

"*I hear you,*" *I whisper, closing my eyes, and goosebumps spread across my skin from the warmth on the other side pressing back.*

"*And I see you—*"

A loud moan brings me back to focus, and I blink a few times at the couple fucking on the bed in room four, almost forgetting I'm at work. It's been a week, and he hasn't returned. No Lennox, no Hunter, and my heart aches that I'm hurting him —that I can't give him what he wants. Me. The man and woman are no longer watching me as they get lost in themselves.

Now, I'm the voyeur, watching their intimacy, their urgent need to please each other, showing how much they love one another, wishing I could act on the same desire I feel deep within my core. Their moans get louder as the man straightens up, driving into his partner harder, grinding, and I squeeze my thighs together on the couch, breathing to suppress the pulsing of my clit, ease the heaviness of my gaze, my cheeks burning, unable to look away as they come face to face, kissing, rocking onto each other to find their release.

Not waiting for them to finish, I'm out of the room, grabbing my robe and heading for the emergency exit, bypassing the cleaning cart next to the door. I can still hear their moans as I walk toward the stairs, slow my steps down when the sound gets louder, and halt once I reach the first landing.

"*Fuck...*" I whisper, leaning against the wall as I tie my robe tight.

Jared's eyes flick up to me mid-stroke along the bottom steps, and he doesn't react—he doesn't stop fucking as Petra's back arches, her scrub pants drawn to her knees, eyes closed, head resting on his shoulder with his grip tight in her unruly curls.

A deep yearning hits me in my gut from their shared intimacy. The lust in Jared's gruff pants and heavy gaze as she backs her ass onto him just as swiftly is one I've never seen on him before—no control, lost in the midst of passion, the need to have one another so intense to not care if someone is watching. I go back up, using the main stairs, my heart racing, hating myself even more, this place, these walls, and I can't find my breath—*breathe, fucking breathe.*

Quickening my steps through the velvet chairs, I push past the eyes on me and the Vixen's working, needing something to ground myself, the bar empty, so I head into the dressing room for my station.

"Where is it—" My eyes widen at my dove torn to shreds, and I hyperventilate, my body running hot while sifting through the pieces. "Please...no," I whimper, grabbing the raven instead, and I lean on the ledge, tears blurring my vision as the paper bird crushes within my grip.

"Hey, Evie, look at me." I don't register who's holding my face until my nose is buried in chestnut brown hair, breathing in deep, shaky breaths of mint and lavender. "Breathe, Everly."

And I do. I inhale deeply, a cry replacing the next, holding on tight as Gin strokes the back of my hair, soothing me with her scent and voice until I'm no longer shaking—I back away from her embrace, staring into the same brown eyes as mine, the same pain. Still, hers has always run deeper, where I learned to suppress emotion.

I am my mother's daughter.

"How are you breathing?" I ask, and her eyes instantly gloss over as she shakes her head.

"Oh, Everly. I don't."

"You don't...help me understand. Why did we leave Cali?" She looks down, but I catch her chin, lifting her back to my eyes. "Mom, please. Tell me."

Her tears release, and she quickly hardens her gentle expression. "I'll tell you, but not here, not today. The time's not right."

I huff a laugh, shaking my head. "When will the time ever be right? You and I both know the secrets eating you inside will be buried with you in your grave."

"Well, my grave won't be the only one holding secrets."

"What?" I blink a few times, Gin watching me for long seconds before walking away, and I let her leave.

Both of us merely exist while time passes by, and I'm sitting at my station with my hand tangled in my hair, scrolling through my contacts. If Gin won't talk, then I'll get my answers elsewhere. Something I should've done a long time ago. Dialing Dad's number, I wait as the line rings nonstop and goes to his voicemail.

"Hey, it's Marco. Leave a message, and I'll get back to you soon. *Ciao.*"

I sigh, my questions stuck on my tongue, being quiet for too long, so I say, "Hey, Dad. You're probably busy now, but I just wanted to hear your voice. If you have time, call me back, but don't worry about it if you're tired. I..." My voice cracks a bit, and I swallow deeply. "I love you. I miss you, and I wish you were here right now, is all."

Ending the call, I drop my phone, wiping my cheeks dry, and groan, walking out of Vivid doors at the end of my shift.

I stare at the ground because I don't want to look for a Mustang, to feel disappointed when he's not here, though I deserve to feel the pain of pushing him away.

When I finally do, I halt my steps, my pulse racing at the black car parked next to mine, the instinct to run as I look back at the closed door, but I force myself to continue forward, removing the elastic from my hair to cover my mascara stained cheeks. Someone gets out of the passenger seat, and Lennox promptly leaves the parking lot, and I watch while continuing to my car, where my best friend leans against my driver's door.

"Sadie?"

"So, I have this one friend who works here. A hell of a woman if you ask me—do you know Evie Russo?" She smirks, crossing her arms over her black sweatshirt.

With my unstable mind, time in the box, and wanting to give her space while she settles into her new life with Kylo, it's been a while since we saw each other. "Shut your face and give me a hug."

We both laugh as we embrace. "I've missed you," she whispers, holding on a second longer before we back away. "Can we sit in your car? I have *big* news."

Nodding a few times, I look her over. Something's different. "Must be huge with that emphasis."

She rolls her eyes, but her grin shows she's anything but annoyed, which eases my nerves a bit.

I unlock the doors as we both get inside the car, then turn to face her when she's settled. "Okay, what's going on?"

"First, things first. Do you prefer to be called auntie or—"

"Sadie—shut your mouth!" My face scrunches as I place the back of my hand over mine. "No you're not," I cry, drawing her in for a hug, feeling her nod as she intakes a shaky breath.

"I am. Twenty-one weeks tomorrow, and we have an ultrasound appointment in the morning. I'm sorry I didn't tell you sooner."

Backing away, I wipe my palms across my raw cheeks. "Wow, I'm so damn happy for you two, and expect me to completely spoil the hell out of this kid."

As much as I am happy for them, my emotional intake is at an overwhelming high, and I'm reaching a breaking point that I'm trying to avoid.

"Wouldn't expect any less from my *maid of honor*...."

My eyes widen as I huff. "You're killing me. What?"

"I know. Kylo asked me to marry him last night. Can you believe it? We haven't made anything official yet, but—" She grins, unable to contain her excitement. "I don't care about a ring. I just love him so much."

As if I have more left to shed, my eyes well, automatically reaching for my bare left hand at the mention of marriage, and I mask the pain with a laugh, focusing on her smile, brushing a few strands of hair off her radiant cheeks because I love this woman. I'm so proud of what she's overcome.

"You are glowing, my dear."

Sadie tips her head to the side, seeing straight through me. "Evie, I have no business pressing you on what happened in Vegas, but I'm here if you ever need to talk."

"I know." I lower my head, waving off her concerns. "It's just easier to ignore the situation right now."

She sighs. "Lennox cares about you a lot. If this certain situation that arose in Vegas made you feel scared, it could mean, maybe, just maybe, you care about him, too."

"Sadie..."

"He once told me, *don't let fear rule you.*" Her hand cradles her little baby bump, which makes me smile. "And I'm glad I took his advice. Perhaps a thought to bear in mind?"

I let out a shaky breath, staring straight at Vivid as the moments between Lennox and me from the last five months rush in at once. Every tear, laugh, moan, already knowing everything she says to be true—the intimacy, to feel the desire, happiness, is what I need, so why am I depriving myself?

Start the car. Don't let fear rule you.

"I know. Thank you."

aky breat

ts between Lenn

months rush in at onc

says to be true—the intimacy

, so why am I depriving myself

f fear rule you. "I know. Thank you

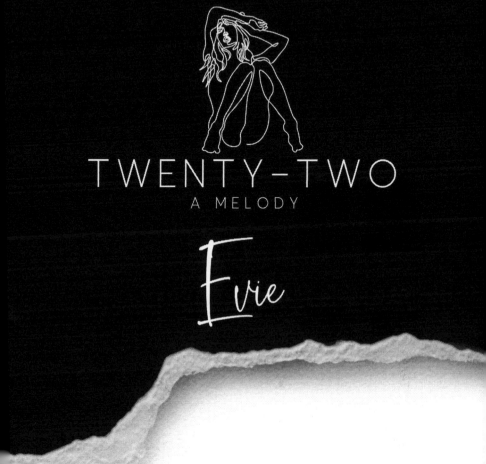

TWENTY-TWO
A MELODY

Evie

For five years, I've come to this cabin to see Kylo. I know the calm that comes upon entering, leaving a little less empty, but the contentment never lasts. Tonight, I take an alternate route, strolling along the pathway toward the guest house, taking my time to give myself a moment to retract, and when it doesn't come, I step faster, my heart fluttering to see Lennox.

The door's open, and I peek inside. "Lex?"

Every light's off as I enter, the moonlight the only source. Sadie's cat is lying on the back of the couch licking her paw, and I stroll by, rubbing her head and making my way toward the stairs. He should be home, or else he wouldn't have cracked the door for Jinx. I slowly take each step and follow the wall to the lounging area on the left, but he's not in there either. It's probably not the best idea, but I check the next door at the end, his bedroom unoccupied, then enter the bathroom last, which is wide open.

Lennox has his eyes closed, lying in the bath with one arm behind his neck and both legs propped on either side of the tub. His moan goes straight to my core, and I grip the door frame, taking him in as he tilts his head back with each grunt while stroking his dick. The way his muscles flex as he takes his time makes my pussy throb, unable to contain the soft moan passing through my lips. He opens his eyes, stops his movements, and stares at me across the room.

"Don't stop on my account," I say, kicking off my shoes.

"What do you want from me, Peaches?" His blunt words make my stomach sink, and I want to break the wall I created.

Pulling my shirt over my bare breasts, I drop it beside me. "I came to apologize."

Lennox takes in my nakedness, his lips parting. "What are you doing?"

Strolling forward, I keep my eyes on him, kneeling by the tub. "I've been a bitch where you've been nothing but nice to me."

I hover my fingers over the water, his chest rising faster,

but his hand gripping his dick stays motionless. "Don't play with me, Evie."

"You said you're not a watch and jerk-off kind of guy." I dip my hand into the water, touching his abs, and glide downward as Lennox lets go of his shaft. "Let me help you in a different way." He tips his head back, breathing out a low moan as I slowly stroke him. "Does that feel good?"

He chuckles, inhaling a sharp breath through his teeth, and hums when I rub down his balls. "More than good."

Leaning over the tub, I smooth my fingers across the goosebumps on his skin, scraping my nails up the nape of his neck, and he groans when I take a fist full of his hair. "How often do you jerk-off to me, Lex?"

"Every fucking night."

"Do I kiss you here?" I place a peck just below his ear, and his moan gets deeper the faster I pump. "Stroke you like this?"

"*Fuck*—yes."

Each kiss along his jaw is an inch closer, wanting a taste of his lips as his heavy breath hits mine. "Tell me what else your wife does for you."

Lennox takes me by the side of my neck and crushes his mouth to mine. I moan as he easily gets me inside the tub, not caring that my pants are soaked—right now, they are only getting in the way. He slips his hands under the waistband, dragging the heavy fabric under my ass, and I lift for him to get them down my legs, the wet bunch plopping to the floor when he tosses it out.

His dick's hard against my stomach as I lie flush to his body, completely submerged, and the water spills over. I straighten up, breaking our kiss to straddle his lap in the tight space, Lennox keeping hold of my hips, breathing harder as I rock my pussy on his thigh, sucking my bottom lip between my teeth as pleasure shoots to my core. He grunts while watching, shifting for me to grind on his knee, and I moan louder.

"Yes, keep going, Peaches. Use me to come."

I arch my back, and he glides his hand up my stomach, squeezing my tit, circling my nipple while urging me to move faster, our breathing erratic, a pulsing building within my core. The sensation's overwhelming, so I pull away, only for him to grip my ass to keep going. He lifts to suck on my nipples, shifting me to where my pussy rocks against his dick pressed along his stomach instead, and I release a deep shuddering moan, gripping the edge of the tub. My head falls back as I grind harder, his grunts rough against my chest, holding me tight, my body shaking, almost there—

"Lex—oh, I can't," I whine on the verge of tears, and he makes me look at him, the lust in those golden hues sending me over while he kisses me hard, swallowing my moans with every buck of my hips. Electricity courses through my body, my voice sharp as the pleasure shocks every nerve ending, never-ending, while he urges me to keep going until the friction becomes too much to bear, and I get him to ease back.

He's breathing hard through his nose, his dick even harder, pulsing between our bodies as I fall limp against his chest, catching my breath, wanting him to be just as spent, so I kiss him. Trailing my hand across his chest, I move toward his abs, continue rubbing down his length, tugging his balls, and a gruff moan passes through his lips when I tear mine away.

I gaze into his heavy eyes while hovering above, caressing the nape of his neck, making him pant, "I need you, baby."

Grinning as he moves in to resume our kiss, I keep him at

a distance, and pleasure grows on his handsome face as I lap my tongue across his swollen lips.

When Lennox tries to claim my mouth again, I back away, and he grips my neck, growling, "Give me that mouth, Peaches." He sucks on my tongue once I give in, our heavy kiss turning erratic the more I stroke his dick, my tits slipping along his chest before he urges me to turn. "Lie back."

Maneuvering around, I rest my head against his shoulder, my lungs racing as Lennox places his palm on my stomach, gliding over each of my breasts to take hold of my throat. I bite my bottom lip once he dips his fingers between my thighs, his grip on my neck tightening while rubbing my pussy, down through my cheeks.

"You want my cock in your ass, baby?"

I giggle, nudging my nose along his jaw to nip his chin. "Hm, we're not there yet, Lex, but my pussy's all yours."

He tilts my head until our lips lock—moaning with our tongues lapping, bodies grinding as I move my ass along his length while he plays with my clit and grunts when I glide along his neck to grip his hair, wanting his mouth closer even if it's not possible. I want to feel him when I wake in the morning, a bittersweet ache that'll bring me back to this moment, reliving how great he makes me feel.

More pleasant sensations creep deep within my core from his strokes, and I don't want him to stop as the urge to release takes over my need to suppress—wanting to enjoy the utter satisfaction that comes with the pleasure he's giving.

My chest presses forward as another orgasm bursts through me, thrusting my pussy against his hand while grinding harder on his dick.

"Don't stop—" he pants, gliding his palm down my stomach to keep me in place, both of our moans echoing around the room, not letting up as he breathes heavy grunts into my cheek, kissing, nipping, and sucking my jaw when I tilt my head back. We're both panting hard as we come to a stop, and I close my eyes, relaxing into his body while he gently explores mine, intertwining our fingers which the water barely covers.

Lennox unlocks the plug with his foot, letting the water flow down the drain before lifting the lever to add more. I turn my body, so my leg rests over his abs, nuzzling my nose in the crook of his neck while grinning at his apparent skill, utterly content as the warmth gradually rises over us.

"I can get used to this," I say, running my fingers through the slight hairs on his chest as he rubs my side.

"Stay with me tonight."

He kisses my temple, my forehead, then my lips, his request is not a question, yet his soft gaze shows it's not a demand either, hoping I'll say yes. I kiss him back and relax further into his hold as his arms strengthen around me—no answer needed.

A nutty aroma draws me from my sleep, and I open my eyes to a clear mug with dark liquid filled to the brim. Lennox is across the dim room in black sweatpants riding low on his hips, sipping coffee, his gaze focused on the lake horizon, maybe deep in thought. With the curtains pulled back, the moon gives just enough light to make out the lines of his abdomen, the way his defined chest gently rises with each subtle breath, his broad back resting against the wall.

Another sip and he looks at me, his once serious expression softening, a bright smile lighting up the room as he pushes off the wall and walks toward me. "Good morning," he says, sitting along the edge of the mattress, brushing a strand of hair behind my ear.

"Early morning."

"Hm. Sleep well?"

I smirk, snuggling further into his pillow and comforter. "Mhm, I don't want to leave your bed. It's so comfortable."

He places his mug on the end table and climbs over me to hold me from behind, resting his nose in the crook of my neck. "Then don't."

Turning to face him, I lift my head to rest on his arm, wiggling closer. "Well, it's Friday, and we both have jobs."

"Jobs are overrated."

Snorting a laugh, I lean in to kiss his lips. "I agree. So is money and bills."

"I'm taking a personal day indefinitely. I'd rather stay in bed with you and continue doing that."

"What? Kiss me?"

He does, then shakes his head. "Make you laugh. Enjoy the after-effects of your beautiful smile."

I bite the inside of my cheek to contain my grin. "Yeah, and what's that?"

He stays quiet, gazing at me with those soft hues before whispering, "A melody."

My brow piques as I eye him. "A melody? Is that really coffee you were drinking?"

Lennox chuckles, smoothing his thumb across my cheek. "Yes. Good coffee." He continues to hold the side of my face, and I nuzzle into his gentle touch, his finger trailing the corner of my mouth. "Because your smile pulls my heart-strings."

"Lex." I bite my lip as tears brim my eyes, trying my hardest to keep them from falling. "That's the sweetest thing anyone has ever said to me."

Pressing forward, I wrap my arms around his neck and breathe against his lips, Lennox returning my kiss just as eagerly, drawing the comforter back from my body to press his chest against mine as he settles between my legs. I moan from his fullness, how small I am beneath his large frame, fitting perfectly within each other, and he feels just right. His touch is gentle yet urgent as if he hates he can't explore every inch of me at once, grunting at the swell of my breast, gliding his thumb over the peak of my hardened nipple.

Breaking our kiss, he dips to lick the hollow of my throat, and his breathing increases the more of me he tastes, traveling downward to tend to my other breast. "You're so perfect, Peaches." He sucks my nipple harder, swirling his tongue, and I moan, threading my fingers into his hair to get him to do that again.

"Keep going."

A jingle sounds in the distance, tiny paws prancing toward the doorway of his room, and Jinx lays along the jamb, rolling around before rubbing her face against the wood a few times. She releases a low meow, coming forward just as Lennox dips further south—his wet kisses and hums down my stomach make goosebumps spread across my skin, my hips rocking with each eager press. Hopping onto the bed, Jinx meows again, stalking toward Lennox, and he shoos her back a few times with her persistence to gain his attention.

"No." He finally looks up, narrowing his eyes as she raises her hind, trilling while rubbing her face into his hand.

I lift to my elbows with a huge smile watching him argue with a cat as she continues jumping onto the bed. "She's probably hungry or horny," I say, giggling.

"Yeah, and so am I." He grips under my hips, nipping below my navel, and I jerk my legs close to his head, intaking a sharp breath through my teeth. "Fucking starving."

Jinx doesn't let up, crying louder, jumps up again, and Lennox huffs, laying his cheek on my pelvis in defeat while staring into the distance. His heavy gaze travels up my naked body as he straightens his stance, and mine trails down, taking in his apparent erection needing relief.

"Go take care of your cat daddy business." I shift onto my side, lifting my knee to accentuate my hip. "Because you have another kitty that needs tending."

"Shit..." He scoops Jinx into his arm and slaps my ass. "I'll be back."

Grinning, I wait a minute after he leaves, then crawl out of his bed, heading straight for his closet. I brush my fingers along the clothes hanging—leather, t-shirt, thermal—his style ranging between man of the forest, and come ride on my Harley. Since the weather is still nippy this early in May, I take down a black thermal, inhaling his faint sweet woodsy scent while dragging the shirt down my body. The hem rests mid-thigh, and I ruffle the sleeves to my elbows since they're too long.

"Mm." My heart races as Lennox breathes into my neck, pressing a kiss while holding me from behind, whispering into my ear, "You look damn sexy wearing my shirt." He cups my pussy, and I release a breathy moan while tilting my head back, my cheeks burning red just as my stomach growls loudly. "Hungry?" He chuckles as I turn into him and nod. "I got pancakes."

"Chocolate chips?"

"Sorry, Peaches. That I don't." I stare up at him with a pout, and he smirks. "Wanna ransack Kylo and Sadie's pantry?"

"Hell yeah. I know that girl got something good."

Lennox leads me out of the room, grabbing my shoes by the bathroom, then to the front door. Jinx bolts toward us from the wooded area, prancing up the deck for the cabin, and I breathe in the crisp, earthy air, leaning into Lennox when our fingers connect. We take our time walking, Lennox using his key to get inside through the side door, and we sneak toward the walk-in pantry in the kitchen area.

Closing the door behind us, Lennox flips the switch, and the decent-sized room lights up, shelves lining the walls stocked with various items. Mostly dried foods and a few cleaning supplies, but Sadie tends to hide her sweets along the top shelf, thinking I never noticed when I'd come to her apartment to grab a bite.

There's a step stool stored beneath the shelves, and I use it to check along the tops, reaching onto my toes but coming down empty-handed. "Damn, I don't see any."

"Go on and check further in the back. I saw some kisses in here once."

"Really?"

I lift again, thoroughly searching behind boxes, and still nothing. There's crinkling behind me, and I glance over my shoulder at Lennox opening a kiss. I place my hands on my hips, pursing my lips when he stares at my bare legs.

"Perve."

He chuckles, raising the bag over his head, and leans

against the door as I press into him in an attempt to grab the chocolates. "A kiss for a kiss. Since I found them, it's only fair if we trade goodies."

"It's like that?" Walking backward, I peer at him from under my lashes, then smile. "I changed my mind. You can keep your kisses."

The foil falls to the floor as he unwraps another and pops the smooth chocolate into his mouth. "Are you sure about that?" He grins, strolling toward me while peeling the silver foil off a third one.

"Mhm. I think I'll find my kiss elsewhere."

His smile fades as his heavy gaze pins me to the shelves, and I swallow hard, goosebumps spreading across my skin the closer he gets. "Peaches, the only kisses touching these lips are mine."

Heat rises along my neck, burning my cheeks. "So I belong to you...." I press my palm on his chest, sliding down to his pants. "Is that what you're saying?"

Lennox rests his forearms on the shelves, his breathing deepening as I tip my head back, our lips inches from touching.

"My woman." He presses a soft kiss, threading his fingers into my hair before giving me another. "My wife." I graze my nails along his trail, dipping inside his waistband, and he tightens his hold while tilting my head back more. "Mine."

Gripping his stiff shaft, I slowly stroke him. "And all this is mine?" He inhales a sharp breath against my lips when I bring him closer by his dick, jerking him with each word. "Property of Everly. Russo. Hunter?"

"God damn, baby—" Our mouths crash, eager for contact, our tongues fighting for dominance. "Yes—" he says with a rough breath. "No one else's."

I hum, forcing myself away from his delicious intent as he slides his hand between my cheeks to bring me into his erection. "Good. You got your kiss. Now we gotta make breakfast."

"My breakfast is already served."

He rubs his middle finger along my pussy, and I close my eyes, suppressing a moan while biting my lip. Shaking my head, I dip under his arm to get away from him, but he reaches the door when I do, pinning my body against the wooden surface with my arms above my head.

"Lex..." I moan as he drags the shirt up my body, his mouth against my ear, each erratic pant making me breathe just as fast while he trails his hand down my back, marking my body with the chocolate.

"Spread your legs, Peaches." Shaking my head again, I back my ass onto his dick when he bucks forward, easing off the hold around my wrists. "You want me to stop?" he asks, inching back, and I nod, twisting around to kiss him.

"I'm hungry. Make me pancakes."

Lennox smirks, looking down at his handprint smudges on my body, chocolate spread all over the door, and wrappers littering the floor. "Kylo and Sadie are gonna kill us." He releases my arms, easing the shirt back to my thighs. "We better leave before they wake."

"Ooh, you dirty boy," I purr, squeezing his cheeks between my fingers to kiss his lips. "I'll come back later to clean before I head to work."

His face falls, but he quickly recovers. "Will you stay with me again?"

My lips twitch with a smile. "Maybe. Depends on how good your pancakes are."

"The best you've ever had."

"Hm, so damn cocky."

My nipples are still hard, my mind replaying how Lennox fed me his pancakes which were the best I've ever had. How he gently grasped my throat, drizzling syrup on my tongue before placing the fluffy cake inside my mouth—though I haven't fed him that compliment just yet, how lunch was just as delicious, wishing we had time for dinner. The more I think of him, the more I regret coming to work tonight, but I can't stop the feeling of not wanting to move too fast, still debating whether to stay over again. Afraid of losing something that's so apparently good.

I whine, rubbing my face as I press my elbows into my lap, and mumble, "Get your shit together, Evie—"

Rosie, one of the Red Vixens who comes to Vivid for holiday purposes, touches my shoulder. "Hey, Jared wants you in his office. Says it's dire."

"For what? I just got here."

She shrugs, removing the clip from her dark brown hair while walking to her station to apply her makeup. "Just passing on the info."

Blowing a heavy breath, I toss my bag inside the locker, then sit at my station. "Well, if it were dire, then he'd be the one to inform me. I have to prepare for my performance."

A beep sounds in the distance, and then a deep voice comes over an intercom I had no idea Vivid had installed. "Ms. Everly Russo, please come to the office immediately."

"What the fuck?" My eyes widen as I turn to look at Rosie, who's staring at me just as confused.

"You've been summoned."

Clenching my jaw, I head for the office and cross my arms once I'm in front of his desk. "Seriously?"

"Take a seat."

"No. What do you want?"

He leans into the chair, tipping his head to rest on the back with his *I've got all day* stance, and I sigh, sitting to leave his presence faster—this pleases him as he smirks. Standing from his seat, he strolls around the desk while fastening his black slacks, and I narrow my eyes once he stops in front of me. My grip on the chair tightens when he dips forward, holding the arms close to my fingertips.

"You know I've always admired you, Evie. Since the first day I saw you from this box, I thought, what was a good girl like you doing within these walls? Such a beautiful little dove, forced to stay in this cage day in and day out."

Goosebumps rise along my skin, and Jared chuckles, catching his step when I push him back from smoothing his index finger over the bumps on my arm. "Don't touch me."

He hums, walks around to sit behind his desk, and opens a side drawer to pull out a sheet of white paper. "Have you ever felt how much you and I are the same?" My gaze stays on him, folding the square, while he speaks, "Two kids who saw too much and experienced too little, growing a hardened exterior at a tender age to withstand a world that is Vivid Vixens. How we slowly drew toward one another, finding ways to talk, needing an escape, which grew into more, promising we'd never end up like our parents, yet look at us today." Jared shakes his head, his face hardening. "No matter how often we spoke this rule, we couldn't stop ourselves from breaking it because deep down, we knew we were destined to be them."

"Why am I here?" I whisper, fighting the tears threatening to build.

"I ask myself that same question every day. Why, why, why...because Vivid is who we are—until both of us decide to fly." He finishes building a paper dove. "Are you going to fly, little dove?"

My face scrunches, and I stand from my seat, heading for the door. "I have to finish getting ready—"

"You're off silks. Rosie's taking over," he states, and I halt my steps.

"What?"

"I'm removing you from the performance. Your schedule is already hectic enough."

"No. Don't you dare act as if you care for my well-being and admit you enjoy tormenting me." My lip trembles as I inhale a shaky breath. "You *never* cared about me, Jared. All you ever wanted was my body for your selfish desires."

"You never belonged here."

I laugh, storming back to his desk. "So that's been your plan all along? Push me until I break and finally leave this place? Continue to use me as a sorry excuse for why *you're* too afraid to leave for yourself. Go ahead, keep taking from me—why do I need anything that gives me even a sliver of joy? I'm too broken to give a fuck."

As I stride for the door, Jared blocks my way, closing it behind him. "Leave," he says, sticking the dove in my hand, and my tears fall.

"What about me is keeping you here—why come back at all? You didn't love me, so what are you hanging on to?"

Jared hesitates to touch my cheek, placing his hands in

his pockets. "I thought I loved you when I didn't know what love was, but now I do—it's a hell of a force that can break you down in a moment's notice, make you feel, do, and say things you never thought possible because with someone you love, rules—"

"Don't exist."

He smirks and licks his lips before staring at the floor. "I'm not a good man, Evie. I've been selfish since I was a kid, even more so when you came to Vivid."

"You weren't always an asshole."

"No. I was good at hiding who I was to keep you here." He looks at the paper bird, his chest rising faster. "You're still here because of me."

"What are you talking about?"

Looking at me with his glossy gaze, he sighs. "Gin was ready to quit that night you went looking for her, she wanted to take you away, and I begged her to stay, made a deal with Red that if he allowed Gin to be an unofficial manager, then I'd take over when I was ready, to ensure you both stayed."

"You...we were gonna leave?"

"I'm sorry."

I push him back when he moves closer. "No. You don't get to be sorry for using me. Why would you do that? Why would you push me away when I needed you, then turn around and keep me close only to bully me?"

"Because I wasn't good for you! Okay...I'm not good for anyone." His voice wavers as he glances at the desk. "Red's a shit father, and the day Gin came along, my life became easier since something in him shifted. I was tired of being alone, and you were an easy target. You're here because of me, and I can't leave until you do."

Shaking my head, I try to keep my breathing under

control while processing everything he just said. "If you believe my leaving is your way out, expect to be here forever because I'd rather stay just so you'd be miserable."

His chest rises faster, jaw clenching before he steps aside, letting me go. I leave to the dressing room, throwing the paper dove in the corner of my station on the verge of breaking down, my head spinning, unsure where to go or what to do. There is so much I regret, and Jared is at the top of my list. Losing my virginity to a boy I thought cared about me, kept seeing him repeatedly until that night—why push me away only to make me stay?

"Gin was leaving." I squeeze my eyes tight, then look at the dove. Something I thought was good turned out to be manipulation, and he's still only looking out for himself.

I stride out of the building, driving to the one slice of joy Jared hasn't taken from me. Entering Lennox's home, I slam the door without thinking, my hands shaking as I stroll toward the couch. He rushes down the stairs, his concerned expression easing once he spots me.

"Hey—"

One look at my lost expression, and he has his arms around me, crashing my lips to his. Lennox lifts me by my ass to straddle his waist, using the back of the couch to lean against. Jinx meows as we almost land on her, kissing him with each shuddering breath I take in between, and he draws back to look at me, his brows furrowing while swiping his thumb under my eyes, catching the tears before they fall. He doesn't question what's wrong—instead, he takes hold of my neck and brings his lips back to mine, carrying me toward the stairs.

There's no hesitation, no resistance, just pure hunger coursing through our veins as he gets me inside his room and kicks the door shut behind him, leaning against it, knowing I don't want the power. Perfecting the assignment at hand.

Make me lose control.

Our kiss breaks, and he rests his forehead on mine. "Yes, Evie. Let it all go."

There's so much more behind his words. For me to trust him, trust my judgment, do what makes *me* happy, and not let anyone push me over.

"I want to." He looks at me, sweeping away more tears. "Show me how."

His brows raise as he stares into my eyes. "Anytime, any day. It's your call, Peaches."

on mine

e. Let it all go.

. For me to trust him

I not let anyone push me ove

way more tears. "Show me how

, any day. It's your call, Peaches

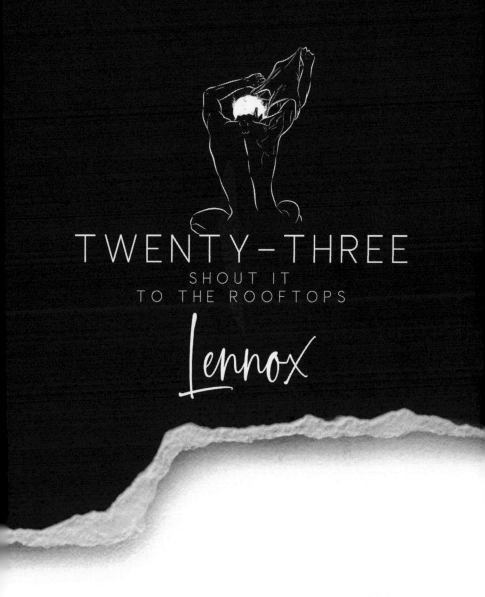

TWENTY-THREE

SHOUT IT
TO THE ROOFTOPS

Lennox

"Take me to your bed," she whispers, and I moan against her mouth, my dick already swelling as I walk to place her on the mattress, stripping her until she's down to her bra and thong.

I've seen Evie naked more times than I've touched her, yet every time, it's like the first, and I want to explore every inch as I flip her to lay on her stomach, starting with her round ass. "Do you like it when I call you Peaches?" I ask, caressing the left cheek and taking a bite.

"No—" Evie gasps, breathing hard as I kiss her spine, stopping at the nape of her neck.

She rolls her hips, making me thrust forward as her ass bucks along my dick. "Hm, I think you do," I whisper into her ear, trailing my palm down her back, making her arch the closer I get to the base. "Deep down, you love the teasing just as much as I love you."

"You want me, Lex. There's a big difference."

I straighten up, grip her hair, and draw her to my chest, her lips parting as her head rests on my shoulder. "When will you get how bad you've got me, Evie?" My tongue glides along her jaw, and she takes a shaky breath. "I am yours as you are mine. My wife, till death do us part."

She lets out a sob, and my stomach drops. Releasing my grip, I spin her around to face me, drawing her close.

"You can't love me, Lex," she cries, clinging to my body. "I'm too flawed. You deserve someone better than me."

"No." I place my hands on her cheeks, wiping under her eyes with my thumbs. "If it's not you in my arms, I don't want her."

Her lip trembles. "Why me?"

Smiling, I say, "Why not you?" Our lips are inches apart, and I add, "You are perfectly flawed." I lay a peck, then another on her cheek. "I love those perfect wrinkles under your eyes when you smile hard." She huffs a laugh, snorting as I nibble on the lobe of her ear, holding back my chuckle. "Your perfect laugh." My hold travels to her waist, my kisses follow to the spot she loves on her neck, and she moans, tilting her head back. "*So damn perfect.*" I glide to her lips, gazing into her eyes. "And all mine."

Our mouths crash the second the words leave my tongue, it's almost painful, but the need to kiss is intense. Evie bites my bottom lip, and I growl as she wraps her legs around my waist, grinding her cunt on my dick. Lifting her, I shift until she's on her back by the pillows, and our kiss breaks as I hover above.

"Is that how you want it?" I nip along her collarbone, making her squirm the lower I go, then stop at her chest. "Rough?" Palming her breast, I rub her nipple through the thin fabric, spread my fingers, then tweak the hardened peak between them, making her gasp. "Yes or no, Peaches?"

"Lex—"

I release, trailing to the other, and draw small circles, waiting for her body to respond before backing away. "Yes. Or no?"

"Yes. Fucking yes. Don't stop."

This time I pull the cup down, swirl my tongue, and suck her nipple into my mouth, dragging my teeth over the sensitive bud. Evie moans, fisting my hair as I blow, then suck again. "I'm gonna taste every inch of you."

She doesn't let up as I continue downward, kissing harder while taking in the sting of her grip, traveling the plains of her stomach, making her squirm when lapping across her hip bones, nipping, grunting, arriving where I'm dying to taste. The thong covering her pussy won't stand a chance, and she hums as I dip my hands under her ass, gripping the strings to tear the fragile fabric off, and fuck is she beautiful. I've yet to see her this close, so open, personal.

I widen her legs as far as they go, her ankles touching the mattress on either side, and I glide my fingers along her smooth skin. My imagination runs wild—all the positions I'll eventually get her in. For now, my attention returns to my prize, admiring what's mine.

Evie rolls her pelvis, urging me forward with her grasp. However, I hold back, grinning when she groans, lets my hair go, and glides her fingers down her pussy, rubbing circles on her clit, needing to ease the ache—I want her wound up, begging, and quickly gather her wrists to pin her arms above her head, nudging my nose along her jaw.

"Keep them here." Her eyes flutter open and closed from my dick pressing against her pussy, trying to find relief with each subtle buck of her hips against my pants and my grip tightening around her wrists, stopping her advance with my weight. "You're tired of taking control, aren't you, baby? You want me to take over, tease your body until you're begging." She's breathing harder while gazing into my eyes, and I trail my hand down her arm to caress her cheek. "Tell me, Peaches," I whisper against her lips. "So I can do everything I've been dying to do to you."

Evie shakes her head. "*Lose control.* Do whatever you want. No rules are holding us back."

"*Fuck*," I moan, my dick straining as I kiss her, our tongues eager, and I force myself to pull away.

Standing, I walk to the foot of the bed, and take in her stretched body, how she's rubbing her thighs together, keeping her arms raised, completely exposed while waiting for me—she's fucking intoxicating.

The mattress dips while I spread her legs and settle between, starting where she left. She bites her bottom lip, whining from my tongue skimming over her slit, and I grab under her thighs, pulling her closer to take her entire pussy into my mouth.

Her moans are loud as I sway my head, wanting to hear more, leaving no area untouched, sucking and lapping until she's fucking my face for more—needing some type of control—my greedy fucking wife. I draw back and slap her cunt, making her cry out.

"Fuck—Lex," Evie pants, digging her nails into the sheets at her sides before placing her hands back over her head, and I hum, pleased at her willingness to comply though she can't help bucking her hips again.

"Are you greedy, Peaches?" Eyes rolling back, she breathes harder when I flick the piercing at the top of her clit. "Should I fill your pussy or that pretty mouth next?"

I don't give her a chance to answer as the urge to feast draws me back, feeling up her stomach, grabbing her perfect tits on the way to her neck, giving a gentle squeeze—testing the waters with a firmer grip, and she loves it, moaning, fucking my face harder until she comes undone, her beautiful body writhing.

She tries to back away, but I don't let up until she stops spasming, though I'm nowhere finished with her as I dip lower, sweeping my tongue between her cheeks. Evie breathes hard, spreading her legs wider as I eat her ass, and a shuddering whine rolls off her tongue—*I'm about to come in my fucking pants.*

"Lex, please—I want to touch you."

I lick the length of her body until our mouths crash, and I bring her hand to my dick. My eyes widen when I hit the mattress, Evie using her tiny frame to get me on my back—she's at my belt, unbuckling and pulling my cock out in seconds. I'm standing tall, hard, and more than ready for her to take me into her mouth. Evie drags my clothes off, then straightens up, unclipping her bra, her nakedness on full display.

"You enjoy eating my pussy?" she asks, climbing onto the bed, trailing her fingers along the ceiling as she walks the mattress and stands above my face.

"More than anything."

"Mm, you want more, baby?"

Lowering herself, she kneels above my mouth, placing her middle finger between me and her slit, teasing her clit as I hold her hips, grunting, urging her to come closer, gripping her harder, my heart pounding I can barely think outside needing to fuck, to eat this sweet cunt she's depriving me—

"God damn, Peaches, give me that pussy," I rasp, swiping my tongue along her fingers.

She chews on her lower lip, looking down at me while shaking her head, and squeezing her tit. "You gotta watch your wife, Lex." Moaning, she rolls her head back the faster she rubs her clit. "Watch her pleasure herself thinking of your mouth."

A low growl leaves my throat as I knead her ass, my chest rising fast while she hovers, slipping her fingers deep into her pussy.

"That's right. Make yourself come, baby."

Her moans fuel the urge as she plays with the piercing above her clit with her thumb, and I swallow deeply, my dick throbbing, begging to be stroked, to be sucked, anything to relieve my aching balls. My gaze flicks between her pussy and face, from the pleasure taken and given, wanting badly to help her, for her to suffocate me in the best way.

She uses my chest to lean back on her hand, moaning while working her cunt as I squeeze her ass, breathing hard against her thigh. Kissing, licking, unable to help myself until she's crying out and drops to my mouth to ride her release on my tongue—I grunt, sucking her pussy as if my life depends on her cum.

Rubbing her ass, I slap both cheeks, making her whimper until her thighs shake, easing away from my mouth, not giving me a chance to breathe as she drags her nails down my body, and I groan the second she grabs my dick and licks base to tip, teasing the bottom of my head with her tongue with light flicks.

"Where's your lube?" she asks, and I stare at her, roughly panting, my pelvis thrusting forward as she gently strokes the base of my shaft.

"Nightstand."

Evie crawls toward the drawer, and I rub her ass as she takes her time searching, smirking at me with the assortment of toys from a dick-shaped vibrator to anal plugs, probes, beads, you name it, still in the packaging—all purchased throughout my voyeur visits. "That's some collection you got."

"Plan on getting familiar with each one. Morning, afternoon, and night."

"Oh?" She removes the probe from the box, eyeing me with a quirked brow. "Well, I accept your proposal, but how hard do *you* want to come tonight?"

"Peaches, you could blow on my dick right now, and I'd come on the spot."

Giggling, she puts the toy back and grabs the lube, biting her lip as she slides to the edge of the bed. "Let's find out."

My smile falls as she leans forward, settling between my legs, my cock rubbing against her stomach, between her cleavage. I close my eyes, humming when she grabs my shaft and rubs the tip along her nipple.

"Eyes on me."

With heavy lids, I open them as she caresses her tits with lube and down the plane of her stomach while she bites her bottom lip, her head rolling back the closer she gets to her pussy, and a low groan leaves my lips when she skips over her mound to grab hold of my dick.

She moves her grip below my head with slick jerks, and I suck in a sharp breath, already getting close again. "Slow down, baby."

Evie spreads my legs wider, rubbing my inner thighs down to my groin, and I let out a deep hum as she sucks my balls, stretching my arms above my head while she gets back to stroking my dick.

"Look how ready you are for me, Lex."

I'm panting harder when she rapidly strokes my head within her fist. The wet pumping on top of the constant building pleasure has me grunting, gripping the pillow behind me, my stomach clenching, almost fucking coming until she pops off, and I whimper—*fucking hell, what is this woman doing to me?*

Evie exhales a deep, shaky breath, her chest rising almost as fast as mine, like she's also on the verge of coming while staring at how deep red my dick has gotten.

"Lex..." she moans, straddling my lap, and I grab her hips as she slowly rocks her pussy on my shaft pressed along my stomach. "I want to feel all of you."

"Condoms are in the drawer. Can't promise I'll last long, but go on. Ride my fucking cock." Evie leans over to grab a rubber, her slit gliding along my length, and she inhales a quick breath as I buck forward from the pleasure—my head tips back, and I grab her thighs hard when my dick slips inside her tight wet pussy raw. "*Fuck, Peaches.*"

She stills, using my chest to keep upright while panting fast, the condom in her hand. I urge her to start moving, lifting to grab her throat while kissing her sweet mouth, guiding her along my dick by her ass until both of us are thrusting, breathing hard, holding on tight.

I break our kiss and moan while watching her pussy take my cock. "That's right, baby. Keep riding me."

She takes sharp breaths while picking up her pace, moaning, gripping the back of my head to bring my mouth to hers, and I match her strive until my balls draw in tighter. Shifting where she's on her back, I spread her legs wide and pound inside her pussy as the need to come takes over, then I slip out. Taking hold of my shaft, I jerk my hips forward, stroking, exhaling a low, gritty moan as pulsating pleasure travels to the tip of my dick, my cum shooting onto her mound, and Evie watches every second with jagged breaths.

Using my cum, I make her squirm, bearing the sharp sensation while tapping her clit with my head, quickly rubbing until she squeezes my thighs with trembling fingers, moaning my name while another rush hits, then pushing me to ease back.

I lie on her chest to wrap her legs around my waist, and we hold each other, relishing in our hearts rapidly beating, her fingers running through my hair while we come down from the high—her gaze stays on mine, seeing the rest of my life in her eyes. It's the best feeling in the world finding my person, and I'll shout it to the rooftops.

I love my fucking wife.

 my wais

 rapidly beating

 hair while we come dow

the rest of my life in her eye

 in the world finding my person

the rooftops. I love my fucking wif

TWENTY-FOUR

BECAUSE YOU'RE HOME

Evie

I can't help the flutters in my stomach as Lennox falls asleep on my chest. I've used various toys for work, and those devices have nothing on the way Lennox claimed my pussy. From his warmth and the after-effects of his wicked mouth, I feel the fatigue. Though, I don't want to sleep. Lennox tightens his hold around my waist as he shifts, breathing out a deep breath of contentment, and I continue to run my fingers through his hair, swiping my thumb along his temple, enjoying this moment as his slight snoring returns.

"Thank you," I whisper, my eyes brimming with tears. "For not giving up on me—for seeing me."

My heart skips when he mumbles something between his deep breaths, unsure what he said, but I can't help smiling. How much I like smiling with him, wanting to create new memories to laugh and hear that melody only we can make. I want all of him.

"Lex..." I rub his cheek when he doesn't wake, entirely spent, and gently shake him. "Baby."

"Hm?" he says, rousing awake, kissing my breast while maneuvering off me. "Am I hurting you?"

I stop him from leaving, the words wanting to spill out stuck on my tongue, and a burn creeps up my throat the longer I hold them in. *Say it. Tell him you love him.*

"No. Stay."

He looks up at me, his gaze still heavy, and I keep massaging his scalp with my nails, holding him close, showing him instead since I can't speak those three simple words. As if I'm incapable when I know I am. I know he loves me, that he's already embraced each syllable and etched our names into his heart.

I glance down at him, still staring at me, now wide awake, and he shifts to rest on the pillow. "Hey, talk to me."

Smiling, I snuggle into his chest. "Hi."

"Are you hungry?"

"A little bit."

Lennox lifts, bringing me to a seated position. "Let's clean up, and I'll make you dinner."

It's still early in the evening, and being with him feels like hours have passed. "Sure."

He kisses my lips, and I squeak when he lifts me into his arms as if I weigh nothing, bringing me to his bathroom, only a few steps away. It's much smaller than the main bathroom down the hall, with only the essentials. Still beautiful, with dark stone floors that extend up the left wall above the white sink and toilet. He places me down in front of the stand-in shower to our right, turns the water on, and grabs two fresh washcloths while waiting for the temperature to warm.

The space is barely spacious enough for him, let alone both of us, but I don't mind being close as I step in after him. He takes up most of the water as it hits his throat, and I lean into the corner of the cool stone to watch the stream drizzle down his body. His hair sticks to the sides of his neck as he rubs water along his face and through his dark strands before he pours a heaping amount of body wash into a cloth to start thoroughly washing himself. I touch the bubbles along the sides of his stomach, and his abs draw in tight.

"Turn around," he says, and I arch a brow.

I do, asking, "Why?"

A bottle clicks open again, and I take a deep breath soon after as a soft terry cloth glides up my back, releasing more of the sweet sandalwood scent into the air. He gathers my hair, rubbing the fabric across the nape of my neck, the soap foaming my shoulders, arms, breasts, and stomach. I giggle as he maneuvers around me, lowering to his knees to get every crevice of my legs, massaging my feet until he drops the cloth at my mound.

Never has a man thoroughly washed me before, Lennox being the first of many things. Grabbing more soap, he uses his hand to dip between my thighs and cheeks. Such intimate touch, yet they aren't sexual as I lift my leg to his shoulder, him finishing the job. However, he stares at my pussy, so damn close, refraining from taking what he clearly wants, and knocks into the showerhead as he stands.

Inhaling a sharp breath through his teeth, he rubs his head, and I bite my lip, taking over soothing away his pain while trying to hold in my laughter. "Aw, come here."

Lennox hums into my neck, holding my waist as I stroke the sore spot, goosebumps rising on my skin as my need to make him feel better gets stronger. How much I want to take care of him. I don't want to leave our little bubble, wishing this moment could exist on a loop, just two people falling deep for one another.

Water trickles around his head, dripping to my face as he lifts to look at me, his heavy breaths rough against my mouth while whispering, "I love you so damn much that the thought of never meeting you hurts."

My lip trembles as I pull myself closer. "I love you, Lex —" I cry, kissing him hard, and he breathes deeply through his nose, his hands gliding along my back and ass to draw me into his skin. "I love you."

"Oh, baby," he moans between our quick pecks, his voice laced with strain, his touch urgent, and it makes my chest tight as he pours his very being into me—every ounce of his love, and I return just as much.

We're panting hard as our kiss breaks, Lennox holding my cheeks, kissing each one before closing his eyes and placing his forehead on mine, utterly content.

"I love this," I say, and he looks at me.

"Hm?"

"Being here with you."

His eyes gloss over as he grins, and the tears he sheds are

full of joy. "I have no words to express how happy that makes me."

"You don't need words, Lex. I feel them in your touch, poured into every kiss, from the way you see me—no one has ever looked at me the way you do, stayed by me through everything I've done to push you away." I smile but can't hold back the sob that breaks through simultaneously. "I love being here with you, but it's hard letting myself feel okay with being open. I hate that I still feel wary of letting you in, even knowing you'd care for me, that even when times are rough, you won't leave."

His hold on my cheeks strengthens. "Do you remember what I told you in Vegas?"

I quickly nod. "Yes."

"Tell me, baby," he breathes against my lips, and I lick the water off them.

"You'll never be far."

"Yes." Lennox takes my hand and places it over his heart. "Because why?"

Staring into his eyes, I smile when he does, hearing that melody. "Because you're home."

The hairs on the back of my neck stand on end from déjà vu, a familiar nutty aroma permeating the air—unable to pinpoint the exact location of the scent because the sudden vibrations between my legs take over every sense in my body. I moan, opening my eyes as Lennox spreads my thighs wide, gliding a sleek vibrator along my slit until he inserts the shaft into my pussy while kissing my clit.

"Mornin'," he mumbles, flicking his tongue, and sucking while slowly working the toy inside me. "Chocolate chip pancakes, hot and ready in the kitchen."

I'm still tender from last night, but the ache is delicious—I'm hungry to feel more and experience every pleasurable sensation this man gives because I've deprived myself for too long. "Hm, keep this up, and you'll turn me spoiled rotten," I say, touching my breasts and bucking my hips forward when he chuckles.

"Say less."

Removing the vibrator, he tosses the device to the side, getting down to business while wrapping my legs around his head and sucking my clit without reservation. There's no time for breathing with a tongue like his—a thorough mouth meant for eating pussy extracts air from my lungs in seconds as an orgasm rips through me. I grip the sheets, my toes curling as I pant, my body squirming beneath his hold, and Lennox moans, lifting his head once I've settled.

"Fucking perfection, baby." He kisses my inner thigh while huffing. "I'll never tire of making you come."

I hum, stretching my body. "Well, I thank you for your service, Mr. Hunter." Scooting to a seated position, I grab the mug off the end table, take a sip of coffee, and use my foot to lift him onto his knees. "Now, be a good boy and fetch me my breakfast, will you," I state, placing the lukewarm beverage down while trying to bite back my laugh.

Lennox groans, kissing the side of my foot. "I've created a monster." Then he nips my ankle, making me giggle as he drags me toward the edge of the bed, dipping forward between my legs. "I love it."

We both laugh, our lips almost touching, and I move in first to press a kiss on his. "Thank you."

"You're welcome, Peaches. Let's get you fed."

As I settle at the island minutes later, wearing my favorite black thermal, Lennox winks at me before heading outside, pulls up a chair to sit on it backward, and draws something out of his pocket. Watching him for a while through the large windows, I finish eating and stroll out into the nippy air, goosebumps rising along my skin until I press into Lennox's warm back. He hums when I rest my chin on his shoulder, warming my fingers under his shirt as I wrap my arms around his front.

"Working on something special?" I ask, peeking down at his hands, which he's taped a few fingers while carving into wood.

"Depends on the outcome of the finished piece. I've been slowly working on this one for a few days, and I'm just about finished."

He's holding an oval object, and I smile, shifting to lay on my cheek as the figure gradually comes to life while he carves in detail, and the finished product is a small bird.

"Wow, amazing," I say, maneuvering to sit in the chair across from him and leaning on my knees to get a closer look.

"Could use a good sanding in some areas and polishing."

"I think it's beautiful the way it is."

"Yeah?" Lennox places the bird on my palm, and I smile, smoothing my thumb over the etched wings, the rough surface along the bottom. "If you like it, then it's yours."

"Thank you."

"I started carving these after reading how when birds attract a mate, they pair for life." He goes into his pocket, pulling out another similar to mine, only smoother in texture.

"So I wanted to make another. If you'd rather have a finished product, you can have this one instead."

I smile and shake my head. "No. The imperfections make the bird all the more beautiful."

"Hm, I'm glad you see it that way—it's refreshing, actually. Looking past perfection."

"I agree." Sighing, I close my hand over the bird and look out into the distance. "Every day, I stand in front of my mirror and tell myself affirmations to end my days in a positive state of mind. Something Kylo taught me. But sometimes I feel like they're words with no real meaning because while I see the beauty, I don't feel beautiful even with daily reminders."

Lennox takes hold of my hand, stroking the back with his thumb. "You are beautiful, Evie."

I smirk, looking at our now interconnected fingers. "It's like the saying goes, *beauty is in the eye of the beholder.* Your vision of beauty is different from mine—like this bird's imperfections. You can polish her up to cover the rough edges, but at what cost? What if she's proud of those ruffled feathers? She fought her way out of a storm and made it to safety, only for someone to say she should cover those flaws. To match what society thinks is beautiful, she wonders why being imperfect is an issue to the point that she loses who she is to please everyone but herself."

Lennox nods, his brows furrowed as he stares at the perfect figure in his hand, then he sighs and looks at me through clearer eyes, having seen the mask I wear every day. However, I smile because Lennox has always seen me for who I am, embracing my imperfections because they are what make me, me. He sees the real Evie outside Vivid doors.

He stands, moving the chair to the side as he draws me to my feet and pulls me toward him. We're close but not flush as he slowly circles my body, goosebumps rising on my skin when he brushes the tips of his fingers across my bare thigh, smelling my hair while passing behind me, his eyes heavy as he rounds to the front and stares into my eyes.

"What are you doing," I ask in a low tone when he holds my cheek in his palm.

"Exploring—I learn something new about you every second we're together, and I want to know every detail."

I wrap my arms around his waist and smile. "I love a thorough man."

He hums, running his thumb across my bottom lip. "And I love your mouth." I raise a brow, and he chuckles. "Not like that—well, yes, like that, but I love your honesty. How you're not afraid to speak your mind, and when you play along with me with your slick tongue. Keeping me on my toes."

"Never a dull moment in our world."

"Dulls not even a word in our vocabulary."

I lick my lips, lifting onto my toes. "Nope, but fuck is... and keep going." Tipping my head back, I let out a breathy moan, "Don't stop, please—"

"Mm, damn, baby." He kisses my neck with a chuckle. "And I fucking love it. Every second."

Staring into the bathroom mirror, I remove the rollers from my long layered hair, finger comb out the beach waves, and love my caramel highlights and side bangs for the summer season. I needed a change. Today's a hot day for mid-July, the last few have been high in the 90s, and I'm counting the weeks until autumn returns. Sweater weather is my favorite season of all.

After applying a bright pink stain to my lips, I'm ready for wherever the day takes me. I've yet to return to Vivid since my talk with Jared, unsure if my time off is permanent. Though a part of me wants that piece of my life to end, the other half knows I'll eventually be back within those walls. Jared was right about one thing, we both have ties to that place that won't allow us to leave, and until we break free from them, we'll always be Vivid.

Closing my eyes, I lean on the sink to get work off my mind and back to my current reality. Two months straight of Lennox Hunter, a man who wakes up before dawn every morning with coffee and his head between my legs—either at his place or mine, which is where we've spent the last few days.

I can still feel the effects of his hands and mouth this morning, the mind-blowing orgasm on my kitchen island, just shy of brunch, still bringing me goosebumps while I begged for him to fuck me. He knows how to work my body better than I do and has no problem showing me how well he does.

Licking my lips, I smile at my flushed cheeks and blow out a long breath to calm my heated body—a quick cold shower is out of the question after already dolling myself up. One last look in the mirror, and I enter my bedroom, walking toward the window that overlooks the backyard, when I hear grunting in the distance. Lennox is digging a hole for a fire pit after I expressed how much I enjoy sitting by one on cooler days. His taking the task upon himself to make me happy makes me love him even more.

Jinx meows behind me, and I look back, not finding her, probably under the bed where she's been relaxing the past two days. It's been hotter than usual, so maybe she feels cooler down there. We've been keeping Jinx to give Sadie and Kylo some alone time while they deal with the stress of what awaits them next month, Kylo's court date for striking Sadie's ex-husband getting pushed back three months. I can't imagine how they are feeling with Declan leaving his trial as a free man after what he did to her.

Another meow draws me to my knees as I crawl by the bed, and she's back hiding under there, only this time, she's heavily panting and too far for me to grab. "Aw, are you feeling hot, Jinxy? Come on out."

When she doesn't budge, laying flat on the ground, I furrow my brows and head back to the window.

"Lex..." I call for him as he tosses dirt to the side.

"Yeah?" He stabs the shovel into the ground, shielding his eyes from the sun as he searches for me. "What's up?"

"Something's up with Jinx. I think she might be over-heating from this heat."

He starts walking toward the house. "Did she drink water today?"

"Last I saw, it was still full—" Jinx meows, and I get on my knees by the bed as she's licking between her legs.

Footsteps sound in the distance, and I glance back as Lennox walks into the room. "She's under there again?"

"I think...do you know if Sadie got her spayed?"

"Not that I know of."

"Call and tell them to hurry over." Jinx spins, lifting her leg again as she lays on her side, her meows sounding more distressful, and my heart skips. "And bring back something soft, please."

He nods, rushing out of the room. I don't want to hurt her, so I pull the bed away from the wall, and Lennox is back with large towels a few moments later.

"Just called them, and they are on their way here."

"Okay." Jinx hisses at me as I approach, only allowing Lennox to be near her.

"Come lay here." Making a fluffy pile, he urges Jinx to settle on top, and she rests on her side again, staring at us while she makes more noise, still panting.

Lennox furrows his brows, sitting beside her while petting her head, and I take in his concerned expression, how much he truly loves this little cat. Only a few minutes pass, and Jinx is bearing down on her hind leg, her tail lifted while pushing—not long after comes a tiny kitten in a sack, and Jinx begins licking it clean.

"Ohh, Lex. She didn't even look pregnant. How many kittens do you think she's carrying?"

He shakes his head, breathing out a shaky breath while swiping away a tear from his cheek. "Fuck, I have no idea."

That's adorable.

"Does this mean you're a grandpa now?" I giggle, and he smirks at me, watching Jinx do her thing, the orange and black kitten already nuzzling into her stomach to feed only moments later.

More footsteps are coming up the stairs, and Sadie appears with Kylo close behind.

Her eyes instantly tear as she covers her mouth. "Aw, Jinx..."

I stand, helping her kneel, and let her and Lennox have their moment alone, walking next to Kylo, smiling just as wide. We keep a close eye on Jinx, and with an internet search, it says if she's no longer panting or bearing down within the next hour, then she's likely done with one kitten.

We converse for a while, and Sadie kisses her cat a few times before she and Kylo leave, feeling Jinx saying here would be best until Jax, the kitten, is old enough to be on his own.

It's nearly sunset when Lennox and I settle on the couch, watching an action movie with the cats in the corner sleeping. Glancing up at him, focused on the screen, I kiss his stubbled jaw while lying on top of him, and he exhales, hugging me closer, utterly content.

for a whil

ne and Kylo lear

enough to be on his own

ne cats in the corner sleeping

ed jaw while lying on top of hir

s, hugging me closer, utterly conten

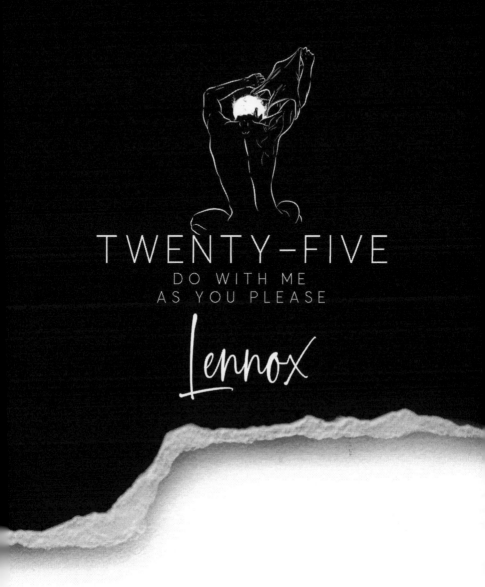

TWENTY-FIVE
DO WITH ME
AS YOU PLEASE

Lennox

E vie's not an early bird person, that's one aspect I learned the last few weeks, and I'm cherishing every second of her gorgeous grumpy face as we drive down the highway on this fine Friday morning. She brings her ball cap down further while I glance at her every so often, then smiles when I hook my arm over her shoulder to kiss her temple. I've been planning this trip since the night she told me at Vivid, the one place she's always wanted to go.

"Lex...why are we here?"

"I have a surprise for you."

Her brow arches. "At the airport?"

I chuckle, parking into the long-term lot, then get out of the car to jog around and open her door. Holding my hand out, I wait for her to take it, and she does with a smirk. I grab the suitcase from the trunk, filled with new outfits and all the traveling essentials, with Sadie's help. Evie stands by with her arms crossed and narrows her eyes.

"What are you up to?"

Draping my arm across her shoulder as we walk toward the building, I say, "What's the one place you've always wanted to visit but never had the chance to?"

Her eyes gloss over, then she shifts to press her cheek into my chest with a tight hug. "No—you're taking me to Italy?"

"Well, we never had a honeymoon."

She giggles, taking hold of my face to place a few kisses on my lips. "Thank you."

"You're welcome, Peaches."

The last time we flew together, we nearly made the mile-high club. Officially, checking that one off my bucket list during our twelve-hour flight. I may have almost thrown my back out in that tiny space, but fuck did Evie's tits look great bouncing in my face. Once we land, I can't hold back my grin the farther we walk into the airport, and she halts her steps.

Enzo's leaning on a white post by the doors, holding a sign that says:

Looking for Bratface.

"What—" Evie gasps, smiling as she runs into his arms, holding him tight. "What are you doing here?"

"Really? Did you think you were coming to the motherland without me?" He pats my back, giving me a side hug over my shoulder. "Your man is very persuasive. Fucker got me all teary-eyed and what not telling me his plan, reminding me how much Gram wanted all of us to come here. How could we refuse?"

"We?"

Enzo wags his brows. "Did I say we? I meant I."

She narrows her eyes, looking between Enzo and me. "You are acting more strangely than usual."

"I take offense to that. Now let's go do some sightseeing shit, and breathe the air as Gram wanted."

Evie grins, hugging him again, then faces me, slowly lifting onto her toes to leave a lingering kiss on my lips. "Thank you."

I draw her in for another, threading my fingers into her hair, and she moans into my mouth, deepening our kiss until I glance up when someone clears their throat. We slowly part, and Evie hums, cleaning her lipstick off my lips while I take in the guy standing next to Enzo with his arms crossed, holding a scowl. They look similar: dark hair, darker eyes, only his form is more muscular, as if he hits the gym a few times a week, possibly in his early thirties, like me.

"What's wrong?" she asks, then looks over her shoulder and quickly spins, holding her hand over her mouth. "Luca."

His expression lightens as she slowly walks toward him and buries her face in his shirt. I smirk as her cousin blinks a few times, stopping the tears threatening to spill by swiping them away with his thumb, then whispers something into her ear. She laughs, then hugs him around his waist before backing up toward me.

"Luca, this is my boyfriend, Lennox."

Heat travels throughout my body, the term bothering me more than it should since we haven't discussed what we'd use in public yet, though her family knows what went down in Vegas already.

He looks at her with a raised brow. "Last I checked, aren't you two married?"

Damn right.

Her cheeks turn bright pink, and then she stares at the floor. "Oh, yes..."

"Lennox," I say, holding my hand to shake, and Luca takes it firmly, that hardened expression returning. "Nice to meet you."

"And let me be straight with you, get my feelings off my chest. For a man who says he was supposedly there to look after Evie, you did a shit job." He looks at Enzo, then back to me. "Both of you."

"Luca—no. Apologize right now because you're not doing that." Evie narrows her eyes at him. "You weren't there, so you have no say in anything that happened in Vegas. Not one. And if you believe it's okay to come here to be disrespectful toward someone I care about, you can go straight home."

I can't stop the smirk that pulls from my lips as I gaze down at Evie. Luca sighs, and I look at him as his jaw ticks, holding out his hand. "My apologies."

"Apology accepted. If there's one thing you should take out of what happened between Evie and me, I love her without a doubt. I understand you're wary of me, but you have nothing to worry about."

Enzo backhands Luca in the chest, making him grunt. "See. What did I tell you? Don't be a dick."

He winks at Evie, then walks outside, Luca grumbling while following, glancing back at Evie and me, then I turn toward her.

"About what I said... I'm sor—"

"It's alright, Peaches. You stood up for me." I move in closer, tipping her chin up. "That showed me all I needed to know."

She smiles. "Thank you for setting all this up. Being here with my family means so much to me."

"Of course. Now is the time to start living, baby. Explore the world together."

Quickly nodding, she asks, "How long are we here?"

"Your cousins are staying for the weekend. Me and you." I dip toward her lips. "We've yet to take our honeymoon, so live up the next forty-eight hours because the moment they go, expect to never leave the hotel room for the rest of the week."

Evie licks her lips, dragging her teeth along the bottom. "I like that plan," she whispers, slipping her hands around my neck and pressing her lips to mine.

We're almost to Amalfi Coast as our driver navigates through traffic, but I'm enjoying every second of Evie taking in her heritage. Our time here will be endless. As we pull into our resort, I tip our driver when he hands us our luggage, which surprises him as he nods and gets back into his vehicle.

"Everything's beautiful." Evie strolls toward the railing with a huge grin, Luca and Enzo standing on either side of her as they take in the ocean view.

She glances back at me as Luca drapes his arm around her shoulder, Enzo her waist, then she faces forward. I give them this moment, entering the resort to check us into our three-bedroom suite, and they walk inside, taking in the beautiful decor. Once we're all settled in our room, we get dressed for dinner, wearing all white, and Evie looks gorgeous in her maxi dress, wishing we were alone right now.

"You look amazing."

Evie smiles, smoothing down the collar of my pressed shirt and tips back my hat. "I like this, but the beanie much more."

"Wait a few months and tell me again if you don't get sick of me wearing one."

She hums, kissing my lips. "Well, if you grow out your hair again, maybe I will since it'll only get in the way."

"Alright, you two have the rest of the week to do all this. I'm starving," Enzo says, standing a foot away and looking between us.

Turning with her hands resting on her hips, she says, "Keep it up, and you'll be sleeping with rocks in your pillow tonight."

"What? Wait, that was—how dare you." Evie presses her lips together to hold in her laugh, and Enzo follows behind her while walking toward the door where Luca's waiting, unable to contain his laughter. "I knew that was you."

I never had a relationship with my half-siblings. We are

years apart, and I'm the only one who stayed in Oregon, growing up as if I was an only child. Watching Evie and her cousins bicker is a bittersweet feeling. One I want to feel more often. When the time is right, I want love to spread in all corners of our home, with children, animals, and cuddles, all the warmth to embrace everyone. I blow out an unsteady breath as my throat burns, and Evie turns to look at me as we walk along the pathway, her smile hitting me the hardest.

My heart is at the fullest it's ever felt.

"You okay?" she asks, intertwining our fingers as she walks next to me.

"Never better, Peaches."

Resting her head on my shoulder, we continue until we reach the restaurant around the corner, just in time for our reservation. The hostess seats us near the ocean view, everything going as planned, though I want to skip dinner and bring my woman back to our room to devour her. Now's not the time to be greedy, so I enjoy our delicious meal. The tension between Luca and I quickly dies out the more we talk, and Evie video calls with Ella—just with the sound of her voice, Luca turns soft, battling with being away from his girlfriend, Enzo just as excited to see his girl, Ashley.

By the end of dinner, the atmosphere shifts as we roam the street toward the ocean. What was once pleasant conversation turns to silence, Evie squeezing my hand every so often. I release her grip, and she glances back as I stop walking.

"Go breathe, baby."

Tears spring to her eyes, and she hugs me tight, kissing me a few times before continuing down the pier with her cousins, resting her head on Lucas' side as he drapes his arm around her shoulder, Enzo strolling further ahead of them. I

lean on the railing overlooking the sea, and moments spent
with Dad on the water come rushing in, missing those years
of our life, and I swallow deeply, wishing for more times like
that.

As much as I've enjoyed getting to know Evie's family, I'm
glad they are gone, and the honeymoon session officially
begins. I've requested guest services to change our reservation to the honeymoon suite, and Evie's beautiful eyes widen
once we enter our new room. Rose petals, candy, candles, the
full experience.

"Lex," she whispers, walking toward the balcony
window with an outdoor hot tub, lounging bed, and ocean
view. "That's it. We are never leaving."

I chuckle, touching her waist as I hum into her neck.
"Whatever you want, baby."

She spins around to face me with a smirk. "Careful.
That's a hell of a statement."

"You have my surrender." Threading my fingers into her
hair, I tilt her head back. "Do with me as you please."

Her breathing deepens as she drags her bottom lip
through her teeth, revealing a wicked grin before stepping
away from me. She continues to stroll around the room,
unbuttoning her blouse, and stops to open the closet by the
bathroom.

Two cream velvet robes are hanging inside, and she
tosses one to me the closer I get. "Put that on."

"We're staying inside the rest of the night if I do."

Evie giggles and takes down hers, walking into the bathroom. "Just wear it."

Removing my clothes down to my drawers, I slip the soft fabric on and lie back on the mattress, taking a deep breath. Who knew traveling could be so tiring as my eyelids fall heavy, but I perk up when the bed dips. Evie crawls toward me, her robe tied tightly around her waist, straddling my lap.

"You look comfortable," she says, rocking along my dick, instantly awakening.

I glide my palms up her bare thighs as she presses her cheek to my chest, and I kiss the top of her head. "I am."

She looks up, stroking my jaw with her index finger, then leans in to kiss me. I follow her lead, letting her take what she wants as I glide further up her thighs, under the velvet robe, then stop when I reach under her ass. Her panties are no longer there, and my breathing deepens, slipping higher until I touch her wet slit. Our kiss heats the more I stroke her, taking in her soft moans against my lips, then I lift us, wrapping her legs around my waist to bring her into the bathroom.

Placing her on the vanity, I release the tie on her robe, the soft fabric falling open, exposing her beautiful body, and I get on my knees to kiss her stomach, licking along her navel. Evie hums, squeezing her legs around my body while gripping my hair, and I stop to look at her. From her long strands casting shadows around her oval face, her rosy nipples, the swell of her tits, and I glide my palm up her side to caress the left one.

"You're so damn perfect, Peaches," I whisper, pressing another kiss below her navel, and she hums, tilting her head back as I brush my thumb over the hardened peak.

I stand, leaning forward to kiss her lips, then head into

the walk-in shower to turn on the water. Evie drives her hands under my arms and presses herself against my back while removing my robe. She kisses along my shoulder blades, and I take deep, shaky breaths as she pulls down my boxer briefs, my erection springing free. Once the water's warm enough, I pull her underneath and get to business, lathering every inch of her body. How much I love taking care of her.

Evie rests on my chest, and we stay this way for who knows how long until the water's no longer hot enough to soothe—then she looks up at me with a smile. "Meet me in the room when you're finished?"

I smile, smack her ass as she leaves me, and take the quickest shower under the frigid water, the cold doing nothing to suppress my hard dick. Drying myself, I walk into the doorway, leaning against it as Evie lies across the bed, touching her pussy. Her heavy gaze lands on me watching her, and she moans, closing her eyes. I push off, sit beside her, and draw her ass onto my lap with her leg resting on my shoulder. She continues to glide her fingers along her slit with no urgency, merely exploring her body, and I enjoy watching her discover just as much as I do pleasuring her.

"Such a beautiful pussy. I love how you play with yourself."

Evie rests her hand on her stomach, gazing at me while baring herself, and I take over, softly circling her clit. Her breathy moan as she rocks her hips forward has my dick stiffening more, but her pleasure is what I desire. I suck my fingers, then keep my strokes at a gentle pace, paying close attention to her breathing when to slow down and draw out her moans, making her squirm with the slightest touch as I do the same to her nipples.

The wetter her pussy gets, the more pressure I give, and the louder she pants, bucking harder, squeezing her tits as her back arches. I press my palm on her stomach to keep her steady while quickly rubbing her clit, bringing her close to the edge, then easing back, lengthening her pleasure, teasing, and showing my beautiful wife the attention she deserves. Inserting a finger inside, I spread her arousal along her slit, grunting as she grinds on my cock, and I strengthen my hold, slapping her clit several times to redden her pretty cunt.

My cock's throbbing from her whimpers and the view that I stop to admire every inch of her.

"Lex—please, baby," she whines, circling her hips for me. "I want more of your touch, your love," she arches her back, "make me feel it."

"Fuck, you're so wet, Peaches."

I slip inside her, fucking her pussy with my middle and ring fingers, drawing out her moans. She intakes a sharp breath as I focus on her g-spot with rapid strokes, letting her suck my fingers as her breathing quickly increases.

"C'mon, baby. Come for me, so I can taste it."

I don't let up, moaning while pushing her over the edge, and she rocks her hips against my hand, sucking hard through her cries of bliss until she's coming all over, squeezing her thighs tight, and I take her sweetness into my mouth.

"Mm, fucking delicious."

She's panting, biting her lip as she lifts to be closer. "Lex, I want you inside me."

Chuckling, I move between her thighs, lifting her ass until she drops back to the mattress. "No, baby," I say, resting her legs on my shoulders. "I'm not done eating yet."

...my all over...

...o into my mouth...

...p as she lifts to be close...

...I move between her thigh...

...til she drops back to the mattress...

...y shoulders. "I'm not done eating yet..."

TWENTY-SIX
I WANT TO HEAR EVERY SOUND YOU MAKE

Evie

I squeeze my thighs together while pressing on Lennox's forehead to give myself a second to recover. Though he continues to lick my pussy, each gentle flick is agonizing bliss as I whine, "Baby—please."

"Fuck, I love it when you beg."

Lennox straightens his stance, grips under my thighs, and drags me closer to the edge of the bed. Taking hold of his shaft, he glides along my slit, hitting my sensitive clit, and my head bucks back as I moan, rocking my pelvis forward.

"You want me to fuck you? Hm?" He inches inside, coating the tip with my wetness, then continues to rub me until I'm squirming, my legs spreading wider as he teases my pussy. "Tell me how badly you want my cock, Peaches."

I wrap my thighs around his hips, pull him down to me by his neck, and nip his bottom lip while our mouths fight for dominance, though I lose when Lennox growls through his teeth, pinning my arms above my head. His shoulders heave while he pants, hovering over me, licking across the blood tinging his lip, and he frees my wrists once my eyes gloss over.

"Lex..." I whisper, easing my thumb across the small cut, lifting to inspect him closer. "Baby."

He grins, wiping away a tear that falls down my cheek. "That bad, huh?"

Snorting a laugh, I smile, nudging my nose along his while gliding my hands up his pecs, slowly working our mouths until we're flush together and making love. Sex with Lennox is beyond anything I've experienced with a man—his drive to please makes it a thousand times better, and I'd fuck him all night if I could—well, I could...

The birds chirp outside as my fingers glide along his length, and Lennox groans, maneuvering away from me. "Peaches, if any more cum shoots out of my dick, it's gonna fall off."

I giggle, kissing his neck as I place my leg over his hip and rub his side. "I can't get enough of you."

"Well, you won't get any more of me if I'm dickless."

"You weren't complaining last night, smashing me over the balcony." I nip below his ear, and he grabs my thigh. "Stretching my leg against that wall." Lennox dips his hand to my ass, breathing deeper as I grind my pussy on his lower back. "I especially loved how you made me come over and over in this very spot." He moans as I glide my tongue along his neck while gently stroking his hardened shaft. "Your cock feels too good. Can you blame me for wanting more?"

He draws my ass forward, my clit rubbing harder against his body, and I let out a breathy hum, gripping his hair tight while I continue to buck my hips. Lennox grunts as I pull his head back, rubbing down his shaft to his balls, knowing how much he enjoys it. I love how dominant he is in bed, but it takes a remarkable man to trust his woman to take control when giving pleasure with no limits.

"I want to make you come just as often as you make me." I sit on top of him, rocking along his shaft, and he grabs my hips when I gently tug his balls. "Do you want to fuck my ass, baby?"

Lennox's gaze lowers, kneading my thighs as I dip to rub his taint with my middle finger and stroke his dick between my cheeks. He shows no hesitance the lower I go, and he moans as I apply more pressure while jerking him, his head tipping back, gripping me harder.

Sucking a breath through his teeth, he straightens up, lifts me by my ass, and gets me on my back. "Fuck, Peaches."

He kisses me hard, sucking my tongue into his mouth. "You almost made me come."

I giggle, pressing another kiss before inching away to twist onto my stomach, peeking back at him. "We better get to it, then." He's gone for a second before returning with a bottle of lube, and a pillow, making my pulse spike. I've never been fucked in my ass by a man, only toys. "Be gentle," I whisper.

The lube is warm as he massages my cheeks and up my back, circling his thumb around my hole with every pass, then tucks the folded pillow under my pelvis. I sway my hips, moaning into the mattress, and he takes hold of my hair, lifting my head to turn my face.

"I want to hear every sound you make."

I hum, licking my lips as I rest my cheek on the bed. Something firm presses into me, a familiar texture, and I grin as he eases in a plug, my nerves dissipating, trusting Lennox knows what he's doing. He leaves the toy in as he enters my pussy a few times before my ass vibrates, making me whine with a low moan. I buck backward onto his body, and Lennox grunts, gripping my sides to draw me in with each pump. Switching the vibration off, he gently pulls the plug out, sticking his thumb in its place while applying a generous amount of lube to his dick.

My heart's racing as he settles in place, then meets my gaze. "Relax, Peaches." Nodding, I rub my clit as he presses his tip at my hole, easing on and off, listening to my body until I'm at ease, and he slips in a bit more. I intake a heavy breath each time he enters, enjoying the pressure, his gentle touch, and how he hums the further his cock goes until he's moving without resistance. Slow and steady.

"Fuck, baby. Such a tight plump ass," he says with a low, gritty tone. "Don't stop rubbing your clit."

We both moan louder as he gradually picks up speed when I quicken mine, then presses his palm on my back to dip me further into the pillow, getting deeper. He inserts two fingers into my pussy, firmly rubbing my wall, a delicious ache forming from the night before, then he backs away to apply more lube.

I turn to face him, needing to feel closer. "Cross your legs."

He doesn't waste time, and I sit on his lap, wrapping my thighs around his hips. Our lips lock in seconds, pressing my tits against his chest, and Lennox strokes his cock while I lift for him to push into my ass again. Keeping a solid hold on my body, he guides me along his shaft as I ride him, hugging him tightly, moaning into each other when he fills me, the sensation unlike any toy I've used, and I want more.

"Harder."

His hold on my body tightens as he gets me onto my back, pinning my legs above my shoulders and increasing the strength of his drive.

"Touch your pussy," he pants, and I do as he says, rubbing my clit with each solid pump until my body bucks from an intense release, rocking faster, my head rolling back with my screams echoing around the spacious room. "Yes, that's it, Peaches." Bending forward, he kisses my neck, all over my face, then my lips while grunting, "God damn, I love my beautiful wife."

He straightens his stance, finishing with a few firm thrusts, breathing out ragged breaths while easing the tip in and out as his cum drips from me, rubbing his head around before lowering my legs. Settling between them, he rests on my breasts, slowly coming down from our high.

"I love you," I whisper, threading my finger through his hair, and he hums, hugging me tighter before lifting me from the bed.

I clutch his shoulders while he walks us to the shower with ease, building our connection and one step closer as husband and wife.

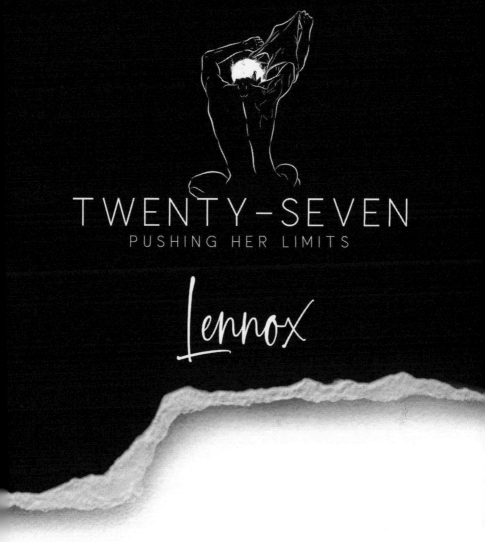

TWENTY-SEVEN
PUSHING HER LIMITS

Lennox

O ur time in Italy ends too soon as we drive to
Evie's place, not ready to drop into regular life.
Evie turns to face me, her sunglasses covering
her eyes, but her contentment shines through. She reaches
for my hand, and I grab hers, placing a kiss on the back.

When we arrive, I park in my spot and hop out to open her car door, which gets me an eye roll with tender cheek slaps.

"Thanks."

Leaving our bags in the trunk, I follow my wife to the front door, waiting for her to unlock it—then she gasps as I lift her into my arms and carry her over the threshold.

"Welcome home."

Evie raises a brow. "As if we haven't walked through the past how many months."

"Today's different," I say, placing her on the floor.

"Explain."

I remove the diamond ring from my pocket and take hold of Evie's hand, gazing into her eyes as I hold the precious metal at the tip of her finger. "Are you feeling lost?"

Evie's quiet for a moment, exhaling a long breath. "No," she whispers.

"Are you happy?"

Her smile is instant. "Yes."

"Are you home?"

Nodding, she looks at me, tears brimming her eyes. "I am."

I slip the ring on, then kiss the back of her hand. "Then today officially marks the beginning of Mr. and Mrs. Hunter."

She doesn't hide the tremble of her smile, allowing her tears to fall along her cheeks. "I love you."

Those three words light a fire within me each time I hear them. "Say it again," I mumble against her lips. "Tell me you love me, baby."

Leaving a peck, she piques a brow while I tug her closer, then whispers, "Hm, are we playing bossy now?"

"We both know who wears the pants." I walk her backward until she's against the door, pinning her arms above her head.

My eyes widen when she hooks her legs around my hips, and I quickly grab her ass with my free hand, preventing her from falling to the floor. "We do."

Chuckling, I kiss her hard, then release her legs from my body, still pressed against her. "I'm going to get us settled. In five minutes, I want you by the silks."

She bites her lip, squirming before me. "What for?"

Letting her wrists go, I hold the side of her neck. "It's been a while, and my beautiful wife has an incredible talent. I miss watching her soar."

Her smile falters. "Lex, I have nothing prepared."

I swipe my thumb across her cheek. "Just fly, baby."

"I...." Her breath quivers as she releases a sigh. "I'm done. They replaced my performance at Vivid."

My brows furrow. "What?"

"Jared. He took me off the day I left, and all I'll have is Voyeur when I return."

"Then don't go back, Evie. You don't need that place. There are so many opportunities out there for you. People who will appreciate your talents."

She scowls. "Which talent, Lex? Making a man come in second just by watching me strip? Or maybe my best fake orgasm performance."

"Don't do that."

"Do what? It's the truth. I've lived at Vivid since I was seven years old. Stripping since I was eighteen. There's no other place for me."

Her eyes gloss over for a different reason, and I hold my tongue, drawing her in for a hug. "Okay," I soothe, "I'm sorry. I understand how you feel."

Shoulders dropping, she returns my hug, nodding into my neck as I kiss her temple. "No, I'm sorry for lashing out. I know there's more to me than being a Red Vixen, but there's also a lot of history within those walls, with unanswered questions, and I need to be there to figure out how to move on."

"Sure, baby. How can I help?"

She lifts to look at me. "When I return, you not coming anymore is a start. Seeing you was the highlight of my night. Then I'll never leave with you there."

I smile and hum. "I knew it."

A snort-giggle releases from deep within her, and I chuckle as she hides her face in my chest. "Stop making me laugh."

"Never."

Her laugh subsides as we slowly sway, staying silent for a moment. "Sadie's birthday is tomorrow," she says, looking at me. "Want to come with me to buy her gifts so I can wrap them later?"

"Nope."

She furrows her brows. "Oh, then I'll go by myself."

"Peaches, you got five seconds to get your butt ready for those silks, or I'll start drinking my morning coffee in the kitchen."

"What?"

"Four."

"Lex—you're not being serious, are you?"

"Three..."

Her eyes open wide. "Okay, I'm going."

I wink at her when she walks past, smack her ass, and she quickens her steps, sticking her tongue out when she's further away, making me chuckle. Grabbing our bags from the trunk, I return to Evie jumping rope in a black sports bra and shorts before stretching on a yoga mat. I set the luggage by the couch and take a seat, watching her work while getting comfortable.

"Do you mind if I record you?" I ask while Evie inspects the fabric minutes later.

She stares at me. "Why?"

"To keep for yourself, or maybe you'd like to spread your talent one day." I draw out my phone and press record when she nods. "Show people what you got."

Evie licks her lips, rubbing her hands on her thighs before saying, "*Alexa*, play *Your Life* by *Stephen.*"

Music flows through the room, a melody serene of nature, and Evie weaves between the white silks like water, her gaze landing on me before she climbs, losing her grip a moment later—I jolt forward, but she catches herself, closing her eyes to compose her thoughts, to breathe. My heart beats fast as she continues, keeping my eyes on her, Evie taking her time switching positions, getting back into an even flow after months of avoiding the air. Once her confidence returns, I continue recording, her moves getting faster, poses harder, pushing her limits, spinning, dropping, stretching...*smiling*, and she looks so damn beautiful in her element.

On the floor, Evie allows the music to guide her body, her smile never faltering as she meets my gaze, then dances toward me, and I hold her when she straddles my lap, ending the recording. "Good job, baby," I whisper into her ear, swiping the damp strands of hair off her temple to press a kiss. "What did I tell you? So damn good."

"Thank you," she pants, locking her arms around my neck, and we sit in our embrace. "I missed that."

"I know." Taking her by the cheeks, I make her look at

me while trying to keep a stern *you know who wears the pants* face. "Now, you have five seconds to get your ass ready for the store before I change my mind about coming along."

She purses her lips and slips off my lap, smirking before sauntering toward the stairs, threading her fingers through her long hair—once she reaches the first step, she glances over her shoulder, sticks her tongue at me, and this time, I chase after her, enjoying her laughter to our bedroom.

keep a ste
rs the pants fac
and about coming along
sauntering toward the stair
o her tongue at me, and this tim
, enjoying her laughter to our bedroo

TWENTY-EIGHT

CAN A GRANDPA DO THAT?

Evie

"**D**on't make me call my auntie." Lennox reads the black onesie over my shoulder, and I peek up with a smirk as I pack the baby item inside the large gift box.

"Damn right."

He hums into my neck, his hold around my waist

strengthening, and my stomach flips when he spreads his hand, rubbing his thumb across my navel. His action speaks well beyond words while I sift through the gifts we got Sadie and Kylo yesterday. I've never thought about starting a family, I've been celibate for years, but with Lennox, him wanting children with me makes the idea less scary. I place my palm over the back of his hand, and he inhales a deep breath through his nose, hoping my small gesture tells him yes.

Not today, not tomorrow, but one day.

Right now, I want us.

To wake up to coffee and his head between my legs. Get to know each other on the deepest level, and explore aspects of ourselves we never knew existed. So when one day comes, our children will grow up experiencing how much their parents love each other. I want them to see affection as ordinary behavior that comes naturally, never forced. Never pretend. That forever type of love because with Lennox, it's that simple.

Spinning to face him, I step onto my toes and thread my fingers into his hair as our lips connect. He glides his hold to my thighs, lifting me to straddle his waist as we fall to the bed, and I suck in a sharp breath when something hard digs into my ass.

"Ow—" I cry, my head falling back as I giggle, and Lennox laughs into my neck, removing the baby item from beneath me.

"Sorry."

"Don't be." I smile, shaking my head. "But I do need to finish wrapping, or we'll be late for the party."

"I'd rather be late with you."

"Yeah?"

"Mhm." He kisses just below my ear, then nips, smirking against my skin as I moan, knowing what his mouth on that spot does to me. "You taste good."

Pressing him back, I purse my lips and straighten up to rest on my elbow. "Tease."

"And you love it."

I smirk, lifting the skirt of my dress while rubbing my thighs together. "So much you got me wet."

"Damn. If I don't step out of the room now, I'm gonna put you to sleep."

"You better, later."

Lennox grins, peeking back at me when he reaches the door just as I spread my legs wide to show my panties, and he groans, "Peaches." Then walks out of the room.

Doesn't take long to finish stuffing the box, hoping Kylo and Sadie get good use out of these items. Only a month left until the baby arrives, time passes by too quickly, and I can't wait to meet him or her.

My phone brightens with an incoming call, and my smile falters at the number. "Hey, Dad."

"How's my baby girl? I feel like we haven't talked in months."

Because it has been.

"I can't talk long. Getting ready for Sadie's birthday party."

"How is she? I tried to call her, but the number is disconnected."

Grabbing the tape, I start covering the box with wrapping paper. "Good. She's getting married and having a baby."

"Oh, wow. I'll have to send Sadie something nice."

I sigh, place the tape on top of the box, and sit on the

edge of the bed. "You could come visit here, you know. I'm sure she'd like to see you instead. I'd like to see you."

"Sweetheart, you know I can't. Come to San Francisco. You're always welcome to come home."

"I am home. I didn't have a choice before, but I've never felt more at home than I do right now, and you don't even know why."

"Know what?"

"What hurts is you were the first person I wanted to call the day my life changed because a girl needs her dad, you know? But as much as you tell me you love me, we aren't as close as we once were, and not knowing how you'd react makes me afraid you'd disapprove. I'm not sure I want to tell you. Or Mom. Neither of you deserves the news with the secrets you've held back over the years, so I'll keep mine."

"Evie, wait. Where is this coming from?"

"Ready?" Lennox asks, poking his head back into the room, and I blink away my tears.

"I gotta go."

Ending the call, I face away from Lennox, using the last of the wrapping to distract me from wanting to cry. I'm done wondering why because wondering hurts, so I no longer care.

"Hey, you okay?" Goosebumps rise along my skin when Lennox smoothes his palms up my arms.

"Yeah." I kiss the back of his hand as he reaches my shoulder. "Let's go."

There's something calming about watching families come together to celebrate a special occasion, a rare commodity nowadays, at least for me. I love watching Kylo and Sadie start their new life together, yet not every happy picture is as it seems—there's a story behind them—one observer won't fully understand. Still, I see through their smiles, a mask hiding the worry, the stress piling onto their shoulders with everything happening behind the scenes. My best friend says she's happy, and I believe her, but the second she's ready to blow out all twenty-nine candles, the mask slips, her worry and all the stress seep through, and she closes her eyes to make her wish that'll hopefully make everything better.

"I love you," I say to Sadie, hugging her tight, her eight-month belly pressing into me. "He's going to win. I know it."

She quickly nods, blowing out a heavy breath. "Me too." Drawing back, she looks at Lennox, and her smile returns when she touches the ring on my finger. "Vegas?"

"Yes. Took a long time to get here, but I'm glad I finally did."

"Wow. That's great, Evie. You deserve every ounce of happiness."

Lennox is talking with Kylo by the back door, and he looks at me just as I do, giving me a wink, and my stomach flutters, embracing the feeling deep to my core. "That I do."

One last hug and I walk toward my man—my husband. I kiss Kylo's cheek, wishing him luck on his trial, and Lennox wraps his arm around my waist when we walk outside, a jingle following behind us as Jinx and Jax come along. Quickly I lift our kitten, kissing the top of his head while holding Lennox's hand, the start of *our* little family, and we head for the guest house. We've been spending most of our time in Portland since it's closer to our jobs, slowly filling it with his items, so there's not much left here besides his couch and a few bedroom furniture.

Drawing me closer as we reach the door, Lennox looks at Jax between us, who grips his shirt to climb, and he inhales a sharp breath. "Okay, those are sharper than last week."

I giggle, chewing on my bottom lip when he places Jax on his shoulder. "Let's go inside, grandpa."

"Nope. Don't like that."

Wagging my brows, I walk backward into the guest house, Jinx and Lennox following, and he places the kitten on the floor, scooping me onto his shoulder next. I squeak, gripping his shirt as he slaps my ass, walks toward the couch, and sits with me on his lap.

"Can a grandpa do that?"

"I don't know. Show me again in thirty years."

His smile fades, and a heavy gaze replaces it as he strokes my cheek. "Peaches, I want nothing more than to start a family with you."

Heat rises within as my breathing deepens, and I press forward while hovering above his lips. "A baby girl on my hip...." I buck on his hardening dick, and Lennox grips my ass tighter. "As you rock our son to sleep?"

"Yes—" Eyes closing, he lets out a low moan, and I place my hands on his chest—his heart's beating fast, and I lower to undo his pants as he shifts them past his hips. "More than anything, baby. Right now—" He presses his lips to mine, breathing hard through his nose. "Later. I'm ready whenever you are."

Now my heart's racing the harder we grind, his dick rock hard, our underwear the only barrier between us. "Lex," I moan when he squeezes my body tight. "I want that for us, but right now, I want you more." Lennox smiles against my lips before we slowly work our tongues together, continuing to rock against one another.

"I don't have condoms here."

I hum from the constant pressure against my clit. "You feel good like this."

He adjusts his dick to be flat on his stomach as I rock my hips faster. "Then keep going, Peaches."

"I want to make you feel good, Lex."

Chuckling, he moans deep within his chest. "Anything you do feels good."

An urge to have him in my mouth arises, and I press my lips on his, then lift his shirt over his head. I take this moment to touch him, across his broad shoulders, down his firm pecs, trailing the indentations along his torso while he watches my every move.

I drag my bottom lip through my teeth, slowly inching off his lap and onto my knees. Kissing his chest, I descend while licking, his stomach drawing in tight the lower I go, pulling his pants down further, his dick begging to be freed. Wanting him to tell me, I stare into his eyes while rubbing his inner thighs with my thumbs, waiting for further instruction.

"You want my cock? Go ahead, show me how bad you want to suck it."

His dick springs free as I draw his boxer briefs down his legs, and I sit on my heels. "Are you ready to put me to sleep? A little choking will do me good."

Heat flushes his cheeks as his head tips back, his eyes open and close while pumping his shaft. "Keep saying shit like that, and I won't last thirty seconds in your mouth."

I smirk, continuing to massage his thighs before taking over his strokes, his legs spreading wider as he adjusts his position on the couch to lean further back. I've sucked his dick plenty of times, but he's never used me to make himself come. Lennox breathes in through his teeth when I tilt my head to lick the cum bead off the tip, keeping my gaze on his handsome face while taking more, humming around his head with the subtle buck of his hips.

There's so much I want to say, tell him I love his cock, the way he feels inside me, but I rather keep my mouth stuffed as I take him to the back of my throat. "Fuck—" Lennox moans, gripping my hair when I lift to take a breath, sucking while stroking the base of his dick.

Sweeping my hair away from my face, he bucks forward again, and I place my hands behind my back, staring into his lust-filled gaze. He stops for a second, his breathing increasing before his bucks continue, stronger, inching deeper into my mouth, bobbing my head along his cock at the firm pace of his choosing. I want more, for him to use me until he loses all self-control, where nothing else around us matters but him chasing his nut.

With a tighter grip, he removes me from his dick, holding my cheeks with his fingers while drawing me close to his face. "You want me to fuck this tight mouth of yours?" he asks, reading my mind.

"Yes."

He presses a firm kiss to my lips. "Hmm, open up, Peaches. Gotta make sure that tongue's nice and slick before I come all over it."

I moan, open for him, and clench my core when he spits inside my mouth, losing all sense of focus as heat radiates my body, melting before him—I've never been more turned on to suck a dick as he guides me back to his length. His grunts fuel the fire within, each pump into my mouth makes my pussy throb, needing relief as I rub my thighs together and Lennox releases his hold on my head.

"Get up here."

We're both breathing hard, his cock jutting from my mouth as he pulls me to kneel on the couch beside him, removing my dress where all that's left is my panties. In seconds I'm upside down with my knees on the back of the couch and my pussy in his face. Lennox kisses my inner thighs, panting against my slit before slipping the fabric to the side, and I inhale a sharp breath, my back arching more when he licks me clit to entrance, his hold on my hips keeping me in place.

"Where does your mouth belong?"

I ease my grip on the cushion, take hold of his shaft, and return to sucking, Lennox rocking upward to match the swipes of his tongue, gentle flicks merely teasing my clit. Needing more power to get me climaxing anytime soon, I circle my hips, and his hold on my ass strengthens to stop my advance.

He slaps both cheeks, and I moan on his cock, slipping off while gripping his ass when he stands. The sudden position change has me holding on tight, but his mouth never leaves my pussy until he has me on my back, my legs pinned by my shoulders, his dick still near my face as he straddles me, my lower half completely exposed for him to take me any way he pleases.

"Lex—" I whine when he spits down my crack, rubbing his thumb along the length and his dick touching my cheek.

Squeezing the base, I tap the tip on my tongue as he lifts his hips, making him grunt, thrusting forward into my mouth and fucking me without holding back. His moans get louder against my pussy the faster he moves, easing back when he makes me gag, and I bring him closer, wanting to feel him at the back of my throat.

"Fuck, Peaches," he pants, forcing his dick out of my mouth as he releases my legs to spread one outward, rapidly stroking my clit, which is my undoing.

My body spasms as he finishes my orgasm with his tongue, then settles on his heels, quickly stroking his dick. I maneuver to my knees right when he comes, thrusting forward while I suck on his head, humming as he fills my mouth. He inhales a sharp breath through his teeth when the sensations become too much, and I back away smiling.

Lennox takes me by my waist and pulls me flush to his body, hugging me, pressing his lips to my temple and cheek, stroking my hair back before kissing me deeply and goose-bumps spread across my skin from the love pouring out of him.

"Did I hurt you, baby?"

I shake my head, and we lie back, side by side, our legs intertwined as we continue to kiss, enjoying each other until he rests his chin on my hair.

"Today was nice," I whisper, stroking his neck.

He hums, rubbing my back until his chest moves slower, his breathing getting deeper, and I smile against his throat— the couch being our means of sleep tonight.

...nue to kiss...

...s chin on my hai...

...hisper, stroking his nec...

... e until his chest moves slowe...

...er, and I smile against his thro...

...couch being our means of sleep tonigh...

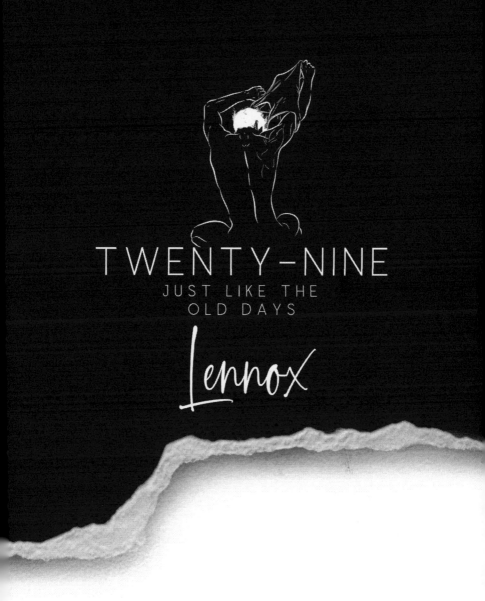

TWENTY-NINE
JUST LIKE THE
OLD DAYS

Lennox

The bright morning sun rouses me awake well past the time I'm usually up, which means I'm late for work, but with Evie still asleep in my arms, the mill is the last place I want to be. Her light snoring makes me smile, and the fuzzy ball snuggled into her neck lifts my lips into a grin. I don't know how Jax got onto the couch at seven weeks old, but this moment can't get any more perfect.

It does when Evie glides her palm up my chest, kissing the hollow of my throat, mumbling with a husky tone, "Good morning."

"Mornin', Peaches. Did you sleep well?"

"Mhm." She nuzzles her nose higher, pressing more kisses. "Very well."

I chuckle, dipping my chin to kiss her forehead. "Good."

Jax stretches his body, and Evie giggles as he tangles his paws within her hair, maneuvering where her back presses against my chest. "Looks like our little man did too."

He brushes his whiskers, letting out a yawn, and Jinx prances toward us from across the room with a trill. Letting him onto the floor, he runs to his ma as she licks his body, but he'd rather eat than have a bath, going straight for his breakfast.

"Poor girl can't catch a break with his hungry ass," I say into Evie's ear, and she glances back at me with a smile.

"Yeah, but she's used to his shenanigans by now."

I hug her closer, letting out a long breath. Happy, content. "I'm going to quit the mill," I whisper, and she moves her fingers through mine. "I have more than enough in my savings, so I'll put in my two weeks, tell my pops I'm not taking over, that I want to pursue something I've never given a chance to succeed in because I was too worried about what he'd think of me if I failed at it. I want to try at least, and if I fail, then I know it was doing something I loved, and I gave my passion my all."

She turns to lie on her back, her head resting on my arm as she looks at me. "And you're going to be amazing. I know it."

"I have you to thank."

"Me?"

"Mhm." I run my hand up her side, across her waist, and glide the pad of my thumb under her breast. "Seeing you in the air, how you love being there, showed me how much passion is important. If you enjoy your work, you'll strive to succeed."

"And you will." Evie lets out a soft moan, dragging her teeth along her bottom lip when I brush my thumb over her nipple. "Plus, you already have your first customer."

I smirk, lifting a brow as I tease her nipple to a hardened peak. "And what does my first customer want?" Touching her finger to her bottom lip, she grins, whispering in my ear, and I hum, gliding my hand to her throat. "That can definitely be arranged."

I ended up spending the rest of yesterday with Evie, though this morning, I woke up at 8 a.m., only getting an hour's worth of sleep as I stayed in bed, thinking of ways to tell Dad my plan without him blowing up on me. A few hours pass until I have the willpower to get up, especially with my wife sleeping naked beside me after our vigorous night. So I make her coffee, leave the mug by the bedside table, and throw on the set of work clothes I left behind, strolling up the pathway toward the cabin. It's quarter to twelve, receiving a text from Kylo to meet him in his office before I leave, so I head inside the cabin through the back sliding door, Jinx running toward me with Jax close on her hind.

"Hey, little man." I pick my guy up, rubbing Jinx's head while walking toward the hallway, letting him down as I meet the office door.

Kylo's focused on his laptop screen, his brows furrowed while reading an email, and he glances at me when I walk toward his desk.

"Hey, what's up?"

He lets out a deep breath, rubbing his forehead. "This morning after the trial, Sadie came home to a package on the steps."

"A package..."

"I didn't tell you before because I would rather you not worry about me, but I had a package come to me a few months back."

I furrow my brows, crossing my arms over my chest. "Kylo, don't start with that bullshit. You know you can come to me for anything."

"Yeah, well, I was trying to comprehend what was happening myself."

"What was in these packages?"

He stares into the distance. "Photos. A video."

"Of?"

"Explicit photos of clients from my sessions. This morning Sadie received a video of Leanna and me during one of our sessions, and I found Sadie watching just as I was...." His jaw clenched while shaking his head. "There's no recording allowed. You know that. Yet, I found multiple cameras around the cabin. I don't know when, or why, but I know it was her."

"Leanna? Shit. What are you going to do?"

He looks back at the computer. "Give in."

"What?"

"I have a plan, one she can't manipulate around this time, and hopefully, once my housekeeper comes in at 2:00, I can proceed with the plan accordingly."

"Okay, so I've missed a lot. Tell me about this plan."

Kylo reads me the email he sent, the one Leanna returned, and what he plans on doing once they meet up at Vivid. It's a good plan, a hell of a good one. I take a seat in the chair across from him. "If you're going, you're not going alone. I'm coming with you."

"I know. I've already discussed my plan with Sadie, and she understands. Giving Leanna the lead is dangerous, but it's only a ploy to make me look desperate. She doesn't know that I figured out Lina's the one behind maintaining the cameras. If I get her to come in and confess, then that's evidence I can use against Leanna."

"Blackmail the blackmailer. I like it."

Adam enters the office carrying a small box and places it on the desk. "I installed the camera in the kitchen corner by the sliding door, which captures the great room. It has up to ten hours of recording footage where you can access the video on the phone app."

Kylo nods. "I won't need that much. Lina's arriving in two hours, and I'll need to be alone with her. If you can, I'd appreciate it if you'd stay here with Sadie tonight while I meet with Leanna."

"I'll be here. No worries."

Standing, Kylo walks toward him to shake his hand. "There are only a few people I trust. Thank you for being one of them."

"Just doing my job, boss," Adam says, patting his shoulder before leaving the room, and I stand next.

"I'll talk to my pops about leaving early. Then I'll be back so we can go over a well-thought-out plan."

"Thanks." He leans against the desk, sighing as he rubs his face.

"Hey." I draw him in for a quick hug, then look him in the eyes, holding the back of his head. "You got this. Alright?"

"Yeah."

"Good. See you in a bit."

Leaving the office, I get on the road, drive to the mill, and park next to Dad's Porsche. My truck's not in the lot, and I sigh, heading inside, already knowing why. Gwyneth looks at me, lifting her brows.

"Lennox didn't expect you'd show up today."

"I know. I've been away for longer than I said. Where's my pops?"

She sighs and lifts her shoulder. "Where else?"

"Are Kevin and Leonel with him?" I ask while clocking in.

"They are, but your father has been working alone, not taking a break to the point he has a hard time catching his breath when he gets back into the office."

I quicken my steps to the locker room, throw on my gear, grab Dad's keys, and get out the door in less than a minute, hoping into the Porsche to drive to the field. Dust clouds fill the air as I park next to my truck, walking toward the buzzing in the distance—Bones is leaning against a tree and perks up when he sees me.

"How long has he been out here?"

"I'm not sure. The last couple of days, he's been here before me. Already got a dozen trees down, trimmed, ready for loading."

"He's gonna put himself in an early grave." I pat his shoulder, walking toward Dad as he's breathing hard, wiping sweat off his forehead with his shirt, then look up at the tree with the saw motor rumbling inside the trunk. "You gonna take that saw out while you're not using it?"

Dad glances at me with a raised brow and then returns to the tree. "You gonna stand there and tell me how to fell a tree? Or pick up a saw and get to work? Last I checked, my son, hasn't been here to get the job done."

"Alright, I get it. Go take a break, and I'll finish this one."

Kevin walks toward us, sweeping sawdust off his shoulders. "Hey, Lex. Long time no see. How was Italy?"

Dad's eyes widen before he narrows them at me. "Italy? You're telling me you've been gone all week because of a vacation? Not the doctor saying you need time off because your knee gave you hell?"

My knee hasn't bothered me for months, a slight ache here and there, but nothing close to what it was when Dad worked me to the bone. "What was I supposed to say? You'd always give me hell for taking time off."

He strides up to me, scowling. "The past eight months, you've been taking time off, distracted, coming to work late, not showing up. What's gotten into you?"

"Life! That's what's happening to me. Something I didn't have before meeting my wife."

His face turns redder. "Wife? What are you talking about? You have a wife?"

"Yes, and you'd know if you took a minute away from this place to actually care about what's happening beyond the mill. How unhappy I was here, how much I don't want to take over when you retire and end up like you, miserable with no one wanting me around."

"This place," he chuckles, shaking his head. "All I hear are excuses for why you'd rather have life easy. That's what's the matter with your generation. Hard work kept a roof over your head, a nice fucking roof." He pushes me back by my shoulder. "You want to live paycheck to paycheck like before, then go ahead, leave, but don't expect a place here when times get rough—"

There's cracking with a pop in the distance, Kevin yelling for everyone to get back while the tree Dad was felling tips toward the area we're standing. My heart leaps while urging Dad to move away when he doesn't, and he's gripping his shoulder when I pull him far enough to where the tree top misses us.

He's gritting his teeth, falling on his knee while hunched over. "Dad—fuck," I huff, looking around as he groans. "Bones, call an ambulance!"

The ride to the hospital is one big blur, hours spent in the waiting room because Dad didn't want me with him, and now I'm watching him struggle to catch his breath with oxygen, still stubborn, saying he doesn't need the assistance even in his fatigued state, clear as day he does. My jaw sets tight as I lean against the wall, crossing my arms over my chest, and I sigh.

"If you're gonna continue to throw a tantrum...get the hell out of my room," he grumbles, and I huff a laugh.

"You're gonna deal with me because I'm not going anywhere."

"Yeah, of course, you ain't. You're stubborn, just like your pops."

A slight smirk pulls at his lips but doesn't stay long when Mom comes rushing into the room with a large overnight bag on her shoulder, her short dark auburn hair clipped back, wearing a tiny apron around her waist, which I'm sure she hasn't realized she's still wearing. Dad looks at me wide-eyed with his *I told you not to call her* stare.

"Thomas. Oh, I told you so many times you're going to kill yourself out in that field!" She places the bag on the floor by the bed, then turns toward me to kiss my cheek. "Hi, honey. How are you? Feels like I haven't seen you in months. Are you hungry?"

"Hey, Ma. I'm Alright." I walk toward the chair and slide it closer to Dad. "Come take a seat. He needs a good earful."

And she does, Dad staring at the ceiling while she unpacks the dinner she was preparing in several Tupperware containers, placing them on his bedside table. "Lucy, I hear you, darlin'...and I love you, but please. I just need a minute."

Mom sighs, holding his hand covered with an IV, and kisses the back. As much as Dad and I butt heads, not seeing eye to eye with a lot of shit, I've always admired the love he shares with his wife—why I've strived for the same and haven't stopped until I finally found it. And just like that, I look at the doorway, and my heart sores when I see her. My beautiful wife, standing wary, with her hands clasped in front of her.

After stewing in that waiting room, I called Evie because I needed to hear her voice since I couldn't stop blaming myself. I called my mother because Dad needed to listen to hers, then Kylo to tell him I couldn't make it tonight, and I'm sorry. The fact that Evie came straight here makes my heart feel even fuller. I walk toward her, and she looks small like she's afraid.

"Hey."

"Is your dad okay?" she whispers. "Are you okay?"

"I'm fine, baby. Come inside. I'd like you to meet my parents." Evie doesn't budge when I take hold of her hand and look back at her. "If this is too much, you don't—"

"No..." She licks her lips, and I gently squeeze her hand as we walk inside.

Neither of my parents turns our way until I clear my throat, wrapping my arm around Evie's waist, and Mom perks up. "Oh—who's this?" She asks with a smile, standing to walk toward us, and Dad cannot look away.

"Mom, Dad, this is Evie. My wife."

"Your...what?" Mom gets teary-eyed, looking between Dad and Evie while holding her hand over her mouth.

"It's nice to meet you both," Evie says, her voice still low and shy, which is a side of her I've yet to meet. I wish I'd introduced Evie sooner to make this moment less uncomfortable for her, but I've enjoyed having her to myself.

Mom takes hold of her hand, looking at the ring, then draws Evie in for a quick hug, holding her at arm's length. "Wow, today's full of surprises. I'm so happy to meet you, Evie."

She smiles. "Me too."

"You should've said something sooner," Dad chimes in, his breathing much better since Mom arrived. "Instead of lying to me. You should've talked to me like an adult."

My shoulders dip as I breathe out a deep sigh. "Yeah, it's hard to get through to you with your head thicker than a log. Even the sharpest blade won't get through to you."

Dad huffs, shaking his head. "Goes both ways, Son—"

"Enough of this bickering." Mom turns to speak into Evie's ear, and she nods. "We're going to grab a coffee. When we return, I want this room to be civil. Got it?"

I smirk when Evie raises her brows, pressing her lips together to hold back her smile—she's enjoying this. Once Dad and I are alone, the room falls silent except for the humming of machines by the bed.

Walking to the chair, I plop down and stare at him with my elbows on my knees. He removes the oxygen from his nose, letting the tube hang by his chin, and exhales a heavy breath. "Son. If you didn't want to take over the mill, you should've told me so. All these years you've been there, and not one word."

"I didn't say I wanted to either or to disappoint you. Yet, I did all the jobs you piled on, even when you knew it was too much for me to do on my own, how you saw the toll the jobs took on my body. I did them because you would've overworked yourself if I didn't. Clearly, I was right."

His jaw clenches as he shakes his head. "Who's right or wrong...that's not the point. Yes, I'm hard on you, just like your grandfather was training me to take over the mill. Hard work builds character, and I'm proud of the man you've become, Son, believe me. I want to pass down the company, so you'll be set, but not by force. Only if you want it."

Nodding a few times, I lean back in my seat, tapping my foot on the floor. "I want to be a carpenter."

His brows raise as he looks straight at me. "Woodworking? Really?"

"Yeah."

"Are you working on anything now? Any finished products? A shop?"

I chuckle, shaking my head. "No shop, but I've been

using the empty office at the mill on Sundays for my bigger projects. Your coffee table is one."

"The river table? Well, I'll be damned—talent right under my nose this whole time. Shows how much I pay attention."

"It's alright, Pops. Old age will do that to ya."

He lets out a gruff laugh as I smirk at him. "Old...right." Glancing at the door, he adds, "Your wife, when did this happen?"

"New Years."

"And you love her?"

My eyes sting just thinking about Evie. "More than anything."

"Good. A piece of advice my father told me is never go to bed on an argument, settle your differences at the end of the night because time is unpredictable, and you're never promised tomorrow. Live up your life, kid. You don't want to be my age, wishing you'd done more, and I'm glad you went to Italy. Shit, I'm more bitter I didn't get an invite."

We both chuckle, and I reach over to rest my hand on his. "Sunday, 6 a.m. You, me, a boat with two rods and a twelve-pack of beer."

"Just like the old days."

"Only this time, I'll be of legal age to drink."

Mom and Evie come into the room giggling while Dad leans close to me. "Let's keep that between you and me, alright?"

"Right."

I walk over to Evie and draw her into me, resting my nose in the crook of her neck. "I missed you."

"And I learned a lot about you." She whispers into my ear, "Dirty boy."

Groaning, I lift my face to glance over my shoulder at Mom sitting by Dad. "What stories?"

Evie shrugs, trying hard to hold back her laugh. "Just a friendly reminder to never leave flour, baby powder, peanut butter, paint, in fact, anything in liquid form unoccupied around our future toddlers to save my sanity."

"Hm, what can I say? I was a wild child."

"Yup. I had a head full of grey hair by the time I was thirty," Mom says with a smirk. "But I wouldn't change a thing of the past. Nothing a bottle of hair dye couldn't fix."

"Also, a bottle of wine with a massage at the end of the night."

Evie chews on her bottom lip, and I raise a brow, saying, "That can be arranged."

Dad lets out a hearty chuckle. "Be careful there. That's how you were made."

My face screws up with the image that popped into my head. "Alright, time to go. Love you guys. See you tomorrow."

We finish our goodbyes, leaving the hospital with a weight lifted from my shoulders. I got my amazing wife by my side and time that needs to be spent with her. However, Dad's words couldn't be more accurate. *Time is unpredictable, and you're never promised tomorrow.* People are just as unpredictable, and plans don't always pan out as you'd hope because someone will always be one step ahead—the incoming call from Kylo is proof of that.

y shoulder.

be spent with he

e. Time is unpredictabl

table, and plans don't alway

ueone will always be one step ahe

coming call from Kylo is proof of tha

THIRTY

ARE YOU JUDGING ME
RIGHT NOW?

Evie

A lot can happen in seventy-two hours, the unimaginable, getting blindsided, completely thrown off your axis, and scurrying to get back to your center, where life should be. However, you come back different, stronger, wiser, and never take life for granted. All the above happened to Kylo and Sadie. Their life was hurled off their axis, and now they are slowly coming back to center with an addition, having to create a new normal.

Watching them navigate their trauma has brought me to light—not wanting to take life for granted. With Lennox reconciling with his father, I found the courage to do the same. To make a change, and it's well past time.

Three months, that's how long it's been since I stepped foot inside Vivid Vixens. To finally rid me of the place that's only holding me back. I run my hand through the rack of outfits, some new, others I've worn countless times, most of them for only seconds. There's more construction happening, an expansion to the building I've yet to see. However, I have no desire to look since today will be the last time I enter the premises.

The dressing room looks updated, with a fresh coat of paint and new lights above each station. Mine still looks how I left it, the paper dove Jared made tossed into the corner behind my makeup. Roni walks out of the locker room buttoning her pearl blouse, the tight black pencil skirt hugging her toned thighs on top of her pattern stockings. She glances at me and continues to her station to finish her hair and makeup. There's still tension between us, and I look at her the same time she does me, then she quickly reverts to her task. Pressing my lips together, I exhale a long breath through my nose and then stroll toward her.

Time to fix what I broke.

"Hey, got a minute?"

Her eyes flick up to mine in the mirror while combing her hair back into a low ponytail. "I got several."

"Alright. I want to clear the air between us."

Pursuing her lips while applying lipstick, she puts the

cover on and stores the tube with the rest of her makeup. "Pretend you didn't take advantage of me while I was brand new, not giving one fuck about how that made me feel?"

"Yes...I wasn't in the best head place at the time of my life." I huff, shaking my head at myself. "Still struggling while I'm here, but that doesn't excuse my behavior. I'm sorry for what I did to you. Truly."

She's still looking through the reflection, pressing her lips together before turning toward me. "You want to start fresh? Then work this session with me."

My brows furrow. "I'm done, Roni. I'm only here to fix my wrongs, and I'm out."

Her eyes gloss over, and she blows out a shaky breath, blinking a few times as she leans onto her station. "Please. A lot has changed, and I don't know if I can do this session alone."

"Why—"

"Clock should be ticking," Julianne says, strolling into the dressing room in her red pantsuit. "Oh, Evie...I didn't know you were here."

Roni pleads, and I sigh. "One session and I'm hitting the road."

A small smile lifts her cheeks, and she nods. "Thanks. Dress like me with red lace and no panties underneath."

"Alright."

"Well, you girls better get a move on it then."

I look at the time on the wall, only five minutes until noon, and Roni walks toward the curtains. "Meet you there?"

"Yeah."

Julianne takes hold of my hand as I walk toward the locker room. "You've been gone a while, kid. Are you prepared for the changes? Read over the new rules in the app?"

"I will," I lie—doesn't matter since I'm leaving after this performance. How much could change in a few weeks?

She blows a heavy breath, seeing through my lie, and whispers, "*Shit.*"

Quickly getting ready, I place my phone and purse inside my locker, then leave for the main floor. Gin glances at me as I pass the bar, the next person I need to speak with, and I pass the regulars who come to vivid on their lunch breaks, up the stairs to room three.

Entering through the employee door, I walk toward Roni, who's holding a stack of papers by the doorway, and she looks at me before sauntering into the room like she owns it. I smirk, walking in a moment later, and my smile falls off my face entirely as I stay by the door, staring at a man sitting behind the desk in a black two-piece suit. Roni raises a brow at me when she looks back, nodding her head to enter further into the room.

Why is there a man here?

"Sorry for keeping you waiting, Mr. Saito. Here are those reports you asked for," she says, her voice low, uncertain.

The guy smiles a perfect grin, lifting his strong cheek-bones, the slant of his ebony eyes thinning until he relaxes back into his seat, continuing to look at his computer screen. "Good. Place them on the desk and take a seat."

His gaze flicks to me, still standing at the entryway, the clock ticking on our thirty-minute session. "Come inside, Ms. Ross."

I don't register the fake name for this session or anything else around me until he stands from his seat, walking toward me while unbuttoning his suit jacket. "Um—" Pressing against the door jamb, I blink a few times as he gets too close for comfort. "I left something outside."

The guy's straight black hair touches his forehead as he leans his forearm above me. "Are you new here?" he asks, touching the first button of my blouse, each one coming undone as he jerks them open with his finger, exposing my tits, then drops his hand on my thigh, lifting the hem of my skirt, and I'm frozen. "Do you need a proper introduction?"

Swallowing deeply, I shake my head, my heart racing, needing to get the fuck out of this room. "No—"

"Why are you here? Leave, now!"

"Tell me which room?!"

There's a commotion outside the voyeur box, my heart skipping at the familiar distressed voices, Gin's muffled tone, and someone else banging on the door. The man steps back, dropping his act when he furrows his brows, and Roni walks toward me as I race for the exit to see.

He can't be here.

"Open this door!"

Instant pins and needles spread across my skin as I halt my step, my pulse skyrocketing when the door opens and Dad walks through, his face turning red when he takes in my outfit.

"Evie." He snaps his head toward Gin with his nose flaring. "You let our daughter work here?"

"Dad..."

"Marco, please, you need to go," Gin says as security enters soon after, but Dad pushes Nate back when he grabs his arm.

Gin shakes her head. "Nate, you don't need to. He's leaving," she says, and he nods, stepping back but staying close by.

"I'm leaving with my daughter. I should've known you'd run back here, but never did I think you'd allow Evie to follow the same path as us—accepting her to stay with you was my biggest mistake."

Her eyes gloss over, getting in between him and me. "You have no say in what I've done to survive since returning home. You knew who I was before we met, what I left behind for us to raise our child miles away from the only place that took care of me, but don't you dare stand here passing judgment when you met me in this very box." Gin pokes his chest. "Do you regret me, too? For not using protection that night, we crossed the line because we were *too deep in love* to care about the rules?"

She met him here?

Dad furrow's his brows. "Our history doesn't shape—"

"Our history has everything to do with this very moment! I don't want to hear excuses—have you told your daughter why I took off to Oregon with her? Or should I tell her?"

His body stiffens. "She doesn't need—"

"Evie's an adult. She deserves to know how you treated me seconds after making the biggest decision of my life. How I lost two people that night."

"There were other options!" Dad shouts, and I jump, my heart hurting at the pain behind his voice, the way he intakes a shaky breath. "Why choose that one?"

Gin huffs a laugh and wipes under her eyes as she shakes her head. "Because not having a second child was the best option for me. I was happy—content living in our little bubble as it was. I'm not like you, wanting the big family you were so passionate about. I was one and done, and you couldn't accept that. It made me feel like shit for terminating the pregnancy, but I did what I had to do. I left to give you what you wanted, freed you so you could find someone with the same mindset as you—"

"I wanted you!" Dad moves in close, touching her face, and my lip trembles when she quickly shakes her head, breathing in a sharp breath. "Dammit, Gin. I wanted you, baby. I loved you."

"No, you didn't. You wouldn't have turned on me when I felt most vulnerable if you truly loved me—you would've understood my reasoning, but you didn't, and now you need to leave."

His jaw clenches, and he takes a step back. "I'm not leaving without Evie."

"She's not a child, Marco."

Dad strides up to me and makes me walk into the hall, where several people stand. Jared included. "Let's go. Get your clothes on now. We're leaving back to San Francisco."

"Wait, Dad, no. I can't just leave."

He stops, turning toward me when I don't move. "You want to stay here? Continue to show your body and let these pigs touch you because you know these men aren't thinking about dating you at the end of the night."

"Dad—"

"Why did you lie to me, Evie?"

"I—" My voice breaks. "That's not what I meant."

"Is this the kind of role model you want to be for your future daughter?" He touches the bra strap on my shoulder. "Do you honestly believe this is a good job? You'll find a man who will respect you working a business like this?"

"Are you judging me right now?"

"No, I'm upset your mother brought you to this place.

I'm disappointed you're still here, and if you stay, then yes, I will because I didn't raise you to be a slut."

Gin gasps, Dad's face falling just as my eyes widen, my vision blurring out the distress in his expression while my tears burn and the back of my throat constricts. "You didn't raise me at all! You left me, or did you forget all the times I called you crying to come back?"

"Evie. I'm sorry, sweetheart, I didn't mean—"

"Leave!" I push him. "Get the fuck out of here now, or I swear today will be the last time you hear my voice—you'll ever see my face again."

"Wait, baby girl, please come home with me. I don't want to leave this way."

I let the tears fall, stepping back into room three while stripping off every layer of clothes until I bump into the guy still behind me. "Can't. I've got a session to finish, and I never leave a performance unsatisfied."

Dad turns away from my nakedness, sidestepping Gin while striding toward the stairs, and I start breathing hard, closing my eyes to block everyone out.

"Everly...look at me."

"No," I breathe, moving away from Gin when she touches my hand. "I'm fine."

She calls my name again, but I'm already walking toward the stairs in a haze, taking each step with no course of action, ending up at my locker. I sit on the bench, staring at my nameplate for several seconds, then down at my naked body. How unfazed I am sitting here nude, walking through a crowded room of people without hesitation because I've become so desensitized where deep down, Dad's words ring true.

I open the door and gather my street clothes, putting

each article on. The ache settling in my gut starts to fester, hurting my heart. Someone sits next to me, touching my hand, and I clench my jaw, staring at Roni while holding back the tears stinging my eyes.

Her hug takes me by surprise, and I breathe out a shaky breath, saying something, maybe another apology, see you later, I don't know what, but I'm standing, walking toward the back exit to my car, on the road heading to wherever my mind knows until I'm parked outside the cabin.

Getting out, I walk toward the front window, staring into Kylo's home as he smiles at Sadie, holding their son Kaden, kissing his little cheek, and Lennox is sitting at the island watching them. I want to join the people I love most, but my chest constricts from their laughter. Looking down at my left hand, feeling furthest from center.

None of this is real—just a vivid fantasy since I don't exist outside the box.

The sob I've been holding cracks through my teeth, my tears breaking as I suck in a loud breath, backing away when Lennox looks straight at me. He stands, walking to the front exit as I rush toward the car, but he takes hold of my hand before I open the door.

"Evie, what happened? What's wrong, baby?"

"I gotta leave."

"What do you mean?"

"I can't...." My hands shake as I go through my keys, searching for the guest house copy to remove.

"What are you doing?" he asks, backing me against the car door, those beautiful eyes glossing over, and I look away.

"It's too much."

"What are you talking about? Look at me." He lifts my

chin, wiping away the tears falling onto my lips. "Talk to me, baby."

I shake my head. "I'm going home."

"I'll meet you there."

"I'm going home. To San Francisco. Tonight." Removing my ring from my finger, I palm the diamond, chewing hard on my bottom lip before placing it in his hand. "You need to stay here, Lex."

"What—" Lennox takes hold of my left hand, but I drop his hold. "Evie, where the fuck is this coming from?"

"I can't play out your fantasy anymore. You deserve someone better than me."

"No." He bangs his closed fists on the hood of the car. "Don't do that. Don't use that excuse because you know that's not true. You know how much I love you, how real our life together is, so why are you doing this?" I shake my head, and Lennox sways while gritting his teeth, breathing hard as he holds the sides of my face, trying to control himself when all he wants to do is draw me closer to kiss his wife. "Evie, stop, please—" his voice cracks, "you're breaking my heart, baby." Taking hold of my hand, he places it on his chest. "Right here. Feel that heart beating for you."

"I do. That's why I can't."

"That doesn't make any sense." More tears spill down his cheeks, and my lip trembles as I kiss each one away, which makes him shake his head, his voice laced with strain, "Why can't I love you? Tell me."

Taking a shaky breath, I say, "Because a Red Vixen is untouchable and always will be."

Lennox walks backward, his hands dropping to his side while palming the diamond ring, and I drop the guest house key on the ground before getting into my car. I make it to my house in Portland, numb deep to the bone as I enter through the front door, slamming it shut, ignoring the numerous phone calls as I lean against the wooden surface behind me. Inside a once empty home and now full to the brim with love...my own fantasy I've continuously pushed away yet yearned to have.

Stripping away my clothes, I drop each layer while wandering across the room, meeting the first step, and taking each one blinded with tears. I grit my teeth as I reach the top, my face scrunching, trying so hard to hold in the pain radiating through me, my chest on fire, and my heart's torn in two because of how fucked up I am in the head.

"You're breaking my heart, baby. Please. Feel that heart beating for you—why can't I love you?"

Because there's no loving somebody who's already gone.

I let the tears fall, roaming to my bedroom and standing in front of my mirror with my eyes closed, another tear dripping down my cheek, and I roughly swipe it away as I whisper, "My work does not define me...." Blowing a shaky breath, I hold my head high and add, "I am brave...." My lip shakes, and I open my eyes to mascara staining my reddened cheeks, willing the words to spill out of me. Anything. "Fucking say it and mean it! I am strong. I'm not a coward incapable of love, of kindness because I am worthy of all the above. I deserve to be happy—to smile until my wrinkles show, laugh until my stomach hurts because living is better than existing." I tip my head higher. "I am Everly Russo, my mother's daughter, and only I can define me."

Sinking to the floor, I hug my knees, allowing the tears to flow, releasing every broken rule in my mind so strength can find me because I love myself and want to be happy—be free.

"I am Evie Russo-Hunter, and I choose us."

My heart leaps as the door slams shut, and I wipe my face, my pulse rising when footsteps race upstairs and Lennox appears at the doorway of our room.

"Evie..."

"I'm sorry—" I weep, and he drops to his knees next to me as I straddle his lap, burying my face in his chest. "I'm sorry, baby."

"Shh, Peaches. Look at me." He strokes the tears off of my cheeks with his thumbs. "I told you before, baby. I fucking told you, no matter what happens between us, no matter how hard times get, I'm not going anywhere. I'm here for the long haul."

I nod as I cry, "I love you."

Our lips press together with a heavy kiss, and I moan into his mouth when our tongues collide, the urgent need to show the other neither of us is leaving. We're right where we need to be. Lennox grunts when I buck my hips forward, adding to the friction as he thrusts back, his hardening dick hitting between my legs. Quickly lifting away his shirt, I fumble with his jeans, and he gets them past his hips, not wasting time filling me to the hilt, and we both moan, our kiss breaking as my head falls back.

Lennox growls, takes hold of my neck, and forces me close to his lips, his hand on my ass keeping me in place, buried deep inside me. "Where do you feel my cock?" His sharp thrust forward when I don't answer makes me clench around him, breathing faster. "Tell me."

"Deep in my pussy."

"No, we're getting technical tonight. Where do you feel me?"

I stare into his eyes and swallow deeply. "My cervix."

"Yes. That ain't no fantasy." Without loosening his hold,

he continues to buck his hips, firm yet pleasurable thrusts, while using his hand to keep me close. "You're gonna milk my cock until every greedy drop of my cum fills your tight cunt—" Another thrust. "Tonight...tomorrow." I pant against his lips when his drive picks up. "Every damn day until our baby grows inside you."

"Lex—" I kiss him hard, gripping his hair tight, and he groans, loosening his hold as I meet him thrust for thrust. "Yes, baby."

"*Fuck*, take my cum, Peaches."

I lock my legs around him as he lifts from the floor, bringing me to our bed. Placing me on top, he kicks off his pants as I crawl toward the middle, and he catches me half-way, dragging me back to the edge, still standing. The length of his dick slips against my pussy from behind, and I hum when he enters me on the third pass, his firm grip on my hips drawing me back, making my ass clap on his body. The sound, mixed with his grunts and possessive actions, heightens my pleasure, relaxing my cheek onto the mattress while he takes total control, fucking me senseless.

Lennox slips out, slapping his dick on my ass, and spreads my wetness along each cheek before moving onto the bed. He lays back on a few pillows, his legs spread wide, cock standing tall as he strokes himself while staring at me.

"Come here."

I crawl closer, my mouth watering as I settle between his legs, but he makes me turn around to where my back is against his chest, straddling his lap. He rubs my clit with each deep breath, and I close my eyes, resting my head on the pillow beside him while trailing my hand up the side of his neck. His slow pace is agonizing, delicious, and even more perfect once he eases the tip of his dick inside me, pressing down on my pussy as his length goes in deeper, then sends a jolt to my core with a sharp thrust to the base of his shaft.

"*Oh—Lex.*"

Lennox squeezes my tit and glides up to my neck as my body squirms. "You belong with me, Evie. Understand?" He slaps my pussy hard when I don't answer, and I let out a raspy moan the more he thrusts while stroking my clit, his mouth against my cheek. "This is my fucking pussy. Do you hear me? Never force me away again."

I chew my bottom lip hard, squirming as my climax builds to the surface. "Yes, I won't."

"That's right." He slaps my pussy again, my eyes rolling back. "My fucking wife."

"Yes—" I whine against his lips when he turns to face me, writhing beneath his strong hold. "Don't stop, please, baby. I'm close."

A deep, gritty moan leaves his throat as he keeps stroking my clit until the need to go appears. My eyes widen as I cry out, an intense wave rocking me deep to the core, my ears ringing, my body convulsing from my head down to the tip of my toes with a vice grip on his hair and the sheets, needing to ground myself. Lennox keeps a firm hold on me, still thrusting deep into my pussy, groaning through his teeth.

"*Good fucking girl, Peaches*—yes, keep coming on my cock."

I finally find my breath, squeezing my legs together when his touch becomes too intense. He forces them apart, diving under to pin my thighs to his while driving his hips upward hard, his breathing erratic, fingers digging into my skin as his rugged groan heats my lips when our mouths crash and his dick throbs inside me, easing his strokes until he slips out. He cups my pussy, slowly kissing me, whispering sweet words with each peck, and I've never felt more in love with this man.

Spinning to face him, I hold him close and smile against his neck as he rubs my back, his arm around my shoulder to draw me closer and hums a heavy breath when a yawn escapes me, point officially taken. No other words needed.

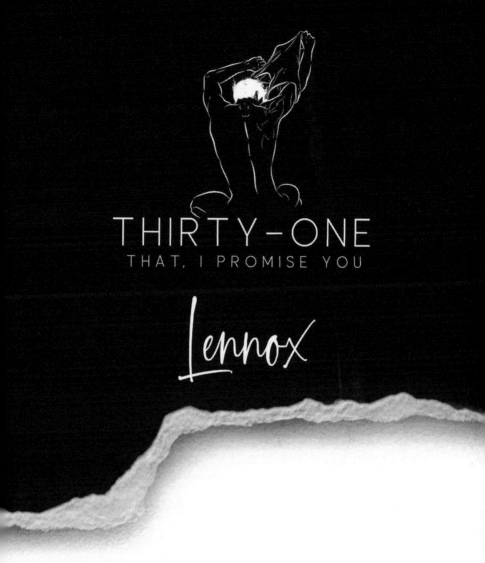

THIRTY-ONE
THAT, I PROMISE YOU

Lennox

I sing softly into Evie's ear while caressing the palm of her left hand, not leaving our bed in hours. There's no point because we are right where we need to be, and nothing else in the world matters outside our bubble. Reaching over to the bedside table, I grab a handful of peach rings from the open bag she always has on hand, feeding one to her. Still singing, I lift her left hand, kissing the palm before inching the candy onto her bare finger, and her giggle is music to my ears.

She takes one from me, does the same, and I lift her chin to kiss her lips, humming from the sweetness on her tongue. "I like these better," I whisper, intertwining our fingers.

"Me too, but they won't last very long. Give or take a few minutes before I suck them off our fingers."

I chuckle, taking hold of her cheek, so utterly in love with this beautiful woman before me. "I love you, Peaches."

"Hm, I love peaches, too."

We continue to hold each other close, but we both know as much as we want to ignore the outside world, we have to talk about what happened. "Are you ready?"

Evie nods, looking up at me as we come to a seated position, then rests her head on my shoulder while leaning into me, both of us looking toward the wall. "The day I got the call that my grandma passed away, I can vividly remember the ache that crept into my stomach. It hurt so bad. I never wanted to feel that way again, ever, but what happened last night hit me just as hard, deep inside my bones."

"What happened, Evie?"

"I'm done with Vivid. You know that, right? I went there with one goal, and everything slowly spiraled out of control like a ripple effect. I couldn't control anything, especially when my dad showed up."

"Your dad's in Portland?"

"Yes...I had no idea what my mom and dad went through, and when he saw me there—" I hold her closer as her voice wavers. "He didn't know I was a Vixen like my mom was and said things to me I'm not sure I can ever forgive him for."

"Oh, Evie. Baby, look at me." She tips her head back, and I wipe the tears before they fall. "Forgiveness is only a step forward in solving a problem. You can stay mad at your father, mother, or anyone close to you, but that feeling will eat you alive until you resolve the issue. That's no way to live."

"So, how should I deal with the problem?"

"Exactly what we're doing. Talking," I say, kissing her. "Communication is the key to happiness." Pressing another, I add, "Go talk to your parents, settle your differences. If you need to do this alone, I'll be here waiting, or if you need me there, I'll be with you every step of the way."

She quickly nods. "Okay, I need you there with me. Please."

With a heavy breath, she scoots off the bed, waiting for me by the bathroom doorway as I follow, taking our time with each other while she mentally prepares, worried if her father is still in Portland, though with past mistakes, I'm positive he's not far. We arrived at Evie's childhood home past midnight, and I was right. While the driveway is empty, a man with dark brown hair is asleep on the front steps.

Evie gasps, leans over, and shuts off my headlights. "Of course, he'd come here."

"We don't have to go yet. Do you want to wait for Gin?"

She glances at me, then stares out the windshield. "Yes."

"Okay." I grab hold of her hand and kiss the back. "There's no rush."

Headlights flash behind us, and her grip tightens around mine as a car pulls inside. "I changed my mind. I can't do this yet. Can we go, please?"

"Are you sure?"

"I'm not in the right headspace to control what comes out of my mouth."

"Sounds like the perfect time, then. Get it all out, and don't hold back."

Her head snaps toward me when Gin knocks on the driver's side window, and her father is now standing, leaning against the front door. "Shit."

"Hey, look at me, Peaches." I move in close, pressing my forehead to hers. "Don't let fear rule you."

A slight smile lifts on her lips as she huffs a laugh. "I won't."

"Good. Come on."

Gin is already by the front door, her arms crossed, clearly pissed the fuck off as she's arguing with Evie's father. "I'm not leaving until I talk to her."

"After your outburst today, I don't want you near my kid. Are you serious, Marco? Say what you want about me, but how could you talk like that to your daughter?"

"Mom...it's okay," Evie says as we walk toward her parents with our hands clasped together. "I need to talk to you both."

"Who is this?" Marco asks, looking at me and then at our hands firmly joined.

"Lennox. Her husband."

"Husband?" His eyes widen, blinking a few times as he looks at Evie, and Gin doesn't seem surprised in the slightest. "Sweetheart, when? Why didn't you tell me?"

"Can you blame her for keeping a secret?" Gin says, shaking her head. "We've kept them for years. Did you ever think our decisions would come back to bite us in the ass?"

Tears pick his dark brown eyes as he rubs the stubble on his jaw. "How did we get here?"

"Question of the fucking ages."

The air is heavy with everyone standing here. "Should we take this conversation inside?" I ask, Evie practically flush to my side.

Marco steps away from the door, and Gin hesitates for a second before unlocking it, allowing me and Evie to enter before herself, then Marco walks in last. Her home is small and tidy. Minimal like Evie's before I moved in. However, her walls are far from bare. There are some paintings, but most of the frames are pictures of Evie.

As if today was the first time in years she stepped foot in here, Evie looks around, taking in every detail, holding back her emotions while reliving each image. She swallows deeply with a vice grip on my hand, and I won't say a word because her discomfort is likely higher than mine.

"Evie," Marco says, still standing by the door, and she looks at her father. "I'm glad you're here."

"I didn't want to come."

He dips his head. "I deserve that, but please listen to me for a moment, sweetheart. I've had time to reflect, not just from the past couple of hours, even days, but over the years. I came here tonight because I need to apologize to your mother in order to ask for forgiveness from you." He takes a step toward Gin, and she steps back. "Virginia, my biggest mistake wasn't leaving Everly here with you. It was giving you a reason to leave San Francisco in the first place."

"Our daughter has always been my highest priority." Gin's voice shakes, and she takes a deep breath when Marco takes a few more steps.

"Yes, but you were mine. You had every right to decide for yourself, just as I was allowed to feel my emotions over losing a child. But you left me because you believed it was what I needed. Even after I repeatedly stated that was farthest from the truth." Gin rapidly shakes her head when Marco reaches her, touching her cheeks. "I never stopped loving you. You and Evie are my life. To this day, I can't stop the ache I feel being away from either of you."

"I can't," Gin whispers, tears escaping down her cheeks.

"But you can, Ginny, baby. I'm right here, pouring my heart out to you." He looks at Evie. "To both of my girls. I'm never leaving you again, and I won't ever give you a reason to leave."

I gently squeeze Evie when she leans further into me, then walks toward her father. "Dad—"

"Oh, Evie," he breathes, embracing her and kissing her temple. "I'm sorry—I'm so sorry, sweetheart. Please, forgive me for those awful words that never should've been a thought in my mind. I have no excuse for my carelessness, but never will I disrespect you again. That, I promise you."

Evie nods into his chest, sniffling, then she walks quickly toward Gin and hugs her tight. She looks up at the ceiling blinking back her tears, and closes her eyes while stroking her daughter's hair as if she believed this moment would never come. Walking closer, Marco takes hold of Gin's hand, both her and Evie still wary. A flawed moment, far from perfection, but it's a step in a better direction for everyone.

When our eyes connect, the weight of the world is no longer behind hers, allowing that mask she held onto to slip away, the real Evie here to stay—I see her once my wife smiles, still feeling that pluck, our melody loud and clear.

Love at first sight is far from bullshit.

ved moment

ection for everyon

is no longer behind her

I see her once my wife smile

t pluck, our melody loud and clea

Love at first sight is far from bullshi

EPILOGUE

Evie

I shake my hands, rubbing them together as I wait for the announcer to call me on stage.

Why am I nervous?

I've been a performer for half my life, but this moment feels different, and I don't want to mess up. Taking another peek from behind the dark curtains, I instantly regret my decision when the company owner looks my way, and my stomach churns. "Get a hold of yourself, Evie."

A deep chuckle sounds from behind me, and goosebumps rise on my skin when warm arms wrap around my waist, my nerves instantly dissipating. "Just do your thing, Peaches."

"Hm, you're late," I say, my high ponytail braid falling past my shoulder when I tilt my neck from Lennox's kiss.

"With good reason." Spinning around, I get lost in my husband's eyes until my name is called. "Show them what you got."

I breathe as Lennox adjusts the cross straps on my matching backless white sports bra and shorts, giving me a love tap on my ass before I walk out onto the stage. Four people are sitting at a table lined with papers, and I'm sure a bunch of aerialists have already auditioned for the part.

"Mrs. Hunter?"

"Yes."

"Whenever you're ready."

The silks are red. Of all colors, it had to be Vivid? All eyes are on me as my palms shake—can they see straight through me? What if someone at the table had been to Vivid and watched me perform on stage nude, inside the box?

Just fly, Evie.

Leaning with one leg forward and my right hand on the silks, I bend backward when the song *Earned It* plays, extending my leg to wrap around the silks and start my climb. The longer I'm up here, the less anxious I feel, working my routine like the dozens of times I practiced at home, yet all it takes is one misstep, losing my footing that ruins all chances of winning over this audition. I gasp, barely landing on my feet as gravity takes me, and I bury my face in the silks. Instead of pushing on, I stride off stage, not one glance at the table, because there's no point in continuing.

Chewing on my bottom lip, I pace the floor, and Lennox comes toward me. "Evie..."

"Can we go, please?"

"Is the audition over? That didn't take long."

"I fell."

Lennox draws me into him, and I breathe heavily into his chest. "I'm sorry, baby. There could still be a chance you'd get the job."

"No." I shake my head, looking up at him. "If falling's not the reason they don't pick me, it's giving up that'll do it."

"Don't beat yourself up over it. If they don't pick you, there will be other opportunities. Okay?"

Only so much his words can do to ease my disappointment, so I just nod. His gaze stays on mine as he takes hold of my cheeks and presses a kiss to my lips, and I smile.

"I'm going to get my stuff. I'll meet you at the car."

"I don't mind waiting for you out here."

"Are you sure?"

Lennox nods, pressing another kiss before releasing our embrace, then takes his phone out of his pocket as he leans against the wall with a view of the table. I head into the bustling backroom, people are getting ready, and I wish I were still back here waiting for my turn to start over with the confidence I know I have. However, wishing will only get me so far. I need to put in the work to make it.

Next time.

I take a brisk shower to ease my mind, quickly get dressed and zip my jacket while leaving the dressing room just as Lennox walks out from the stage. He jogs up to me with a grin, lifting me into a bear hug before placing me back on the floor. "Ready?"

"Yes. What were you doing back there?"

"I was getting a closer look at the last audition."

"How did they do?"

"Eh."

I giggle and intertwine our fingers while we stroll toward the door, my shoulders dipping when I release a sigh and glance up at Lennox when he gives me a gentle squeeze and a wink. We drive the half hour home as I stare out the passenger window, trying not to think about today.

"I have a surprise for you."

Tilting my head toward him, I smile. "Your reason for being late?"

"Yup. My first customer was top priority. With my dad still on limited physical activity, getting your purchase up the stairs and setting up took longer than I anticipated."

My cheeks heat. "It's ready?"

"The question is," he moves close to my ear, "are you ready to go to bed?"

I blow out a shaky breath, my heart skipping. "Yes—wait, you had your dad help you bring it!?"

Lennox hums, kissing me just below my ear, and I moan, kneading my thighs as I squeeze them together. "Well, Kylo's in Florida, but don't worry, Peaches. My dad has no clue."

"Are you sure?" I ask, capturing his lips when he nips my skin.

"Completely." He grunts when I maneuver to straddle his lap, the horn sounds as my ass hits the steering wheel, and we laugh, breathing hard into each other, needing to be closer.

Urging me to grind on his growing erection, Lennox tilts

his head back as I slowly buck forward, his grip on my hips strengthening, gazing into his eyes while teasing him harder, getting him ready.

"Arms behind the headrest," I whisper against his lips, my hair surrounding his handsome face. He quirks a brow, gliding his hands up my sides before complying, and I nibble on his lower lip while rocking on his dick faster, his grunts getting louder as I hold his throat—touching the door handle, I say, "First one upstairs wears the pants."

In seconds I'm out of the Mustang, looking back at his furrowed expression before he grins, booking it toward me. I squeak a laugh while trying to get the front door unlocked and jet inside, Jinx and Jax dashing across the room as I drop my keys on the floor when he grabs hold of my waist, drawing my back flush to his body. Moaning, I caress his cheek while he kisses my neck, cupping my pussy to pull my ass closer to his hard dick.

"Wait—" I breathe, my heart racing. "I need a second."

Lennox loosens his hold, and I break free, dropping my coat, huffing while backing up against the wall. "You have five seconds."

I grin and yank my shirt over my head, his heavy gaze darting to my bare tits. "I only needed one."

Racing for the stairs, I glance back at Lennox hot on my heels, lifting away his shirt in one swoop, and he gets me onto my knees halfway up the stairs when he secures his arm around my body. My leggings and thong are around my thighs as Lennox yanks them down, baring my ass while gliding his palm over the right cheek—I moan when he leaves a sharp slap.

"You like being chased, Peaches?" He takes my arms behind my back, my cheek pressed against the step while his buckle jingles, unfastening his zipper. "Or do you enjoy the effects of being caught?"

"Why choose—" I moan, dragging my teeth over my bottom lip when he enters my pussy in one swift thrust.

A gruff pant leaves him before he laughs, grunting while I back into his body, making him pick up his pace. Each eager thrust has me whining, my legs slipping wider to take him in deeper as he presses onto my lower back, hitting the same spot, over and over—my heavy breaths pick up, my clit pulsing, so damn close to coming, then he withdraws.

"No—keep going," I whimper, and he hums, my eyes rolling back as he glides his fingers along my slit.

"Not here."

There's no way I'm making it to the bedroom with my pussy still throbbing, and he knows it while kicking off his jeans and lifting me into his arms, taking each careful step with his tongue down my throat. Walking to the doorway, he places me on the floor, easing me against the door as he deepens our kiss—this man will suck my face for hours if I'd let him, and as much as I enjoy his mouth on mine, right now I want that tongue between my legs.

I break our kiss, gripping his hair tight, and he groans as I force him to his knees, Lennox already having my leg on his shoulder, biting my inner thigh while licking the length to my pussy, and my head bucks backward.

"I have to tell you something," Lennox says between kissing my clit.

"I can't hear you right now, Lex." He chuckles, staring at me with his mouth full, and my eyes flutter, grinding my hips toward his face the harder he sucks, gripping his hair tighter when he pulls away. "Don't you fucking stop."

Lennox growls, both my legs now securely around his

shoulders as he supports me by my waist, grunting with the brutal lashes of his tongue, and I can almost taste the finish line. He's stronger than me, pulling away to take a breath through his teeth from the sting, and if I didn't love this man, I would kill him for stopping again.

"Lex, please, baby—let me come."

"Not here. You and I know what your body is capable of, and I'm bringing you there again tonight."

Pins and needles prickle my skin, last night flooding to the forefront of my mind, and Lennox glides his finger across the bumps. We've been exploring everything about each other, and that orgasm still shakes me to the core when I think about it.

"Then bring me inside."

My feet planted on the floor, Lennox stands, backing me into the room as he opens the door, towering over my naked body. The blackout curtains are closed, the only source of light coming from the hallway, bright enough to see the surrounding area, yet I can't pull my gaze away from him— his presence puts me in a trance until the back of my legs hit something hard, and I look back.

He takes hold of my chin, making me look at him as he cocks his head to the side. "Eyes on me."

I lick my lips, blowing out a shaky breath when he rubs his thumb across the bottom. "I want to see."

A shiver shoots up my spine when he trails his fingers down my arms, taking hold of my wrists and raising them. "There's a bar above your head. Grab it."

I reach but feel nothing. "Where?" He lifts me by my ass, and I grab onto the metal pole, my body stretching as I hang at least a foot off the floor. "Lex..."

"Tell me your safe word, Peaches."

"Socks."

Lennox smiles, then lowers to draw something out from under the bed, my toes just barely touching the platform below, then he leaves me to hang. My heart's pounding as he opens a drawer to my left, metal clinking while walking back to me, securing cuffs around my wrists and connecting the chain links to the bar.

"If you get tired, let go and use the platform to gather your strength." Leaning against the bar, he lingers above my lips. "The longer you hang, the faster we'll come." He presses a feather-light kiss. "Each time you let go, I'll stop."

"Stop what?" I breathe.

Leaving me again, he returns to run something smooth along my pussy, and I hum once he slips the hard object inside me. "You're in charge of our pleasure tonight."

He moves back before I can kiss him, then walks across the room to sit in a chair with a small remote in his hand. There's a bottle of lube on the table beside him, and he drizzles a good amount on his palm—mine feel slick once he slowly strokes his dick, and I squeeze my thighs together, moaning when vibrations rock me to my core.

I drop, and the pulsing stops, the restraints pulling my wrists taunt. He watches me as I catch my breath, and I grab hold again, more put together this time. I keep eye contact as he presses the button, the settings still low, yet the rumbling is tantalizing, an ache slowly settling in my muscles, which adds to my pleasure, needing more.

He resumes jerking off, tipping his head against the chair, and ups the speed to medium. "We gotta talk, Peaches."

I grip the pole harder, moaning louder, trying not to let go. "Lex—"

His moans increase, bucking his hips forward when he adjusts his position to lean further back, and he stops when I slip again, both of us breathing hard while he grips the arms of the chair.

"You can hold on longer. Don't let anything distract you from your goal. You're in control of your body, your mind."

I nod, chewing on my bottom lip, understanding where he's taking me. "Okay."

Grabbing the bar, I squeeze my core, hollowing my body to feel weightless, and close my eyes as the vibrations return. "Watch me."

I breathe through my nose, my toes curling as I peel my eyes open, heat flushing my skin as Lennox continues to stroke himself, each pump making my pussy pulse more, his rhythm becoming sporadic, his chest rising fast like my racing heart.

"The owner of the company you auditioned for...he saw you perform."

My eyes widen as my stomach sinks. "Where—" I ask, dropping, and he switches the bullet off. Breathing hard, I blink a few times as the night Lennox recorded me comes to mind, and him leaving the stage with a grin. "You showed them?"

"I did."

Swallowing deeply, I blow out a shaky breath. "And they liked my performance?"

"Peaches, they are giving you another chance to show them what you got."

My heart beats faster for an entirely new reason. "When?"

"Tomorrow." I open my mouth to protest, but my head

bucks back when he switches the vibrator on high. "Get back up there."

"Lex..."

Doing as he says, I twist my legs to help ease the sensations while focusing on staying up, and he lets out a husky moan as he grabs himself, his head tipping back the faster he strokes.

"Attagirl, keep at it, baby."

I grit my teeth, looking at my hands as my fingers start slipping, grunting from the intense pleasure and wanting to succeed. Just before I drop, Lennox holds and lifts me by my ass to straddle his waist, unhooking the chain from the bar, then places me onto the bed to remove the bullet from between my legs.

"I got you," he whispers against my lips, kissing me softly, and I cling to him, needing my husband. "I got you, baby."

Continuing to kiss down my body, he reaches my mound, and I inch away from his mouth to get further onto the bed, his hungry gaze meeting mine as he follows, dragging me back to finish the job properly. His heavy hands pin my hips as I buck forward, my moans increasing between him sucking and finger fucking my pussy, and I grip his hair as he pushes me over the edge, rapidly rubbing inside me until I'm coming all over the sheets.

"There we go, Peaches."

I bite my bottom lip as he kisses my inner thigh, smiling while trailing my fingers through his hair, then tip my head back the more he presses his lips on my skin. A sheer black fabric covers the rectangular top of the four post bed, with several bars running across and anchors on each one.

"Lex, there's no way your dad doesn't know what kind of bed this is."

"Oh yeah," he says, kissing up my stomach. "One hundred percent he knows about our kinky ways."

I groan and hide my face in my hands. "Just so you know I'm never going over to their place again."

Lennox chuckles in the crook of my neck. "You'll be alright."

"I bet he'll want one next," I say, rolling onto my hip as he settles beside me.

"Don't—don't do that." There's no hiding my laugh when he slaps my ass. "My dick just permanently shriveled."

A snort laugh escapes me, and Lennox chuckles, drawing me closer, and releasing me from the cuffs. I roll on top of him and intertwine our fingers above his head.

"Doesn't feel like it," I say, rocking on his stiff shaft.

"Are you sure?" He thrusts his pelvis upward, making me moan. "Maybe you should keep checking."

Lennox has always been dominant in bed, but so am I—hovering above his mouth, I grin, slowly inching onto his length, and he inhales a sharp breath through his teeth as I ride him while securing a cuff to his wrist. There's no hesitation, no resistance as I bound my husband, merely scratching the surface of exploring our bodies, our life together full of endless possibilities because we've only just begun.

"My turn."

on my body

over to my mouth

w delicious you are. Pet

in a man who loves to degrad

-every whispering kiss has a tast

in sinful sweet bites that aim to pleas

PROLOGUE

Petra

Multiple people have approached me, and I don't know why. I'm wearing white, which means I'm here to observe—what's the point of wearing colors if people don't follow the rules?

"If you sit on my lap, they won't come to you."

I side-eye Jared, who's wearing all black, and politely

decline the next couple who ask if I'm interested in joining them. "Only in your wildest dreams."

"Suit yourself."

That beautiful woman from the munch, Keondra, strolls toward me wearing a white babydoll slip, her red lips tugging high as her gaze flicks to my dress. "Hey, baby." She steps in closer, smelling delectable, like cotton candy, which makes my mouth water. "Are you aware of the color system in place for the Velvet Room?"

"I am. I'm only here to watch."

"To watch?" Her perfectly arched brow moves up a notch, the golden shimmer along her deep brown skin warming her dark eyes. "Your companion is an observer tonight." I look at Jared, then back to the host, who gently holds my chin to focus on her. "But did *you* read the rules? What does your color signify?"

Her closeness spikes my pulse, so I inch back to distance myself from the overwhelming sensation. "From what I remember, white was for those interested in watching."

"And you didn't care to inform her?" she asks Jared, and they stare at each other for long seconds, speaking without words before he nods at me, leaning further into his seat.

"I advised her to change, but she didn't care for being told what to wear."

"Yet you allowed her to enter anyway?"

I search between the both of them for context. "Okay, did I do something wrong?"

Keondra reaches for my hand as if to take me away. "Honey, if you're interested in attending my parties or entering the kink lifestyle, for that matter, I suggest finding someone more trustworthy than Jared for guidance."

Her warning sends a chill down my spine, yet I have an

urge to defend Jared, who merely shrugs at her comment. "You should listen to her."

My head screams for me to have sense, yet my heart declares there has to be more to this man than what his reputation perceives him. "Shouldn't I be the judge of that?"

Keondra smiles, stepping back when I remove her hold. "Of course. You certainly should be. Have a pleasant evening. Refreshments are on the house."

She glances at me over her shoulder before strolling away to greet other guests, and I search around the room, observing what others are wearing and their activities. While doing so, an older gentleman makes eye contact with me a second too long, and once he walks in my direction, panic sets in as I quickly plant my ass on Jared's lap.

He chuckles behind me, adjusting his position on the couch while placing his large palm on my thigh to squeeze the meat. "Seems I must've fallen asleep."

I glare at Jared, sucking my teeth before swatting his hand away. "Shut up."

His eyes darken, such a stern look making me shift. "Be mindful, Pet. Your smart mouth will only get you punished."

Daring, I maneuver my leg to the side, straddling him backward before leaning into his chest. "Sorry to say, boss, but you don't have that power over me."

"Maybe not yet." Jared touches my stomach, his other hand resting on my throat, and I lose my breath on a moan when he gently nips below my ear. "But you have no idea how capable I am of getting my way."

I hum, grinding my ass against his growing dick until he dips to stop my advance with a firm hold on my pelvis. "Having a big head will only slow you down. You'll never catch me otherwise."

"Ms. Beckett, think wisely of your next words before you find yourself bent over my knee."

"Yeah? Well, I believe you're all threats and no bite," I say, snapping my teeth at his chin.

"Ooh," Jared chuckles, his grip firming around my throat before drawing me close to his lips. "Be a good girl, Pet, and run, now." He trails his index finger across my jaw as his steel eyes captivate me entirely. "Steer clear of me because I'm not a good man."

I shake my head, gliding my palms down his thighs while lapping my tongue along his top lip. "Still not convincing."

Taking my bottom lip between his teeth, he growls, kissing me with such heat while sucking my tongue into his mouth, the moment ending too soon as he forces us inches apart. "My bite is lethal. I'll only have you until you kneel before me, then I'll tear your fragile heart out with no remorse once I'm bored enough."

I'm panting at this point, not hearing a word he says as I remove myself from his hold to face him. I stare into his cold eyes, hovering above his parted lips while gliding my palm down his chest. His heart's pounding, warm, very much telling, and I smirk once I meet his hard dick through his pants.

His eyelids close, head falling back against the cushion as I slowly stroke him and say, "Prove it."

I APPRECIATE YOU!

Thank you for taking the time to read Broken Rules! I hope you enjoy Evie and Lex's story as much as I've enjoyed writing it.

Next is book three, Ground Rules, Jared & Petra's story in the Don't Fall in Love Series.

Info to my social media pages are in the about the author section. Stay updated on future books, enjoy teasers, and more.

If you've enjoyed Broken Rules and would like to leave a review, it's much appreciated!

Don't Fall in Love Series

Rule Breaker: Book One

I had one rule...

then she came along.

Sadie Oakley

The client I shouldn't have taken.

My escort business has always come first, working with women who are searching for that extra *boost* in their life, and I enjoy the gratification of a successful weekend.

Building trust.

Satisfying needs.

Yet, Sadie makes me reckless, willing to risk everything, and each day we're together, I'm falling harder, my rule becoming damn near impossible to keep.

I'm close to breaking.

I don't know how much more of her I can take with every urge to draw her close while keeping her at a distance.

INSATIABLE SERIES

Whiskey Lullaby: Book one

Whiskey will forever taste like him.

One glance created an insatiable urge, and a drunken kiss sealed my desire for a stranger where the smallest drop of Whiskey reminds me of our moment, even if I don't know his name.

The odds of finding him were low until life dropped me on his doorstep with a resume, waiting for a job interview. I'm to be his son's live-in nanny, and Carter Anderson is far from a pleasant boss.

He's stern, to the point, no in-betweens, yet every glance my way still has my pulse racing—that desire loud and greedy for more. However, Mr. Anderson is off-limits. My job must come first, though staying away is a challenge whenever *Whiskey* calls my name.

ACKNOWLEDGMENTS

To my family and friends, I love and appreciate you all! Thank you for being so supportive and encouraging me to keep writing.

To Andrea, you've been my rock throughout writing this series, helping me create these characters from bare bones. Thank you for the pep talks, brainstorming, and laughs. For sharing your characters with me, because you know I can't get enough of Enzo!

To my Beta readers: Brenna Fowler, Margo Brialis & Hallie Niumalu Yim Gannon. Thank you for your wonderful feedback and for helping me strengthen this story to its full potential. I look forward to working with you again!

If you want to learn more about Enzo and Luca Russo, Evie's cousins, keep an eye out for Andi McClane's RomCom **Picture This Series,** due later this year. You're going to laugh and love these stories to bits!

ABOUT THE AUTHOR

S.J. Rosalie is a romance author from Rhode Island who enjoys writing slow-burn books, creating obstacles with twists before her characters find their happily ever after. When she's not writing, you'll find her relaxing with her three children and husband, cozying up under a warm blanket with a book, or binge-watching a TV series.

- amazon.com/S.J.-Rosalie/e/B092L3KKMP
- tiktok.com/@sjrosalie_author
- instagram.com/sjrosalie_author
- goodreads.com/sjrosalie

Made in the USA
Columbia, SC
06 October 2024

4cf70a1c-2d55-40c8-9b2b-0e5b74e322ceR01